westland publications ltd

Amish is a 1974-born, IIM (Kolkata)-educated, boring banker turned happy author. The success of his debut book, *The Immortals of Meluha* (Book 1 of the Shiva Trilogy), encouraged him to give up a fourteen-year-old career in financial services to focus on writing. He is passionate about history, mythology and philosophy, finding beauty and meaning in all world religions. Amish's books have sold more than 4 million copies and have been translated into over 19 languages.

Amish lives in Mumbai with his wife Preeti and son Neel.

www.authoramish.com
www.facebook.com/authoramish
www.twitter.com/authoramish

'I wish many more would be inspired by Amish Tripathi ...'
— *Amitabh Bachchan, Indian actor and living legend*

'Amish is India's Tolkien'

— *Business Standard*

'Amish is India's first literary popstar'
— *Shekhar Kapur, renowned filmmaker*

'Amish is ... the Paulo Coelho of the east.'

— *Business World*

'Amish's mythical imagination mines the past and taps into the possibilities of the future. His book series, archetypal and stirring, unfolds the deepest recesses of the soul as well as our collective consciousness.'

— *Deepak Chopra, world-renowned spiritual guru and bestselling author*

'Amish is a fresh new voice in Indian writing — steeped in myth and history, with a fine eye for detail and a compelling narrative style.'

— *Shashi Tharoor, Member of Parliament and celebrated author*

'… Amish has mastered the art of gathering, interpreting and presenting India's many myths, folklores and legends, and blending all of that into fast-paced thrillers that change your views about Gods, cultures, histories, demons and heroes, forever.'

– Hi Blitz

'Amish's philosophy of tolerance, his understanding of mythology and his avowed admiration for Shiva are evident in his best-selling works.'

– Verve

'Tripathi is part of an emerging band of authors who have taken up mythology and history in a big way, translating bare facts into delicious stories.'

– The New Indian Express

'… one must congratulate Amish on reintroducing Hindu mythology to the youth of this country.'

– First City

Sita
Warrior of Mithila

Book 2
of the
Ram Chandra Series

Amish

www.authoramish.com

westland publications ltd

61, II Floor, Silverline Building, Alapakkam Main Road, Maduravoyal, Chennai 600095

93, I Floor, Sham Lal Road, Daryaganj, New Delhi 110002

www. westlandbooks.in

Published by westland publications ltd 2017

ISBN: 978-93-86224-58-3

Cover Concept and Design by Sideways

Illustration by Arthat studio

Inside book formatting and typesetting by SÜRYA, New Delhi

Printed at Thomson Press (India) Ltd.

To Himanshu Roy
My brother-in-law,
A man who exemplifies the ancient Indian path of Balance,
A proud Lord Ganesh devotee who also respects
all other faiths,
A sincere Indian patriot,
A man with wisdom, courage, and honour.
A hero.

Om Namah Shivāya
The universe bows to Lord Shiva.
I bow to Lord Shiva.

From the Adbhuta Rāmāyana
(credited to Maharishi Valmikiji)

Yadā yadā hi dharmasya glanirbhavati suvrata |
Abhyutthānamadharmasya tadā prakṛtisambhavaḥ ||

O keeper of righteous vows, remember this,
Whenever dharma is in decline,
Or there is an upsurge of adharma;
The Sacred Feminine will incarnate.

She will defend dharma.
She will protect us.

List of Characters and Important Tribes
(In Alphabetic Order)

Arishtanemi: Military chief of the Malayaputras; right-hand man of Vishwamitra

Ashwapati: King of the northwestern kingdom of Kekaya; father of Kaikeyi and a loyal ally of Dashrath

Bharat: Ram's half-brother; son of Dashrath and Kaikeyi

Dashrath: Chakravarti king of Kosala and emperor of the Sapt Sindhu; husband of Kaushalya, Kaikeyi, and Sumitra; father of Ram, Bharat, Lakshman and Shatrughan

Hanuman: Radhika's cousin; son of Vayu Kesari; a Naga and a member of the Vayuputra tribe

Janak: King of Mithila; father of Sita and Urmila

Jatayu: A captain of the Malayaputra tribe; Naga friend of Sita and Ram

Kaikeyi: Daughter of King Ashwapati of Kekaya; the second and favourite wife of Dashrath; mother of Bharat

Kaushalya: Daughter of King Bhanuman of South Kosala and his wife Maheshwari; the eldest queen of Dashrath; mother of Ram

Kumbhakarna: Raavan's brother; also a Naga

Kushadhwaj: King of Sankashya; younger brother of Janak

Lakshman: One of the twin sons of Dashrath; born to Sumitra; faithful to Ram; later married to Urmila

Malayaputras: The tribe left behind by Lord Parshu Ram, the sixth Vishnu

Manthara: The richest merchant of the Sapt Sindhu

Mara: An independent assassin for hire

Naarad: A trader from Lothal; Hanuman's friend

Nagas: Human beings born with deformities

Raavan: King of Lanka; brother of Vibhishan, Shurpanakha and Kumbhakarna

Radhika: Sita's friend; Hanuman's cousin

Ram: Son of Emperor Dashrath of Ayodhya (capital city of Kosala) and his eldest wife Kaushalya; eldest of four brothers, later married to Sita

Samichi: Police and protocol chief of Mithila

Shatrughan: Twin brother of Lakshman; son of Dashrath and Sumitra

Shurpanakha: Half-sister of Raavan

Shvetaketu: Sita's teacher

Sita: Adopted daughter of King Janak and Queen Sunaina of Mithila; also the prime minister of Mithila; later married to Ram

Sumitra: Daughter of the king of Kashi; the third wife of Dashrath; mother of the twins Lakshman and Shatrughan

Sunaina: Queen of Mithila; mother of Sita and Urmila

Vali: The king of Kishkindha

Varun Ratnakar: Radhika's father; chief of the Valmikis

Vashishtha: Raj guru, the royal priest of Ayodhya; teacher of the four Ayodhya princes

Vayu Kesari: Hanuman's father; Radhika's uncle

Vayuputras: The tribe left behind by Lord Rudra, the previous Mahadev

Vibhishan: Half-brother of Raavan

Vishwamitra: Chief of the Malayaputras, the tribe left behind by Lord Parshu Ram, the sixth Vishnu; also temporary guru of Ram and Lakshman

Urmila: Younger sister of Sita; blood-daughter of Janak and Sunaina; later married to Lakshman

Note on the Narrative Structure

Thank you for picking up this book and giving me the most important thing you can share: your time.

I know this book has taken long to release, and for that I offer my apologies. But when I tell you the narrative structure of the Ram Chandra Series, perhaps you will understand why it took so long.

I have been inspired by a storytelling technique called hyperlink, which some call the multilinear narrative. In such a narrative, there are many characters; and a connection brings them all together. The three main characters in the Ram Chandra Series are Ram, Sita, and Raavan. Each character has life experiences which mould who they are and their stories converge with the kidnapping of Sita. And each has their own adventure and riveting back-story.

So, while the first book explored the tale of Ram, the second and third will offer a glimpse into the adventures of Sita and then Raavan respectively, before all three stories merge from the fourth book onwards into a single story.

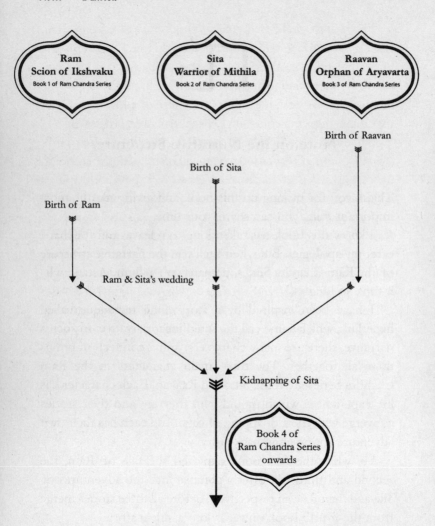

Ram
Scion of Ikshvaku
Book 1 of Ram Chandra Series

Sita
Warrior of Mithila
Book 2 of Ram Chandra Series

Raavan
Orphan of Aryavarta
Book 3 of Ram Chandra Series

Birth of Raavan

Birth of Sita

Birth of Ram

Ram & Sita's wedding

Kidnapping of Sita

Book 4 of
Ram Chandra Series
onwards

I knew it would be a complicated and time consuming affair, but I must confess, it was thoroughly exciting. I hope this will be as rewarding and thrilling an experience for you as it was for me. Understanding Sita and Raavan as characters helped me inhabit their worlds and explore the maze of plots and stories that make this epic come alive. I feel truly blessed for this.

Since this was the plan, I had left clues in the first book (***Ram – Scion of Ikshvaku***) which will tie up with the stories in the second and third books. Needless to say, there are surprises and twists in store for you in books 2 and 3 as well!

In fact, there was a very big clue in the last paragraph of ***Ram – Scion of Ikshvaku***. Some had caught on to it. And for those who didn't, a big revelation awaits you in the first chapter of the second book, ***Sita – Warrior of Mithila***.

I hope you like reading ***Sita – Warrior of Mithila***. Do tell me what you think of it, by sending me messages on my Facebook or Twitter accounts listed below.

Love,
Amish

www.facebook.com/authoramish
www.twitter.com/authoramish

Acknowledgements

When one writes, one pours one's soul out on paper. They say it takes courage to do that. They also say that courage comes only when one knows that many stand with him. I'd like to acknowledge those who stand with me: Who give me courage: Who make me realise that I am not alone.

Neel, my 8-year-old son, my pride and joy. He reads a lot already. I can't wait for him to read my books!

Preeti, my wife; Bhavna, my sister; Himanshu, my brother-in-law; Anish and Ashish, my brothers, for all their inputs to the story. They read the first draft, usually as each chapter is written. And I discuss many of the philosophies with them in detail. I also wrote much of this book in Anish and Meeta's house in Delhi. I must have done something good in my previous life to be blessed with these relationships.

The rest of my family: Usha, Vinay, Meeta, Donetta, Shernaz, Smita, Anuj, Ruta. For their consistent faith and love.

Sharvani, my editor. She is as committed to my stories as I am. She is as stubborn as I am. She reads a lot, just like I do. She's as technologically-challenged as I am. We must have been siblings in a previous life!

Gautam, Krishnakumar, Neha, Deepthi, Satish, Sanghamitra, Jayanthi, Sudha, Vipin, Srivats, Shatrughan, Sarita, Arunima, Raju, Sanyog, Naveen, Jaisankar, Sateesh, Divya, Madhu, Sathya Sridhar, Christina, Preeti and the fantastic team at Westland, my publisher. In my humble opinion, they are the best publisher in India.

Anuj, my agent. A friend and a partner from the very beginning.

Abhijeet, an old friend and senior corporate executive, who worked with Westland to drive the marketing efforts for this book. The man is brilliant!

Mohan and Mehul, my personal managers, who manage everything so that I can have the time to write.

Abhijit, Sonali, Shruti, Roy, Kassandra, Joshua, Purva, Nalin, Nivedita, Neha, Nehal, and the team at Sideways, an exceptional company that applies creativity across all aspects of a business. Sideways helped formulate the business and marketing strategy for the book. They've also made most of the marketing material, including the cover. Which I think is one of the best covers I have ever seen. They were helped in the cover design by the Arthat team (Jitendra, Deval, Johnson) who are thoroughly outstanding designers.

Mayank, Priyanka Jain, Deepika, Naresh, Vishaal, Danish and the Moe's Art team, who have driven media relations and marketing alliances for the book. They have been strong partners and among the best agencies I have worked with.

Hemal, Neha and the Oktobuzz team, who have helped manage many of the social media activities for the book. Hardworking, super smart and intensely committed. They are an asset to any team.

Mrunalini and Vrushali, Sanskrit scholars, who work with me on research. My discussions with them are enlightening. What I learn from them helps me develop many theories which go into the books.

And last, but certainly not the least, you, the reader. It is only due to your support that I have been given the privilege of living the kind of life I do; where I can do what I love and actually earn my living from it. I can never thank you enough!

Chapter 1

3400 BCE, somewhere near the Godavari River, India

Sita cut quickly and efficiently, slicing through the thick leaf stems with her sharp knife. The dwarf banana trees were as tall as she was. She did not need to stretch. She stopped and looked at her handiwork. Then she cast a look at Makrant, the Malayaputra soldier, a short distance away. He had cut down perhaps half the number of leaves that Sita had.

The weather was calm. Just a little while ago, the wind had been howling through this part of the forest. Unseasonal rain had lashed the area. Sita and Makrant had stood under a thick canopy of trees to save themselves from the rain. The winds had been so loud that it had been almost impossible for them to talk to each other. And just as suddenly, calm had descended. The rain and winds had vanished. They'd quickly headed to a patch of the woods with an abundance of dwarf banana trees. For the entire purpose of the excursion was to find these leaves.

'That's enough, Makrant,' said Sita.

Makrant turned around. The wetness had made it hard to cut the leaf stems. Under the circumstances, he had thought that he had done a good job. Now, he looked at the stack of leaves by Sita's side. And then down at his own much smaller pile. He smiled sheepishly.

Sita smiled broadly in return. 'That's more than enough. Let's go back to the camp. Ram and Lakshman should be returning from their hunt soon. Hopefully, they would have found something.'

Sita, along with her husband Prince Ram of Ayodhya and her brother-in-law Lakshman, had been racing through the *Dandakaranya*, or forest of Dandak, to escape the expected vengeance of the demon-king of Lanka, Raavan. Captain Jatayu, leading a small company of the Malayaputra tribe, had sworn to protect the three Ayodhya royals. He had strongly advised that flight was the only available course of action. Raavan would certainly send troops to avenge his sister, Princess Shurpanakha, who had been injured by Lakshman.

Secrecy was essential. So, they were cooking their food in pits dug deep into the ground. For fire, they used a specific type of coal — anthracite. It let out smokeless flames. For abundant caution, the sunk cooking pot was covered with a thick layer of banana leaves. It ensured that no smoke escaped even by accident. For that could give their position away. It was for this reason that Sita and Makrant had been cutting down banana leaves. It was Sita's turn to cook.

Makrant insisted on carrying the larger pile, and she let him. It made the Malayaputra soldier feel like he was balancing his contribution. But it was this act that would eventually prove fatal for poor Makrant.

Sita heard it first. A sound that would have been inaudible a little while ago, with the howling winds. It was unmistakable now: the menacing creak of a bow being stretched. A common bow. Many of the more accomplished soldiers and senior officers used the more expensive composite bows. But the frontline soldiers used the common variety, made entirely of wood. These bows were usually more rigid. And, they made a distinct sound when stretched.

'Makrant, duck!' screamed Sita, dropping the leaves as she leapt to the ground.

Makrant responded quickly enough, but the heavier load made him trip. An arrow shot in quickly, slamming into his right shoulder as he fell forward. Before he could react, a second arrow struck his throat. A lucky shot.

Sita rolled as she fell to the ground and quickly steadied herself behind a tree. She stayed low, her back against the tree, protected for now. She looked to her right. The unfortunate Makrant lay on the ground, drowning rapidly in his own blood. The arrow point had exited through the back of his neck. He would soon be dead.

Sita cursed in anger. And then realised it was a waste of energy. She began to breathe deeply. Calming her heart down. Paying attention. She looked around carefully. Nobody ahead of her. The arrows had come from the other direction, obscured by the tree that protected her. She knew there had to be at least two enemies. There was no way a single archer could have shot two arrows in such rapid succession.

She looked at Makrant again. He had stopped moving. His soul had moved on. The jungle was eerily quiet. It was almost impossible to believe that just a few short moments ago, brutal violence had been unleashed.

Farewell, brave Makrant. May your soul find purpose once again.

She caught snatches of commands whispered in the distance. 'Go to ... Lord Kumbhakarna ... Tell ... she's ... here ...'

She heard the hurried footsteps of someone rushing away.

There was probably just one enemy now. She looked down at the earth and whispered, 'Help me, mother. Help me.'

She drew her knife from the scabbard tied horizontally to the small of her back. She closed her eyes. She couldn't afford to look around the tree and expose herself. She would probably be shot instantly. Her eyes were useless. She had to rely on her ears. There were great archers who could shoot arrows by relying on sound. But very few could throw knives at the source of a sound. Sita was one of those very few.

She heard a loud yet surprisingly gentle voice. 'Come out, Princess Sita. We don't want to hurt you. It's better if ...'

The voice stopped mid-sentence. It would not be heard ever again. For there was a knife buried in the throat that had been the source of that voice. Sita had, without bringing herself into view, turned quickly and flung the knife with unerring and deadly accuracy. The Lankan soldier was momentarily surprised as the knife thumped into his throat. He died in no time. Just like Makrant had, drowning in his own blood.

Sita waited. She had to be sure there was no one else. She had no other weapon. But her enemies didn't know that. She listened intently. Hearing no sound, she threw herself to the ground, rolling rapidly behind low shrubs. Still no sign of anyone.

Move! Move! There's nobody else!

Sita quickly rose to her feet and sprinted to the slain Lankan, surprised that his bow was not nocked with an arrow. She tried to pull her knife out, but it was lodged too deep in the dead Lankan's vertebra. It refused to budge.

The camp is in trouble! Move!

Sita picked up the Lankan's quiver. It contained a few arrows. She quickly tied it around her back and shoulder. She lifted the bow. And ran. Ran hard! Towards the temporary camp. She had to kill the other Lankan soldier before he reached his team and warned them.

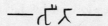

The temporary camp showed signs of a massive struggle. Most of the Malayaputra soldiers, except Jatayu and two others, were already dead. Lying in pools of blood. They had been ruthlessly massacred. Jatayu was also badly injured. Blood seeped out from numerous wounds that covered his body. Some made by blades, some by fists. His arms were tied tightly behind his back. Two Lankan soldiers held him up in a tight grip. A giant of a man loomed in front, questioning the great Naga.

Naga was the name given to people of the Sapt Sindhu born with deformities. Jatayu's malformation gave his face the appearance of a vulture.

The other two Malayaputras knelt on the ground, also bloodied. Their hands were similarly tied at the back. Three Lankan soldiers surrounded each one, while two more held them down. The Lankan swords were dripping with blood.

Raavan and his younger brother, Kumbhakarna, stood at a distance. Looking intently at the interrogation. Focused. Their hands clean of any blood.

'Answer me, Captain,' barked the Lankan. 'Where are they?'

Jatayu shook his head vehemently. His lips were sealed.

The Lankan leaned within an inch of the Naga's ear and whispered, 'You were one of us, Jatayu. You were loyal to Lord Raavan once.'

Jatayu cast a malevolent look at the Lankan. His smouldering eyes gave the reply.

The Lankan continued. 'We can forget the past. Tell us what we want to know. And come back to Lanka with honour. This is the word of a Lankan. This is the word of Captain Khara.'

Jatayu looked away and stared into the distance. Anger fading. A blank expression on his face. As if his mind was somewhere else.

The Lankan interrogator signalled one of his soldiers.

'As you command, Captain Khara,' said the soldier, wiping his sword clean on his forearm band and slipping it back into his scabbard. He walked up to an injured Malayaputra, and drew out his serrated knife. He positioned himself behind the youth, yanked his head back and placed the knife against his throat. Then he looked at Khara, awaiting the order.

Khara took hold of Jatayu's head such that his eyes stared directly at his fellow Malayaputra. The knife at his throat.

'You may not care for your own life, Captain Jatayu,' said Khara, 'but don't you want to save at least two of your soldiers?'

The Malayaputra looked at Jatayu and shouted, 'I am ready to die, my Captain! Don't say anything!'

The Lankan hit the young soldier's head with the knife hilt. His body slouched and then straightened again with courage. The blade swiftly returned to his throat.

Khara spoke with silky politeness, 'Come on, Captain. Save your soldier's life. Tell us where they are.'

'You will never catch them!' growled Jatayu. 'The three of them are long gone!'

Khara laughed. 'The two princes of Ayodhya can keep going, for all I care. We are only interested in the Vishnu.'

Jatayu was shocked. *How do they know?*

'Where is the Vishnu?' asked Khara. 'Where is she?'

Jatayu's lips began to move, but only in prayer. He was praying for the soul of his brave soldier.

Khara gave a curt nod.

Jatayu suddenly straightened and loudly rent the air with the Malayaputra cry. *'Jai Parshu Ram!'*

'Jai Parshu Ram!' shouted both the Malayaputras. The fear of death could not touch them.

The Lankan pressed the blade into the throat of the Malayaputra. Slowly. He slid the serrated knife to the side, inflicting maximum pain. Blood spurted out in a shower. As the youth collapsed to the ground, life slowly ebbing out of him, Jatayu whispered within the confines of his mind.

Farewell, my brave brother …

— ᚱᚷ —

Sita slowed as she approached the camp. She had already killed the other Lankan soldier. He lay some distance away. An arrow pierced in his heart. She had grabbed his arrows and added them to her quiver. She hid behind a tree and surveyed the camp. Lankan soldiers were everywhere. Probably more than a hundred.

All the Malayaputra soldiers were dead. All except Jatayu. Two lay close to him, their heads arched at odd angles. Surrounded by large pools of blood. Jatayu was on his knees, held by two Lankans. His hands were tied behind his back. Brutalised, injured and bleeding. But not broken. He was defiantly staring into the distance. Khara stood near him, his knife placed on Jatayu's upper arm. He ran his knife gently along the triceps, cutting into the flesh, drawing blood.

Sita looked at Khara and frowned. *I know him. Where have I seen him before?*

Khara smiled as he ran the knife back along the bloodied line he had just drawn, slicing deep into some sinew.

'Answer me,' said Khara, as he slid the knife along Jatayu's cheek this time, drawing some more blood. 'Where is she?'

Jatayu spat at him. 'Kill me quickly. Or kill me slowly. You will not get anything from me.'

Khara raised his knife in anger, about to strike and finish the job. It was not to be. An arrow whizzed in and struck his hand. The knife fell to the ground as he screamed aloud.

Raavan and his brother Kumbhakarna whirled around, startled. Many Lankan soldiers rushed in and formed a protective cordon around the two royals. Kumbhakarna grabbed Raavan's arm to restrain his impulsive elder brother.

Other soldiers raised their bows and pointed their arrows in the direction of Sita. A loud 'Don't shoot!' was heard from Kumbhakarna. The bows were swiftly lowered.

Khara broke the shaft, leaving the arrowhead buried in his hand. It would stem the blood for a while. He looked into the impenetrable line of trees the arrow had emerged from, and scoffed in disdain. 'Who shot that? The long-suffering prince? His oversized brother? Or the Vishnu herself?'

A stunned Sita stood rooted to the spot. *Vishnu?! How do the Lankans know? Who betrayed me?!*

She marshalled her mind into the present moment. This was not the time for distractions.

She moved quickly, without a sound, to another location. *They must not know that I'm alone.*

'Come out and fight like real warriors!' challenged Khara.

Sita was satisfied with her new position. It was some distance away from where she had shot her first arrow. She slowly pulled another arrow out of her quiver, nocked it on the bowstring and took aim. In the Lankan army, if the commander fell, the rest of the force was known to quickly retreat. But

Raavan was well protected by his soldiers, their shields raised high. She could not find an adequate line of sight.

Wish Ram was here. He would have gotten an arrow through somehow.

Sita decided to launch a rapid-fire attack on the soldiers to create an opening. She fired five arrows in quick succession. Five Lankans went down. But the others did not budge. The cordon around Raavan remained resolute. Ready to fall for their king.

Raavan remained protected.

Some soldiers began to run in her direction. She quickly moved to a new location.

As she took position, she checked the quiver. Three arrows left.

Damn!

Sita deliberately stepped on a twig. Some of the soldiers rushed towards the sound. She quickly moved again, hoping to find a breach in the protective circle of men around Raavan. But Khara was a lot smarter than she had suspected.

The Lankan stepped back and, using his uninjured left hand, pulled out a knife from the sole of his shoe. He moved behind Jatayu and held the knife to the Naga's throat.

With a maniacal smile playing on his lips, Khara taunted, 'You could have escaped. But you didn't. So I'm betting you are among those hiding behind the trees, *great* Vishnu.' Khara laid sarcastic emphasis on the word 'great'. 'And, you want to protect those who worship you. So inspiring ... so touching ...'

Khara pretended to wipe away a tear.

Sita stared at the Lankan with unblinking eyes.

Khara continued, 'So I have an offer. Step forward. Tell your husband and that giant brother-in-law of yours to also step forward. And we will let this captain live. We will even let the two sorry Ayodhya princes leave unharmed. All we want is your surrender.'

Sita remained stationary. Silent.

Khara grazed the knife slowly along Jatayu's neck, leaving behind a thin red line. He spoke in a sing-song manner, 'I don't have all day ...'

Suddenly, Jatayu struck backwards with his head, hitting Khara in his groin. As the Lankan doubled up in pain, Jatayu screamed, 'Run! Run away, My Lady! I am not worth your life!'

Three Lankan soldiers moved in and pushed Jatayu to the ground. Khara cursed loudly as he got back on his feet, still bent over to ease the pain. After a few moments, he inched towards the Naga and kicked him hard. He surveyed the treeline, turning in every direction that the arrows had been fired from. All the while, he kept kicking Jatayu again and again. He bent and roughly pulled Jatayu to his feet. Sita could see the captive now. Clearly.

This time Khara held Jatayu's head firmly with his injured right hand, to prevent any headbutting. The sneer was back on his face. He held the knife with his other hand. He placed it at the Naga's throat. 'I can cut the jugular here and your precious captain will be dead in just a few moments, great Vishnu.' He moved the knife to the Malayaputra's abdomen. 'Or, he can bleed to death slowly. All of you have some time to think about it.'

Sita was still. She had just three arrows left. It would be foolhardy to try anything. But she could not let Jatayu die. He had been like a brother to her.

'All we want is the Vishnu,' yelled Khara. 'Let her surrender and the rest of you can leave. You have my word. You have the word of a Lankan!'

'Let him go!' screamed Sita, still hidden behind the trees.

'Step forward and surrender,' said Khara, holding the knife to Jatayu's abdomen. 'And we will let him go.'

Sita looked down and closed her eyes. Her shoulders slumped with helpless rage. And then, without giving herself any time for second thoughts, she stepped out. But not before her instincts made her nock an arrow on the bow, ready to fire.

'Great Vishnu,' sniggered Khara, letting go of Jatayu for a moment, and running his hand along an ancient scar at the back of his head. Stirring a not-so-forgotten memory. 'So kind of you to join us. Where is your husband and his giant brother?'

Sita didn't answer. Some Lankan soldiers began moving slowly towards her. She noticed that their swords were sheathed. They were carrying *lathis, long bamboo sticks*, which were good enough to injure but not to kill. She stepped forward and lowered the bow. 'I am surrendering. Let Captain Jatayu go.'

Khara laughed softly as he pushed the knife deep into Jatayu's abdomen. Gently. Slowly. He cut through the liver, a kidney, never stopping ...

'Nooo!' screamed Sita. She raised her bow and shot an arrow deep into Khara's eye. It punctured the socket and lodged itself in his brain, killing him instantly.

'I want her alive!' screamed Kumbhakarna from behind the protective Lankan cordon.

More soldiers joined those already moving toward Sita, their bamboo *lathis* held high.

'Raaaam!' shouted Sita, as she pulled another arrow from her quiver, quickly nocked and shot it, bringing another Lankan down instantly.

It did not slow the pace of the others. They kept rushing forward.

Sita shot another arrow. Her last. One more Lankan sank to the ground. The others pressed on.

'Raaaam!'

The Lankans were almost upon her, their bamboo *lathis* raised.

'Raaam!' screamed Sita.

As a Lankan closed in, she lassoed her bow, entangling his *lathi* with the bowstring, snatching it from him. Sita hit back with the bamboo *lathi*, straight at the Lankan's head, knocking him off his feet. She swirled the *lathi* over her head, its menacing sound halting the suddenly wary soldiers. She stopped moving, holding her weapon steady. Conserving her energy. Ready and alert. One hand held the stick in the middle, the end of it tucked under her armpit. The other arm was stretched forward. Her feet spread wide, in balance. She was surrounded by at least fifty Lankan soldiers. But they kept their distance.

'Raaaam!' bellowed Sita, praying that her voice would somehow carry across the forest to her husband.

'We don't want to hurt you, Lady Vishnu,' said a Lankan, surprisingly polite. 'Please surrender. You will not be harmed.'

Sita cast a quick glance at Jatayu. *Is he still breathing?*

'We have the equipment in our *Pushpak Vimaan* to save him,' said the Lankan. 'Don't force us to hurt you. Please.'

Sita filled her lungs with air and screamed yet again, 'Raaaam!'

She thought she heard a faint voice from a long distance. 'Sitaaa …'

A soldier moved suddenly from her left, swinging his *lathi* low. Aiming for her calves. Sita jumped high, tucking her feet in to avoid the blow. While in the air, she quickly released the right-hand grip on the *lathi* and swung it viciously with her left hand. The *lathi* hit the Lankan on the side of his head. Knocking him unconscious.

As she landed, she shouted again, 'Raaaam!'

She heard the same voice. The voice of her husband. Soft, from the distance. 'Leave … her … alone …'

As if electrified by the sound of his voice, ten Lankans charged in together. She swung her *lathi* ferociously on all sides, rapidly incapacitating many.

'Raaaam!'

She heard the voice again. Not so distant this time. 'Sitaaaa ….'

He's close. He's close.

The Lankan onslaught was steady and unrelenting now. Sita kept swinging rhythmically. Viciously. Alas, there were one too many enemies. A Lankan swung his *lathi* from behind. Into her back.

'Raaa …'

Sita's knees buckled under her as she collapsed to the ground. Before she could recover, the soldiers ran in and held her tight.

She struggled fiercely as a Lankan came forward, holding a neem leaf in his hand. It was smeared with a blue-coloured paste. He held the leaf tight against her nose.

As darkness began to envelop her, she sensed some ropes against her hands and feet.

Ram … Help me …

And the darkness took over.

Chapter 2

'Wait a minute,' whispered Sunaina, as she pulled the reins on her horse.

Janak, the king of Mithila, and his wife, Sunaina, had travelled a long way to the Trikut Hills, nearly a hundred kilometres south of the Ganga River. They sought to meet the legendary *Kanyakumari*, the *Virgin Goddess*. A divine child. It was believed across the *Sapt Sindhu, land of the seven rivers*, that the blessings of the Living Goddess helped all who came to her with a clean heart. And the royal family of Mithila certainly needed Her blessings.

Mithila, founded by the great king Mithi, on the banks of the mighty Gandaki River, was once a thriving river-port town. Its wealth was built on agriculture, owing to its exceptionally fertile soil, as well as river trade with the rest of the Sapt Sindhu. Unfortunately, fifteen years ago, an earthquake and subsequent flood had changed the course of the Gandaki. It also changed the fortunes of Mithila. The river now flowed farther to the west, by the city of Sankashya. Ruled by Janak's younger brother Kushadhwaj, Sankashya was a nominally subsidiary kingdom of Mithila. To add to the woes of Mithila, the rains had failed repeatedly for a few years after the change of Gandaki's course. Mithila's loss was Sankashya's gain. Kushadhwaj rapidly rose in stature as the *de facto* representative of the clan of Mithi.

Many had suggested that King Janak should invest some of the old wealth of Mithila in an engineering project to redirect the Gandaki back to its old course. But Kushadhwaj had advised against it. He had argued that it made little sense to spend money on such a massive engineering project. After all, why waste money to take the river from Sankashya to Mithila, when the wealth of Sankashya was ultimately Mithila's.

Janak, a devout and spiritual man, had adopted a philosophical approach to his kingdom's decline in fortune. But the new queen, Sunaina, who had married Janak just two years earlier, was not the idle sort. She planned to restore Mithila to its old glory. And a big part of that plan was to restore the old course of the Gandaki. But after so many years, it had become difficult to find logical reasons to justify the costly and difficult engineering project.

When logic fails, faith can serve a purpose.

Sunaina had convinced Janak to accompany her to the temple of the *Kanyakumari* and seek her blessings. If the Child Goddess approved of the Gandaki project, even Kushadhwaj would find it difficult to argue against it. Not just the Mithilans, but many across the length and breadth of India believed the *Kanyakumari*'s word to be that of the Mother Goddess Herself. Unfortunately, the *Kanyakumari* had said no. 'Respect the judgement of nature,' she had said.

It was a disappointed Sunaina and a philosophical Janak, along with their royal guard, who were travelling north from the Trikut Hills now, on their way home to Mithila.

'Janak!' Sunaina raised her voice. Her husband had ridden ahead without slowing.

Janak pulled his horse's reins and looked back. His wife pointed wordlessly to a tree in the distance. Janak followed her direction. A few hundred metres away, a pack of wolves had surrounded a solitary vulture. They were trying to close in and were being pushed back repeatedly by the huge bird. The vulture was screaming and squawking. A vulture's squawk is naturally mournful; but this one sounded desperate.

Sunaina looked closely. It was an unfair fight. There were six wolves, weaving in and out, attacking the vulture in perfect coordination. But the brave bird stood its ground, pushing them back repeatedly. The aggressors were gradually drawing close. A wolf hit the vulture with its claws, drawing blood.

Why isn't it flying away?

Sunaina began to canter towards the fight, intrigued. Her bodyguards followed at a distance.

'Sunaina ...' cautioned her husband, staying where he was, holding his horse's reins tight.

Suddenly, using the distraction of the vulture with another attack from the left, a wolf struck with lethal effect. It charged in from the right and bit the bird's left wing brutally. Getting a good hold, the wolf pulled back hard, trying to drag the vulture away. The bird squawked frantically. Its voice sounding like a wail. But it held strong. It did not move, pulling back with all its strength. However, the wolf had strong jaws and a stronger grip. Blood burst forth like a fountain. The wolf let go, spitting parts of the severed wing as it stepped back.

Sunaina spurred her horse and began to gallop towards the scene. She had expected the vulture to escape through the opening the two wolves had provided. But, surprisingly, it stood in place, pushing another wolf back.

Use the opening! Get away!

Sunaina was speeding towards the animals now. The royal bodyguards drew their swords and raced after their queen. A few fell back with the king.

'Sunaina!' said Janak, worried about his wife's safety. He spurred his horse, but he was not the best of riders. His horse blithely continued its slow trot.

Sunaina was perhaps fifty metres away when she noticed the bundle for the first time. The vulture was protecting it from the pack of wolves. It was lodged in what looked like a little furrow in the dry mud.

The bundle moved.

'By the great *Lord Parshu Ram!*' exclaimed Sunaina. 'That's a baby!'

Sunaina pressed forward, rapidly goading her horse into a fierce gallop.

As she neared the pack of wolves, she heard the soft, frantic cries of a human baby, almost drowned out by the howling animals.

'*Hyaah!*' screamed Sunaina. Her bodyguards rode close behind.

The wolves turned tail and scampered into the woods as the mounted riders thundered towards the wounded bird. A guard raised his sword to strike the vulture.

'Wait!' ordered Sunaina, raising her right hand.

He stopped in his tracks as his fellow bodyguards reined their horses to a halt.

Sunaina was raised in a land to the east of Branga. Her father was from Assam, sometimes called by its ancient name, *Pragjyotisha,* the land of *Eastern Light.* And her mother belonged to *Mizoram*, the land of the *High People of Ram.* Devotees of the sixth Vishnu, Lord Parshu Ram, the Mizos were fierce warriors. But they were most well known for their instinctive understanding of animals and the rhythms of nature.

Sunaina intuitively knew that the 'bundle' was not food for the vulture, but a responsibility to be protected.

'Get me some water,' ordered Sunaina, as she dismounted her horse.

One of the guards spoke up as the group dismounted. 'My Lady, is it safe for you to …'

Sunaina cut him short with a withering look. The queen was short and petite. Her round, fair-complexioned face conveyed gentleness to the observer. But her small eyes betrayed the steely determination that was the core of her being. She repeated softly, 'Get me some water.'

'Yes, My Lady.'

A bowl filled with water appeared in an instant.

Sunaina locked her eyes with the vulture's. The bird was breathing heavily, exhausted by its battle with the wolves. It was covered in blood from the numerous wounds on its body. The wound on its wing was especially alarming, blood gushing out of it at a frightening rate. Loss of blood made it unsteady on its feet. But the vulture refused to move, its eyes fixed on Sunaina. It was squawking aggressively, thrusting its beak forward. Striking the air with its talons to keep the Queen of Mithila away.

Sunaina pointedly ignored the bundle behind the vulture. Focused on the massive bird, she began to hum a soft, calming tune. The vulture seemed to ease a bit. It withdrew its talons. The squawking reduced in volume and intensity.

Sunaina crept forward. Gently. Slowly. Once close, she bowed her head and submissively placed the bowl of water in front of the bird. Then she crept back just as slowly. She spoke in a mellifluous voice. 'I have come to help ... Trust me ...'

The dumb beast understood the tone of the human. It bent to sip some water, but instead, collapsed to the ground.

Sunaina rushed forward and cradled the head of the now prone bird, caressing it gently. The child, wrapped in a rich red cloth with black stripes, was crying desperately. She signalled a soldier to pick up the precious bundle as she continued to soothe the bird.

— ௴ —

'What a beautiful baby,' cooed Janak, as he bent his tall, wiry frame and edged close to his wife, his normally wise but detached eyes full of love and attention.

Janak and Sunaina sat on temporarily set up chairs. The baby slept comfortably in Sunaina's arms, swaddled in a soft cotton cloth. A massive umbrella shaded them from the scorching sun. The royal doctor had examined the baby, and bandaged a wound on her right temple with some herbs and neem leaves. He had assured the royal couple that the scar would largely disappear with time. Along with the other physician, the doctor now tended to the vulture's wounds.

'She's probably just a few months old. She must be strong to have survived this ordeal,' said Sunaina, gently rocking the baby in her arms.

'Yes. Strong and beautiful. Just like you.'

Sunaina looked at her husband and smiled as she caressed the baby's head. 'How can anyone abandon a child like her?'

Janak sighed. 'Many people are not wise enough to count life's blessings. They keep focusing instead on what the world has denied them.'

Sunaina nodded at her husband and turned her attention back to the child. 'She sleeps like an angel.'

'That she does,' said Janak.

Sunaina pulled the baby up close and kissed her gently on the forehead, careful to avoid the injured area.

Janak patted his wife's back warmly. 'But are you sure, Sunaina?'

'Yes. This baby is ours. Devi *Kanyakumari* may not have given us what we wanted. But she has blessed us with something much better.'

'What will we call her?'

Sunaina looked up at the sky and drew in a deep breath. She had a name in mind already. She turned to Janak. 'We found her in a furrow in Mother Earth. It was like a mother's womb for her. We will call her Sita.'

— ◌ —

Sunaina rushed into Janak's private office. Reclining in an easy chair, the king of Mithila was reading the text of the *Jabali Upanishad*. It was a treatise on wisdom by the great Maharishi Satyakam Jabali. Shifting attention to his wife, he put down the text. 'So, has the Emperor won?'

It had been five years since Sita had entered their lives.

'No,' said a bewildered Sunaina, 'he lost.'

Janak sat up straight, stunned. 'Emperor Dashrath lost to a trader from Lanka?'

'Yes. Raavan has almost completely massacred the Sapt Sindhu Army at Karachapa. Emperor Dashrath barely escaped with his life.'

'Lord Rudra be merciful,' whispered Janak.

'There's more. Queen Kaushalya, the eldest wife of the Emperor, gave birth to a son on the day that he lost the Battle of Karachapa. And now, many are blaming the little boy for the defeat. Saying that he's an ill omen. For the Emperor had never lost a battle till this boy was born.'

'What nonsense!' said Janak. 'How can people be so stupid?'

'The little boy's name is Ram. Named after the sixth Vishnu, Lord Parshu Ram.'

'Let's hope it's lucky for him. Poor child.'

'I am more concerned about the fate of Mithila, Janak.'

Janak sighed helplessly. 'What do you think will happen?'

Sunaina had been governing the kingdom practically single-handedly, of late. Janak was spending more and more time lost in the world of philosophy. The queen had become increasingly popular in the kingdom. Many believed that she had been lucky for Mithila. For the rains had poured down in all their glory every year since she had come to the city as King Janak's wife.

'I am worried about security,' said Sunaina.

'And what about money?' asked Janak. 'Don't you think Raavan will enforce his trade demands on all the kingdoms? Money will flow out of the Sapt Sindhu into Lanka's coffers.'

'But we hardly trade these days. He cannot demand anything from us. The other kingdoms have a lot more to lose. I am more worried about the decimation of the armies of the Sapt Sindhu. Lawlessness will increase everywhere. How safe can we be if the entire land falls into chaos?'

'True.'

A thought crossed Janak's mind. *Who can prevent that which is written by Fate, be it of people or of countries? Our task is but to understand, not fight, what must be; and learn the lessons for our next life. Or prepare for moksha.*

But he knew Sunaina disliked 'helplessness'. So he remained silent.

The queen continued, 'I did not expect Raavan to win.'

Janak laughed. 'It's all very well to be a victor. But the vanquished get more love from their women!'

Sunaina narrowed her eyes and stared at Janak. Not impressed by her husband's attempt at wit. 'We must make some plans, Janak. We must be ready for the inevitable.'

Janak was tempted to respond with another humorous remark. Wisdom dictated restraint.

'I trust you completely. You'll think of something, I'm sure,' smiled Janak, as he turned his attention back to the *Jabali Upanishad*.

Chapter 3

While the rest of India was suffering the aftershocks of Dashrath's defeat to Raavan, Mithila itself was relatively unaffected. There was not much trade in any case to be negatively impacted. Sunaina had initiated some reforms that had worked well. For instance, local tax collection and administration had been devolved to the village level. It reduced the strain on the Mithila bureaucracy and improved efficiency.

Using the increased revenue from agriculture, she had retrained the excess bureaucracy and expanded the Mithila police force, thus improving security within the kingdom. Mithila had no standing army and did not need one; by treaty, the Sankashya Army of Kushadhwaj was supposed to fight the external enemies of Mithila, when necessary. These were not major changes and were implemented relatively smoothly, without disturbing the daily life of the Mithilans. There were mass disturbances in the other kingdoms though, which required gut-wrenching changes to comply with the treaties imposed by Raavan.

Sita's birthday had been established as a day of celebration by royal decree. They didn't know her actual date of birth. So they celebrated the day she had been found in the furrow. Today was her sixth birthday.

Gifts and alms were distributed to the poor in the city. Like it was done on every special day. With a difference. Until Sunaina had come and toned up the administration, much of the charity was grabbed by labourers who were not rich, but who were not exactly poor either. Sunaina's administrative reforms had ensured that the charity first went to those who were truly poor and needy; those who lived in the slums close to the southern gate of the inner, secondary fort wall.

After the public ceremonies, the royal couple had arrived at the massive temple of Lord Rudra.

The Lord Rudra temple was built of red sandstone. It was one of the tallest structures in Mithila, visible from most parts of the city. It had a massive garden around it — an area of peace in this crowded quarter of the city. Beyond the garden were the slums, spreading all the way to the fort walls. Inside the main *garba griha, the sanctum sanctorum* of the temple, a large idol of Lord Rudra and Lady Mohini had been consecrated. Seemingly in consonance with a city that had come to symbolise the love of knowledge, peace, and philosophy, the image of Lord Rudra was not in his normally fierce form. In this form, he looked kind, almost gentle. He held the hand of the beauteous Lady Mohini, who sat next to him.

After the prayers, the temple priest offered *prasad* to the royal family. Sunaina touched the priest's feet and then led Sita by the hand to a wall by the side of the *garba griha*. On the wall, a plaque had been put up in memory of the vulture that had valiantly died defending Sita from a pack of wolves. A death mask of its face had been made before the bird was cremated with honour. Cast in metal, the mask recorded the last expression of the vulture as it left its mortal body. It was a haunting look: determined and noble. Sita had made her mother relate the entire story on several occasions. Sunaina had been happy to oblige. She wanted her daughter to remember. To know that nobility came in many a form and face. Sita touched the death mask gently, reverentially. And as always, she shed a tear for the one who had also given her the gift of life.

'Thank you,' whispered Sita. She said a short prayer to the great God *Pashupati, Lord of the Animals*. She hoped the vulture's brave soul had found purpose again.

Janak discreetly signalled his wife, and the royal family slowly walked out of the Lord Rudra temple. The priests led the family down the flight of steps. The slums were clearly visible from the platform height.

'Why don't you ever let me go there, *Maa*?' asked Sita, pointing at the slums.

Sunaina smiled and patted her daughter's head. 'Soon.'

'You always say that,' Sita protested, a grumpy expression on her face.

'And, I mean it,' laughed Sunaina. 'Soon. I just didn't say how soon!'

— ᚺᛉ —

'Alright,' said Janak, ruffling Sita's hair. 'Run along now. I have to speak with Guru*ji*.'

The seven-year-old Sita had been playing with her father in his private office when Janak's chief guru, Ashtaavakra, had walked in. Janak had bowed to his guru, as was the tradition, and had requested him to sit on the throne assigned for him.

Mithila, not being a major player in the political arena of the Sapt Sindhu anymore, did not have a permanent *raj guru*. But Janak's court hosted the widest range of eminent seers, scholars, scientists and philosophers from India. Intellectuals loved the Mithilan air, wafting with the fragrance of knowledge and wisdom. And one of the most distinguished of these thinkers, Rishi Ashtaavakra, was Janak's chief guru. Even the great Maharishi Vishwamitra, Chief of the Malayaputra tribe, visited Mithila on occasion.

'We can speak later, if you so desire, Your Highness,' said Ashtaavakra.

'No, no. Of course not,' said Janak. 'I need your guidance on a question that has been troubling me, Guru*ji*.'

Ashtaavakra's body was deformed in eight places. His mother had met with an accident late in her pregnancy. But fate and karma had balanced the physical handicap with an extraordinary mind. Ashtaavakra had shown signs of utter brilliance from a very young age. As a youth, he had visited Janak's court and defeated the king's then chief guru, Rishi Bandi, in a scintillating debate. In doing so, he had redeemed his father, Rishi Kahola, who had lost a debate to Bandi earlier. Rishi Bandi had gracefully accepted defeat and retired to an ashram near the Eastern Sea to acquire more knowledge. Thus it was that the young Ashtaavakra became Janak's chief guru.

Ashtaavakra's deformities did not attract attention in the liberal atmosphere of Mithila, the kingdom of the pious king, Janak. For the sage's luminous mind was compelling.

'I will see you in the evening, *Baba*,' said Sita to her *father* as she touched his feet.

Janak blessed her. She also touched the feet of Rishi Ashtaavakra and walked out of the chamber. As she crossed the threshold, Sita stopped and hid behind the door. Out of Janak's eyesight, but within earshot. She wanted to hear what question had been troubling her father.

'How do we know what reality is, Guru*ji*?' asked Janak.

The young Sita stood nonplussed. Confused. She had heard whisperings in the corridors of the palace. That her father was becoming increasingly eccentric. That they were lucky to have a pragmatic queen in Sunaina to look after the kingdom. *What is reality?*

She turned and ran towards her mother's chambers. '*Maa!*'

— ᚱᚷ —

Sita had waited long enough. She was eight years old now. And her mother had still not taken her to the slums adjoining the fort walls. The last time she had asked, she had at least been offered an explanation. She had been told that it could be dangerous. That some people could get beaten up over there. Sita now believed that her mother was just making excuses.

Finally, curiosity had gotten the better of her. Disguised in the clothes of a maid's child, Sita slipped out of the palace. An oversized *angvastram* was wrapped around her shoulder and ears, serving as a hood. Her heart pounded with excitement and nervousness. She repeatedly looked behind to ensure that no one noticed her embark on her little adventure. No one did.

Late in the afternoon, Sita passed the Lord Rudra temple gardens and stole into the slums. All alone. Her mother's words ringing in her ears, she had armed herself with a large stick. She had been practising stick-fighting for over a year now.

As she entered the slum area, she screwed up her nose. Assaulted by the stench. She looked back at the temple garden, feeling the urge to turn back. But almost immediately, the excitement of doing something forbidden took over. She had waited a long time for this. She walked farther into the slum quarters. The houses were rickety structures made of bamboo sticks and haphazardly spread cloth awnings. The cramped space between the wobbly houses served as the 'streets' on which people walked through the slums. These streets also served as open drains, toilets, and open-air animal shelters. They were covered with garbage. There was muck and excreta everywhere. A thin film of animal and human urine made it difficult to walk. Sita pulled her *angvastram* over her nose and mouth, fascinated and appalled at the same time.

People actually live like this? Lord Rudra be merciful.

The palace staff had told her that things had improved in the slums after Queen Sunaina had come to Mithila.

How much worse could it have been for this to be called an improvement?

She soldiered on, gingerly side-stepping the muck on the muddy walkways. Till she saw something that made her stop.

A mother sat outside a slum house, feeding her child from a frugal plate. Her baby was perhaps two or three years old. He sat in his mother's lap, gurgling happily as he dodged the morsels from her hand. Every now and then, he obliged the mother and opened his mouth with theatrical concession, allowing her to stuff small morsels of food into his mouth. It would then be the mother's turn to coo in delight. Pleasing as it was, this wasn't what fascinated Sita. A crow sat next to the woman. And she fed every other morsel to the bird. The crow waited for its turn. Patiently. To it, this wasn't a game.

The woman fed them both. Turn by turn.

Sita smiled. She remembered something her mother had said to her a few days back: *Often the poor have more nobility in them than the actual nobility.*

She hadn't really understood the words then. She did now.

Sita turned around. She'd seen enough of the slums for her first trip. She promised herself that she would return soon. Time to go back to the palace.

There were four tiny lanes ahead. *Which one do I take?*

Uncertain, she took the left-most one and began to walk. She kept moving. But the slum border was nowhere in sight. Her heartbeat quickened as she nervously hastened her pace.

The light had begun to fade. Every chaotic lane seemed to end at a crossroads of several other paths. All haphazard, all disorganised. Confused, she blindly turned into a quiet lane. Beginning to feel the first traces of panic, she quickened her steps. But it only took her the wrong way, faster.

'Sorry!' cried Sita, as she banged into someone.

The dark-skinned girl looked like an adolescent; perhaps older. She had a dirty, unkempt look about her. The stench from her tattered clothes suggested that she had not changed them for a while. Lice crawled over the surface of her matted, unwashed hair. She was tall, lean, and surprisingly muscular. Her feline eyes and scarred body gave her a dangerous, edgy look.

She stared at Sita's face and then at her hands. There was a sudden flash of recognition in her eyes, as though sensing an opportunity. Sita, meanwhile, had darted into an adjacent lane. The Princess of Mithila picked up pace, almost breaking into a desperate run. Praying that this was the correct path out of the slum.

Sweat beads were breaking out on her forehead. She tried to steady her breath. She couldn't.

She kept running. Till she was forced to stop.

'Lord Rudra be merciful.'

She had screeched to a halt, confronted by a solid barrier

wall. She was now well and truly lost, finding herself at the other end of the slum which abutted the inner fort wall. The inner city of Mithila was as far as it could be. It was eerily quiet, with scarcely anyone around. The sun had almost set, and the faint snatches of twilight only emphasised the darkness. She did not know what to do.

'Who is this now?' A voice was heard from behind her.

Sita whirled around, ready to strike. She saw two adolescent boys moving towards her from the right. She turned left. And ran. But did not get far. A leg stuck out and tripped her, making her fall flat on her face. Into the muck. There were more of them. She got up quickly and grabbed her stick. Five boys had gathered around her. Casual menace on their faces.

Her mother had warned her about the crimes in the slums. Of people getting beaten up. But Sita had not believed those stories, thinking that the sweet people who came to collect charity from her mother would never hurt anyone.

I should have listened to Maa.

Sita looked around nervously. The five boys were now in front of her. The steep fort wall was behind her. There was no escape.

She brandished the stick at them, threateningly. The boys let out a merry laugh, amused by the antics of the little girl.

The one in the centre bit a fingernail in mock fear, and said in a sing-song voice, 'Ooh ... we're so scared ...'

Raucous laughter followed.

'That's a precious ring, noble girl,' said the boy, with theatrical politeness. 'I'm sure it's worth more than what the five of us will earn in our entire lives. Do you think that ...'

'Do you want the ring?' asked Sita, feeling a sense of relief as she reached for it. 'Take it. Just let me go.'

The boy sniggered. 'Of course we will let you go. First throw the ring over here.'

Sita gulped anxiously. She balanced her stick against her body, and quickly pulled the ring off her forefinger. Holding it in her closed fist, she pointed the stick at them with her left hand. 'I know how to use this.'

The boy looked at his friends, his eyebrows raised. He turned to the girl and smiled. 'We believe you. Just throw the ring here.'

Sita flung the ring forward. It fell a short distance from the boy.

'Your throwing arm could do with more strength, noble girl,' laughed the boy, as he bent down to pick it up. He looked at it carefully and whistled softly, before tucking it into his waistband. 'Now, what more do you have?'

Suddenly, the boy arched forward and fell to the ground. Behind him stood the tall, dark-skinned girl Sita had crashed into earlier. She held a big bamboo stick with both hands. The boys whirled around aggressively and looked at the girl; the bravado evaporated just as quickly. She was taller than they were. Lean and muscular.

More importantly, it appeared the boys knew her. And her reputation.

'You have nothing to do with this, Samichi ...' said one of the boys, hesitantly. 'Leave.'

Samichi answered with her stick and struck his hand. Ferociously. The boy staggered back, clutching his arm.

'I'll break the other one too, if you don't get out of here,' growled Samichi.

And, the boy ran.

The other four delinquents, however, stood their ground.

The one that was felled earlier was back on his feet. They faced Samichi, their backs to Sita. The apparently harmless one. They didn't notice Sita gripping her stick, holding it high above her head and creeping up on the one who had her ring. Judging the distance perfectly, she swung her weapon viciously at the boy's head.

Thwack!

The boy collapsed in a heap, blood spurting from the crack on the back of his head. The three others turned around. Shocked. Paralysed.

'Come on! Quick!' screamed Samichi, as she rushed forward and grabbed Sita by the hand.

As the two girls ran around the corner, Samichi stole a glance back at the scene. The boy lay on the ground, unmoving. His friends had gathered around him, trying to rouse him.

'Quickly!' shouted Samichi, dragging Sita along.

Chapter 4

Sita stood, her hands locked behind her back. Her head bowed. Muck and refuse from the Mithila slums all over her clothes. Her face caked with mud. The very expensive ring on her finger missing. Shivering with fear. She had never seen her mother so angry.

Sunaina was staring at her daughter. No words were spoken. Just a look of utter disapproval. And worse, disappointment. Sita felt like she had failed her mother in the worst possible way.

'I'm so sorry, *Maa*,' wailed Sita, fresh tears flowing down her face.

She wished her mother would at least say something. Or, slap her. Or, scold her. This silence was terrifying.

'*Maa* …'

Sunaina sat in stony silence. Staring hard at her daughter.

'My Lady!'

Sunaina looked towards the entrance to her chamber. A Mithila policeman was standing there. His head bowed.

'What is the news?' asked Sunaina, brusquely.

'The five boys are missing, My Lady,' said the policeman. 'They have probably escaped.'

'All five?'

'I don't have any new information on the injured boy, My Lady,' said the policeman, referring to the one hit on the head by Sita. 'Some witnesses have come forward. They say that he was carried away by the other boys. He was bleeding a lot.'

'A lot?'

'Well... one witness said he would be surprised if that boy ...'

The policeman, wisely, left the words 'made it alive' unsaid.

'Leave us,' ordered Sunaina.

The policeman immediately saluted, turned, and marched out.

Sunaina turned her attention back to Sita. Her daughter cowered under the stern gaze. The queen then looked beyond Sita, at the filthy adolescent standing near the wall.

'What is your name, child?' asked Sunaina.

'Samichi, My Lady.'

'You are not going back to the slums, Samichi. You will stay in the palace from now on.'

Samichi smiled and folded her hands together into a *Namaste*. 'Of course, My Lady. It will be my honour to ...'

Samichi stopped speaking as Sunaina raised her right hand. The queen turned towards Sita. 'Go to your chambers. Take a bath. Have the physician look at your wounds; and Samichi's wounds. We will speak tomorrow.'

'*Maa* ...'

'Tomorrow.'

— ᚱᚼ —

Sita was standing next to Sunaina, who was seated on the ground. Both Sunaina and she were outside the private temple room in the queen's chambers. Sunaina was engrossed in making a fresh *rangoli* on the floor; *made of powdered colours, it was an ethereal mix of fractals, mathematics, philosophy, and spiritual symbolism.*

Sunaina made a new *rangoli* early every morning at the entrance of the temple. Within the temple, idols of the main Gods who Sunaina worshipped had been consecrated: Lord Parshu Ram, the previous Vishnu; Lord Rudra, the great Mahadev; Lord Brahma, the creator-scientist. But the pride of place at the centre was reserved for the Mother Goddess, Shakti *Maa.* The tradition of Mother Goddess worship was especially strong in the land of Sunaina's father, Assam; a vast, fertile and fabulously rich valley that embraced the upper reaches of the largest river of the Indian subcontinent, Brahmaputra.

Sita waited patiently. Too scared to talk.

'There is always a reason why I ask you to do or not do something, Sita,' said Sunaina. Not raising her eyes from the intricate *rangoli* that was emerging on the floor.

Sita sat still. Her eyes pinned on her mother's hands.

'There is an age to discover certain things in life. You need to be ready for it.'

Finishing the *rangoli*, Sunaina looked at her daughter. Sita relaxed as she saw her mother's eyes. They were full of love. As always. She wasn't angry anymore.

'There are bad people too, Sita. People who do criminal things. You find them among the rich in the inner city and the poor in the slums.'

'Yes *Maa*, I ...'

'Shhh ... don't talk, just listen,' said Sunaina firmly. Sita fell silent. Sunaina continued. 'The criminals among the rich are mostly driven by greed. One can negotiate with greed. But the criminals among the poor are driven by desperation and anger. Desperation can sometimes bring out the best in a human being. That's why the poor can often be noble. But desperation can also bring out the worst. They have nothing to lose. And they get angry when they see others with so much when they have so little. It's understandable. As rulers, our responsibility is to make efforts and change things for the better. But it cannot happen overnight. If we take too much from the rich to help the poor, the rich will rebel. That can cause chaos. And everyone will suffer. So we have to work slowly. We must help the truly poor. That is dharma. But we should not be blind and assume that all poor are noble. Not everyone has the spirit to keep their character strong when their stomachs are empty.'

Sunaina pulled Sita onto her lap. She sat comfortably. For the first time since her foolhardy foray into the slums, she breathed a little easier.

'You will help me govern Mithila someday,' said Sunaina. 'You will need to be mature and pragmatic. You must use your heart to decide the destination, but use your head to plot the journey. People who only listen to their hearts usually fail. On the other hand, people who only use their heads tend to be selfish. Only the heart can make you think of others before yourself. For the sake of dharma, you must aim for equality and balance in society. Perfect equality can never be achieved but we must try to reduce inequality as much as we can. But don't fall into the trap of stereotypes. Don't assume that the powerful are always bad or that the powerless are always good. There is good and bad in everyone.'

Sita nodded silently.

'You need to be liberal, of course. For that is the Indian way. But don't be a blind and stupid liberal.'

'Yes, *Maa.*'

'And do not wilfully put yourself in danger ever again.'

Sita hugged her mother, as tears flowed out of her eyes.

Sunaina pulled back and wiped her daughter's tears. 'You frightened me to death. What would I have done if something bad had happened to you?'

'Sorry, *Maa.*'

Sunaina smiled as she embraced Sita again. 'My impulsive little girl …'

Sita took a deep breath. Guilt had been gnawing away at her. She needed to know. '*Maa*, that boy I hit on the head … What …'

Sunaina interrupted her daughter. 'Don't worry about that.'

'But …'

'I said don't worry about that.'

— ॐ —

'Thank you, *chacha*!' Sita squealed, as she jumped into her *uncle* Kushadhwaj's arms.

Kushadhwaj, Janak's younger brother and the king of Sankashya, was on a visit to Mithila. He had brought a gift for his niece. A gift that had been a massive hit. It was an Arabian horse. Native Indian breeds were different from the Arab variety. The Indian ones usually had thirty-four ribs while the Arabian horses often had thirty-six. More importantly, an Arabian horse was much sought after as it was smaller, sleeker, and easier to train. And its endurance level was markedly superior. It was a prized possession. And expensive too.

Sita was understandably delighted.

Kushadhwaj handed her a customised saddle, suitable for

her size. Made of leather, it had a gold-plated horn on top of the pommel. The saddle, though small, was still heavy for the young Sita. But she refused the help of the Mithila royal staff in carrying it.

Sita dragged the saddle to the private courtyard of the royal chambers, where her young horse waited for her. It was held by one of Kushadhwaj's aides.

Sunaina smiled. 'Thank you so much. Sita will be lost in this project for the next few weeks. I don't think she will eat or sleep till she's learnt how to ride!'

'She's a good girl,' said Kushadhwaj.

'But it is an expensive gift, Kushadhwaj.'

'She's my only niece, *Bhabhi*,' said Kushadhwaj to his *sister-in-law*. 'If I won't spoil her, then who will?'

Sunaina smiled and gestured for them to join Janak in the veranda adjoining the courtyard. The king of Mithila set the *Brihadaranyak Upanishad* manuscript aside as his wife and brother joined him. Discreet aides placed some cups filled with buttermilk on the table. They also lit a silver lamp, placed at the centre of the table. Just as noiselessly, they withdrew.

Kushadhwaj cast a quizzical look at the lamp and frowned. It was daytime. But he remained quiet.

Sunaina waited till the aides were out of earshot. Then she looked at Janak. But her husband had picked up his manuscript again. Deeply engrossed. After her attempts to meet his eyes remained unsuccessful, she cleared her throat. Janak remained focused on the manuscript in his hands.

'What is it, *Bhabhi*?' asked Kushadhwaj.

Sunaina realised that she had no choice. She would have to be the one to speak up. She pulled a document out of the large pouch tied to her waist and placed it on the table. Kushadhwaj resolutely refused to look at it.

'Kushadhwaj, we have been discussing the road connecting Sankashya to Mithila for many years now,' said Sunaina. 'It was washed away in the Great Flood. But it has been more than two decades since. The absence of that road has caused immense hardship to the citizens and traders of Mithila.'

'What traders, *Bhabhi*?' said Kushadhwaj, laughing gently. 'Are there any in Mithila?'

Sunaina ignored the barb. 'You had agreed in principle to pay for two-thirds of the cost of the road, if Mithila financed the remaining one-third.'

Kushadhwaj remained silent.

'Mithila has raised its share of the money,' said Sunaina. She pointed to the document. 'Let's seal the agreement and let the construction begin.'

Kushadhwaj smiled. 'But *Bhabhi*, I don't see what the problem is. The road is not that bad. People use it every day. I myself took that road to Mithila yesterday.'

'But you are a king, Kushadhwaj,' said Sunaina pleasantly, her tone studiously polite. 'You are capable of many things that ordinary people are not. Ordinary people need a good road.'

Kushadhwaj smiled broadly. 'Yes, the ordinary people of Mithila are lucky to have a queen as committed to them as you are.'

Sunaina did not say anything.

'I have an idea, *Bhabhi*,' said Kushadhwaj. 'Let Mithila begin the construction of the road. Once your share of the one-third is done, Sankashya will complete the remaining two-third.'

'All right.'

Sunaina picked up the document and a quill from a side table and scribbled a line at the end. She then pulled out the royal seal from her pouch and marked the agreement.

She offered the document to Kushadhwaj. It was then that Kushadhwaj realised the significance of the lamp.

Lord Agni, the God of Fire, as witness.

Every Indian believed that *Agni* was the great purifier. It was not a coincidence that the first hymn of the first chapter of the holiest Indian scripture, the *Rig Veda*, celebrated Lord Agni. All promises that were sealed with the God of Fire as witness could never be broken; promises of marriage, of *yagnas*, of peace treaties ... and even a promise to build roads.

Kushadhwaj did not take the agreement from his sister-in-law. Instead, he reached into his pouch and pulled out his own royal seal. 'I trust you completely, *Bhabhi*. You can mark my agreement on the document.'

Sunaina took the seal from Kushadhwaj and was about to stamp the agreement, when he softly spoke, 'It's a new seal, *Bhabhi*. One that reflects Sankashya properly.'

Sunaina frowned. She turned the seal around and looked at its markings. Even though it was a mirror image of the symbol that would be marked on the agreement, the Queen of Mithila recognised it immediately. It was a single dolphin; the seal symbol of Mithila. Sankashya had historically been a subsidiary kingdom of Mithila, ruled by the younger members of the royal family. And it had a different seal: a single *hilsa* fish.

Sunaina stiffened in anger. But she knew that she had to control her temper. She slowly placed the document back on the table. The Sankashya seal had not been used.

'Why don't you give me your actual seal, Kushadhwaj?' said Sunaina.

'This is my kingdom's seal now, *Bhabhi*.'

'It can never be so unless Mithila accepts it. No kingdom will recognise this as your seal till Mithila publicly does so.

Every Sapt Sindhu kingdom knows that the single dolphin is the mark of the Mithila royal family's direct line.'

'True, *Bhabhi*. But you can change that. You can legitimise this seal across the land by using it on that document.'

Sunaina cast a look at her husband. The king of Mithila raised his head, looked briefly at his wife, and then went back to the *Brihadaranyak Upanishad*.

'This is not acceptable, Kushadhwaj,' said Sunaina, maintaining her calm expression and voice to hide the anger boiling within. 'This will not happen for as long as I'm alive.'

'I don't understand why you are getting so agitated, *Bhabhi*. You have married into the Mithila royal family. I was born into it. The royal blood of Mithila flows in *my* veins, not yours. Right, Janak *dada*?'

Janak looked up and finally spoke, though the tone was detached and devoid of anger. 'Kushadhwaj, whatever Sunaina says is my decision as well.'

Kushadhwaj stood up. 'This is a sad day. Blood has been insulted by blood. For the sake of …'

Sunaina too rose to her feet. Abruptly interrupting Kushadhwaj, though her tone remained unfailingly polite. 'Be careful what you say next, Kushadhwaj.'

Kushadhwaj laughed. He stepped forward and took the Sankashya seal from Sunaina's hand. 'This is mine.'

Sunaina remained silent.

'Don't pretend to be a custodian of the royal traditions of Mithila,' scoffed Kushadhwaj. 'You are not blood family. You are only an import.'

Sunaina was about to say something when she felt a small hand wrap itself around hers. She looked down. The young Sita stood by her side, shaking with fury. In her other hand was the saddle that Kushadhwaj had just gifted her. She threw the saddle at her uncle. It fell on his feet.

As Kushadhwaj doubled up in pain, the Sankashya seal fell from his hand.

Sita leapt forward, picked up the seal and smashed it to the ground, breaking it in two. The breaking of a royal seal was considered a very bad omen. This was a grievous insult.

'Sita!' shouted Janak.

Kushadhwaj's face contorted with fury. 'This is an outrage, *Dada*!'

Sita now stood in front of her mother. She faced her uncle, daring him with her eyes. Spreading her arms out to cover her mother protectively.

The king of Sankashya picked up the broken pieces of his royal seal and stormed out. 'You have not heard the last of this, *Dada*!'

As he left, Sunaina went down on her knees and turned Sita around. 'You should not have done that, Sita.'

Sita looked at her mother with smouldering eyes. Then turned to look at her father, defiant and accusing. There was not a trace of apology on her face.

'You should not have done that, Sita.'

— ᚷᚷ —

Sita held on to her mother, refusing to let go. She wept with wordless anguish. A smiling Janak came up to her and patted her head. The royal family had gathered in the king's private office. A few weeks had passed since the incident with Kushadhwaj. Sita, her parents had decided, was old enough to leave for *gurukul*; literally, the *Guru's family*, but in effect a residential school.

Janak and Sunaina had chosen Rishi Shvetaketu's *gurukul* for their daughter. Shvetaketu was the uncle of Janak's chief guru, Ashtaavakra. His *gurukul* offered lessons in the core subjects of Philosophy, Mathematics, Science, and Sanskrit. Sita would also receive education in other specialised subjects like Geography, History, Economics, and Royal Administration, among others.

One subject that Sunaina had insisted Sita be taught, overriding Janak's objections, was warfare and martial arts. Janak believed in non-violence. Sunaina believed in being practical.

Sita knew that she had to go. But she was a child. And the child was terrified of leaving home.

'You will come home regularly, my dear,' said Janak. 'And we will come and see you too. The *ashram* is on the banks of the Ganga River. It's not too far.'

Sita tightened her grip on her mother.

Sunaina prised Sita's arms and held her chin. She made her daughter look at her. 'You will do well there. It will prepare you for your life. I know that.'

'Are you sending me away because of what I did with *chacha*?' sobbed Sita.

Sunaina and Janak immediately went down on their knees and held her close.

'Of course not, my darling,' said Sunaina. 'This has nothing to do with your uncle. You have to study. You must get educated so that you can help run this kingdom someday.'

'Yes, Sita,' said Janak. 'Your mother is right. What happened with Kushadhwaj uncle has nothing to do with you. It is between him, and your mother and I.'

Sita burst into a fresh bout of tears. She clung to her parents like she'd never let them go.

Chapter 5

Two years had passed since Sita had arrived in Shvetaketu's *gurukul*. While the ten-year-old student had impressed her guru with her intelligence and sharpness, it was her enthusiasm for the outdoors that was truly extraordinary. Especially noteworthy was her skill in stick-fighting.

But her spirited temperament also created problems on occasion. Like the time when a fellow student had called her father an ineffectual king, more suited to being a teacher than a ruler. Sita's response had been to thrash the living daylights out of him. The boy had been confined to the *gurukul Ayuralay* for almost a month. He had limped for two months after that.

A worried Shvetaketu had arranged for extra classes on the subjects of non-violence and impulse control. The hot-headed girl had also been strictly reminded of the rules against physical violence on the *gurukul* premises. The art of warfare was taught to inculcate self-discipline and a code of conduct for future royal duties. Within the school, they were not allowed to hurt one another.

To ensure that the message went home, Sunaina had also been told of this incident on one of her visits to the *gurukul*. Her strong words had had the desired impact on Sita. She had refrained from beating other students since then, though her resolve was tested at times.

This was one such time.

'Aren't you adopted?' taunted Kaaml Raj, a fellow classmate.

Five students from the *gurukul* had gathered close to the pond on the campus. Three sat around Sita, who had drawn a geometric shape on the ground, using some ropes. Engrossed in explaining a theorem from the *Baudhayana Shulba Sutra*, she had been studiously ignoring Kaaml. As were the others. He was hovering around as usual, trying to distract everyone. Upon hearing his words, all eyes turned to Sita.

Radhika was Sita's best friend. She immediately tried to prevent a reaction. 'Let it be, Sita. He is a fool.'

Sita sat up straight and closed her eyes for a moment. She had often wondered about her birth mother. Why had she abandoned her? Was she as magnificent as her adoptive mother? But there was no doubt in her mind about one fact: She was Sunaina's daughter.

'I am my mother's daughter,' muttered Sita, looking defiantly at her tormentor as she pointedly ignored her friend's advice.

'Yes, yes, I know that. We are all our mothers' children. But aren't you adopted? What will happen to you when your mother has a real daughter?'

'Real daughter? I am not unreal, Kaaml. I am *very* real.'

'Yes, yes. But you are not ...'

'Just get lost,' said Sita. She picked up the twig with which she had been explaining the *Baudhayana* theorem.

'No, no. You aren't understanding what I'm saying. If you are adopted, you can be thrown out at any time. What will you do then?'

Sita put the twig down and looked at Kaaml with cold eyes.

This would have been a good moment for the boy to shut up. Regrettably, he did not have too much sense.

'I can see that the teachers like you. Guru*ji* likes you a lot. You can come back here and teach all day when you get thrown out of your home!' Kaaml broke into maniacal laughter. No one else laughed. In fact, the tension in the air was crackling dangerously.

'Sita ...' pleaded Radhika, again advising calm. 'Let it be ...'

Sita ignored Radhika's advice yet again. She slowly got up and walked towards Kaaml. The boy swallowed hard, but he did not step back. Sita's hands were locked tightly behind her back. She stopped within an inch of her adversary. She looked at him and glared. Straight into his eyes. Kaaml's breath had quickened nervously, and the twitch in his temple showed that his courage was rapidly disappearing. But he stood his ground.

Sita took one more threatening step. Dangerously close to Kaaml. Her toe was now touching the boy's. The tip of her nose was less than a centimetre from his face. Her eyes flashed fire.

Sweat beads had formed on Kaaml's forehead. 'Listen ... you are not allowed to hit anyone ...'

Sita kept her eyes locked with his. She kept staring. Unblinking. Cold. Breathing heavily.

Kaaml's voice emerged in a squeak. 'Listen ...'

Sita suddenly screamed loudly; an ear-splitting sound right in Kaaml's face. A forceful, strong, high-pitched bellow. A startled Kaaml fell back, flat on the ground and burst into tears.

And, the other children burst into laughter.

A teacher appeared seemingly from nowhere.

'I didn't hit him! I didn't hit him!'

'Sita ...'

Sita allowed herself to be led away by the teacher. 'But I didn't hit him!'

— ᠌ᡶᠵ —

'Hanu *bhaiya*!' cooed Radhika as she hugged her *elder brother*. Or more specifically, her elder *cousin* brother.

Radhika had asked Sita along to meet her favourite relative. The meeting place was around an hour's walk from the *gurukul*, deep in the jungles to the south, in a well-hidden clearing. This was where the cousins met. In secret. Her brother had good reasons to remain invisible to the *gurukul* authorities.

He was a Naga; a person born with deformities.

He was dressed in a dark-brown *dhoti* with a white *angvastram*. Fair-skinned. Tall and hirsute. An outgrowth jutted out from his lower back, almost like a tail. It flapped with rhythmic precision, as though it had a mind of its own. His massive build and sturdy musculature gave him an awe-inspiring presence. Almost a godly aura. His flat nose was pressed against his face, which in turn was outlined with facial hair, encircling it with neat precision. Strangely though, the skin above and below his mouth was hairless, silken smooth and light pink in colour; it had a puffed appearance. His lips were a thin, barely noticeable line. Thick eyebrows drew a sharp, artistic curve above captivating eyes that radiated intelligence and a meditative calm. It almost seemed like the Almighty had taken the face of a monkey and placed it on a man's head.

He looked at Radhika with almost paternal affection. 'How are you, my little sister?'

Radhika stuck her lower lip out in mock anger. 'How long has it been since I saw you last? Ever since father allowed that new *gurukul* to come up …'

Radhika's father was the chief of a village along the river Shon. He had recently given permission for a *gurukul* to be set up close to the village. Four young boys had been enrolled. There were no other students. Sita had wondered why Radhika was still in Rishi Shvetaketu's *gurukul*, when another was now so close to home. Maybe a small, four-student *gurukul* was not as good as their Guru*ji*'s renowned school.

'Sorry Radhika, I've been very busy,' said the man. 'I've been given a new assignment and ...'

'I don't care about your new assignment!'

Radhika's brother quickly changed the topic. 'Aren't you going to introduce me to your new friend?'

Radhika stared at him for a few more seconds, then smiled in surrender and turned to her friend. 'This is Sita, the princess of Mithila. And this is my elder brother, Hanu *bhaiya*.'

He gave his new acquaintance a broad smile as he folded his hands into a *Namaste*. 'Hanu *bhaiya* is what little Radhika calls me. My name is Hanuman.'

Sita folded her hands too, and looked up at the kindly face. 'I think I prefer Hanu *bhaiya*.'

Hanuman laughed warmly. 'Then Hanu *bhaiya* it is!'

— ᳵ —

Sita had spent five years in the *gurukul*. She was thirteen years old now.

The *gurukul* was built on the southern banks of the holy Ganga, a short distance downriver from Magadh, where the feisty Sarayu merged into the sedate Ganga. Its location was so convenient that many *rishis* and *rishikas* from various *ashrams* used to drop into this *gurukul.* They, usually, even taught for a few months as visiting teachers.

Indeed, Maharishi Vishwamitra himself was on a visit to the *gurukul* right now. He and his followers entered the frugal *ashram,* home to almost twenty-five students.

'*Namaste,* great Malayaputra,' said Shvetaketu, folding his hands together and bowing to the legendary *rishi,* chief of the tribe left behind by the sixth Vishnu, Lord Parshu Ram. The Malayaputras were tasked with two missions: to help the next Mahadev, Destroyer of Evil, if and when he or she arose. And, to give rise to the next Vishnu, Propagator of Good, when the time was right.

The *gurukul* was electrified by the presence of the great Maharishi Vishwamitra; considered a *Saptrishi Uttradhikari, successor to the legendary seven rishis.* It was a singular honour, greater than receiving any of the men and women of knowledge who had visited before.

'*Namaste,* Shvetaketu,' said Vishwamitra imperiously, a hint of a smile playing on his face.

The staff at the *gurukul* had immediately set to work. Some helped the sage's followers with their luggage and horses, while others rushed to clean the already spick-and-span guest quarters. Arishtanemi, the military chief of the Malayaputras and the right-hand man of Vishwamitra, organised the efforts like the battle commander that he was.

'What brings you to these parts, Great One?' asked Shvetaketu.

'I had some work upriver,' said Vishwamitra, enigmatically, refusing to elaborate.

Shvetaketu knew better than to ask any more questions on this subject to the fearsome Malayaputra chief. But an attempt at conversation was warranted. 'Raavan's trade treaties are causing immense pain to the kingdoms of the Sapt Sindhu, noble Guru. People are suffering and being impoverished. Somebody has to fight him.'

Almost seven feet tall, the dark-skinned Vishwamitra was altogether of unreal proportions, both physically and in intellect. His large belly lay under a sturdy chest, muscular shoulders, and powerful arms. A flowing white beard grazed his chest. Brahminical, tuft of knotted hair on an otherwise shaven head. Large, limpid eyes. And the holy *janau, sacred thread*, tied over his shoulder. In startling contrast were the numerous battle scars that lined his face and body. He looked down at Shvetaketu from his great height.

'There are no kings today who can take on this task,' said Vishwamitra. 'They are all just survivors. Not leaders.'

'Perhaps this task is beyond that of mere kings, Illustrious One ...'

Vishwamitra's smile broadened mysteriously. But no words followed.

Shvetaketu would not let down his need for interaction with the great man. 'Forgive my impertinence, Maharishi*ji*, but how long do you expect to stay with us? It would be wonderful if my students could get the benefit of your guidance.'

'I will be here for only a few days, Shvetaketu. Teaching your children may not be possible.'

Shvetaketu was about to repeat his request, as politely as possible, when a loud sound was heard.

A speedy whoosh followed by a loud thwack!

Vishwamitra had once been a Kshatriya warrior prince. He recognised the sound immediately. Of a spear hitting a wooden target. Almost perfectly.

He turned in the direction that the sound had emerged from, his brows lifted slightly in admiration. 'Someone in your *gurukul* has a strong throwing arm, Shvetaketu.'

Shvetaketu smiled proudly. 'Let me show you, Guru*ji*.'

— ᚱᚷ —

'Sita?' asked Vishwamitra, surprised beyond words. 'Janak's daughter, Sita?'

Vishwamitra and Shvetaketu were at one end of the sparse but well-equipped outdoor training arena, where students practised archery, spear-throwing and other *ananga* weapon techniques. At the other end was a separate area set aside for the practice of *anga* weapons like swords and maces. Sita, immersed in her practice, did not see the two *rishis* as they silently walked in and watched her get ready for the next throw.

'She has the wisdom of King Janak, great Malayaputra,' answered Shvetaketu. 'But she also has the pragmatism and fighting spirit of Queen Sunaina. And, dare I say, my *gurukul* teachers have moulded her spirit well.'

Vishwamitra observed Sita with a keen eye. Tall for a thirteen-year old, she was already beginning to build muscle. Her straight, jet-black hair was braided and rolled into a practical bun. She flicked a spear up with her foot, catching it expertly in her hand. Vishwamitra noticed the stylish flick. But he was more impressed by something else. She had caught the spear exactly at the balance point on the shaft. Which had not been marked, unlike in a normal training spear. She judged it, instinctively perhaps. Even from a distance, he could see that her grip was flawless. The spear shaft lay flat on the palm of her hand, between her index and middle finger. Her thumb pointed backwards while the rest of the fingers faced the other direction.

Sita turned to the target with her left foot facing it. It was a wooden board painted with concentric circles. She raised her left hand, again in the same direction. Her body twisted ever so slightly, to add power to the throw. She pulled her right hand back, parallel to the ground; poised as a work of art.

Perfect.

Shvetaketu smiled. Though he did not teach warfare to his students, he was personally proud of Sita's prowess. 'She doesn't take the traditional few steps before she throws. The twist in her body and strength in her shoulders give her all the power she needs.'

Vishwamitra looked dismissively at Shvetaketu. He turned his attention back to the impressive girl. Those few steps may add power, but could also make you miss the target. Especially if the target was small. He did not bother to explain that little detail to Shvetaketu.

Sita flung hard as she twisted her body leftward, putting the power of her shoulder and back into the throw. Whipping the spear forward with her wrist and finger. Giving the final thrust to the missile.

Whoosh and thwack!

The spear hit bang on target. Right at the centre of the board. It jostled for space with the earlier spear which had pierced the same small circle.

Vishwamitra smiled slightly. 'Not bad ... Not bad at all ...'

What her two spectators did not know was that Sita had been taking lessons from Hanuman, on his regular visits to see his two sisters. He had helped perfect her technique.

Shvetaketu smiled with the pride of a parent. 'She is exceptional.'

'What is her status in Mithila now?'

Shvetaketu took a deep breath. 'I can't be sure. She is their adopted daughter. And, King Janak and Queen Sunaina have always loved her dearly. But now that ...'

'I believe Sunaina was blessed with a daughter a few years back,' interrupted Vishwamitra.

'Yes. After more than a decade of marriage. They have their own natural-born daughter now.'

'Urmila, right?'

'Yes, that is her name. Queen Sunaina has said that she does not differentiate between the two girls. But she has not visited Sita for nine months. She used to come every six months earlier. Admittedly, Sita has been called to Mithila regularly. She last visited Mithila six months ago. But she didn't return very happy.'

Vishwamitra looked at Sita, his hand on his chin. Thoughtful. He could see her face now. It seemed strangely familiar. But he couldn't place it.

— ᚜ᚉ —

It was lunchtime at the *gurukul*. Vishwamitra and his Malayaputras sat in the centre of the courtyard, surrounded by the simple mud huts that housed the students. It also served as an open-air classroom. Teaching was always done in the open. The small, austere huts for the teachers were a short distance away.

'Guru*ji*, shall we begin?' asked Arishtanemi, the Malayaputra military chief.

The students and the *gurukul* staff had served the honoured guests on banana leaf plates. Shvetaketu sat alongside

Vishwamitra, waiting for the Chief Malayaputra to commence the ceremony. Vishwamitra picked up his glass, poured some water into the palm of his right hand, and sprinkled it around his plate, thanking Goddess Annapurna for her blessings in the form of food and nourishment. He scooped the first morsel of food and placed it aside, as a symbolic offering to the Gods. Everyone repeated the action. At a signal from Vishwamitra, they began eating.

Vishwamitra, however, paused just as he was about to put the first morsel into his mouth. His eyes scanned the premises in search of a man. One of his soldiers was a Naga called Jatayu. The unfortunate man had been born with a condition that led to deformities on his face over time, classifying him as a Naga. His deformities were such that his face looked like that of a vulture. Many ostracised Jatayu. But not Vishwamitra. The Chief Malayaputra recognised the powerful warrior and noble soul that Jatayu was. Others, with prejudiced eyes, were blind to his qualities.

Vishwamitra knew the biases that existed in the times. He also knew that in this *ashram*, it was unlikely that anybody would have bothered to take care of Jatayu's meals. He looked around, trying to find him. He finally saw Jatayu, sitting alone in the distance, under a tree. Even as he was about to signal a student, he saw Sita heading towards the Naga, a banana-leaf plate in one hand, and a tray full of food in the other.

The *Maharishi* watched, as Jatayu stood up with coy amazement.

From the distance, Vishwamitra could not hear what was being said. But he read the body language. With utmost respect, Sita placed the banana-leaf plate in front of Jatayu, then served the food. As Jatayu sat down to eat with an embarrassed smile, she bowed low, folded her hands into a *Namaste* and walked away.

Vishwamitra watched Sita, lost in thought. *Where have I seen that face before?*

Arishtanemi, too, was observing the girl. He turned to Vishwamitra.

'She seems like a remarkable girl, Guru*ji*,' said Arishtanemi.

'Hmm,' said Vishwamitra, as he looked at his lieutenant very briefly. He turned his attention to his food.

Chapter 6

'Kaushik, this is not a good idea,' said Divodas. 'Trust me, my brother.'

Kaushik and Divodas sat on a large boulder outside their gurukul, on the banks of the Kaveri River. The two friends, both in their late thirties, were teachers at the Gurukul of Maharishi Kashyap, the celebrated Saptrishi Uttradhikari, successor to the seven legendary seers. Kaushik and Divodas had been students of the gurukul in their childhood. Upon graduation, they had gone their separate ways. Divodas had excelled as a teacher of great renown and Kaushik, as a fine Kshatriya royal. Two decades later, they had joined the prestigious institution again, this time as teachers. They had instantly rekindled their childhood friendship. In fact, they were like brothers now. In private, they still referred to each other by the gurukul names of their student days.

'Why is it not a good idea, Divodas?' asked Kaushik, his massive, muscular body bent forward aggressively, as usual. 'They are biased against the Vaanars. We need to challenge this prejudice for the good of India!'

Divodas shook his head. But realised that further conversation was pointless. He had long given up trying to challenge Kaushik's stubborn streak. It was like banging your head against an anthill. Not a good idea!

He picked up a clay cup kept by his side. It contained a bubbly, milky liquid. He held his nose and gulped it down. 'Yuck!'

Kaushik burst into laughter as he patted his friend heartily on his back. 'Even after all these years, it still tastes like horse's piss!'

Divodas wiped his mouth with the back of his hand and smiled. 'You need to come up with a new line! How do you know it tastes like horse's piss, anyway? Have you ever drunk horse's piss?!'

Kaushik laughed louder and held his friend by the shoulder. 'I have had the Somras *often. And I'm sure even horse's piss can't taste worse!'*

Divodas smiled broadly and put his arm around his friend's shoulder. They sat on the boulder in companionable silence, watching the sacred Kaveri as it flowed gently by Mayuram, the small town that housed their gurukul. The town was a short distance from the sea, and the perfect location for this massive gurukul, which taught hundreds of young students. More importantly, it also offered specialised courses in higher studies in different fields of knowledge. Being close to the sea, students from the Sapt Sindhu in the North could conveniently sail down the eastern coast of India to the gurukul. Thus, they did not need to cross the Narmada River from the north to south, and violate the superstitious belief that instructed against it. Furthermore, this gurukul was close to the submerged, prehistoric land of Sangamtamil, which along with the submerged ancient land of Dwarka in western India, was one of the two fatherlands of Vedic culture. This made its location uniquely holy to the students.

Divodas braced his shoulders, as if gathering resolve.

Kaushik, knowing well the non-verbal cues of his friend, remarked, 'What?'

Divodas took a deep breath. He knew this would be a difficult conversation. But he decided to try one more time. 'Kaushik, listen to me. I know you want to help Trishanku. And, I agree with you. He needs help. He is a good man. Perhaps immature and naive, but a good man nonetheless. But he cannot become a Vayuputra. He failed their examination. He must accept that. It has nothing to do with how he looks or where he was born. It is about his capability.'

The Vayuputras were the tribe left behind by the previous Mahadev,

Lord Rudra. *They lived far beyond the western borders of India in a place called Pariha. The Vayuputras were tasked with supporting the next Vishnu, whenever he or she arose. And, of course, one of them would become the next Mahadev whenever Evil raised its dangerous head.*

Kaushik stiffened. 'The Vayuputras are intolerant towards the Vaanars *and you know it.'*

The Vaanars *were a large, powerful, and reclusive tribe living on the banks of the great Tungabhadra River, north of the Kaveri. The Tungabhadra was a tributary of the Krishna River farther to the north. The tribe had a distinctly different appearance: Mostly short, stocky and very muscular, some of them were giant-like too. Their faces were framed with fine, facial hair, which ballooned into a beard at the jaw. Their mouths protruded outwards, and the skin around it was silken smooth and hairless. Their hirsute bodies sported thick, almost furry hair. To some prejudiced people, the* Vaanars *appeared like monkeys and thus, somehow, less human. It was said that similar tribes lived farther to the west of Pariha. One of their biggest and most ancient settlements was a land called Neanderthal or the valley of Neander.*

'What intolerance are you talking about?' asked Divodas, his hand raised in question. 'They accepted young Maruti into their fold, didn't they? Maruti is a Vaanar *too. But he has merit. Trishanku doesn't!'*

Kaushik would not be dissuaded. 'Trishanku has been loyal to me. He asked for my help. I will help him!'

'But Kaushik, how can you create your own version of Pariha? This is not wise ...'

'I have given him my word, Divodas. Will you help me or not?'

'Kaushik, of course I will help! But, brother, listen ...'

Suddenly a loud, feminine voice was heard from a distance. 'Hey, Divodas!'

Kaushik and Divodas turned around. It was Nandini. Another teacher at the gurukul. *And a friend to both. Kaushik cast a dark, injured look at Divodas, gritting his teeth softly.*

'Guru*ji* ...'

Vishwamitra's eyes flew open, bringing him back to the present from an ancient, more-than-a-century-old memory.

'I am sorry to disturb you, Guru*ji*,' said Arishtanemi, his hands joined in a penitent *Namaste*. 'But you had asked me to wake you when the students assembled.'

Vishwamitra sat up and gathered his *angvastram*. 'Is Sita present?'

'Yes, Guru*ji*.'

— ⚔ —

Shvetaketu sat on a chair placed in a discreet corner. He was clearly elated to see all the twenty-five students of his *gurukul* gathered in the open square. Vishwamitra sat on the round platform built around the trunk of the main *peepal* tree. It was the seat of the teacher. The great Chief Malayaputra would teach his students, if only for one class. This was a rare honour for Shvetaketu and his students.

The teachers of the *gurukul* and the Malayaputras stood in silence behind Shvetaketu.

'Have you learnt about our great ancient empires?' asked Vishwamitra. 'And the reasons for their rise and fall?'

All the students nodded in the affirmative.

'All right, then someone tell me, why did the empire of the descendants of the great Emperor Bharat decline? An empire that flourished for centuries, was annihilated within just two generations. Why?'

Kaaml Raj raised his hand. Shvetaketu groaned softly.

'Yes?' asked Vishwamitra.

'Guru*ji*,' answered Kaaml, 'they were attacked by foreigners and had internal rebellions at the same time. They were like the *kancha* marbles we play with. Everyone from everywhere was hitting them again and again. How could the empire survive?'

Saying this, Kaaml guffawed uncontrollably, laughing as if he had just cracked the funniest joke in human history. Everyone else remained silent. A few students at the back held their heads in shame. Vishwamitra stared at Kaaml with a frozen expression. The same expression was then directed towards Shvetaketu.

Not for the first time, Shvetaketu considered sending young Kaaml back to his parents. He really was a strange, untrainable child.

Vishwamitra did not deign to respond to Kaaml and repeated his question, this time looking directly at Sita. But the princess of Mithila did not answer.

'Bhoomi, why don't you answer?' asked Vishwamitra, using her *gurukul* name.

'Because I am not sure, Guru*ji*.'

Vishwamitra pointed to the front row. 'Come here, child.'

Since her last visit to Mithila, Sita had preferred to be alone. She mostly sat at the back of the class. Her friend Radhika patted her back, encouraging her to go. As Sita came forward, Vishwamitra gestured for her to sit. Then he stared at her eyes closely. Very few sages were adept at reading people's minds through their eyes. Vishwamitra was one such rare sage.

'Tell me,' said Vishwamitra, his eyes piercing through her mind. 'Why did the *Bhaaratas*, the descendants of the great Emperor Bharat, disintegrate so suddenly?'

Sita felt very uncomfortable. She felt an overpowering urge to get up and run. But she knew she could not insult the great *Maharishi*. She chose to answer. 'The *Bhaaratas* had a massive standing army. They could have easily fought on multiple battle fronts. But their warriors were ...'

'They were useless,' said Vishwamitra, completing Sita's thought. 'And, why were they useless? They had no shortage of money, of training, of equipment, or of war weapons.'

Sita repeated something she had heard Samichi say. 'What matters is not the weapon, but the woman who wields that weapon.'

Vishwamitra smiled in approval. 'And why were their *warriors* incapable of wielding weapons? Do not forget, these were weapons of far superior technology than those of their enemies.'

Sita had not thought about this. She remained silent.

'Describe the *Bhaarat* society at the time of their downfall,' Vishwamitra demanded.

Sita knew this answer. 'It was peaceful. A liberal and polite society. It was a haven for arts, culture, music, conversations, debates ... They not only practised but proudly celebrated non-violence. Both verbal and physical. It was a perfect society. Like heaven.'

'True. But there were some for whom it was hell.'

Sita did not say anything. But her mind wondered: *For whom?*

Vishwamitra read her mind as if she had spoken aloud. He answered, 'The warriors.'

'The warriors?'

'What are the chief qualities of warriors? What drives them? What motivates them? Yes, there are many who fight for honour, for the country, for a code. But equally, there are those who simply want a socially sanctioned way to kill. If not given an outlet, such people can easily turn to crime. Many great warriors, celebrated by humanity, narrowly escaped being remembered as social degenerates. What saved them from becoming criminals and instead, turned them into soldiers? The answer is the warrior code: The *right* reason to kill.'

It's difficult for a child to surrender certainties and understand nuances. Sita, after all just a thirteen-year-old, stiffened.

'Warriors thrive on admiration and hero worship. Without these, the warrior spirit, and with it, the warrior code, dies. Sadly, many in the latter-day *Bhaarat* society despised their soldiers and preferred to condemn them. Every action of the army was vehemently criticised. Any form of violence, even dharmic violence, was opposed. The warrior spirit itself was berated as a demonic impulse that had to be controlled. It didn't stop there. Freedom of speech was curtailed so that verbal violence could also be controlled. Disagreement was discouraged. This is how the *Bhaaratas* felt that heaven could be created on earth; by making strength powerless, and weakness powerful.'

Vishwamitra's voice became softer, almost as if he was speaking only to Sita. The assembly listened in rapt attention.

'Essentially, the *Bhaaratas* curbed their Kshatriya class drastically. Masculinity was emasculated. Great sages of yore who preached absolute non-violence and love were glorified and their messages amplified. But then, when barbaric invaders attacked from foreign lands, these pacifist, non-violent *Bhaarat* men and women were incapable of fighting back. These civilised people appeared like weak wimps to the brutal warriors from abroad.' With an ironic laugh, Vishwamitra continued, 'Unexpectedly, for the people of *Bhaarat* society, the *Hiranyaloman Mlechcha* warriors did not care for their message of love. Their answer to love was mass murder. They were barbarians, incapable of building their own empire. But they destroyed *Bhaarat* power and prestige. Internal rebels finished the job of destruction.'

'Guru*ji*, are you saying that to fight foreign monsters, you need your own monsters?'

'No. All I'm saying is that society must be wary of extremes. It must constantly strive towards attaining a balance among competing ideologies. Criminals must be removed from society, and meaningless violence must be stopped. But the warrior spirit must not be demonised. Do not create a society that demeans masculinity. Too much of anything creates an imbalance in life. This is true even of virtues such as non-violence. You never know when the winds of change strike; when violence may be required to protect your society, or to even survive.'

There was pin-drop silence.

It was time.

Vishwamitra asked the question he had steered the conversation towards. 'Is there an extremism that the Sapt Sindhu surrendered to which allowed Raavan to defeat them?'

Sita considered the question carefully. 'Yes, resentment and hatred towards the trading class.'

'Correct. In the past, because of a few monsters among their warriors, the *Bhaaratas* attacked the entire Kshatriya way of life. They became pathologically non-violent. There have been societies that have attacked the Brahmin way of life, becoming proudly anti-intellectual, because a few of their Brahmins became closed-minded, elitist and exclusivist. And the Sapt Sindhu in our age began to demean trading itself when a few of their Vaishyas became selfish, ostentatious, and money-grubbing. We gradually pushed trade out of the hands of the 'evil-moneyed capitalists' of our own society, and into the hands of others. Kubaer, and later Raavan, just gathered the money slowly, and economic power flowed naturally to them. The Battle of Karachapa was only a formality that sealed long historical trends. A society must always aim for balance. It needs intellectuals, it needs warriors, it needs traders, it needs artists, and it needs skilled workers. If it empowers one group too much or another too little, it is headed for chaos.'

Sita recalled something she had heard in one of the *dharma sabhas* of her father. 'The only "ism" I believe in, is pragmatism.'

It was said by a Charvak philosopher.

'Are you committed to Charvak philosophy?' asked Vishwamitra.

The Charvak School of philosophy was named after their ancient founder, an atheist who believed in materialism. He had lived near Gangotri, the source of the holy Ganga. The Charvaks only believed in what could be sensed by the physical senses. According to them, there was neither a soul, nor any Gods. The only reality was this body, a mix of the elements, which would return to the elements once it died. They lived for the day and enjoyed life. Their admirers saw them as liberal, individualistic and non-judgemental. On the other hand, their critics saw them as immoral, selfish and irresponsible.

'No, I am not committed to the Charvaks, Guru*ji*. If I am pragmatic, then I should be open to *every* school of philosophy. And accept only those parts that make sense to me, while rejecting other bits that don't. I should learn from any philosophy that can help me fulfil my karma.'

Vishwamitra smiled. *Smart, very smart for a thirteen-year-old.*

Chapter 7

Sita sat by the pond, reading *Nyayasutra*, the classic text which introduced a key school of Indian philosophy, *Nyaya Darshan*. A few months had passed since Vishwamitra had visited Rishi Shvetaketu's *gurukul*.

'Bhoomi,' said Radhika, using the *gurukul* name of Sita, 'someone from your home has come to meet you.'

Sita sighed with irritation. 'Can't they wait?'

She was compiling a list of questions she wanted to ask Rishi Shvetaketu. Now the exercise would be delayed.

— ᚸᚵ —

Samichi stood patiently, close to the jetty. Waiting for Sita.

A posse of ten men stood behind her. They were under her command.

Samichi was not the girl from the slums anymore. Having joined the police, she was a rapidly rising star there. It was common knowledge that the royal family liked her, indebted as they were to her for having saved Princess Sita in the Mithila slums. People were guarded in her presence. Nobody knew her exact age, including Samichi herself. Her appearance suggested that she was in her early twenties now. For a woman of her age, not born into nobility, to be commanding a posse in the police force was a rare honour. But then, she had saved the princess.

'Samichi!'

Samichi groaned as she recognised the voice. It was that ridiculous boy, Kaaml Raj. He was panting by the time he ran up to her. Excited.

'Someone told me you were here. I came as fast as I could.'

Samichi looked at the twelve-year-old. He held a red rose in his hands. She narrowed her eyes and resisted the temptation to shove him. 'I've told you ...'

'I thought you'd like this rose,' said Kaaml shyly. 'I saw you enjoy the fragrance of the flowers the last time you were here.'

Samichi spoke in a cold whisper. 'I'm not interested in odours of any kind.'

Not to be deterred, Kaaml held out a hand, showing her his bleeding finger. A pathetic attempt to extract sympathy. He had pricked himself repeatedly with thorns before yanking the flower from the rose bush. Seeing that it wasn't working, he stepped closer. 'Do you have some medicine for my finger?'

Samichi stepped back to put some distance between them. In doing so, she stumbled on a stone. Just a little. Kaaml rushed forward to grab her. The poor boy genuinely wanted to help. What happened next was blinding in its speed. Samichi screamed in anger, twisted his arm, and viciously kicked him in the leg. As Kaaml fell forward, she brought her elbow up in a brutal jab. It cracked his nose. Instantly.

Kaaml clutched his bleeding nose, as Samichi shouted in anger, 'DO NOT TOUCH ME, EVER!'

Kaaml was crying desperately now. He lay on the ground in a frightened heap. Bloodied. Trembling. The policemen rushed forward and helped the boy to his feet. They cast a surreptitious, horror-filled glance at their leader. All of them had the same thought.

He's only a boy! What is wrong with her?

Samichi's stony face showed no trace of regret. She signalled a Mithila policeman with a dismissive wave of a hand. 'Get this idiot out of here.'

The policeman lifted the boy gingerly and walked away to find the *gurukul* doctor. The other policemen walked back to the jetty in a fearful procession. The air was thick with unspoken words about their captain.

Something is not right with Samichi.

'Samichi.'

All turned to see Princess Sita emerge from the trees. And, Samichi transformed like a chameleon. Smiling broadly, she rushed forward with warmth oozing from her eyes.

'How are you, Samichi?' asked Sita, as she embraced her friend.

Before Samichi could answer, Sita turned to the policemen standing at a distance and pulled her hands together into a *Namaste,* along with a warm smile. The policemen bowed low, also folding their hands into a *Namaste.*

'I wonder why your men always look so scared,' whispered Sita.

Samichi grinned and shook her head, holding Sita's hand, pulling her away, out of earshot of the policemen. 'Forget them, Princess,' said Samichi, her smile affectionate.

'I've told you before, Samichi,' said Sita, 'when we are alone, call me Sita. Not Princess. You are my friend. Anyway, it's not as if anyone thinks of me as a princess anymore.'

'Whatever anyone may think, I have no doubt that you are a princess of Mithila.'

Sita rolled her eyes. 'Yeah, right.'

'Princess, I have been sent to ...'

Sita interrupted Samichi. 'Sita. Not Princess.'

'Apologies, Sita, you must come home.'

Sita sighed. 'You know I can't, Samichi. I have caused enough trouble for *maa*.'

'Sita, don't do this to yourself.'

'Everyone knows about the incident with *chacha*. When I broke his royal seal,' Sita recalled her *uncle* Kushadhwaj's last visit to Mithila. 'He is endlessly troubling *maa* and Mithila. Everyone blames me for it. And rightly so. I should just stay away.'

'Sita, your father and mother miss you. Queen Sunaina is very sick. You really should ...'

'Nothing can happen to *maa*. She is a superwoman. You are just saying this to make me leave the *gurukul* and come home.'

'But ... it's the truth.'

'The truth is that *maa* should focus on Urmila and the kingdom. You know that *baba* is ... distracted. You yourself have told me what the people say about me. She doesn't need me to increase her problems.'

'Sita ...'

'Enough,' said Sita, raising her hand. 'I don't feel like talking about this anymore.'

'Sita ...'

'I feel like practising stick-fighting. Are you game?'

Anything to change the subject, thought Samichi.

'Come on,' said Sita, turning around.

Samichi followed.

— ༒ —

Vishwamitra sat in the lotus position in his austere hut at the Ganga *ashram* of the Malayaputras.

He was meditating. Trying to keep all thoughts out of his mind. But he was failing today.

He heard a whistling sound. And recognised it immediately. It was a common hill myna. A bird that has often been called the most amazing vocalist. It can whistle, warble, shriek, and even mimic.

What is it doing so far away from home? In the plains?

His mind wandered to an incident from the past. When he had heard the myna in a place he should not have.

Amazing how the mind wanders ... So flighty and unpredictable ...

The memory of that day, many decades ago, now came flooding back.

It was the day he had received the news of his former friend, Vashishtha, being appointed the *raj guru* of Ayodhya.

Vishwamitra felt his chest constrict. In anger. And pain.

That backstabber ... I did so much for him ...

His mind wandered to the exact moment he had heard the news. At the *ashram* of ...

Vishwamitra's eyes suddenly flew open.

By the great Lord Parshu Ram ...

He remembered where he had seen that face. Sita's face. He smiled. This only reinforced his decision.

Thank you, Lord Parshu Ram. You made my mind wander only to help me find my path.

— ᚱᚷ —

'Guru*ji* ...' whispered Arishtanemi.

He stood next to Vishwamitra at the balustrade of the lead ship. They were in a five-vessel convoy that was sailing down the sacred Ganga, on their way to supervise a search being conducted by their miners for some special material. It would help them acquire a powerful weapon called the *Asuraastra*, leaving them less dependent on the Vayuputras.

Centuries ago, Lord Rudra, the previous Mahadev, had restricted the use of *daivi astras*. The approval of the Vayuputras, the living representatives of Lord Rudra, was mandatory for using the *divine weapons*. This was not to Vishwamitra's liking or comfort.

The great *Maharishi* had made elaborate plans. Plans which involved, perhaps, the use of the *Asuraastra*. He knew the Vayuputras did not like him. Not since the episode with Trishanku. They tolerated him because they had no choice. He was, after all, chief of the Malayaputras.

While the search was a slow and tedious process, Vishwamitra was confident that the material would be found, eventually.

It was time to move to the next phase of his plan. He had to select a Vishnu. He had just revealed his choice to Arishtanemi, his trusted lieutenant.

'You disagree?' asked Vishwamitra.

'She is exceptionally capable, Guru*ji*. No doubt about it. One can sense it, even at her tender age. But …' Arishtanemi's voice trailed off.

Vishwamitra put his hand on Arishtanemi's shoulder. 'Speak freely. I am talking to you because I want to hear your views.'

'I spent some time watching her carefully, Guru*ji*. I think she is too rebellious. I am not sure the Malayaputras will be able to manage her. Or, control her.'

'We will. She has no one else. Her city has abandoned her. But she has the potential to be great. She *wants* to be great. We will be her route to realising it.'

'But can't we also keep searching for other candidates?'

'Your trusted aides gathered information on her in Mithila, right? Most of it was very encouraging.'

'But there was that case of her probably killing a boy in the Mithila slums when she was eight.'

'I see in that incident her ability to survive. Your investigators also said the boy was probably a criminal. She fought her way through, even as a small child. That's a positive. She has the fighting spirit. Would you rather she had died like a coward?'

'No, Guru*ji*,' said Arishtanemi. 'But I am wondering if there are possibly other candidates that we have not yet stumbled upon.'

'You personally know almost every royal family in India. Most of them are completely useless. Selfish, cowardly, and weak. And their next generation, the royal children, are even worse. They are nothing but genetic garbage.'

Arishtanemi laughed. 'Few countries have had the misfortune of being saddled with such a worthless elite.'

'We have had great leaders in the past. And we will have a great leader in the future too. One who will pull India out of its present morass.'

'Why not from the common folk?'

'We have been searching for a long time. Had that been Lord Parshu Ram's will, we would have found one by now. And don't forget, Sita is only an adopted royal. Her parentage is unknown.'

Vishwamitra did not feel the need to tell Arishtanemi what he suspected about Sita's birth.

Arishtanemi overcame his hesitation. 'I have heard that the Ayodhya princes ...'

The Malayaputra military chief stopped mid-sentence when

he saw Vishwamitra bristle. His famed courage vanished into thin air. Arishtanemi had indeed heard positive reports about the young princes of Ayodhya, particularly Ram and Bharat. Ram was a little less than nine years old. But Vashishtha was the *raj guru* of Ayodhya. And, Vashishtha was a subject Arishtanemi had learned to avoid.

'That snake has taken the Ayodhya princes to his *gurukul*,' said Vishwamitra, anger boiling within. 'I don't even know where his *ashram* is. He has kept it a secret. If *I* don't know then nobody knows. We only hear about the four brothers when they return to Ayodhya on holiday.'

Arishtanemi stood like a statue, barely breathing.

'I know how Vashishtha's mind works. I had made the mistake of considering him my friend once. He is up to something. Either with Ram or Bharat.'

'Sometimes, things don't work out as planned, Guru*ji*. Our work in Lanka inadvertently ended up helping …'

'Raavan has his uses,' interrupted Vishwamitra. 'Don't ever forget that. And, he is moving in the direction we need him to. It will all work out.'

'But Guru*ji*, can the Vayuputras oppose the Malayaputras? It is our prerogative to choose the next Vishnu. Not that of the *raj guru* of Ayodhya.'

'For all their sham neutrality, the Vayuputras will do everything they can to help that rat. I know it. We do not have much time. We must start preparing now!'

'Yes, Guru*ji*.'

'And, if she is to be trained for her role, it too must begin now.'

'Yes, Guru*ji*.'

'Sita will be the Vishnu. The Vishnu will rise during my

reign. The time has come. This country needs a leader. We cannot allow our beloved India to suffer endlessly.'

'Yes, Guru*ji*,' said Arishtanemi. 'Should I tell the Captain to …'

'Yes.'

— ॐ —

'Where are you taking me, Radhika?' asked Sita, smiling, as her friend led her by the hand.

They were walking deep into the forest to the south of the *gurukul*.

'Hanu *bhaiya*!' screamed Sita in delight, as they entered a small clearing.

Hanuman stood next to his horse, rubbing the tired animal's neck. The horse was tied to a tree.

'My sisters!' said Hanuman affectionately.

The gentle giant walked up to them. He enclosed them together in a warm embrace. 'How are the two of you doing?'

'You have been away for far too long!' Radhika complained.

'I know,' sighed Hanuman. 'I'm sorry. I was abroad …'

'Where do you keep going?' asked Sita, who found Hanuman's mysterious life very exciting. 'Who sends you on these missions?'

'I will tell you when the time is right, Sita … But not now.'

Hanuman reached into the saddlebag tied to the horse and pulled out a delicate necklace made of gold, in a style that was obviously foreign.

Radhika squealed with delight.

'You guess correctly,' smiled Hanuman, as he handed it to her. 'This one is for you …'

Radhika admired the necklace in detail, turning it around several times in her hands.

'And for you, my serious one,' said Hanuman to Sita. 'I've got what you've always wanted ...'

Sita's eyes widened. 'An *ekmukhi Rudraaksh*?!'

The word *Rudraaksh* literally meant the *teardrop of Rudra*. In reality, it was a brown elliptical seed. All who were loyal to the Mahadev, Lord Rudra, wore threaded *Rudraaksh* beads or kept one in their *puja* rooms. A common *Rudraaksh* seed had many grooves running across it. An *ekmukhi Rudraaksh* was rare, and had only one groove on its surface. Very difficult to find. Expensive too. Priceless for Sita, a staunch Lord Rudra devotee.

Hanuman smiled as he reached into the saddlebag.

Suddenly, the horse became fidgety and nervous, its ears flicking back and forth. Within moments its breathing was rapid and shallow. Conveying panic.

Hanuman looked around carefully. And he caught sight of the danger.

Very slowly, without any sign of alarm, he pulled Radhika and Sita behind him.

The girls knew better than to talk. They, too, could sense danger. Something was seriously wrong.

Hanuman suddenly made a loud, screeching sound; like that of an agitated monkey. The tiger hidden behind the tree immediately knew that its element of surprise was gone. It walked out slowly. Hanuman reached for the scabbard tied to his cummerbund and drew out his curved knife. Made in the style of the *khukuris* of the fierce Gorkhas, the blade of the knife was not straight. It thickened at mid-length, and then the thick section curved downwards. Like a sloping shoulder. At the hilt-end, the sharp side of the blade had a double-wave notch. Shaped like a cow's foot. It served a practical purpose. It allowed the blood from the blade to drip to the ground, instead of spreading to the hilt and making the knife-hold slippery. The cow's foot indentation also signified that the weapon could never be used to kill a holy cow. The handle was made of ivory. At the halfway mark, a protrusion emerged from all sides of the hilt. It served as a peg between the middle finger and the ring finger, making the grip secure. The *khukuri* had no cross-guard for a thrusting action. A less-skilled warrior's hand could slip forward onto the blade, in a thrust. It could cause serious injury to the knife-wielder.

But nobody in their right mind would call Hanuman less than supremely skilled.

'Stay behind me,' whispered Hanuman to the girls, as the tiger edged forward slowly.

Hanuman spread his legs apart and bent, maintaining his balance. Waiting. For what was to follow. Keeping his breathing steady.

With an ear-splitting roar, the tiger suddenly burst forward, going up on its hind legs, spreading its front legs out. Ready to hold the massive Hanuman in its grip. Its jaws opened wide, it headed straight for Hanuman's throat.

The tiger's tactic was sound: topple the human with its massive weight, pin him to the ground with its claws, and rely on its jaws to finish the job.

Against a lesser enemy, it would have prevailed. But, to its misfortune, it had attacked the mighty Hanuman.

The giant Naga was almost as big as the tiger. With one foot back, he arched his spine, flexed his powerful muscles; and, remained on his feet. Using his left hand, he held the tiger by its throat, and kept its fearsome jaws away. Hanuman allowed the tiger to claw his back. It would not cause much damage. He pulled his right hand back, flexed his shoulder muscles and brutally thrust the *khukuri* deep into the tiger's abdomen. Its outrageously sharp-edged blade sliced in smoothly. The beast roared in pain. Its eyes wide in shock.

Hanuman sucked in his breath and executed a draw-cut to the right, ripping deep into the beast's abdominal cavity. All the way from one end to the other. Vicious, but effective. Not only did most of the beast's abdominal organs get slashed, the knife even sliced through a bit of the backbone and the nerves protected inside.

The tiger's slippery intestines slid out of its cleaved abdomen, its hind legs locked in paralysis. Hanuman pushed the beast back. It fell to the ground, roaring in agony as its front legs lashed out in all directions.

Hanuman could have avoided further injury from its claws had he waited for the tiger to weaken. And let its front legs go down. But the animal was in agony. He wanted to end its suffering. Hanuman bent closer even as the tiger's claws dug deep into his shoulders. The Naga stabbed straight into the animal's chest. The blade cut right through, sliding deep into the beast's heart. It struggled for a few moments and then its soul escaped its body.

Hanuman pulled the blade out and whispered softly, 'May your soul find purpose once again, noble beast.'

— ௴ᚷ —

'These things happen, Radhika,' said Hanuman. 'We're in the middle of a jungle. What do you expect?'

Radhika was still shaking with fear.

Sita had quickly pulled out the medical aid kit from the saddlebag and dressed Hanuman's injuries. They were not life-threatening but a few of them were deep. Sita stitched a couple of gaping wounds. She found some rejuvenating herbs around the clearing and made an infusion, using stones to grind the leaves with some water. She gave it to Hanuman to drink.

As Hanuman gulped the medicine down and wiped his mouth with the back of his hand, he watched Sita.

She is not nervous … She didn't get scared … This girl is special …

'I would not have imagined that a tiger could be brought down with such ease,' whispered Sita.

'It helps if you're my size!' laughed Hanuman.

'Are you sure that you can ride? Your wounds aren't serious, but …'

'I can't stay here either. I have to get back …'

'Another of your mysterious missions?'

'I have to go.'

'You have to do what you have to do, Hanu *bhaiya*.'

Hanuman smiled. 'Don't forget your *Rudraaksh*.'

Sita reached into the saddlebag and pulled out a silk pouch. She opened it slowly, carefully picking up the *ekmukhi Rudraaksh*. She stared at it in awe. Then she held it to her forehead with reverence before slipping it into the pouch tied to her waist.

Chapter 8

Shvetaketu could not believe his luck. The great Vishwamitra had arrived at his *gurukul* for the second time this year! He rushed to the gates of the *ashram* as the Malayaputras marched in.

'*Namaste*, Great One,' said Shvetaketu, smiling broadly, his hands joined together in respect.

'*Namaste*, Shvetaketu,' said Vishwamitra, smiling just enough to not intimidate his host.

'What an honour to have you call on our *gurukul* so soon after your last visit.'

'Yes,' said Vishwamitra, looking around.

'It is unfortunate that my students are not here to gain from your presence,' said Shvetaketu, his expression reflecting heartfelt regret. 'Most of them are away on vacation.'

'But I believe a few have stayed back.'

'Yes, Illustrious One. Sita is here … And …'

'I would like to meet Sita.'

'Of course.'

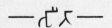

Sita stood with Maharishi Vishwamitra near the balustrade at the edge of the main deck of his anchored ship, facing the far bank of the Ganga. Vishwamitra had wanted privacy, away from the curious eyes of the teachers in the *gurukul*. A small brick-laid *yagna kund* was being readied by the Malayaputra *pandits* on the main deck of the ship, a little distance away from Sita and Vishwamitra.

Sita was confused. *Why does the* Maharishi *want to speak to me?*

'How old are you now, Sita?'

'I will turn fourteen soon, Guru*ji*.'

'That's not too old. We can begin, I think.'

'Begin what, Guru*ji*?'

Vishwamitra took a deep breath. 'Have you heard of the institution of the Vishnu?'

'Yes, Guru*ji*.'

'Tell me what you know.'

'It is a title given to the greatest of leaders, who are Propagators of Good. They lead their people into a new way of life. There have been six Vishnus in this present Vedic age that we live in. The previous Vishnu was the great Lord Parshu Ram.'

Jai Parshu Ram.'

Jai Parshu Ram.'

'What else do you know?'

'The Vishnus normally work in partnership with the Mahadevs, who are Destroyers of Evil. The Mahadevs assign a tribe as their representatives once their *karma* in a particular life is over. The tribe of the previous Mahadev, Lord Rudra, is the Vayuputras who live in faraway Pariha. The Vishnu of our age will work in close partnership with …'

'This partnership thing is not necessarily important,' interrupted Vishwamitra.

Sita fell silent. Surprised. This was not what she had learnt.

'What else do you know?'

'I know that the previous Vishnu, Lord Parshu Ram, left behind a tribe as well — the Malayaputras. And you, *Maharishiji,* are the chief of the Malayaputras. And if a Vishnu must rise in our age, to fight the darkness that envelops us, it must be you.'

'You are wrong.'

Sita frowned. Confused.

'The assumption you made in your last statement is wrong,' clarified Vishwamitra. 'Yes, I am the chief of the Malayaputras. But I cannot be the Vishnu. My task is to decide who the next Vishnu will be.'

Sita nodded silently.

'What do you think is the main problem corroding India today?'

'Most people will say Raavan, but I won't.'

Vishwamitra smiled. 'Why not?'

'Raavan is only a symptom. He is not the disease. If it hadn't been Raavan, it would have been someone else torturing us. The fault lies in us, that we allow ourselves to be dominated. Raavan may be powerful, but if we …'

'Raavan is not as powerful as the people of Sapt Sindhu think he is. But he revels in this image of the monster that he has created for himself. That image intimidates others. But that image is useful for us as well,' said Vishwamitra.

Sita didn't understand that last line. And, Vishwamitra chose not to explain.

'So, you say that Raavan is only a symptom. Then, what is the disease afflicting the Sapt Sindhu today?'

Sita paused to formulate her thoughts. 'I've been thinking about this since you spoke to us at the *gurukul* last year, Guru*ji.*

You said society needs balance. It needs intellectuals, warriors, traders, and skilled workers. And that ideally, the scale should not be tipped against any group. That there should be a fair balance between all.'

'And ...'

'So, why is it that society always moves towards imbalance? That's what I was thinking. It gets unbalanced when people are not free to live a life that is in alignment with their innate *guna*, their *attributes*. It can happen when a group is oppressed or belittled, like the *Vaishyas* in Sapt Sindhu today. It makes those with *Vaishya gunas* frustrated and angry. It can also happen when you're made to follow the occupation of your parents and clan, rather than what you may want to pursue. Raavan was born a Brahmin. But he clearly did not want to be a Brahmin. He is a Kshatriya by nature. It must have been the same with ...'

Sita stopped herself in time. But Vishwamitra was staring directly into her eyes, reading her thoughts. 'Yes, it happened with me too. I was born a Kshatriya but wanted to be a Brahmin.'

'People like you are rare, Guru*ji*. Most people surrender to the pressure of society and family. But it builds terrible frustration within. These are unhappy and angry people, living unbalanced, dissatisfied lives. Furthermore, society itself suffers. It may get stuck with Kshatriyas who do not possess valour, and cannot protect their society. It may get stuck with Brahmins who prefer to be skilled Shudras like medical surgeons or sculptors, and therefore will be terrible teachers. And ultimately, society will decline.'

'You have diagnosed the problem well. So, what is the solution?'

'I don't know. How does one change society? How do we break down this birth-based caste system that is destroying our noble land?'

'I have a solution in mind.'

Sita waited for an explanation.

'Not now,' said Vishwamitra. 'I will explain one day. When you are ready. For now, we have a ceremony to conduct.'

'Ceremony?'

'Yes,' said Vishwamitra, as he turned towards the *yagna kund,* which had been built at the centre of the main deck. Seven Malayaputra *pandits* waited at the other end of the deck. Upon a signal from Vishwamitra, they walked up to the *yagna kund.*

'Come,' said Vishwamitra, as he led her forward.

The *yagna* platform was built in an unorthodox manner, or at least one with which Sita was not familiar. It had a square, outer boundary, made of bricks. Encased within it was a circular inner boundary, made of metal.

'This *yagna kund* represents a type of *mandal,* a symbolic representation of spiritual reality,' Vishwamitra explained to Sita. 'The square boundary symbolises *Prithvi,* the earth that we live on. The four sides of the square represent the four directions. The space inside the square represents *Prakruti* or nature. It is uncultured and wild. The circle within represents the path of consciousness; of the *Parmatma.* The task of the Vishnu is to find the *Parmatma* within this earthly life. The Vishnu lights a path to God. Not through detachment from the world, but through profound and spiritual attachment to this great land of ours.'

'Yes, Guru*ji.*'

'You will sit on the southern side of the square.'

Sita sat in the seat indicated by Vishwamitra. The Chief

Malayaputra sat with his back to the north, facing Sita. A Malayaputra *pandit* lit the fire within the circular inner boundary of the *yagna* platform. He was chanting a hymn dedicated to Lord Agni, the God of Fire.

A *yagna* signifies a sacrificial exchange: you sacrifice something that you hold dear, and receive benediction in return. Lord Agni, the purifying fire, is witness to this exchange between humans and the divine.

Vishwamitra folded his hands together into a *Namaste*. So did Sita. He began chanting a hymn from the *Brihadaranyak Upanishad*. Sita and the seven Malayaputra *pandits* joined in.

Asato mā sadgamaya
Tamasomā jyotir gamaya
Mrityormāamritam gamaya
Om shāntishānti shāntih
Lead me from untruth to truth
Lead me from darkness to light
Lead me from death to immortality
For Me and the Universe, let there be peace, peace, peace

Vishwamitra reached into a pouch tied to his waist and withdrew a small scabbard. Holding it reverentially in the palm of his hand, he pulled out a tiny silver knife. He ran his finger over the edge, bringing it to rest on the tip of the blade. Sharp. He checked the markings on the handle. It was the correct one. He reached over the fire and handed the knife to Sita. It had to be passed from the northern to the southern direction.

'This *yagna* will be sealed in blood,' said Vishwamitra.

'Yes, Guru*ji*,' said Sita, accepting the knife with both hands as a mark of respect.

Vishwamitra reached into his pouch and retrieved another small scabbard. He pulled out the second knife and checked its blade. Perfectly sharp. He looked at Sita. 'The blood must only drop within the circular inner boundary of the *yagna kund*. Under no circumstances must it spill in the space between the metal and bricks. Is that clear?'

'Yes, Guru*ji*.'

Two Malayaputra *pandits* approached them silently and handed two pieces of cloth each to Vishwamitra and Sita. Each had been doused in neem-juice disinfectants. Without waiting for further instructions, Sita placed the sharp knife-edge on her left palm and folded her hand over the blade. Then, in a swift, clean motion, she pulled the knife back, cutting open the skin from edge to edge. Blood dribbled freely into the sacred fire. She did not flinch.

'*Arrey*, we needed just a drop of blood,' exclaimed Vishwamitra. 'A little nick would have been enough.'

Sita looked at Vishwamitra, unperturbed. She pressed the disinfectant cloth into her injured hand, careful not to spill any blood.

Vishwamitra quickly pricked his thumb with the knife edge.

He held his hand over the inner boundary of the *yagna kund*, and pressed his thumb to let a drop of blood fall into the flames. Sita also held out her left hand and removed the cloth, letting her blood drip into the fire.

Vishwamitra spoke in a clear voice. 'With the pure Lord Agni as my witness, I swear that I will honour my promise to Lord Parshu Ram. Always. To my last breath. And beyond.'

Sita repeated the words. Exactly.

'*Jai Parshu Ram*,' said Vishwamitra.

'*Jai Parshu Ram*,' repeated Sita.

The Malayaputra *pandits* around them chimed in. '*Jai Parshu Ram*.'

Vishwamitra smiled and withdrew his hand. Sita too pulled her hand back and covered it with the disinfectant cloth. A Malayaputra *pandit* walked up to her and tied the cloth tight around her hand, staunching the blood flow.

'It is done,' said Vishwamitra, looking at Sita.

'Am I a Malayaputra now?' asked Sita expectantly.

Vishwamitra looked amused. He pointed to Sita's knife. 'Look at the markings on your knife.'

Sita picked up the silver knife. Its blade-edge was stained with her blood. She examined the handle. It had three intricate letters engraved on it. Sages of yore, in their wisdom, had suggested that Old Sanskrit should not have a written script. They felt that the written word was inferior to the spoken; that it reduced the ability of the mind to understand concepts. Rishi Shvetaketu had had another explanation: the sages preferred that scriptures were not written down and remained oral so that as times changed, they could change easily as well. Writing things down brought rigidity into the scriptures. Whatever the reason, the fact was that writing was not valued in the Sapt Sindhu. As a result, there were many scripts that existed across the land. Scripts that changed from time to time and place to place. There was no serious attempt to develop a standard script.

The word on the handle was written in a common script from the upper reaches of the Saraswati River. Sita recognised it.

The symbols represented Parshu Ram.

'Not that side, Sita,' said Vishwamitra. 'Turn it around.'

Sita flipped the knife. Her eyes widened with shock.

The fish was the most common symbol across all scripts in India. A giant fish had helped Lord Manu and his band escape when the sea had devastated their land. Lord Manu had decreed that the great fish would be honoured with the title of Lord Matsya, the first Vishnu. The symbol of the fish represented a follower of the Vishnu. This was the symbol on Vishwamitra's knife handle.

But the symbol on Sita's handle was a modified version. It was a fish, no doubt, but it also had a crown on top.

The fish symbol minus the crown on it meant that you were a follower of the Vishnu. But if the fish symbol had a crown on top, it meant that you *were* the Vishnu.

Sita looked at Vishwamitra, bewildered.

'This knife is yours, Sita,' said Vishwamitra softly.

Chapter 9

The student quarters in Shvetaketu's *gurukul* were frugal. In keeping with the general atmosphere of the place. Each student occupied a small windowless mud hut, barely large enough to accommodate a single bed, some clothes pegs and a place for study materials. The huts had no doors, just doorways.

Sita was lying in bed, recalling the events of the previous day on the Malayaputra ship.

She held the knife in her hand. She was in no danger of getting cut since the blade was safely in the scabbard. Again and again, her eyes were drawn to the knife handle. And the beautiful symbol etched on its surface.

Vishnu?

Me?

Vishwamitra had said that her training would begin soon. She would be old enough to leave the *gurukul* in a few months. She would then take a trip to Agastyakootam, the capital of the Malayaputras, deep in the south of India. After that, she would travel across India, incognito. Vishwamitra wanted her to understand the land that she would redeem and lead one day. Along with his Malayaputras, he would guide her through this. In the interim, she and Vishwamitra would prepare a blueprint for the task ahead. For a new way of life.

It was all quite overwhelming.

'My Lady.'

Sita slipped out of bed and came to the doorway. Jatayu was standing at some distance.

'My Lady,' he repeated.

Sita folded her hands into a *Namaste*. 'I am like your younger sister, Jatayu*ji*. Please don't embarrass me. Just call me by my name.'

'No, I can't do that, My Lady. You are the ...'

Jatayu fell silent. Strict instructions had been given to the Malayaputras. Nobody was to speak of Sita as the next Vishnu. It would be announced at the right time. Even Sita had been prohibited from speaking about it with anyone. Not that she would have, in any case. She felt anxious, almost afraid, of what the title implied.

'Well then, you can call me your sister.'

Jatayu smiled. 'That is fair, my sister.'

'What did you want to talk about, Jatayu*ji*?'

'How is your hand now?'

Sita grinned as she touched the neem-leaf bandage with her other hand. 'I was a little too enthusiastic about drawing blood.'

'Yes.'

'I am all right now.'

'That is good to hear,' said Jatayu. He was a shy man. Taking a slow, long breath in, he softly continued, 'You are one of the very few people, besides the Malayaputras, who have shown kindness towards me. Even though Lord Vishwamitra had not ordered you to do so.'

All those months ago, Sita had served Jatayu some food simply because his face reminded her of the noble vulture who had saved her life. But she kept that to herself.

'You are probably unsure about this new situation,' said Jatayu. 'It's natural to feel overwhelmed.'

What he didn't tell her was that even some Malayaputras had their doubts about the choice of Sita as a Vishnu, but wouldn't dare openly challenge their formidable chief.

Sita nodded silently.

'It must be even more difficult because you cannot talk to anyone other than a Malayaputra about this.'

'Yes,' Sita smiled.

'If you ever need any advice, or even someone to talk to, you always have me. It is my duty to protect you from now onwards. My platoon and I will always be nearby,' said Jatayu, gesturing behind him.

Around fifteen men stood quietly at a distance.

'I will not embarrass you by revealing myself in public, in Mithila or anywhere else,' said Jatayu. 'I understand that I am a Naga. But I will never be more than a few hours' ride away. My people and I will always be your shadow from now on.'

'You could never embarrass me, Jatayu*ji*,' said Sita.

'Sita!'

The princess of Mithila looked to her left. It was Arishtanemi.

'Sita,' said Arishtanemi, 'Guru*ji* would like to have a word with you.'

'Excuse me, Jatayu*ji*,' said Sita, as she folded her hands into a polite *Namaste*.

Jatayu returned her salutation and Sita walked away, trailing Arishtanemi. As she faded into the distance, Jatayu bent down, picked up some dust from her footprint, and touched it respectfully to his forehead. He then turned in the direction that Sita had walked.

She is such a good soul ...

I hope Lady Sita does not become a pawn in the battle between Guru Vishwamitra and Guru Vashishtha.

—— ↿⅄ ——

Two months had passed. The Malayaputras had left for their capital, Agastyakootam. As instructed, Sita spent most of her free time reading texts that the chief of the Malayaputras had given her. They chronicled the lives of some of the previous Vishnus: Lord Narsimha, Lord Vaaman, Lord Parshu Ram, among others. He wanted her to learn from their lives, their challenges; and, how to overcome them and establish a new path that led to the Propagation of Good.

She took up this task with utmost seriousness and conducted it in privacy. Today, she sat by a tiny pond not frequented by other students. It was therefore with irritation that she reacted to the disturbance.

'Bhoomi, you need to come to the main *gurukul* clearing right away,' said Radhika, using Sita's *gurukul* name. 'Someone from your home is here.'

Sita waved her hand in annoyance. 'I'll be there, soon.'

'Sita!' said Radhika loudly.

Sita turned around. Her friend looked and sounded agitated. 'Your mother is here. You need to go. Now.'

—— ↿⅄ ——

Sita walked slowly towards the main *gurukul* clearing. Her heart beating hard. She saw two elephants tied close to the walkway, which led to the *gurukul* jetty. She knew her mother liked bringing her elephants along. On Sunaina's visits, Sita and she would go on elephant rides deep into the jungle. Sunaina loved to educate her daughter on animals in their natural habitat.

Sunaina knew more about animals than anyone Sita had met. The trips into the jungle were among Sita's most cherished memories. For they involved the two most important entities in her life: Mother Earth and her own mother.

Pain shot through her heart.

Because of her, Kushadhwaj had imposed severe restrictions on Mithila trade. Her uncle's kingdom, Sankashya, was the main conduit for trade with her father's kingdom; and the prices of most commodities, even essentials, had shot through the roof. Most Mithilans blamed Sita for this. Everyone knew that she had broken Kushadhwaj's royal seal. And, that retaliation was inevitable. According to ancient tradition, the royal seal was the representation of the king; breaking it was comparable to regicide.

The blame had also seamlessly passed on to her mother, Sunaina. For everyone knew that it was Sunaina's decision to adopt Sita.

I have given her nothing but trouble. I have destroyed so much of what she spent her life building.

Maa *should forget me.*

Sita was even more convinced of her decision by the time she reached the clearing.

It was unusually crowded, even for a royal visit. Eight men were gathered around a heavy, empty palanquin. It was a palanquin she hadn't seen before: longer and broader. It appeared to be designed so that the person travelling in it could lie down. To the left, she saw eight women crowding around a low platform built around an *Ashok* tree. She looked all over for her mother, but did not see her anywhere.

She moved towards the women, about to ask where her mother was. Just then, a few of them moved aside, revealing Queen Sunaina.

It knocked the wind out of Sita.

Her mother was a shadow of her former self. She had been reduced to bare skin and bones. Her round, moon-shaped face had turned gaunt, with cheeks sunken in. She had always been short and petite, but had never looked unhealthy. Now, her muscles had wasted away, and her body was stripped of the little fat she had once had. Her eyes looked hollow. Her lustrous, rich black hair had turned sparse and a ghostly white. She could barely hold herself up. She needed her aides to support her.

As soon as Sunaina saw her precious daughter, her face lit up. It was the same warm smile where Sita had always found comfort and sanctuary.

'My child,' said Sunaina, in a barely audible voice.

The queen of Mithila held out her hands, her deathly pallor temporarily reduced by the abundance of a mother's love-filled heart.

Sita stood rooted to her spot. Hoping the earth would swallow her.

'Come here, my child,' said Sunaina. Her arms, too weak to be held up, fell on her sides.

Sunaina coughed. An aide rushed forward and wiped her mouth with a handkerchief. Specks of red appeared on the white cloth.

Sita stumbled towards her mother. Dazed. She fell to her knees and rested her head on Sunaina's lap. One that had always been soft, like Mother Earth immediately after the rains. It was bony and hard now, like the same earth after a series of devastating droughts.

Sunaina ran her fingers through Sita's hair.

Sita trembled in fear and sorrow, like a little sparrow about to see the fall of the mighty *Banyan* tree that had sheltered not just her body but also her soul.

Continuing to run her hand through Sita's hair, Sunaina bent down, kissed her head and whispered, 'My child …'

Sita burst out crying.

— ༺ༀ —

The Mithila physician-in-attendance had vehemently opposed it. Even though severely weakened, Sunaina was still a formidable creature. She would not be denied the elephant ride into the jungle with her daughter.

The physician had played his final card. He had whispered into the queen's ear, 'This may well be your last elephant ride, Your Highness.'

And Sunaina had replied, 'That is precisely why I must go.'

The queen had rested in the palanquin while the two elephants were prepared for the ride. One would carry the physician and a few attendants, while the other would carry Sunaina and Sita.

When it was time, Sunaina was carried to the howdah of the seated elephant. A maid tried to clamber aboard, next to the queen.

'No!' a firm Sunaina decreed.

'But, My Lady …' pleaded the maid, holding up a handkerchief and a small bottle. The fumes from the dissolved herbal medicine helped boost her energy for short periods of time.

'My daughter is with me,' said Sunaina. 'I don't need anyone else.'

Sita immediately took the handkerchief and bottle from the maid and climbed aboard the howdah.

Sunaina signalled the mahout, who tenderly stroked the elephant behind its ears with his foot. The elephant rose very slowly, causing the least amount of discomfort to Sunaina.

'Let's go,' she ordered.

The two elephants ambled off into the jungle, accompanied by fifty armed Mithila policemen, on foot.

Chapter 10

The howdah swayed like a cradle with the animal's gentle walk. Sita held her mother's hand and huddled close. The mahout steered the elephants in the shade, under the trees. Nonetheless, it was dry and warm.

Sita, though, was shivering. With guilt. And fear.

Sunaina lifted her hand slightly. Sita instinctively knew what her mother wanted. She lifted Sunaina's arm higher, and snuggled in close. And wrapped her mother's arm around her shoulder. Sunaina smiled with satisfaction and kissed Sita on her forehead.

'Sorry that your father couldn't come, Sita,' said Sunaina. 'He had to stay back for some work.'

Sita knew her mother was lying. She did not wish to cause her daughter further pain.

Perhaps, it was just as well.

Sita had, in a fit of anger, told Janak the last time she had been in Mithila that he should stop wasting his time on spirituality and help Sunaina govern the kingdom. That it was his duty. Her outburst had angered Sunaina more than her father.

Also, little Urmila, Sita's four-year-old younger sister, was a sickly child. Janak had probably stayed behind with her, while their mother travelled to Shvetaketu's *gurukul.* In debilitating illness. To meet her troubled elder daughter. And, to make her come back home.

Sita closed her eyes, as another guilty tear rolled down her cheek.

Sunaina coughed. Sita immediately wiped her mother's mouth with the cloth. She looked at the red stains — signs that her mother's life was slowly slipping away.

Tears began to flow in a rush.

'Everyone has to die someday, my darling,' said Sunaina.

Sita continued crying.

'But the fortunate ones die with their loved ones around them.'

— 𒀹𒀹 —

The two elephants were stationary, expertly stilled by their mahouts. The fifty Mithilan guards, too, were immobile, and silent. The slightest sound could prove dangerous.

Ten minutes back, Sunaina had spotted a scene rarely witnessed by human eyes: The death of the matriarch of a large elephant herd.

Sita remembered her mother's lessons on elephant herds. They tended to be matriarchal, led by the eldest female. Most herds comprised adult females with calves, both male and female, nurtured as common children. Male elephants were normally exiled from the herd when they came of age.

The matriarch was more than the leader of the herd. She was a mother to all.

The death of the matriarch, therefore, would be a devastating event for the herd. Or so one would imagine.

'I think it's the same herd that we saw a few years ago,' whispered Sunaina.

Sita nodded.

They watched from a safe distance, hidden by the trees.

The elephants stood in a circle around the corpse of the matriarch. Solemn. Motionless. Quiet. The gentle afternoon breeze struggled to provide relief as the sun shone harshly on the assembly. Two calves stood within the circle, near the body. One was tiny, the other slightly older.

'We saw that little one being born, Sita,' said Sunaina.

Sita nodded in the affirmative.

She remembered the birth of the matriarch's child. Her mother and she had witnessed it on another elephant ride a few years ago.

Today, that baby elephant, a male calf, was down on his knees next to his dead mother. His trunk was entwined with hers, his body shaking. Every few minutes, he would pull on the trunk of his mother's corpse, as though trying to wake her up.

The older calf, his sister, stood next to the baby. Calm. Still. Like the other members of the herd.

'Watch now ...' whispered Sunaina.

An adult female, perhaps the new matriarch, slowly ambled up to the corpse. She stretched her trunk and touched the forehead of the dead body with utmost respect. Then she walked around the corpse solemnly, turned and simply walked away.

The other elephants in the circle followed her lead, one by one. Doing the exact same thing — touching the forehead of the dead former matriarch with their trunks, performing a circumambulation and then walking away.

With dignity. With respect.

None of them looked back. Not once. Not once.

The little male calf, however, refused to leave. He clung to his mother. Desperately. He pulled at her with helpless ferocity. His sister stood quietly by his side.

The rest of the herd came to a halt at a distance, not once turning around. Patiently, they waited.

After some time, the sister touched her little brother with her trunk.

The male calf pushed it away. With renewed energy, he stood on his feet and wrapped his trunk around his mother's. And pulled hard. He slipped. He got up again. Held his mother's trunk and pulled. Harder. He cast a beseeching look at his sister, begging for her help. With a gut-wrenching cry, he turned back to his mother, willing her to get up.

But his mother had succumbed to the long sleep now. She would wake up only in her next life.

The child refused to give up. Shifting from side to side, he pulled his mother's trunk. Repeatedly.

The sister finally walked up to her mother's corpse, and touched the forehead with her trunk, just like the others had. She then walked around the body of her mother. She came up to her brother, held his trunk and tried to pull him away.

The male calf began to screech heartbreakingly. He followed his sister. But he kept looking back. Again. And again. He offered no resistance, however, to his sister.

The sister, like every other elephant in the herd, walked steadily ahead. She did not look back. Not once. Not once.

Sita looked up at her mother, tears flowing down her cheeks.

'Society moves on, my child,' whispered Sunaina. 'Countries move on. Life moves on. As it should.'

Sita couldn't speak. She could not look at her mother. She held Sunaina close, burying her head in her mother's bosom.

'Clinging to painful memories is pointless, Sita,' said Sunaina. 'You must move on. You must live...'

Sita listened. But the tears did not stop.

'There's no escape from problems and challenges. They're a part of life. Avoiding Mithila does not mean that your troubles will disappear. It only means that other challenges will appear.'

Sita tightened her grip on her mother.

'Running away is never the solution. Confront your problems. Manage them. That is the way of the warrior.' Sunaina lifted Sita's chin and looked into her eyes. 'And, you are a warrior. Don't ever forget that.'

Sita nodded.

'You know your sister was born weak. Urmila is no warrior. You must take care of her, Sita. And, you must look after Mithila.'

Sita made a promise to herself within the confines of her mind. *Yes. I will.*

Sunaina caressed Sita's face and smiled. 'Your father has always loved you. So does your younger sister. Remember that.'

I know.

'As for me, I don't just love you, Sita. I also have great expectations from you. Your karma will ensure our family's name survives for many millennia. You will go down in history.'

Sita uttered her first words since she had seen her mother at the *gurukul.* 'I am so sorry, *Maa.* I'm so sorry. I ...'

Sunaina smiled and held Sita tight.

'Sorry ...' sobbed Sita.

'I have faith in you. You will live a life that will make me proud.'

'But I can't live without you, *Maa.*'

Sunaina pulled back and held Sita's face up. 'You can and you will.'

'No ... I will not live without you ...'

Sunaina's expression became firm. 'Listen to me, Sita. You will not waste your life mourning me. You will live wisely and make me proud.'

Sita continued crying.

'Don't look back. Look to the future. Build your future, don't grieve for your past.'

Sita did not have the strength to speak.

'Promise me.'

Sita stared at her mother, her eyes brimming with misery.

'Promise me.'

'I promise, *Maa*. I promise.'

— ऱॐ —

It had been four weeks since Sunaina's visit to Shvetaketu's *gurukul*. Sita had returned home with her mother. Sunaina had manoeuvred for Sita to be appointed prime minister of Mithila, with all the executive powers necessary to administer the kingdom.

Sita now spent most of her time with Sunaina, looking after her mother's failing health. Sunaina guided Sita's meetings with the ministers of the kingdom in her private chambers, by her bedside.

Sita was aware that Sunaina was greatly concerned about her relationship with her younger sister. Thus, she made a concerted effort to bond with Urmila. The queen of Mithila wanted her daughters to build a strong relationship that would tide them over the difficult years ahead. She had spoken to them about the need for them to stand by each other. And the love and loyalty they must share.

One evening, after a long meeting in Sunaina's chambers, Sita entered Urmila's room, next to their mother's. She had asked an aide to arrange a plate of black grapes. Urmila loved black grapes. Dismissing the aide, she carried the plate into the chamber.

The room was dimly lit. The sun had set but only a few lamps were aglow.

'Urmila!'

She was not in bed. Sita began looking for her sister. She stepped into the large balcony overlooking the palace garden.

Where is she?

She came back into the room. Irritated with the minimal light, she was about to order for some more lamps to be lit, when she noticed a shaking figure bundled in a corner.

'Urmila?'

Sita walked over.

Urmila sat in the corner, her knees pulled against her chest. Her head down on her knees.

Sita immediately set the plate aside and sat down on the floor next to Urmila. She put her arm around her baby sister.

'Urmila …' she said, gently.

Urmila looked up at her *elder sister*. Her tear-streaked face was lined with misery.

'*Didi* …'

'Talk to me, my child,' said Sita.

'Is …'

Sita squeezed Urmila's shoulders gently. 'Yes …'

'Is *maa* leaving us and going to heaven?'

Sita swallowed hard. She wished *maa* was here to answer Urmila's questions. Almost immediately, she realised that Sunaina would soon not be here at all. Urmila was her responsibility. She had to be the one to answer her.

'No, Urmila. *Maa* will always be here.'

Urmila looked up. Confused. Hopeful. 'But everyone is telling me that *maa* is going away. That I have to learn to ...'

'Everyone doesn't know what you and I know, Urmila. *Maa* will just live in a different place. She won't live in her body anymore.' Sita pointed to Urmila's heart and then her own. '*Maa* will live in these two places. She will always be there in our hearts. And, whenever we are together, she will be complete.'

Urmila looked down at her chest, feeling her heart pick up pace. Then she looked at Sita. 'She will never leave us?'

'Urmila, close your eyes.'

Urmila did as her sister ordered.

'What do you see?'

She smiled. 'I see *maa*. She is holding me. She is caressing my face.'

Sita ran her fingers down Urmila's face. She opened her eyes, smiling even more broadly.

'She will always be with us.'

Urmila held Sita tightly. '*Didi* ...'

'The both of us, together, are now our mother.'

— ☬ —

'My journey in this life is drawing to an end,' said Sunaina.

Sita and Sunaina were alone in the queen's chambers. Sunaina lay in bed. Sita sat beside her, holding her hand.

'*Maa* ...'

'I'm aware of what people in Mithila say about me.'

'*Maa*, don't bother about what some idiots ...'

'Let me speak, my child,' said Sunaina, pressing Sita's hand. 'I know they think my achievements of the past have evaporated in the last few years. Ever since Kushadhwaj began to squeeze our kingdom dry.'

Sita felt the familiar guilt rise in her stomach.

'It is not your fault,' said Sunaina, emphatically. 'Kushadhwaj would have used any excuse to hurt us. He wants to take over Mithila.'

'What do you want me to do, *Maa?*'

Sunaina knew her daughter's aggressive nature. 'Nothing to Kushadhwaj… He is your father's brother. But I want you to redeem my name.'

Sita kept quiet.

'It is said that we come with nothing into this world, and take nothing back. But that's not true. We carry our karma with us. And we leave behind our reputation, our name. I want my name redeemed, Sita. And I want *you* to do it. I want *you* to bring back prosperity to Mithila.'

'I will, *Maa.*'

Sunaina smiled. 'And, once you have done that… you have my permission to leave Mithila.'

'*Maa?*'

'Mithila is too small a place for one such as you, Sita. You are meant for greater things. You need a bigger stage. Perhaps, a stage as big as India. Or, maybe history itself …'

Sita considered telling Sunaina about the Malayaputras having recognised her as the next Vishnu.

It took her only a few moments to decide.

— ॐ —

The head *pandit* walked up to Sita, holding a torch in his right hand. Other *pandits* were lined up at the back, chanting hymns from the *Garuda Purana*. 'It's time, My Lady.'

Sita nodded at him and looked down to her left. Urmila had not stopped crying since Sunaina's death. She held on to Sita's arm with both her hands. Sita tried to pry them open, but her sister clung on, even stronger. Sita looked at her father, who walked up, picked Urmila up in his arms and stood beside his elder daughter. Janak looked as devastated and lost as the young Urmila. He had lost the human shield that had guarded him, as he had soared the heights of philosophical wisdom. Reality had intruded rudely into his life.

Sita turned to the *pandit* and took the torch.

It had only been three months since Sunaina's visit to the *gurukul*.

Sita had thought she'd have more time with Sunaina. To learn. To live. To love.

But that was not to be.

She moved forward as she heard the *pandits* chant from the *Isha Vasya Upanishad*.

Vayur anilam amritam; Athedam bhasmantam shariram

Let this temporary body be burned to ashes. But the breath of life belongs elsewhere. May it find its way back to the Immortal Breath.

She walked up to the sandalwood logs that entombed her mother's body. She closed her eyes as she pictured her mother's face. She must not cry. Not here. Not in public. She knew that many Mithilans secretly blamed her for further weakening her mother in her illness, by making her travel to Shvetaketu's *gurukul*. She also knew that they blamed her for the troubles caused by Kushadhwaj.

She must be strong. For her mother. She looked to her friend, Samichi, who stood at a distance. Next to her stood Radhika, her friend from the *gurukul*. She drew strength from their support.

She stuck the burning log into the pyre. Washed with ghee, the wood caught fire immediately. The pyre burned bright and strong, as if honoured to be the purifying agent for one so noble.

Farewell, Maa.

Sita stepped back and looked at the sky, to the One God, *Brahman.*

If anyone ever deserved moksha, it is her, my mother.

Sita remembered her mother's words as they had witnessed the mourning of the elephant matriarch.

Don't look back. Look to the future.

Sita whispered softly to the cremation pyre. 'I *will* look back, *Maa.* How can I not? You are my life.'

She remembered her last coherent conversation with her mother. Sunaina had warned Sita to not trust either the Malayaputras or the Vayuputras completely if she were to fulfil her destiny as the Vishnu. Both tribes would have their own agenda. She needed partners.

Her mother's voice resonated in her mind. *Find partners you can trust; who are loyal to your cause. Personal loyalty is not important. But they must be loyal to your cause.*

She remembered her mother's last statement.

I will always be looking at you. Make me proud.

Sita took a deep breath and clenched her fists, making a vow. 'I will, *Maa.* I will.'

Chapter 11

Sita and Samichi sat on the edge of the outer fort wall. Sita moved forward and looked down at the moat that surrounded the city. It was a long way down. Not for the first time, she wondered what it would be like to fall, all the way to the ground. Would it hurt? Would she be released from her body instantly? Would she finally be free? What happens after death?

Why do these stupid thoughts enter my mind?

'Sita ...' whispered Samichi, breaking the silence.

They had been seated together for some time. There were hardly any words exchanged between the two, as a distracted Sita kept looking beyond the wall. Samichi could understand Sita's pain. After all, it had just been a day since the princess had cremated her mother's dead body. Despite her recently reduced popularity, almost the entire kingdom was in mourning for their Queen Sunaina. Not just Sita, but all of Mithila had lost its mother.

Sita did not respond.

'Sita ...'

Instinct kicked in. Samichi reached her arm out and held it in front of Sita. Attempting to prevent some unspoken fear from coming true. Samichi understood, only too well, the power of dark thoughts.

Sita shook her head. Pushing the unnecessary thoughts out of her head.

Samichi whispered again, 'Sita ...'

Sita spoke distractedly. To herself. '*Maa*, as always, was right ... I need partners ... I will complete my karma ... But I can't do it alone. I need a partner ...'

Samichi held her breath, thinking that Sita had plans for her. Thinking that Sita was talking about what Sunaina had wanted for Mithila. And, the karma the dying queen had asked of her. But Sita was, in fact, dwelling on what the chief of the Malayaputras had tasked her with.

Sita touched the scar on her left palm, recalling the blood oath she had made with Vishwamitra. She whispered to herself, 'I swear by the great Lord Rudra and by the great Lord Parshu Ram.'

Samichi did not notice that Sita had, for the first time, taken an oath in the name of Lord Parshu Ram as well. Usually, the princess only invoked Lord Rudra's name. But how could she have registered the change? Her thoughts, too, had drifted; to her *True Lord,* the *Iraiva.*

Does Sita intend to make me her second-in-command in Mithila? Iraiva be praised ... Iraiva will be happy ...

— ௭௫ —

A year had passed since the death of Sunaina. The sixteen-year-old Sita had been administering the kingdom reasonably well. She had consolidated her rule by retaining the team that had advised Sunaina, careful to continue systems that her mother had instituted. The only major change she had made was to appoint her trusted aide, Samichi, as the Chief of Police. An appointment necessitated by the sudden death of the previous police chief, who had had an unexpected and fatal heart attack.

Jatayu, the Malayaputra captain, had been true to his word, and shadowed Sita along with his team of soldiers. They had been tasked with being her bodyguards. Sita did not feel the need for this extra protection. But who can shake off a shadow? In fact, she had had to give in to Jatayu's request and induct some Malayaputra soldiers into the Mithila police force. Their true identity was kept a secret from all, including Samichi. They followed Sita. Always.

Over the last year, Sita had grown to trust Jatayu. Almost like a brother. He was the senior most Malayaputra officer that she interacted with on a regular basis. And, the only person she could openly discuss her Vishnu responsibilities with.

'I'm sure you understand, don't you, Jatayu*ji*?' asked Sita.

Sita and Jatayu had rendezvoused an hour's ride away from Mithila, near an abandoned bangle-making factory. Her Malayaputra bodyguards had accompanied her, disguised as Mithila policemen. Jatayu had just told her that Vishwamitra expected her to come to Agastyakootam, the capital of the Malayaputras, a hidden city deep in the south of India. She was to be trained there for some months to prepare her for her role as the Vishnu. After that, for the next few years, she would remain in her hometown, Mithila, for half the year and spend the other half travelling around the Sapt Sindhu, understanding the land she had to save.

However, Sita had just told Jatayu that she was not ready to leave Mithila yet. There was a lot left to be done. Mithila had to be stabilised and made secure; not the least of all, from the threat posed by Kushadhwaj.

'Yes, my sister,' said Jatayu. 'I understand. You need a few more years in Mithila. I will convey this to Guru*ji*. I am sure he, too, will understand. In fact, even your work here is training, in a way, for your mission.'

'Thank you,' said Sita. She asked him something she had been meaning to for some time. 'By the way, I have heard that Agastyakootam is close to Raavan's Lanka. Is that true?'

'Yes, it is. But do not worry, you will be safe there. It's a hidden city. And, Raavan would not dare attack Agastyakootam even if he knew where it was.'

Sita was not worried about Agastyakootam's security. It was something else that troubled her. But she decided not to seek further clarification. At least for now.

'Have you decided what to do with the money?' asked Jatayu.

The Malayaputras had donated a grand sum of one hundred thousand gold coins to Mithila, to help Sita speedily establish her authority in the kingdom. It was a relatively small amount for the tribe; but for Mithila, it had been a windfall. The Malayaputras had officially called it an endowment to a city that had dedicated itself to knowledge and was the beloved of the *rishis*.

No one was surprised by this unprecedented generosity. Why wouldn't great *rishis* nurture the saintly king Janak's city of knowledge? In fact, Mithilans had gotten used to seeing many of the Malayaputras, and even the great *maharishi*, Vishwamitra, visit their city often.

There were two potential projects that needed investment. One was the road that connected Mithila to Sankashya. The other was cheap, permanent and liveable housing for the slum dwellers.

'The road will revive trade to a great extent,' said Jatayu. 'Which will bring in more wealth to the city. A big plus.'

'Yes, but that wealth will largely go to a small number of already rich people. Some of them may even leave, taking their wealth along with them to more trade-friendly cities. The road will not rid us of our dependency on the Sankashya port. Nor will it stymie my uncle's ability to freeze supplies to Mithila whenever he feels like. We must become independent and self-reliant.'

'True. The slum redevelopment project, on the other hand, will provide permanent homes to the poor. It will also remove an eyesore at one of the main city gates, making it accessible to traffic.'

'Hmm.'

'And, you will earn the loyalty of the poor. They are the vast majority in Mithila. Their loyalty will prove useful, my sister.'

Sita smiled. 'I am not sure if the poor are always loyal. Those who are capable of loyalty will be loyal. Those who are not will not, no matter what I may do for them. Be that as it may, we must help the poor. And we can generate so many jobs with this project, making many more people productive locally. That is a good thing.'

'True.'

'I have other ideas related to this project, which would increase our self-reliance. At least with regard to food and other essentials.'

'I have a feeling that you've made up your mind already!'

'I have. But it is good to listen to other wise opinions before taking the final decision. This is exactly what my mother would have done.'

'She was a remarkable woman.'

'Yes, she was,' smiled Sita. She hesitated a moment, took one more look at Jatayu, and then broached another sensitive topic. 'Jatayu*ji*, do you mind if I ask you a question?'

'Anytime you wish to, great Vishnu,' said Jatayu. 'How can I not answer?'

'What is the problem between Maharishi Vishwamitra and Maharishi Vashishtha?'

Jatayu smiled ruefully. 'You have a rare ability to discover things that you are not supposed to. Things that are meant to be a secret.'

Sita smiled with disarming candour. 'That is not an answer to my question, Jatayu*ji*.'

'No, it's not, my sister,' laughed Jatayu. 'To be honest, I don't know much about it. But I do know this: they hate each other viscerally. It is unwise to even mention the name of Maharishi Vashishtha in the presence of Maharishi Vishwamitra.'

— ᚱᚷᚷ —

'Good progress,' whispered Sita. She was standing in the garden of the Lord Rudra temple in Mithila, looking at the ongoing work of rebuilding the city slums.

A few months ago, Sita had ordered that the slums at the southern gate of Mithila be demolished and new, permanent houses be built for the poor on the same land. These houses, built with the money given by the Malayaputras, would be given to the poor free of cost.

Samichi preened at the compliment from her prime minister. In an unorthodox move, Sita had assigned her, rather than the city engineer, with the task of implementing the project rapidly and within budget. Sita knew that her Police Chief was obsessively detail-oriented, with an ability to push her subordinates ruthlessly to get the job done. Also, having spent her early years in the slums, Samichi was uniquely qualified to understand the problems faced by the people living there.

Though the execution had been entrusted to Samichi, Sita had involved herself in the planning and design of the project after consulting the representatives of the slum dwellers. She had eventually worked out an innovative solution for not only their housing needs, but also providing them with sustainable livelihood.

The slum dwellers had been unwilling to vacate their land for even a few months. They had little faith in the administration. For one, they believed the project would be under construction for years, rendering them homeless for a long time. Also, many were superstitious and wanted their rebuilt homes to stand exactly where the old ones had been. This, however, would leave no excess space for neatly lined streets. The original slum had no streets to begin with, just small, haphazard pathways.

Sita had conceived a brilliant solution: building a honeycomb-like structure, with houses that shared walls on all sides. Residents would enter from the top, with steps descending into their homes. The 'ceilings' of all the homes would, from the outside, be a single, joint, level platform; a new 'ground level' above all the houses; an artificial ground that was four floors above the actual ground. It would be an open-to-sky space for the slum dwellers, with a grid of 'streets' marked in paint. The 'streets' would contain hatch doors serving as entries to their homes. This would address their superstitions; each one would get a house exactly at the same location as their original hovel. And, since the honeycomb structure would extend four floors below, each inhabitant would, in effect, have four rooms. A substantially bigger home than earlier.

Because of its honeycomb-like structure, Samichi had informally named the complex Bees Quarter. Sita had liked it so much that it had become the official name!

There was still the problem of temporary accommodation for the slum dwellers, while their new homes were being constructed. Sita had had another innovative idea. She converted the moat outside the fort wall into a lake, to store rain water and to aid agriculture. The uninhabited area between the outer fort wall and the inner fort wall was partly handed over to the slum dwellers. They built temporary houses for themselves there with bamboo and cloth. They used the remaining land to grow food crops, cotton and medicinal herbs. This newly allotted land would remain in their possession even after they moved back into the Bees Quarter, which would be ready in a few months.

This had multiple benefits. Firstly, the land between the outer fort wall and the inner fort wall, which had been left unoccupied as a security measure, was put to good use. Agricultural productivity improved. This provided additional income for the slum dwellers. Moving agriculture within the city wall would also provide food security during times of siege; unlikely though it seemed that impoverished Mithila would ever be attacked.

Most importantly, Mithilans became self-reliant in terms of food, medicines and other essentials. This reduced their dependence on the Sankashya river port.

Samichi had warned Sita that this might tempt Kushadhwaj to militarily attack them. But Sita doubted it. It would be politically difficult for her uncle to justify his army attacking the saintly king of Mithila. It would probably stoke rebellion even among the citizens of Sankashya. Notwithstanding this, it was wise to be prepared for even the most unlikely event.

Sita had always been uneasy about the outer moat being the city's main water supply. In the unlikely event of a siege, an enemy could poison the water outside and cause havoc. She decreed that a deep lake be constructed within the city as a precaution. In addition to this, she also strengthened the two protective walls of Mithila.

She organised the chaotic central market of the city. Permanent, uniform stalls were given to the vendors, ensuring cleanliness and orderliness. Sales increased, along with a reduction in pilferage and wastage. This led to a virtuous cycle of decrease in prices, further enhancing business.

All these moves also dramatically increased Sita's popularity. At least, among the poor. Their lives had improved considerably, and the young princess was responsible.

— ᛞᚴ —

'I must admit, I am surprised,' said Jatayu. 'I didn't expect a police chief to efficiently oversee the construction of your Bees Quarter so smoothly.'

Sita sat with Jatayu outside the city limits. The day had entered the third *prahar*. The sun still shone high in the sky.

She smiled. 'Samichi is talented. No doubt.'

'Yes. But ...'

Sita looked at him and frowned. 'But what, Jatayu*ji*?'

'Please don't misunderstand me, great Vishnu. It is your kingdom. You are the prime minister. And, we Malayaputras concern ourselves with the whole country, not just Mithila ...'

'What is it, Jatayu*ji*?' interrupted Sita. 'You know I trust you completely. Please speak openly.'

'My people in your police force talk to the other officers. It's about Samichi. About her ...'

Sita sighed. 'I know ... It's obvious that she has a problem with men ...'

'It's more like hatred for men, rather than just a problem.'

'There has to be a reason for it. Some man must have ...'

'But hating all men because of one man's actions, whatever they may have been, is a sign of an unstable personality. Reverse-bias is also bias. Reverse-racism is also racism. Reverse-sexism is also sexism.'

'I agree.'

'If she kept her feelings to herself that would be fine. But her prejudice is impacting her work. Men are being targeted unfairly. You don't want to trigger a rebellion.'

'She does not allow me to help her in the personal space. But I will ensure that her hatred does not impact her work. I'll do something.'

'I am only concerned about your larger interest, great Vishnu. There is no doubt in my mind that she is personally very loyal to you.'

'I guess it helps that I am not a man!'

Jatayu burst out laughing.

— ट॒ᴊ —

'How are you, Naarad?' asked Hanuman.

Hanuman had just returned from a trip to Pariha. He had sailed into the port of Lothal in Gujarat, on his way eastward, deeper into the heart of India. He had been met at the port by his friend Naarad, a brilliant trader in Lothal who was also a lover of art, poetry and the latest gossip! Naarad had immediately escorted his friend, along with his companions, to the office behind his shop.

'I'm all right,' said Naarad heartily. 'Any better would be a sin.'

Hanuman smiled. 'I don't think you try too hard to stay away from sin, Naarad!'

Naarad laughed and changed the topic. 'The usual supplies, my friend? For you and your band?'

A small platoon of Parihans accompanied Hanuman on his travels.

'Yes, thank you.'

Naarad nodded and whispered some instructions to his aide.

'And, I thank you further,' continued Hanuman, 'for not asking where I am going.'

The statement was too obvious a bait, especially for Naarad. He swallowed it hook, line, and sinker.

'Why would I ask you? I already know you are going to meet Guru Vashishtha!'

Vashishtha was the royal guru of the kingdom of Ayodhya. It was well known that he had taken the four princes of Ayodhya — Ram, Bharat, Lakshman and Shatrughan— to his *gurukul* to train and educate them. The location of the *gurukul*, however, was a well-kept secret.

Hanuman stared at Naarad, not saying anything.

'Don't worry, my friend,' said Naarad, smiling. 'Almost nobody, besides me of course, knows who you are going to meet. And nobody, not even me, knows where the *gurukul* is.'

Hanuman smiled. He was about to retort when a loud feminine voice was heard.

'Hans!'

Hanuman closed his eyes for a moment, winced and turned around. It was Sursa, an employee of Naarad who was obsessed with him.

Hanuman folded his hands together into a *Namaste* and

spoke with extreme politeness, 'Madam, my name is Hanuman, not Hans.'

'I know that,' said Sursa, sashaying towards Hanuman. 'But I think Hans sounds so much better. Also, don't you think Sur is better than madam?'

Naarad giggled with mirth as Sursa came uncomfortably close to Hanuman. The Naga glared at his friend before taking a few steps back and distancing himself from his admirer. 'Madam, I was engaged in an important conversation with Naarad and ...'

Sursa cut him short. 'And, I've decided to interrupt. Deal with it.'

'Madam ...'

Sursa arched her eyebrows and swayed her hip seductively to the side. 'Hans, don't you understand the way I feel about you? The things I can do for you ... And, to you ...'

'Madam,' interrupted Hanuman, blushing beet-red, and stepping back farther. 'I have told you many times. I am sworn to celibacy. This is inappropriate. I am not trying to insult you. Please understand. I cannot ...'

Naarad was leaning against the wall now, covering his mouth, shoulders shaking, laughing silently. Trying hard not to make a sound.

'Nobody needs to know, Hans. You can keep up the appearance of your vow. You don't have to marry me. I only want you. Not your name.' Sursa stepped forward and reached out for Hanuman's hand.

With surprising agility for a man his size, Hanuman sidestepped quickly, deftly avoiding Sursa's touch. He raised his voice in alarm, 'Madam! Please! I beg you! Stop!'

Sursa pouted and traced her torso with her fingers. 'Am I not attractive enough?'

Hanuman turned towards Naarad. 'In Lord Indra's name, Naarad. Do something!'

Naarad was barely able to control his laughter. He stepped in front of Hanuman and faced the woman. 'Listen Sursa, enough is enough. You know that …'

Sursa flared up. Suddenly aggressive. 'I don't need your advice, Naarad! You know I love Hans. You had said you would help me.'

'I am sorry, but I lied,' said Naarad. 'I was just having fun.'

'This is fun for you?! What is wrong with you?'

Naarad signalled a couple of his employees. Two women walked up and pulled an irate Sursa away.

'I will make sure you lose half your money in your next trade, you stupid oaf!' screamed Sursa, as the women dragged her out.

As soon as they were alone again, Hanuman glared at his friend. 'What *is* wrong with you, Naarad?'

'I was just having fun, my friend. Sorry.'

Hanuman held the diminutive Naarad by his shoulder, towering over him. 'This is not fun! You were insulting Sursa. And, harassing me. I should thrash you to your bones!'

Naarad held Hanuman's hands in mock remorse, his eyes twinkling mischievously. 'You won't feel like thrashing me when I tell you who the Malayaputras have appointed as the Vishnu.'

Hanuman let Naarad go. Shocked. '*Appointed?*'

How can Guru Vishwamitra do that? Without the consent of the Vayuputras!

Naarad smiled. 'You won't survive a day without the information I give you. That's why you won't thrash me!'

Hanuman shook his head, smiled wryly, hit Naarad playfully on his shoulder and said, 'Start talking, you stupid nut.'

Chapter 12

'Radhika!' Sita broke into a broad smile.

Sita's friend from her *gurukul* days had made a surprise visit. The sixteen-year-old Radhika, a year younger than Sita, had been led into the princess' private chambers by Samichi, the new protocol chief of Mithila. The protocol duties, a new addition to Samichi's responsibilities, kept her busy with non-police work of late. Sita had therefore appointed a Deputy Police Chief to assist Samichi. This deputy was male. A strong but fair-minded officer, he had ensured that Samichi's biases did not affect real policing.

Radhika had not travelled alone, this time. She was accompanied by her father, Varun Ratnakar, and her uncle, Vayu Kesari.

Sita had met Varun Ratnakar in the past, but this was her first meeting with Radhika's uncle and Ratnakar's cousin, Vayu Kesari. The uncle did not share any family resemblance with his kin. Substantially short, stocky and fair-complexioned, his muscular body was extraordinarily hairy.

Perhaps he is one of the Vaanars, thought Sita.

She was aware that Radhika's tribe, the Valmikis, were matrilineal. Their women did not marry outside the community.

Men, however, could marry non-Valmiki women; of course, on the condition that if they did, they would leave the tribe. Perhaps Vayu Kesari was the son of one such excommunicated Valmiki man and a Vaanar woman.

Sita bent down and touched the feet of the elderly men.

Both blessed Sita with a long life. Varun Ratnakar was a respected intellectual and thinker, revered by those who valued knowledge. Sita knew he would love to spend time with her father, who was, perhaps, the most intellectual king in the Sapt Sindhu. With the departure of his chief guru, Ashtaavakra, to the Himalayas, Janak missed philosophical conversations. He would be happy to spend some quality time in the company of fellow intellectuals.

The men soon departed for King Janak's chambers. Samichi, too, excused herself. Her busy schedule did not leave her with much time for social niceties. Sita and Radhika were soon alone in the Mithila princess' private study.

'How is life treating you, Radhika?' asked Sita, holding her friend's hands.

'I am not the one leading an exciting life, Sita,' smiled Radhika. 'You are!'

'Me?!' laughed Sita, rolling her eyes with exaggerated playfulness. 'Hardly. All I do is police a small kingdom, collect taxes and redevelop slums.'

'Only for now. You have so much more to do …'

Sita instantly became guarded. There seemed to be more to this conversation than was obvious at the surface level. She spoke carefully. 'Yes, I do have a lot to do as the prime minister of Mithila. But it's not unmanageable, you know. We truly are a small and insignificant kingdom.'

'But India is a big nation.'

Sita spoke even more carefully, 'What can this remote corner do for India, Radhika? Mithila is a powerless kingdom ignored by all.'

'That may be so,' smiled Radhika. 'But no Indian in his right mind will ignore Agastyakootam.'

Sita held her breath momentarily. She maintained her calm demeanour, but her heart was thumping like the town crier's drumbeat.

How does Radhika know? Who else does? I have not told anyone. Except Maa.

'I want to help you, Sita,' whispered Radhika. 'Trust me. You are a friend and I love you. And, I love India even more. You are important for India. *Jai Parshu Ram.*'

'*Jai Parshu Ram,*' whispered Sita, hesitating momentarily before asking, 'Are your father and you ...'

Radhika laughed. 'I'm a nobody, Sita. But my father ... Let's just say that he's important. And, he wants to help you. I am just the conduit, because the universe conspired to make me your friend.'

'Is your father a Malayaputra?'

'No, he is not.'

'Vayuputra?'

'The Vayuputras do not live in India. The tribe of the Mahadev, as you know, can visit the sacred land of India anytime but cannot live here. So, how can my father be a Vayuputra?'

'Then, who is he?'

'All in good time ...' smiled Radhika. 'Right now, I have been tasked with checking a few things with you.'

— ᚱᚷ —

Vashishtha sat quietly on the ground, resting against a tree. He looked at his *ashram* from the distance, seeking solitude in the early morning hour. He looked towards the gently flowing stream. Leaves floated on the surface, strangely even-spaced, as if in a quiet procession. The tree, the water, the leaves ... nature seemed to reflect his deep satisfaction.

His wards, the four princes of Ayodhya — Ram, Bharat, Lakshman, and Shatrughan — were growing up well, moulding ideally into his plans. Twelve years had passed since the demon king of Lanka, Raavan, had catastrophically defeated Emperor Dashrath, changing the fortunes of the Sapt Sindhu in one fell blow.

It had convinced Vashishtha that the time for the rise of the Vishnu had arrived.

Vashishtha looked again at his modest *gurukul*. This was where the great Rishi Shukracharya had moulded a group of marginalised Indian royals into leaders of one of the greatest empires the world had ever seen: the *AsuraSavitr*, the Asura Sun.

A new great empire shall rise again from this holy ground. A new Vishnu shall rise from here.

Vashishtha had still not made up his mind. He wasn't sure which of the two — Ram or Bharat — he would push for as the next Vishnu. One thing was certain; the Vayuputras supported him. But there were limits to what the tribe of Lord Rudra could do. The Vayuputras and Malayaputras had their fields of responsibility; after all, the Vishnu was supposed to be officially recognised by the Malayaputras. And the chief of the Malayaputras ... His former friend ...

Well ...

I'll manage it.

'Guru*ji*.'

Vashishtha turned. Ram and Bharat had quietly approached him.

'Yes,' said Vashishtha. 'What did you find out?'

'They are not there, Guru*ji*,' said Ram.

'They?'

'Not only Chief Varun, but many of his advisers are also missing from their village.'

Varun was the chief of the tribe that managed and maintained this *ashram,* situated close to the westernmost point of the River Shon's course. His tribe, the Valmikis, rented out these premises to *gurus* from time to time. Vashishtha had hired this *ashram* to serve as his *gurukul* for the duration that the four Ayodhya princes were with him.

Vashishtha had hidden the true identity of his wards from the Valmikis. But of late he had begun to suspect that perhaps the tribe knew who the students were. It also seemed to him that the Valmikis had their own carefully kept secrets.

He had sent Ram and Bharat to check if Chief Varun was in the village. It was time to have a talk with him. Vashishtha would then decide whether to move his *gurukul* or not.

But Varun had left. Without informing Vashishtha. Which was unusual.

'Where have they gone?' asked Vashishtha.

'Apparently, Mithila.'

Vashishtha nodded. He knew that Varun was a lover and seeker of knowledge, especially the spiritual kind. Mithila was a natural place for such a person.

'All right, boys,' said Vashishtha. 'Get back to your studies.'

— ༺༻ —

'We heard that the Vishnu blood oath has been taken,' said Radhika.

'Yes,' answered Sita. 'In Guru Shvetaketu's *gurukul*. A few years ago.'

Radhika sighed.

Sita frowned. 'Is there a problem?'

'Well, Maharishi Vishwamitra is a little … unorthodox.'

'Unorthodox? What do you mean?'

'Well, for starters, the Vayuputras should have been present.'

Sita raised her eyebrows. 'I didn't know that …'

'The tribes of the Vishnu and the Mahadev are supposed to work in partnership.'

Sita looked up as she realised something. 'Guru Vashishtha?'

Radhika smiled. 'For someone who hasn't even begun training, you have picked up quite a lot already!'

Sita shrugged and smiled.

Radhika held her friend's hand. 'The Vayuputras do not like or trust Maharishi Vishwamitra. They have their reasons, I suppose. But they cannot oppose the Malayaputra chief openly. And yes, you guessed correctly, the Vayuputras support Maharishi Vashishtha.'

'Are you telling me that Guru Vashishtha has his own ideas about who the Vishnu should be?'

Radhika nodded. 'Yes.'

'Why do they hate each other so much?'

'Very few know for sure. But the enmity between Guru Vishwamitra and Guru Vashishtha is very old. And, very fierce …'

Sita laughed ruefully. 'I feel like a blade of grass stuck between two warring elephants.'

'Then you wouldn't mind another species of grass next to you for company while being trampled upon, I suppose!'

Sita playfully hit Radhika on her shoulders. 'So, who is this other blade of grass?'

Radhika took a deep breath. 'There are two, actually.'

'Two?'

'Guru Vashishtha is training them.'

'Does he plan to create two Vishnus?'

'No. Father believes Guru Vashishtha will choose one of them.'

'Who are they?'

'The princes of Ayodhya. Ram and Bharat.'

Sita raised her eyebrows. 'Guru Vashishtha has certainly aimed high. The family of the emperor himself!'

Radhika smiled.

'Who is better among the two?'

'My father prefers Ram.'

'And who do you prefer?'

'My opinion doesn't matter. Frankly, father's opinion doesn't count either. The Vayuputras will back whomsoever Guru Vashishtha chooses.'

'Is there no way Guru Vashishtha and Guru Vishwamitra can be made to work together? After all, they are both working for the greater good of India, right? I am willing to work in partnership with the Vishnu that Guru Vashishtha selects. Why can't they partner each other?'

Radhika shook her head. 'The worst enemy a man can ever have is the one who was once his best friend.'

Sita was shocked. 'Really? Were they friends once?'

'Maharishi Vashishtha and Maharishi Vishwamitra were childhood friends. Almost like brothers. Something happened to turn them into enemies.'

'What?'

'Very few people know. They don't speak about it even with their closest companions.'

'Interesting …'

Radhika remained silent.

Sita looked out of the window and then at her friend. 'How do you know so much about Guru Vashishtha?'

'You know that we host a *gurukul* close to our village, right? It is Guru Vashishtha's *gurukul*. He teaches the four princes in the *ashram* we have rented out.'

'Can I come and meet Ram and Bharat? I'm curious to know if they are as great as Guru Vashishtha thinks they are.'

'They are still young, Sita. Ram is five years younger than you. And, don't forget, the Malayaputras keep track of you. They follow you everywhere. We cannot risk revealing the location of Guru Vashishtha's *gurukul* to them …'

Sita was constrained to agree. 'Hmm.'

'I will keep you informed about what they are doing. I think father intends to have an honest conversation with Guru Vashishtha in any case. Perhaps, even offer his help.'

'Help Guru Vashishtha? Against me?'

Radhika smiled. 'Father hopes for the same partnership that you do.'

Sita bent forward. 'I have told you much of what I know. I think I deserve to know … Who is your father?'

Radhika seemed hesitant.

'You would not have spoken about the Ayodhya princes had your father not allowed you to do so,' said Sita. 'And, I am sure that he would have expected me to ask this question. So, he wouldn't have sent you to meet me unless he was prepared to reveal his true identity. Tell me, who is he?'

Radhika paused for a few moments. 'Have you heard of Lady Mohini?'

'Are you serious?' asked Sita. 'Who hasn't heard of her, the great Vishnu?'

Radhika smiled. 'Not everyone considers her a Vishnu. But the majority of Indians do. I know that the Malayaputras revere her as a Vishnu.'

'So do I.'

'And so do we. My father's tribe is the one Lady Mohini left behind. We are the Valmikis.'

Sita sat up straight. Shocked. 'Wow!' Just then another thought struck her. 'Is your uncle, Vayu Kesari, the father of Hanu *bhaiya*?'

Radhika nodded. 'Yes.'

Sita smiled. 'That's why ...'

Radhika interrupted her. 'You are right. That is one of the reasons. But it's not the only one.'

Chapter 13

'Chief Varun,' said Vashishtha, as he came to his feet and folded his hands into a respectful *Namaste*.

Varun had just returned from Mithila. And, Guru Vashishtha had been expecting a visit from him.

Vashishtha was much taller than Varun. But far thinner and leaner compared to the muscular and sturdy tribal chief.

'Guru Vashishtha,' said Varun, returning Vashishtha's greeting politely. 'We need to talk in private.'

Vashishtha was immediately wary. He led the chief out to a quieter spot.

Minutes later, they sat by the stream that flowed near the *ashram*, away from the four students, as well as others who might overhear them.

'What is it, Chief Varun?' asked Vashishtha, politely.

Varun smiled genially. 'You and your students have been here for many years, Guru*ji*. I think it's time we properly introduce ourselves to each other.'

Vashishtha stroked his flowing, snowy beard carefully, feigning a lack of understanding. 'What do you mean?'

'I mean... for example, the princes of Ayodhya do not have to pretend to be the children of some nobles or rich traders anymore.'

Vashishtha's thoughts immediately flew to the four boys. Where were they? Were they being rounded up by Varun's warriors? Chief Varun's tribe was not allowed, according to their traditional law, to help any Ayodhyan royals.

Perhaps, I wasn't so clever after all. I thought we would be safe if we just stayed away from the areas under Lankan or Malayaputra influence.

Vashishtha leaned forward. 'If you are concerned about your laws, you must also remember the one that states that you cannot harm the people you accept as your guests.'

Varun smiled. 'I intend no harm either to you or your students, Guru*ji*.'

Vashishtha breathed easy. 'My apologies, if I have offended you. But I needed a place that was ... safe. We will leave immediately.'

'There is no need to do that either,' said Varun, calm. 'I do not intend to kick you out. I intend to help you, Guru*ji*.'

Vashishtha was taken aback. 'Isn't it illegal for you to help the Ayodhya royalty?'

'Yes, it is. But there is a supreme law in our tribe that overrides every other. It is the primary purpose of our existence.'

Vashishtha nodded, pretending to understand, though he was confused.

'You must know our war cry: Victory at all costs ... When war is upon us, we ignore all the laws. And a war is coming, my friend ...'

Vashishtha stared at him, completely flummoxed.

Varun smiled. 'Please don't think I am unaware that my Vayuputra nephew steals into your *ashram* regularly, late at night, thinking we wouldn't notice. He thinks he can fool his uncle.'

Vashishtha leaned back, as a veil seemed to lift from his eyes. 'Hanuman?'

'Yes. His father is my cousin.'

Vashishtha was startled, but he asked in an even tone. 'Is Vayu Kesari your brother?'

'Yes.'

Varun was aware of the bond that Hanuman and Vashishtha shared. Many years ago, the guru had helped his nephew. He chose not to mention it. He knew the situation was complicated.

'Who are you?' Vashishtha finally asked.

'My full name is Varun Ratnakar.'

Suddenly, everything fell into place. Vashishtha knew the significance of that second name. He had found allies. Powerful allies. By pure chance.

There was only one thing left to do. Vashishtha clasped his right elbow with his left hand and touched his forehead with the clenched right fist, in the traditional salute of Varun's tribe. Respectfully, he uttered the ancient greeting. *'Jai Devi Mohini!'*

Varun held Vashishtha's forearm, like a brother, and replied, *'Jai Devi Mohini!'*

— ॐ —

Indians in the Sapt Sindhu have a strange relationship with the Sun God. Sometimes they want him, at other times, they don't. In summer, they put up with his rage. They plead with him, through prayers, to calm down and, if possible, hide behind the clouds. In winter, they urge him to appear with all his force and drive away the cold fury of the season.

It was on one such early winter day, made glorious by the energising sun, when Sita and Samichi rode out into the main palace garden. It had been refurbished recently on Sita's orders.

The two had decided on a private competition — a chariot race. It was a sport Sita truly enjoyed. The narrow lanes of the garden would serve as the racing track. They had not raced together in a long time. And, they had never done so in the royal garden before.

The garden paths were narrow, hemmed in with trees and foliage. It would require considerable skill to negotiate them in a chariot. The slightest mistake would mean crashing into trees at breakneck speed. Dangerous … And, exhilarating.

The risk of it, the thrill, made the race worthwhile. It was a test of instinct and supreme hand-eye coordination.

The race began without any ceremony.

'*Hyaah*!' screamed Sita, whipping her horses, instantly urging them forward.

Faster. Faster.

Samichi kept pace, close behind. Sita looked back for an instant. She saw Samichi swerving her chariot to the right. Sita looked ahead and pulled her horses slightly to the right, blocking Samichi's attempt to sneak past her at the first bend.

'Dammit!' screamed Samichi.

Sita grinned and whipped her horses. 'Move!'

She swung into the next curve without reining her horses in. Speeding as her chariot swerved left. The carriage tilted to the right. Sita expertly balanced her feet, bending leftwards to counter the centrifugal forces working hard on the chariot at such fast speeds. The carriage balanced itself and sped ahead as the horses galloped on without slowing.

'*Hyaah*!' shouted Sita again, swinging her whip in the air.

It was a straight and narrow path now for some distance. Overtaking was almost impossible. It was the best time to generate some speed. Sita whipped her horses harder. Racing forward. With Samichi following close behind.

Another bend lay farther ahead. The path broadened before the curve, giving a possible opportunity for Samichi to forge ahead. Sita smoothly pulled the reins to the right, guiding the horses to the centre, leaving as little space as possible on either side. Samichi simply could not overtake.

'*Hyaah!*'

Sita heard Samichi's loud voice. Behind her. To the left. Her voice was much louder than normal. Like she was trying to announce her presence.

Sita read her friend correctly.

A few seconds later, Sita quickly swerved. But, unexpectedly, to the right, covering that side of the road. Samichi had feigned the leftward movement. She had actually intended to overtake from the right. As Sita cut in, that chance was lost.

Sita heard a loud curse from Samichi.

Grinning, Sita whipped her horses again. Taking the turn at top speed. Ahead of the curve, the path would straighten out. And become narrower. Again.

'*Hyaah!*'

'Sita!' screamed Samichi loudly.

There was something in her voice.

Panic.

As if on cue, Sita's chariot flipped.

Sita flew up with the momentum. High in the air. The horses did not stop. They kept galloping.

Instinctively, Sita tucked in her head and pulled her legs up, her knees close to her chest. She held her head with her hands. In brace position.

The entire world appeared to flow in slow motion for Sita. Her senses alert. Everything going by in a blur.

Why is it taking so long to land?

Slam!

Sharp pain shot through her as she landed hard on her shoulder. Her body bounced forward, in the air again, hurled sickeningly with the impact.

'Princess!'

Sita kept her head tucked in. She had to protect her head.

She landed on her back. And was hurled forward, repeatedly rolling on the tough ground, brutally scraping her body.

A green blur zipped past her face.

Wham!

She slammed hard against a tree. Her back felt a sharp pain. Suddenly stationary.

But to her eyes, the world was still spinning.

Dazed, Sita struggled to focus on her surroundings.

Samichi brought her chariot to a halt, dismounted rapidly, and ran towards the princess. Sita's own chariot was being dragged ahead. Sparks flew in the air due to the intense friction generated by the chariot metal rubbing against the rough road. The disoriented horses kept galloping forward wildly.

Sita looked at Samichi. 'Get … my … chariot …'

And then, she lost consciousness.

— ᛞᚷ —

It was dark when Sita awoke. Her eyelids felt heavy. A soft groan escaped her lips.

She heard a panic-stricken squeal. '*Didi* … Are you alright …? Talk to me …'

It was Urmila.

'I'm alright, Urmila …'

Her father gently scolded the little girl. 'Urmila, let your sister rest.'

Sita opened her eyes and blinked rapidly. The light from the various torches in the room flooded in. Blinding her. She let her eyelids droop. 'How long… have I been …'

'The whole day, *Didi.*'

Just a day? It feels longer.

Her entire body was a mass of pain. Except her left shoulder. And her back. They were numb.

Painkillers. May the Ashwini Kumars bless the doctors.

Sita opened her eyes again. Slowly. Allowing the light to gently seep in. Allowing her pupils to adjust.

Urmila stood by the bedside, clutching the bedsheet with both hands. Her round eyes were tiny pools of water. Tears streamed down her face. Her father, Janak, stood behind his younger daughter. His normally serene face was haggard, lined with worry. He had just recovered from a serious illness. The last thing he needed was this additional stress.

'*Baba* …' said Sita to her father. 'You should be resting… You are still weak …'

Janak shook his head. 'You are my strength. Get well soon.'

'Go back to your room, *Baba* …'

'I will. You rest. Don't talk.'

Sita looked beyond her family. Samichi was there. As was Arishtanemi. He was the only one who looked calm. Unruffled.

Sita took a deep breath. She could feel her anger rising. 'Samichi …'

'Yes, princess,' said Samichi, as she quickly walked up to the bed.

'My chariot …'

'Yes, princess.'

'I want to… see it …'

'Yes, princess.'

Sita noticed Arishtanemi hanging back. There was a slight smile on his face now. A smile of admiration.

— ᚦᚷ —

'Who do you think tried to kill you?' asked Arishtanemi.

It had been five days since the chariot accident. Sita had recovered enough to be able to sit up in bed. Even walk around a bit. She ate like a soldier, quickly increasing her energy levels and boosting her alertness. A full recovery would take a few weeks.

Her left arm was in a sling. Her back was plastered with thick *neem* paste, mixed with tissue-repairing Ayurvedic medicines. Miniature bandages covered most parts of her body, protecting nicks and cuts to make them heal quickly.

'One doesn't need to be Vyomkesh to figure this out,' said Sita, referring to a popular fictional detective from folk stories.

Arishtanemi laughed softly.

The chariot had been brought to Sita's large chamber in the *Ayuralay*. Sita had examined it thoroughly. It had been very cleverly done.

Wood from another type of tree had been used to replace the two suspension beams. It was similar in appearance to the wood used in the rest of the carriage. It looked hardy. But was, in fact, weak. The nail marks that fixed the beams on the main shaft were fresh, despite care being taken to use old nails. One beam had cracked like a twig when strained by the speed of movement on uneven ground and the sharp turns. The beam had collapsed and jammed into the ground, seizing up the axle. This had brought the wheels to an abrupt halt when at a great speed. The chariot had levered up on the broken suspension beam as its front-end had rammed into the ground.

Very cleverly done.

Whoever had done this had the patience of a stargazer. It could have been done many months ago. It had been made to look like an old construction flaw, a genuine error. To make the death appear like an accident. And not an assassination. Sita had uncovered the conspiracy only through a close inspection of the nail marks.

The chariot was Sita's. The target obvious. She was the only one who stood between Mithila and its expansionary enemies. Urmila could simply be married off. And Janak ... Well. After Sita, it would only be a matter of time.

She had been extremely lucky. The accident had occurred when the last bend had almost been negotiated, making the chariot drag in a direction different from where Sita was flung due to the inertia of her bodily movement. Otherwise, she would have been crushed under the wheels and metal of her chariot. It would have been an almost certain death.

'What do you want to do?' asked Arishtanemi.

Sita had no doubt in her mind about who the perpetrator was behind her supposed accident. 'I was willing to consider an alliance. Frankly, he could have become the head of the royal family, too. After all, I have bigger plans. All I had asked for was that my father and sister be safe and treated well. And, my citizens be taken care of. That's it. Why did he do this?'

'People are greedy. They are stupid. They misread situations. Also, remember, outside of the Malayaputras, no one knows about your special destiny. Perhaps, he sees you as a future ruler and a threat.'

'When is Guru Vishwamitra coming back?'

Arishtanemi shrugged. 'I don't know.'

So we have to do this ourselves.

'What do you want to do?' repeated Arishtanemi.

'Guru Vishwamitra was right. He had told me once ... Never wait. Get your retaliation in first.'

Arishtanemi smiled. 'A surgical strike?'

'I can't do it openly. Mithila cannot afford an open war.'

'What do you have in mind?'

'It must look like an accident, just like mine was meant to be.'

'Yes, it must.'

'And, it cannot be the main man.'

Arishtanemi frowned.

'The main man is just the strategist. In any case, I can't attack him directly ... My mother had prohibited it ... We must cut off his right hand. So that he loses the ability to execute such plans.'

'Sulochan.'

Sulochan was the prime minister of Sankashya. The right-hand man of Sita's uncle Kushadhwaj. The man who ran practically everything for his king. Kushadhwaj would be paralysed without Sulochan.

Sita nodded.

Arishtanemi's face was hard as stone. 'It will be done.'

Sita did not react.

Now, you are truly worthy of being a Vishnu, thought Arishtanemi. *A Vishnu who can't fight for herself would be incapable of fighting for her people.*

— ᚛ᚉ᚜ —

Mara had chosen his day and time well.

The boisterous *nine-day* festivities of the Winter *Navratra* always included the day that marked the *Uttarayan*, the beginning of the *northward movement* of the sun. This was the day the nurturer of the world, the sun, was farthest away from the northern hemisphere. It would now begin its six-month journey back to the north. *Uttarayan* was, in a sense, a harbinger of renewal. The death of the old. The birth of the new.

It was the first hour of the first *prahar*. Just after midnight. Except for the river port area, the city of Sankashya was asleep. The peaceful sleep of the tired and happy. Festivals manage to do that. The city guards, though, were among the few who were awake. Throughout the city, one could hear their loud calls on the hour, every hour: All is well.

Alas, not all the guards were as duty-conscious.

Twenty such men sat huddled in the guard room at Prime Minister Sulochan's palace; it was the hour of their midnight snack. They should not have left their posts. But this had been a severe winter. And, the snack was only an excuse. They had, in fact, gravitated to the warm fireplace in the room like fireflies. It was just a break, they knew. They would soon be back on guard.

Sulochan's palace was perched on a hill, skirting the royal garden of Sankashya at one end. At the other end was the generous River Gandaki. It was a truly picturesque spot, apt for the residence of the second-most powerful man in the city. But not very kind to the guards. The palace's elevation increased the severity of the frosty winds. It made standing at the posts a battle against the elements. So, the men truly cherished the warmth of the guard room.

Two guards lay on the palace rooftop, towards the royal garden end. Their breathing even and steady. Sleeping soundly. They would not remember anything. Actually, there was nothing to remember. An odourless gas had gently breezed in and nudged them into a sound sleep. They would wake up the next morning, guiltily aware that they had dozed off on duty. They wouldn't admit this to any investigator. The punishment for sleeping while on guard duty was death.

Mara was not a crass assassin. Any brute with a bludgeon could kill. He was an artist. One hired Mara only if one wanted to employ a shadow. A shadow that would emerge from the darkness, for only a little while, and then quickly retreat. Leaving not a trace. Leaving just a body behind. The right body; always, the right body. No witnesses. No loose ends. No other 'wrong' body. No unnecessary clues for the mind of a savvy investigator.

Mara, the artist, was in the process of crafting one of his finest creations.

Sulochan's wife and children were at her maternal home. The Winter *Navratra* was the period of her annual vacation with her family. Sulochan usually joined them after a few days, but had been held back this time by some urgent state business. The prime minister was home alone. Indeed, Mara had chosen the day and time well. For he had been told strictly: avoid collateral damage.

He looked at the obese form of Prime Minister Sulochan. Lying on the bed. His hands on his sides. Feet flopped outwards. As he would ordinarily sleep. He was wearing a beige *dhoti*. Bare-chested. He had placed his *angvastram* on the bedside cabinet. Folded neatly. As he ordinarily would have done before going to sleep. His rings and jewellery had been removed and placed inside the jewellery box, next to the *angvastram*. Again, as he ordinarily would.

But, he was not breathing as he ordinarily would. He was already dead. A herbal poison had been cleverly administered through his nose. No traces would be left behind. The poison had almost instantly paralysed the muscles in his body.

The heart is a muscle. So is the diaphragm, located below the lungs. The victim asphyxiated within minutes.

Perhaps, Sulochan had been conscious through it. Perhaps not. Nobody would know.

And Mara didn't care to know.

The assassination had been carried out.

Mara was now setting the scene.

He picked up a manuscript from a shelf. It chronicled the doomed love story of a courtesan and a peripatetic trader. The story was already a popular play throughout the Sapt Sindhu. It was well known that Sulochan liked reading. And that he especially loved a good romance. Mara walked over to Sulochan's corpse and placed the dog-eared manuscript on the bed, by the side of his chest.

Sulochan had fallen asleep while reading.

He picked up a glass-encased lamp, lit the wick, and placed it on the bedside cabinet.

His reading lamp …

He picked up the decanter of wine lying on a table-top at the far end of the room and placed it on the cabinet, along with a glass. He poured some wine into the empty glass.

Prime Minister Sulochan had been drinking wine and reading a romantic novel at the end of a tiring day.

He placed a bowlful of an Ayurvedic paste on the bedside cabinet. He dipped a wooden tong in the paste, opened Sulochan's mouth and spread it evenly inside, taking care to include the back of his throat. A doctor would recognise this paste as a home remedy for stomach ache and gas.

The prime minister was quite fat. Stomach trouble would surely have been common. And he was also known to have enough Ayurvedic knowledge for home remedies for minor diseases and afflictions.

He walked towards the window.

Open window. Windy night.

He retraced his steps and pulled the covering sheet up to Sulochan's neck.

Sulochan had covered himself up. He was feeling cold.

Mara touched the sheet and the *angvastram*. And cast a careful glance around the room. Everything was as it should be.

Perfect.

Sulochan had, it would be deduced, confused the beginnings of a heart attack for a stomach and gas problem. A regrettably common mistake. He had had some medicine for it. The medicine had relieved his discomfort. Somewhat. He had then picked up a book to read and poured himself some wine. He had begun to feel the chill, typical of a heart attack. He had pulled up his sheet to cover himself. And then the heart attack had struck with its full ferocity.

Unfortunate.

Perfectly unfortunate.

Mara smiled. He looked around the scene and took a final mental picture. As he always did.

He frowned.

Something's not right.

He looked around again. With animal alertness.

Damn! Bloody stupid!

Mara walked up to Sulochan and picked up his left arm. *Rigor mortis* was setting in and the body had already begun to stiffen. With some effort, Mara placed Sulochan's left hand on his chest. With strain, he spread the fingers apart. As if the man had died clutching his chest in pain.

I should have done this earlier. Stupid! Stupid!

Satisfied with his work now, Mara once again scanned the room. Perfect.

It looked like a simple heart attack.

He stood in silence, filled with admiration for his creation. He kissed the fingertips of his right hand.

No, he was not just a killer. He was an artist.

My work here is done.

He turned and briskly walked up to the window, leapt up and grabbed the parapet of the roof. Using the momentum, he somersaulted and landed on his feet above the parapet. Soon he was on the rooftop.

Mara was the invisible man. The dark, non-transferable polish that he had rubbed all over his skin, along with his black *dhoti*, ensured that he went unseen in the night.

The maestro sighed with satisfaction. He could hear the sounds of the night. The chirping crickets. The crackling fire from the guard room. The rustling wind. The soft snores of the guards asleep on the roof ... Everything was as it should be. Nothing was amiss.

He ran in the direction of the royal garden. Without any hesitation. Building up speed. As he neared the edge of the roof, he leapt like a cat and glided above the ground. His outstretched arms caught an overhanging branch of a tree. He swung onto the branch, balanced his way to the tree trunk and smoothly slid to the ground.

He began running. Soft feet. Silent breaths. No unnecessary sound.

Mara, the shadow, disappeared into the darkness. Lost to the light. Again.

Chapter 14

Mithila was more stable than it had been in years. The rebuilt slums, along with the ancillary opportunities it provided, had dramatically improved the lives of the poor. Cultivation in the land between the two fort walls had led to a spike in agricultural production. Inflation was down. And, the unfortunate death of the dynamic prime minister of Sankashya had neutralised Kushadhwaj substantially. No one grudged the now popular Sita her decision to carry out a spate of diplomatic visits across the country.

Of course, few knew that the first visit would be to the fabled capital of the Malayaputras: Agastyakootam.

The journey was a long and convoluted one. Jatayu, Sita, and a large Malayaputra company first travelled to Sankashya by the dirt road. Thereafter, they sailed on river boats down the Gandaki till its confluence with the mighty Ganga. Then, they sailed up the Ganga to its closest point to the Yamuna. They then marched over land to the banks of the Yamuna and sailed down the river till it met the Sutlej to form the Saraswati. From there, they sailed farther down the Saraswati till it merged into the Western Sea. Next, they boarded a seaworthy ship and were presently sailing down the western coast of India, towards the southwestern tip of the Indian subcontinent. Destination: Kerala. Some called it God's own country. And why not, for this was the land the previous Vishnu, Lord Parshu Ram, had called his own.

On an early summer morning, with a light wind in its sails, the ship moved smoothly over calm waters. Sita's first experience of the sea was pleasant and free of discomfort.

'Was Lord Parshu Ram born in Agastyakootam?' asked Sita.

Sita and Jatayu stood on the main deck, their hands resting lightly on the balustrade. Jatayu turned to her as he leaned against the bar. 'We believe so. Though I can't give you proof. But we can certainly say that Lord Parshu Ram belongs to Kerala and Kerala belongs to him.'

Sita smiled.

Jatayu pre-empted what he thought Sita would say. 'Of course, I am not denying that many others in India are as devoted to Lord Parshu Ram as we are.'

She was about to say something but was distracted as her eyes fell upon two ships in the distance. Lankan ships. They were moving smoothly, but at a startling speed.

Sita frowned. 'Those ships look the same as ours. They have as many sails as ours. How are they sailing so much faster?'

Jatayu sighed. 'I don't know. It's a mystery. But it's a huge maritime advantage for them. Their armies and traders travel to faraway regions faster than anyone else can.'

Raavan must have some technology that the others do not possess.

She looked at the mastheads of the two ships. Black-coloured Lankan flags, with the image of the head of a roaring lion emerging from a profusion of fiery flames, fluttered proudly in the wind.

Not for the first time, Sita wondered about the relationship between the Malayaputras and the Lankans.

— ᚱᚴ —

As they neared the Kerala coast, the travellers were transferred to a ship with a lesser draught, suitable for the shallower backwaters they would now sail into.

Sita had been informed in advance by Jatayu and knew what to expect as they approached the landmass. They sailed into the maze-like water bodies that began at the coast. A mix of streams, rivers, lakes and flooded marshes, they formed a navigable channel into the heart of God's own country. Charming at first glance, these waters could be treacherous; they constantly changed course in a land blessed with abundant water. As a result, new lakes came into being as old ones drained every few decades. Fortuitously, most of these backwaters were inter-connected. If one knew how, one could navigate this watery labyrinth into the hinterland. But if one was not guided well, it was easy to get lost or grounded. And, in this relatively uninhabited area, populated with all kinds of dangerous animals, that could be a death sentence.

Sita's ship sailed in this confusing mesh of waterways for over a week till it reached a nondescript channel. At first, she did not notice the three tall coconut trees at the entrance to the channel. The creepers that spread over the three trunks seemed fashioned into a jigsaw of axe-parts.

The channel led to a dead end, covered by a thick grove of trees. No sight of a dock where the ship could anchor. Sita frowned. She assumed that they would anchor mid-stream and meet some boats soon. Amazingly, the ship showed no signs of slowing down. In fact, the drumbeats of the pace-setters picked up a notch. As the rowers rowed to a faster beat, the vessel gathered speed, heading straight for the grove!

Sita was alone on the upper deck. She held the railings nervously and spoke aloud, 'Slow down. We are too close.'

But her voice did not carry to Jatayu, who was on the secondary deck with his staff, supervising some intricate operations.

How can he not see this! The grove is right in front of us!

'Jatayu*ji*!' screamed Sita in panic, sure now that the ship would soon run aground. She tightened her grip on the railing, bent low and braced herself. Ready for impact.

No impact. A mild jolt, a slight slowing, but the ship sailed on.

Sita raised her head. Confused.

The trees moved, effortlessly pushed aside by the ship! The vessel sailed deep into what should have been the grove. Sita bent over and looked into the water.

Her mouth fell open in awe.

By the great Lord Varun.

Floating trees were pushed aside as the ship moved into a hidden lagoon ahead. She looked back. The floating trees had moved back into position, hiding the secret lagoon as the ship sailed forward. Later, Jatayu would reveal to her that they were a special sub-species of the Sundari tree.

Sita smiled with wonder and shook her head. 'What mysteries abound in the land of Lord Parshu Ram!'

She faced the front again, her eyes aglow.

And then, she froze in horror.

Rivers of blood!

Bang in front of her, in the distance, where the lagoon

ended and the hills began, three streams of blood flowed in from different directions and merged into the cove.

It was believed that a long time ago, Lord Parshu Ram had massacred all the evil kings in India who were oppressing their people. Legend had it that when he finally stopped, his blood-drenched axe had spewed the tainted blood of those wicked kings in an act of self-purification. It had turned the river Malaprabha red.

But it's just a legend!

Yet here she was, on a ship, seeing not one, but three rapid streams of blood disgorging into the lagoon.

Sita clutched her *Rudraaksh* pendant in fear as her heart rate raced. *Lord Rudra, have mercy.*

— ॐ —

'Sita is on her way, Guru*ji*,' said Arishtanemi, as he entered the Hall of Hundred Pillars. 'She should be in Agastyakootam in two or three weeks at most.'

Vishwamitra sat in the main *ParshuRamEshwar* temple in Agastyakootam. The temple was dedicated to the one that Lord Parshu Ram worshipped: Lord Rudra. He looked up from the manuscript he was reading.

'That's good news. Are all the preparations done?

'Yes, Guru*ji*,' said Arishtanemi. He extended his hand and held out a scroll. The seal had been broken. But it could still be recognised. It was the royal seal of the descendants of Anu. 'And King Ashwapati has sent a message.'

Vishwamitra smiled with satisfaction. Ashwapati, the king of Kekaya, was the father of Kaikeyi and Emperor Dashrath's father-in-law. That also made him the grandfather of Dashrath's second son, Bharat. 'So, he has seen the light and seeks to build new relationships.'

'Ambition has its uses, Guru*ji*,' said Arishtanemi. 'Whether the ambition is for oneself or one's progeny. I believe, an Ayodhya nobleman called General Mrigasya has shown ...'

'Guru*ji*!' A novice ran into the hall, panting with exertion. Vishwamitra looked up, irritated.

'Guru*ji*, she is practising.'

Vishwamitra immediately rose to his feet. He quickly folded his hands together and paid his respects to the idols of Lord Rudra and Lord Parshu Ram. Then, he rushed out of the temple, followed closely by Arishtanemi and the novice.

They quickly mounted their horses and broke into a gallop. There was precious little time to lose.

Within a short while, they were exactly where they wanted to be. A small crowd had already gathered. On hallowed ground. Under a tower almost thirty metres in height, built of stone. Some heads were tilted upwards, towards a tiny wooden house built on top of the tower. Others sat on the ground, their eyes closed in bliss. Some were gently crying, rocking with emotions coursing through their being.

A glorious musical rendition wafted through the air. Divine fingers plucked the strings of an instrument seemingly fashioned by God himself. A woman, who had not stepped out of that house for years, was playing the *Rudra Veena*. An instrument named after the previous Mahadev. What was being performed was a *raga* that most Indian music aficionados would recognise. Some called it *Raga Hindolam*, others called it *Raga Malkauns*. A composition dedicated to the great Mahadev himself, Lord Rudra.

Vishwamitra rushed in as the others made way. He stopped

at the base of the staircase at the entrance to the tower. The sound was soft, filtered by the wooden walls of the house. It was heavenly. Vishwamitra felt his heart instantly settle into the harmonic rhythm. Tears welled up in his eyes.

'*Wah*, Annapoorna *devi*, *wah*,' mouthed Vishwamitra, as though not wanting to break the spell with any superfluous sound, even that of his own voice.

According to Vishwamitra, Annapoorna was undoubtedly the greatest stringed-instrument player alive. But if she heard any such words of praise, she might stop her practice.

Hundreds had gathered, as if risen from the ground. Arishtanemi looked at them uncomfortably. He had never been happy about this.

Offering refuge to the estranged wife of the chief court musician of Lanka? A former favourite of Raavan himself?

Arishtanemi possessed a military mind. Given to strategic thought. Not for him the emotional swings of those passionately in love with music.

But he knew that his Guru did not agree with him. So he waited, patiently.

The *raga* continued to weave its ethereal magic.

— ༺༻ —

'It's not blood, my sister,' said Jatayu, looking at Sita.

Though Sita had not asked any question regarding the 'rivers of blood', the terror on her face made Jatayu want to ease her mind. She did not let go of her *Rudraaksh* pendant, but her face relaxed.

The Malayaputras, meanwhile, were anchoring the vessel to the floating jetty.

'It's not?' asked Sita.

'No. It's the effect of a unique riverweed which grows here. It lines the bottom of the stream and is reddish-violet in colour. These streams are shallow, so they appear red from a distance. As if it's a stream full of blood. But the 'blood' doesn't discolour the lagoon, don't you see? Because the riverweeds are too deep in the lagoon to be seen.'

Sita grinned in embarrassment.

'It can be alarming, the first time one sees it. For us, it marks Lord Parshu Ram's territory. The legendary river of blood.'

Sita nodded.

'But blood can flow by other means, in this region. There are dangerous wild animals in the dense jungles between here and Agastyakootam. And we have a two-week march ahead of us. We must stick together and move cautiously.'

'All right.'

Their conversation was cut short by the loud bang of the gangway plank crashing on the floating jetty.

— ᚱᚦᚴ —

A little less than two weeks later, the company of five platoons neared their destination. They had cut through unmarked, dense forests along the way, where no clear pathway had been made. Sita realised that unless one was led by the Malayaputras, one would be hopelessly lost in these jungles.

Excitement coursed through her veins as they crested the final hill and beheld the valley that cradled Lord Parshu Ram's city.

'Wow ...' whispered Sita.

Standing on the shoulders of the valley, she admired

the grandiose beauty spread out below her. It was beyond imagination.

The Thamiravaruni river began to the west and crashed into this huge, egg-shaped valley in a series of massive waterfalls. The valley itself was carpeted with dense vegetation and an impenetrable tree cover. The river snaked its way through the vale and exited at the eastern, narrower end; flowing towards the land where the Tamil lived.

The valley was deep, descending almost eight hundred metres from the peaks in the west, from where the Thamiravaruni crashed into it. The sides of the valley fell sharply from its shoulders to its floor, giving it steep edges. The shoulders of the valley were coloured red; perhaps the effect of some metallic ore. The river picked up some of this ore as it began its descent down the waterfall. It lent a faint, red hue to the waters. The waterfalls looked eerily bloody. The river snaked through the valley like a lightly coloured red snake, slithering across an open, lush green egg.

Most of the valley had been eroded over the ages by the river waters, heavy rainfall, and fierce winds. All except for one giant monolith, a humongous tower-like mountain of a single rock. It stood at a proud height of eight hundred and fifty metres from the valley floor, towering well above the valley's shoulders. Massive in breadth as well, it covered almost six square kilometres. The monolith was coloured grey, signifying that it was made of granite, one of the hardest stones there is. Which explained why it stood tall, like a sentinel against the ravages of time, refusing to break even as Mother Nature constantly reshaped everything around it.

Early evening clouds obstructed her view, yet Sita was overwhelmed by its grandeur.

The sides of the monolith were almost a ninety-degree drop from the top to the valley floor. Though practically vertical, the sides were jagged and craggy. The crags sprouted shrubs and ferns. Some creepers clung on bravely to the sides of the monolith. Trees grew on the top, which was a massive space of six square kilometres in area. Besides the small amount of vegetation clinging desperately to the monolith's sides, it was a largely naked rock, standing in austere glory against the profusion of green vegetation that populated every other nook and cranny of the valley below.

The *ParshuRamEshwar* temple was at the top of the monolith. But Sita could not get a very clear view because it was hidden behind cloud cover.

The monolith was *Agastyakootam*; literally, the *hill of Agastya*. The Malayaputras had eased the otherwise impossible access to Agastyakootam with a rope-and-metal bridge from the valley shoulders to the monolith.

'Shall we cross over to the other side?' asked Jatayu.

'Yes,' answered Sita, tearing her gaze away from the giant rock.

Jai Parshu Ram.'

Jai Parshu Ram.'

— ᘰ᙭ —

Jatayu led his horse carefully over the long rope-and-metal bridge. Sita followed with her horse in tow. The rest of the company fell in line, one behind the other.

Sita was amazed by the stability of the rope bridge. Jatayu explained that this was due to the innovatively designed hollow metal planks that buttressed the bottom of the bridge. The foundations of these interconnected planks lay buried deep on both sides; one at the valley-shoulder end, the other at the granite monolith.

Intriguing as the bridge design was, it did not hold Sita's attention for long. She peered over the rope-railing at the Thamiravaruni, flowing some eight hundred metres below her. She steadied herself; it was a long and steep drop. The Thamiravaruni crashed head-on into the monolith that Sita was walking towards. The river then broke into two streams, which, like loving arms, embraced the sheer rock. They re-joined on the other side of the monolith; and then, the Thamiravaruni continued flowing east, out of the valley. The monolith of granite rock was thus, technically, a riverine island.

'What does the name Thamiravaruni mean, Jatayu*ji*?' asked Sita.

Jatayu answered without turning around. '*Varuni* is *that which comes from Lord Varun*, the God of Water and the Seas. In these parts, it is simply another word for *river*. And *Thamira*, in the local dialect, has two meanings. One is red.'

Sita smiled. 'Well, that's a no-brainer! The red river!'

Jatayu laughed. 'But *Thamira* has another meaning, too.'

'What?'

'Copper.'

— ᚱᚷᚷ —

As Sita neared the other side, the clouds parted. She came to a sudden halt, making her horse falter. Her jaw dropped. In sheer amazement and awe.

'How in Lord Rudra's name did they build this?'

Jatayu smiled as he looked back at Sita and gestured that

she keep moving. He turned quickly and resumed his walk. He had been trained to be careful on the bridge.

A massive curvilinear cave had been carved into the monolith. Almost fifteen metres in height and probably around fifty metres deep, the cave ran all along the outer edge of the monolith, in a continuous line, its floor and ceiling rising gently as it spiralled its way to the top of the stone structure. It therefore served as a road, built into the monolith itself. The 'road' spiralled its way down to a lower height as well, till it reached the point of the monolith where it was two hundred metres above the valley floor. But this long continuous cave, which ran within the surface of the structure, with the internal monolith rock serving as its road and roof, did not just serve as a passage. On the inner side of this cave were constructions, again carved out of the monolith rock itself. These constructions served as houses, offices, shops and other buildings required for civilised living. This innovative construction, built deeper into the inner parts of the monolith itself, housed a large proportion of the ten thousand Malayaputras who lived in Agastyakootam. The rest lived on top of the monolith. There were another ninety thousand Malayaputras, stationed in camps across the great land of India.

'How can anyone carve something this gigantic into stone as hard as granite?' asked Sita. 'That too in a rock face that is almost completely vertical? This is the work of the Gods!'

'The Malayaputras represent the God, Lord Parshu Ram, himself,' said Jatayu. 'Nothing is beyond us.'

As he stepped off the bridge onto the landing area carved into the monolith, Jatayu mounted his horse again. The ceiling of the cave was high enough to comfortably allow a mounted soldier to ride along. He turned to see Sita climbing onto her horse as well. But she did not move. She was admiring the intricately engraved railings carved out at the edge of the cave, along the right side of the 'road'. The artistry imposed on it distracted one from the sheer fall into the valley that the railing prevented. The railing itself was around two metres high. Pillars had been carved into it, which also allowed open spaces in between for light. The 'fish' symbol was delicately carved into each pillar's centre.

'My sister,' whispered Jatayu.

Sita had steered her horse towards the four-floor houses on the left inner side of the cave road. She turned her attention back to Jatayu.

'Promise me, my sister,' said Jatayu, 'you will not shrink or turn back, no matter what lies ahead.'

'What?' frowned Sita.

'I think I understand you now. What you're about to walk into may overwhelm you. But you cannot imagine how important this day is for us Malayaputras. Don't pull back from anyone. Please.'

Before Sita could ask any further questions, Jatayu had moved ahead. Jatayu steered his horse to the right, where the road rose gently, spiralling its way to the top.

Sita too kicked her horse into action.

And then, the drumbeats began.

As the road opened ahead, she saw large numbers of people lined on both sides. None of them wore any *angvastrams*. The people of Kerala dressed this way, when they entered temples to worship their Gods and Goddesses. The absence of the *angvastram* symbolised that they were the servants of their Gods and Goddesses. And, they were dressed this way today, as their living Goddess had come home.

At regular intervals stood drummers with large drums hanging from cloth ropes around their shoulders. As Sita emerged, they began a rhythmic, evocative beat. Next to each drummer was a *veena* player, stringing melody to the rhythm of the drummers. The rest of the crowd was on their knees, heads bowed. And, they were chanting.

The words floated in the air. Clear and precise.

Om Namo Bhagavate Vishnudevaya
Tasmai Saakshine namo namah
Salutations to the great God Vishnu
Salutations, Salutations to the Witness

Sita looked on, unblinking. Unsure of what to do. Her horse, too, had stopped.

Jatayu pulled up his horse and fell behind Sita. He made a clicking sound and Sita's horse began to move. Forward, on a gentle gradient to the top.

And thus, led by Sita, the procession moved ahead.

Om Namo Bhagavate Vishnudevaya
Tasmai Matsyaaya namo namah
Salutations to the great God Vishnu
Salutations, Salutations to Lord Matsya

Sita's horse moved slowly, but unhesitatingly. Most of the faces in the crowd were filled with devotion. And many had tears flowing down their eyes.

Some people came forward, bearing rose petals in baskets. They flung them in the air. Showering roses on their Goddess, Sita.

Om Namo Bhagavate Vishnudevaya
Tasmai Kurmaaya namo namah
Salutations to the great God Vishnu
Salutations, Salutations to Lord Kurma

One woman rushed in, holding her infant son in her arms. She brought the baby close to the horse's stirrups and touched the child's forehead to Sita's foot.

A confused and troubled Sita tried her best to not shrink back.

The company, led by Sita, kept riding up the road, towards the summit of the monolith.

The drumbeats, the veenas, the chanting continued... ceaselessly.

Om Namo Bhagavate Vishnudevaya
Tasyai Vaaraahyai namo namah
Salutations to the great God Vishnu
Salutations, Salutations to Lady Varahi

Ahead of them, some people were down on their knees with their heads placed on the ground, their hands spread forward. Their bodies shook with the force of their emotions.

Om Namo Bhagavate Vishnudevaya
Tasmai Narasimhaaya namo namah
Salutations to the great God Vishnu
Salutations, Salutations to Lord Narsimha

The gently upward-sloping cave opened onto the top of the monolith. The railing continued to skirt the massive summit. People from the spiral cave road followed Sita in a procession.

The large area at the top of the monolith was well organised with grid-like roads and many low-rise buildings. The streets were bordered with dugouts on both sides that served as flower beds, the soil for which had been painstakingly transported from the fertile valley below. At regular intervals, the dugouts were deep, for they held the roots of larger trees. It was a carefully cultivated naturalness in this austere, rocky environment.

At the centre of the summit lay two massive temples, facing each other. Together, they formed the *ParshuRamEshwar* temple complex. One temple, red in colour, was dedicated to the great Mahadev, Lord Rudra. The other, in pristine white, was the temple of the sixth Vishnu, Lord Parshu Ram.

The other buildings in the area were uniformly low-rise, none built taller than the temples of *ParshuRamEshwar*. Some served as offices and others as houses. Maharishi Vishwamitra's house was at the edge of the summit, overlooking the verdant valley below.

Om Namo Bhagavate Vishnudevaya
Tasmai Vaamanaaya namo namah
Salutations to the great God Vishnu
Salutations, Salutations to Lord Vaaman
The chanting continued.

Jatayu held his breath as his eyes fell on a gaunt old lady. Her flowing white hair let loose in the wind, she sat on a platform in the distance. Her proud, ghostly eyes were fixed on Sita. With her felicitous fingers, she plucked at the strings of the *Rudra Veena*. Annapoorna *devi*. The last time she had been seen was the day that she had arrived at Agastyakootam, many years ago. She had stepped out of her home, today. She was playing the *Veena* in public, consciously breaking her oath. A terrible oath, compelled by a husband she had loved. But there was good reason to break the oath today. It was not every day that the great Vishnu came home.

Om Namo Bhagavate Vishnudevaya
Tasyai Mohinyai namo namah
Salutations to the great God Vishnu
Salutations, Salutations to Lady Mohini
Some purists believed that a Mahadev and a Vishnu could

not exist simultaneously. That at any given time, either the Mahadev exists with the tribe of the previous Vishnu, or the Vishnu exists with the tribe of the previous Mahadev. For how could the need for the destruction of Evil coincide with the propagation of Good? Therefore, some refused to believe that Lady Mohini was a Vishnu. Clearly, the Malayaputras sided with the majority that believed that the great Lady Mohini was a Vishnu.

The chanting continued.

Om Namo Bhagavate Vishnudevaya
Tasmai Parshuramaaya namo namah
Salutations to the great God Vishnu
Salutations, Salutations to Lord Parshu Ram

Sita pulled her horse's reins and stopped as she approached Maharishi Vishwamitra. Unlike the others, he was wearing his *angvastram*. All the Malayaputras in Agastyakootam were on top of the monolith now.

Sita dismounted, bent and touched Vishwamitra's feet with respect. She stood up straight and folded her hands together into a *Namaste*. Vishwamitra raised his right hand.

The music, the chanting, all movement stopped instantly.

A gentle breeze wafted across the summit. The soft sound it made was all that could be heard. But if one listened with the soul, perhaps the sound of ten thousand hearts beating as one would also have been heard. And, if one possessed the power of the divine, one would have also heard the cry of an overwhelmed woman's heart, as she silently called out to the beloved mother she had lost.

A Malayaputra *pandit* walked up to Vishwamitra, holding two bowls in his hands. One contained a thick red viscous liquid; and, the other, an equal amount of thick white liquid.

Vishwamitra dipped his index and ring finger into the white liquid and then the middle finger in the red liquid.

Then he placed his wrist on his chest and whispered, 'By the grace of the Mahadev, Lord Rudra, and the Vishnu, Lord Parshu Ram.'

He placed his three colour-stained fingers together in between Sita's eyebrows, then slid them up to her hairline, spreading the outer fingers gradually apart as they moved. A trident-shaped *tilak* emerged on Sita's forehead. The outer arms of the *tilak* were white, while the central line was red.

With a flick of his hand, Vishwamitra signalled for the chanting to resume. Ten thousand voices joined together in harmony. This time, though, the chant was different.

Om Namo Bhagavate Vishnudevaya
Tasyai Sitadevyai namo namah
Salutations to the great God Vishnu
Salutations, Salutations to Lady Sita

Chapter 15

Late in the evening, Sita sat quietly in the Lord Parshu Ram temple. She had been left alone. As she had requested.

The grand *ParshuRamEshwar* temple grounds spread over nearly one hundred and fifty acres on the summit of the granite monolith. At the centre was a man-made square-shaped lake, its bottom lined with the familiar reddish-violet riverweeds. It reminded her of the three apparently 'blood-filled' streams she had seen at the hidden lagoon. The riverweeds had been grafted here, so that they could survive in these still waters. The lake served as a store for water for the entire city built into this rock formation. The water was transported into the houses through pipes built parallel to the spiral pathway down the curvilinear cave structure.

The two temples of the *ParshuRamEshwar* complex were constructed on opposite sides of this lake. One was dedicated to Lord Rudra and the other to Lord Parshu Ram.

The Lord Rudra temple's granite inner structure had been covered with a single layer of red sandstone, transported in ships from a great distance. It had a solid base, almost ten metres in height, forming the pedestal on which the main temple structure had been built. The exterior face of the base was intricately carved with figures of *rishis* and *rishikas*. A broad staircase in the centre led to a massive veranda. The main temple was surrounded by delicate lattice, made from thin strips of a copper alloy; it was brown in colour, rather than the natural reddish-orange of the metal. The lattice comprised tiny square-shaped openings, each of them shaped into a metallic lamp at its base. With thousands of these lamps festively lit, it was as if a star-lit sky screened the main temple.

Ethereal.

Beyond the metallic screen holding thousands of lamps, was the Hall of Hundred Pillars. Each pillar was shaped to a near-perfect circular cross-section using elephant-powered lathes. These imposing pillars held the main temple spire, which itself shot up a massive fifty metres. The towering temple spire was carved on all sides with figures of great men and women of the ancient past. People from many groups such as the Sangamtamils, Dwarkans, Manaskul, Adityas, Daityas, Vasus, Asuras, Devas, Rakshasas, Gandharvas, Yakshas, Suryavanshis, Chandravanshis, Nagas and many more. The forefathers and foremothers of this noble Vedic nation of India.

At the centre of the Hall was the *sanctum sanctorum*. In it were life-size idols of Lord Rudra and the woman he had loved, Lady Mohini. Unlike their normal representations, these idols did not carry weapons. Their expressions were calm, gentle, and loving. Most fascinatingly, Lord Rudra and Lady Mohini held hands.

On the other side of the square lake, facing the Lord Rudra temple, was the temple dedicated to Lord Parshu Ram. Almost exactly similar to the Lord Rudra temple, there was one conspicuous difference: Lord Parshu Ram temple's granite inner structure was layered on top with white marble.

The *sanctum sanctorum* in the middle of the Hall of Hundred Pillars had life-sized idols of the great sixth Vishnu and his wife, Dharani. And, these idols were armed. Lord Parshu Ram held his fearsome battle axe and Lady Dharani sat with the long bow in her left hand and a single arrow in the other.

Had Sita paid close attention, she might have recognised the markings on the bow that Lady Dharani held. But she was lost in her own thoughts. Leaning against a pillar. Staring at the idols of Lord Parshu Ram and Lady Dharani.

She recalled the words of Maharishi Vishwamitra as he had welcomed her to Agastyakootam, earlier today. That they would wait for nine years. Till the stars aligned with the calculations of the Malayaputra astrologers. And then, her Vishnuhood would be announced to the world. She had been told that she had time till then to prepare. To train. To understand what she must do. And that the Malayaputras would guide her through it all.

Of course, until that auspicious moment, it was the sworn duty of every single Malayaputra to keep her identity secret. The risks were too high.

She looked back. Towards the entrance. Nobody had entered the temple. She had been left alone.

She looked at the idol of Lord Parshu Ram.

She knew that not every Malayaputra was convinced of her potential as the Vishnu. But none would dare oppose the formidable Vishwamitra.

Why is Guru Vishwamitra so sure about me? What does he know that I don't?

— ल्ऱ —

A month had passed since Sita had arrived in Agastyakootam. Vishwamitra and she had had many extended conversations.

Some of these were purely educational; on science, astronomy and medicine. Others were subtle lessons designed to help her clearly define, question, confront or affirm her views on various topics like masculinity and femininity, equality and hierarchy, justice and freedom, liberalism and order, besides others. The debates were largely enlightening for Sita. But the ones on the caste system were the most animated.

Both teacher and student agreed that the form in which the caste system currently existed, deserved to be completely destroyed. That it corroded the vitals of India. In the past, one's caste was determined by one's attributes, qualities and deeds. It had been flexible. But over time, familial love distorted the foundations of this concept. Parents began to ensure that their children remained in the same caste as them. Also, an arbitrary hierarchy was accorded to the castes, based on a group's financial and political influence. Some castes became 'higher', others 'lower'. Gradually, the caste system became rigid and birth-based. Even Vishwamitra had faced many obstacles when, born a Kshatriya, he had decided to become a Brahmin; and, in fact, a *rishi*. This rigidity created divisions within society. Raavan had exploited these divisions to eventually dominate the Sapt Sindhu.

But what could be the solution for this? The *Maharishi* believed that it was not possible to create a society where all were completely and exactly equal. It may be desirable, but would remain a utopian idea, always. People differed in skills, both in degree and kind. So, their fields of activity and achievements also had to differ. Periodic efforts at imposing exact equality had invariably led to violence and chaos.

Vishwamitra laid emphasis on freedom. A person must be enabled to understand himself and pursue his dreams. In his scheme of things, if a child was born to Shudra parents, but with the skills of a Brahmin, he should be allowed to become a Brahmin. If the son of a Kshatriya father had trading skills, then he should train to become a Vaishya.

He believed that rather than trying to force-fit an artificial equality, one must remove the curse of birth determining one's life prospects. Societies would always have hierarchies. They existed even in nature. But they could be fluid. There would be times when Kshatriya soldiers comprised the elite, and then, there would be times when skilful Shudra creators would be the elite. The differences in society should be determined by merit. That's all. Not birth.

To achieve this, Vishwamitra proposed that families needed to be restructured. For it was inheritance that worked most strongly against merit and free movement in society.

He suggested that children must compulsorily be adopted by the state at the time of birth. The birth-parents would have to surrender their children to the kingdom. The state would feed, educate and nurture the in-born talents of these children. Then, at the age of fifteen, they would appear for an examination to test them on their physical, psychological and mental abilities. Based on the result, appropriate castes would be allocated to them. Subsequent training would further polish their natural skills. Eventually, they would be adopted by citizens of the same caste as the one assigned to the adolescents through the examination process. The children would not know their birth-parents, only their adoptive caste-parents. The birth-parents, too, would not know the fate of their birth-children.

Sita agreed that this would be a fair system. But she also felt that it was harsh and unrealistic. It was unimaginable to her that parents would willingly hand over their birth-children to the kingdom. Permanently. Or that they would ever stop trying to learn what happened to them. It was unnatural. In fact, times were such that it was impossible to make Indians follow even basic laws for the greater good. It was completely far-fetched to think that they would ever make such a big sacrifice in the larger interest of society.

Vishwamitra retorted that it was the Vishnu's task to radically transform society. To convince society. Sita responded that perhaps the Vishnu would need to be convinced, first. The guru assured her that he would. He laid a wager that over time, Sita would be so convinced that she would herself champion this 'breathtakingly fair and just organisation of society'.

As they ended another of their discussions on the caste system, Sita got up and walked towards the end of the garden, thinking further about it. The garden was at the edge of the monolith summit. She took a deep breath, trying to think of some more arguments that would challenge her guru's proposed system. She looked down at the valley, eight hundred and fifty metres below. Something about the Thamiravaruni startled her. She stopped thinking. And stared.

Why have I not noticed this before?

The river did not appear to flow out of the valley at all. At the eastern end of the egg-shaped valley, the Thamiravaruni disappeared underground.

What in Lord Rudra's name …

'The river flows into a cave, Sita.' Vishwamitra had quietly walked up to his student.

— रुद्र —

Vishwamitra and Sita stood at the mouth of the natural cave, carved vertically into the rock face.

Intrigued by the flow of the Thamiravaruni, Sita had wished to see the place where it magically disappeared, at the eastern end of the valley. From a distance, it had seemed as if the river dropped into a hole in the ground. But, as she drew near, she had seen the narrow opening of the cave. A vertical cave. It was incredible that an entire river entered the small aperture. The thunderous roar of the river within the cave suggested that the shaft expanded underground.

'But where does all this water go?' asked Sita.

A company of Malayaputra soldiers stood behind Sita and Vishwamitra. Out of earshot. But close enough to move in quickly if needed.

'The river continues to flow east,' said Vishwamitra. 'It drains into the Gulf of Mannar which separates India from Lanka.'

'But how does it emerge from the hole it has dug itself into?'

'It bursts out of this underground cavern some ten kilometres downstream.'

Sita's eyes widened in surprise. 'Is this cave that long?'

Vishwamitra smiled. 'Come. I'll show you.'

Vishwamitra led Sita to the edge of the mouth of the cave. She hesitated. It was only around twenty-five metres across at the entry point. This forced constriction dramatically increased the speed of the river. It tore into the underground causeway with unreal ferocity.

Vishwamitra pointed to a flight of stairs to the left side of the cave mouth. It was obviously man-made. Steps had been carved into the sloping side wall. A railing thoughtfully provided on the right side, preventing a steep fall into the rapids.

Torrents of foam and spray from the rapidly descending river diminished vision. It also made the stairs dangerously slippery.

Vishwamitra pulled his *angvastram* over his head to shield himself from water droplets that fell from the ceiling. Sita followed suit.

'Be careful,' said Vishwamitra, as he approached the staircase. 'The steps are slippery.'

Sita nodded and followed her guru. The Malayaputra soldiers stayed close behind.

They wended their way in silence. Descending carefully. Deeper and deeper, into the cave. Sita huddled into her *angvastram*. Daylight filtered through. But she expected pitch darkness as they descended farther. The insistent spray of water made it impossible to light a torch.

Sita had always been afraid of the dark. Added to which was this confined, slippery space. The looming rock structure and the loud roar of the descending river combined altogether into a terrifying experience.

Her mother's voice called out to her. A memory buried deep in her psyche.

Don't be afraid of the dark, my child. Light has a source. It can be snuffed out. But darkness has no source. It just exists. This darkness is a path to That, *which has no source: God.*

Wise words. But words that didn't really provide much comfort to Sita at this point. Cold fear slowly tightened its grip on her heart. A childhood memory forced itself into her consciousness. Of being confined in a dark basement, the sounds of rats scurrying about, the frantic beat of her heart.

Barely able to breathe. She pulled her awareness into the present. An occasional glimpse of Vishwamitra's white robe disturbed the void they had settled into. Suddenly, she saw him turn left. She followed. Her hand not letting go of the railing.

Disoriented by sudden blinding light, her eyes gradually registered the looming figure of Vishwamitra standing before her. He held aloft a torch. He handed it to her. She saw a Malayaputra soldier hand another torch to Vishwamitra.

Vishwamitra started walking ahead again, continuing to descend. The steps were much broader now. Though the sound of the river reverberated against the wall and echoed all around.

Too loud for such a small cave.

But Sita could not see much since there were only two torches. Soon, all the Malayaputras held a torch each and light flooded into the space.

Sita held her breath.

By the great Lord Rudra!

The small cave had opened into a cavern. And it was huge. Bigger than any cave Sita had ever seen. Perhaps six hundred metres in width. The steps descended farther and farther while the ceiling remained at roughly the same height. When they reached the bottom of the cavern, the ceiling was a good two hundred metres above. A large palace, fit for a king, could have been built in this subterranean space. And still have room left over. The Thamiravaruni flowed on the right-hand side of this cavern, descending rapidly with great force.

'As you can see, the river has eroded this cave over the ages,' explained Vishwamitra. 'It is huge, isn't it?'

'The biggest I have ever seen!' said Sita in wonder.

There was a massive white hill on the left. The secret behind the well-lit interior. It reflected light from the numerous torches and spread it to all the corners of the cave.

'I wonder what material that hill is made up of, Guru*ji*,' said Sita.

Vishwamitra smiled. 'A lot of bats live here.'

Sita looked up instinctively.

'They are all asleep now,' said Vishwamitra. 'It's daytime. They will awaken at night. And that hill is made from the droppings of billions of bats over many millennia.'

Sita grimaced. 'Yuck!'

Vishwamitra's laughter echoed in the vastness.

It was then that Sita's eyes fell on something behind Vishwamitra. Many rope ladders hanging from the walls; so many that she gave up the attempt to count them. Hammered into place on top, they fell from the roof, all the way to the floor.

Sita pointed. 'What's that, Guru*ji*?'

Vishwamitra turned around. 'There are some white semi-circular bird nests in the nooks and crannies of these walls. Those nests are precious. The material they are made from is precious. These ladders allow us to access them.'

Sita was surprised. 'What could be so valuable about the material that a nest is made from? These ladders go really high. Falling from that height must mean instant death.'

'Indeed, some have died. But it is a worthy sacrifice.'

Sita frowned.

'We need some hold over Raavan. The material in those nests gives us that control.'

Sita froze. The thought that had been troubling her for some time made its reappearance: *What is the relationship between the Malayaputras and the Lankans?*

'I will explain it to you, someday,' said Vishwamitra, reading her thoughts as usual. 'For now, have faith in me.'

Sita remained silent. But her face showed that she was troubled.

'This land of ours,' continued Vishwamitra, 'is sacred. Bound by the Himalayas in the north, washed by the Indian Ocean at its feet and the Western and Eastern Seas at its arms, the soil in this great nation is hallowed. All those born in this land carry the sacred earth of Mother India in their body. This nation cannot be allowed to remain in this wretched state. It is an insult to our noble ancestors. We must make India great again. I will do anything, anything, to make this land worthy of our great ancestors. And, so shall the Vishnu.'

— ᚱᚷ —

Sita, Jatayu, and a company of Malayaputra soldiers were sailing back up the western coast towards the Sapt Sindhu. Sita was returning to Mithila. She had spent more than five months in Agastyakootam, educating herself on the principles of governance, philosophies, warfare and personal history of the earlier Vishnus. She had also acquired advanced training in other subjects. This was in preparation for her Vishnuhood. Vishwamitra had been personally involved in her training.

Jatayu and she sat on the main deck, sipping a hot cup of ginger *kadha*.

Sita set her cup down and looked at the Malayaputra. 'Jatayu*ji*, I hope you will answer my question.'

Jatayu turned towards Sita and bowed his head. 'How can I refuse, great Vishnu?'

'What is the relationship between the Malayaputras and the Lankans?'

'We trade with them. As does every kingdom in the Sapt

Sindhu. We export a very valuable material mined in the cavern of Thamiravaruni to Lanka. And they give us what we need.'

'I'm aware of that. But Raavan usually appoints sub-traders who are given the licence to trade with Lanka. No one else can conduct any business with him. But there is no such sub-trader in Agastyakootam. You trade directly with him. This is strange. I also know that he strictly controls the Western and Eastern Seas. And that no ship can set sail in these waters without paying him a cess. This is how he maintains a stranglehold over trade. But Malayaputra ships pay nothing and yet, pass unharmed. Why?'

'Like I said, we sell him something very valuable, great Vishnu.'

'Do you mean the bird's nest material?' asked Sita, incredulously. 'I am sure he gets many equally valuable things from other parts of the Sapt Sindhu ...'

'This material is *very, very* valuable. Far more than anything he gets from the Sapt Sindhu.'

'Then why doesn't he just attack Agastyakootam and seize it? It's not far from his kingdom.'

Jatayu remained silent, unsure of how much to reveal.

'I have also heard,' continued Sita, choosing her words carefully, 'that, apparently, there is a shared heritage.'

'That there may be. But every Malayaputra's primary loyalty is to you, Lady Vishnu.'

'I don't doubt that. But tell me, what is this common heritage?'

Jatayu took a deep breath. He had managed to sidestep the first question, but it seemed he would be unable to avoid this one. 'Maharishi Vishwamitra was a prince before he became a *Brahmin Rishi*.'

'I know that.'

'His father, King Gaadhi, ruled the kingdom of Kannauj. Guru Vishwamitra himself was the king there for a short span of time.'

'Yes, so I have heard.'

'Then he decided to renounce his throne and become a Brahmin. It wasn't an easy decision, but nothing is beyond our great Guru*ji*. Not only did he become a Brahmin, he also acquired the title of *Maharishi*. And, he scaled great heights to reach the peak by ultimately becoming the chief of the Malayaputras.'

Sita nodded. 'Nothing is beyond Guru Vishwamitra. He is one of the all-time greats.'

'True,' said Jatayu. Hesitantly, he continued. 'So, Guru Vishwamitra's roots are in Kannauj.'

'But what does that have to do with Raavan?'

Jatayu sighed. 'Most people don't know this. It is a well-kept secret, my sister. But Raavan is also from Kannauj. His family comes from there.'

Chapter 16

At twenty years of age, Sita may have had the energy and drive of a youngster, but her travels through much of India and the training she had received at Agastyakootam, had given her wisdom far beyond her years.

Samichi was initially intrigued by Sita's repeated trips around the country. She was told that they were for trade and diplomatic purposes. And, she believed it. Or, pretended to. As she practically governed Mithila with a free hand in the absence of the princess. But Sita was now back in Mithila and the reins of administration were back in the hands of the prime minister.

Radhika was on one of her frequent visits to Mithila.

'How are you doing, Samichi?' asked Radhika.

Sita, Radhika and Samichi were in the private chambers of the prime minister of Mithila.

'Doing very well!' smiled Samichi. 'Thank you for asking.'

'I love what you have done with the slums at the southern gate. A cesspool has transformed into a well-organised, permanent construction.'

'It would not have been possible without the guidance of the prime minister,' said Samichi with genuine humility. 'The idea and vision were hers. I just implemented it.'

'Not prime minister. Sita.'

'Sorry?'

'I have told you many times,' said Sita, 'when we are alone, you can call me by my name.'

Samichi looked at Radhika and then at Sita.

Sita rolled her eyes. 'Radhika is a friend, Samichi!'

Samichi smiled. 'Sorry. No offence meant.'

'None taken, Samichi!' said Radhika. 'You are my friend's right hand. How can I take offence at something you say?'

Samichi rose to her feet. 'If you will excuse me, Sita, I must go to the inner city. There is a gathering of the nobles that I need to attend.'

'I have heard,' said Sita, gesturing for Samichi to wait, 'that the rich are not too happy.'

'Yes,' said Samichi. 'They are richer than they used to be, since Mithila is doing well now. But the poor have improved their lot in life at a faster pace. It is no longer easy for the rich to find cheap labour or domestic help. But it's not just the rich who are unhappy. Ironically, even the poor aren't as happy as they used to be, before their lives improved. They complain even more now. They want to get richer, more quickly. With greater expectations, they have discovered higher dissatisfaction.'

'Change causes disruption ...' Sita said, thoughtfully.

'Yes.'

'Keep me informed of the early signs of any trouble.'

'Yes, Sita,' said Samichi, before saluting and walking out of the room.

As soon as they were alone, Sita asked Radhika, 'And what else has been happening with the other Vishnu candidates?'

'Ram is progressing very well. Bharat is a little headstrong. It's still a toss-up!'

— दॅ人 —

It was late in the evening at the gurukul of Maharishi Kashyap. Five friends, all of them eight years old, were playing a game with each other. A game suitable for the brilliant students who populated this great centre of learning. An intellectual game.

One of the students was asking questions and the others had to answer. The questioner had a stone in his hand. He tapped it on the ground once. Then he paused. Then he tapped once again. Pause. Then two times, quickly. Pause. Three times. Pause. Five times. Pause. Eight times. Pause. He looked at his friends and asked, 'Who am I?'

His friends looked at each other, confused.

A seven-year-old boy stepped up gingerly from the back. He was dressed in rags and clearly looked out of place. 'I think the stone taps represented 1, 1, 2, 3, 5, 8, right? That's the Pingala Series. Therefore, I am Rishi Pingala.'

The friends looked at the boy. He was an orphan who lived in the minuscule guard cabin of the local Mother Goddess temple. The boy was weak, suffering from malnutrition and poor health. But he was brilliant. A gurukul student named Vishwamitra had managed to convince the principal to enrol this poor orphan in the school. Vishwamitra had leveraged the power of the massive endowment that his father, the King of Kannauj, had given to the gurukul, to get this done.

The boys turned away from the orphan, even though his answer was correct.

'We're not interested in what you say, Vashishtha,' sneered the boy who had asked the question. 'Why don't you go and clean the guard's cabin?'

As the boys burst out laughing, Vashishtha's body shrank in shame. But he stood his ground. Refusing to leave.

The questioner turned to his friends again and tapped the earth once. Then drew a circle around the spot he had tapped. Then he drew the circle's diameter. Then, outside the circle, he tapped sharply once. Then, he placed the stone flat on the ground. Pause. Then he tapped the stone sharply again. Quickly. Eight times. 'Who am I?'

Vashishtha immediately blurted out, 'I know! You tapped the ground and drew a circle. That's Mother Earth. Then you drew the diameter. Then you tapped 1-0-8 outside. What is 108 times the diameter of the Earth? The diameter of the Sun. I am the Sun God!'

The friends did not even turn to look at Vashishtha. Nobody acknowledged his answer.

But Vashishtha refused to be denied. 'It's from the Surya Siddhanta *... It's the correct answer ...'*

The questioner turned to face him in anger. 'Get lost, Vashishtha!'

A loud voice was heard. 'Hey!'

It was Vishwamitra. He may have been only eight years old, but he was already huge. Powerful enough to scare the five boys.

'Kaushik ...' said the boy questioner nervously, using the gurukul *name for Vishwamitra, 'this has nothing to do with you ...'*

Vishwamitra walked up to Vashishtha and held his hand. Then, he turned to the five boys. Glaring. 'He is a student of the gurukul *now. You will call him by his* gurukul *name. With respect.'*

The questioner swallowed. Shaking in fear.

'His gurukul *name is Divodas,' said Vishwamitra, holding Vashishtha's hand tighter. Divodas was the name of a great ancient king. It was Vishwamitra who had selected this* gurukul *name for Vashishtha and then convinced the principal to make it official. 'Say it.'*

The five friends remained paralysed.

Vishwamitra stepped closer, menace oozing from every pore of his body. He had already built a reputation with his fierce temper. 'Say my friend's gurukul *name. Say it. Divodas.'*

The questioner sputtered, as he whispered, 'Divo...das.'

'Louder. With respect. Divodas.'

All five boys spoke together, 'Divodas.'

Vishwamitra pulled Vashishtha towards himself. 'Divodas is my friend. You mess with him, you mess with me.'

'Guru*ji*!'

Vashishtha was pulled back from the ancient, more than a hundred-and-forty-year-old memory. He quickly wiped his eyes. Tears are meant to be hidden.

He turned to look at Shatrughan, who was holding up a manuscript of the *Surya Siddhanta*.

Of all the books in the entire world ... What are the odds?

Vashishtha would have smiled at the irony. But he knew it was going to be a long discussion. The youngest prince of Ayodhya was by far the most intelligent of the four brothers. So, he looked with a serious expression at Shatrughan and said, 'Yes, my child. What is your question?'

— ᚱ ᚤ —

Sita and Radhika were meeting after a two-year gap.

Over this time, Sita had travelled through the western parts of India, all the way to Gandhar, at the base of the Hindukush mountains. While India's cultural footprints could be found beyond these mountains, it was believed that the Hindukush, peopled by the Hindushahi Pashtuns and the brave Baloch, defined the western borders of India. Beyond that was the land of the *Mlechchas*, the *foreigners*.

'What did you think of the lands of Anu?' asked Radhika.

Kekaya, ruled by Ashwapati, headed the kingdoms of the Anunnaki, descendants of the ancient warrior-king, Anu. Many of the kingdoms around Kekaya, bound by Anunnaki clan ties, pledged fealty to Ashwapati. And Ashwapati, in turn, was loyal to Dashrath. Or, at least so it was publicly believed. After all, Ashwapati's daughter, Kaikeyi, was Dashrath's favourite wife.

'Aggressive people,' said Sita. 'The Anunnaki don't do anything by half measures. Their fire, put to good use, can help the great land of India achieve new heights. But, when uncontrolled, it can also lead to chaos.'

'Agreed,' said Radhika. 'Isn't Rajagriha beautiful?'

Rajagriha, the capital of Kekaya, was on the banks of the river Jhelum, not far from where the Chenab River merged into it. Rajagriha extended on both sides of the river. The massive and ethereally beautiful palace of its king was on the eastern bank of the Jhelum.

'It is, indeed,' said Sita. 'They are talented builders.'

'And, fierce warriors. Quite mad, too!' Radhika giggled.

Sita laughed loudly. 'True ... There is a thin dividing line between fierceness and insanity!'

Sita noted that Radhika seemed happier than usual. 'Tell me about the princes of Ayodhya.'

'Ram is doing well. My father is quite certain that Guru Vashishtha will choose him.'

'And Bharat?'

Radhika blushed slightly. And, Sita's suspicions were confirmed.

'He's growing up well too,' whispered Radhika, a dreamy look on her face.

'That well?' joked Sita.

Her crimson face a giveaway, Radhika slapped her friend on her wrists. 'Shut up!'

Sita laughed in delight. 'By the great Lady Mohini, Radhika is in love!'

Radhika glared at Sita, but did not refute her friend.

'But what about the law …'

Radhika's tribe was matrilineal. Women were strictly forbidden from marrying outside the tribe. Men could marry outside their tribe on condition that they would be excommunicated.

Radhika waved her hand in dismissal. 'All that is in the future. Right now, let me enjoy the company of Bharat, one of the most romantic and passionate young men that nature has ever produced.'

Sita smiled, then changed the subject. 'What about Ram?'

'Very stoic. Very, very serious.'

'Serious, is it?'

'Yes. Serious and purposeful. Relentlessly purposeful. Almost all the time. He has a strong sense of commitment and honour. Hard on others and on himself. Fiercely patriotic. In love with every corner of India. Law-abiding. Always! And not one romantic bone in his body. I am not sure he will make a good husband.'

Sita leaned back in her couch and rested her arms on the cushions. She narrowed her eyes and whispered to herself. *But he will probably make a good Vishnu.*

— ᚱᚷ —

A year had lapsed since the friends had last met. Her work having kept her busy, Sita had not travelled out of Mithila. She was delighted, therefore, when Radhika returned, unannounced.

Sita embraced her warmly. But pulled back as she noticed her friend's eyes.

'What's wrong?'

'Nothing,' said Radhika, shaking her head. Withdrawn.

Sita immediately guessed what must have happened. She held her friend's hands. 'Did he leave you?'

Radhika frowned and shook her head. 'Of course not. You don't know Bharat. He is an honourable man. In fact, he begged me not to leave him.'

She left him?!

'In the name of Lady Mohini, why? Forget about your tribe's silly law. If you want him then you have to fight for him ...'

'No. It's not about the laws ... I would have left the tribe if ... if I had wanted to marry him.'

'Then, what is the problem?' asked Sita.

'It wouldn't have worked out ... I know. I don't want to be a part of this "greatness project", Sita. I know Ram, Bharat, and you will do a lot for India. I also know that greatness usually comes at the cost of enormous personal suffering. That is the way it has always been. That is the way it will always be. I don't want that. I just want a simple life. I just want to be happy. I don't want to be great.'

'You are being too pessimistic, Radhika.'

'No, I am not. You can call me selfish but ...'

Sita cut in, 'I would never call you selfish. Realistic, maybe. But not selfish.'

'Then speaking realistically, I know what I am up against. I have observed my father all my life. There is a fire within him. I see it in his eyes, all the time. I see the same fire in you. And in Ram. A desire to serve Mother India. I didn't expect it initially, but now I see the same fire in Bharat's eyes. You are all the same. Even Bharat. And just like all of you, he is willing to sacrifice everything for India. I don't want to sacrifice anything. I just want to be happy. I just want to be normal ...'

'But can you be happy without him?'

Radhika's sad smile did not hide her pain. 'It would be even worse if I married him and all my hopes for happiness were tied to nagging him to give up his dreams for India and for himself. I'd eventually make him unhappy. I'd make myself unhappy as well.'

'But …'

'It hurts right now. But time always heals, Sita. Years from now, what will remain are the bittersweet memories. More sweet, less bitter. No one can take away the memories of passion and romance. Ever. That'll be enough.'

'You've really thought this through?'

'Happiness is not an accident. It is a choice. It is in our hands to be happy. Always in our hands. Who says that we can have only one soulmate? Sometimes, soulmates want such radically different things that they end up being the cause of unhappiness for each other. Someday I will find another soulmate, one who also wants what I want. He may not be as fascinating as Bharat. Or, even as great as Bharat will be. But he will bring me what I want. Simple happiness. I will find such a man. In my tribe. Or, outside of it.'

Sita gently placed a hand on her friend's shoulder.

Radhika took a deep breath and shook her head. Snapping out of her blues. She had been sent to Mithila with a purpose. 'By the way, Guru Vashishtha has made his decision. So have the Vayuputras.'

'And?'

'It's Ram.'

Sita took a long, satisfied breath. Then, she smiled.

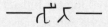

Another year passed by. Sita was twenty-four years old now. She had visited the entire length of the western coast of India, the previous year. From the beaches of Balochistan all the way down to Kerala, which cradled Agastyakootam. She was finally back in Mithila, engaged in mounds of pending royal duties. Whatever little time she could spare, she spent with her younger sister, Urmila, and her father, Janak.

Kushadhwaj had not visited Mithila for a while. He wasn't in Sankashya either. Which was strange. Sita had tried to make inquiries about his whereabouts, but had not been successful so far. What she did know was that the Sankashya administration had lost much of its efficiency after Sulochan's death, universally believed to be the result of an unfortunate heart attack.

Sita was used to Radhika's unexpected visits, by now. Hence, she was delighted to receive her friend, whom she was meeting after a few months.

'How are things in your village, now that the excitement of hosting the princes of Ayodhya is gone?'

Radhika laughed. 'It's all right …'

'Are *you* all right?'

'I'm getting there …'

'And how is Ram doing in Ayodhya?'

'He has been made the chief of police. And Bharat the chief of diplomatic relations.'

'Hmm … So Queen Kaikeyi still has her grip on Ayodhya. Bharat is better placed to catapult into the role of Crown Prince. The chief of police is a tough and thankless job.'

'So it would seem. But Ram is doing exceedingly well. He has managed to bring crime under visible control. This has made him popular among the people.'

'How did he manage that miracle?'

'He just followed the laws. Ha!'

Sita laughed, befuddled. 'How does Ram abiding by the law make any difference? The people also have to follow it. And, Indians will never do that. In fact, I think we enjoy breaking rules. Pointlessly. For the heck of it. One must be pragmatic when dealing with Indians. Laws must be enforced, yes. But this cannot be an end in itself. You may sometimes need to even misuse the law to achieve what you want.'

'I disagree. Ram has shown a new way. By simply ensuring that he, too, is accountable and subject to the law. No shortcuts are available to the Ayodhyan nobility anymore. This has electrified the common folk. If the law is above even a prince, then why not them?'

Sita leaned into her chair. 'Interesting ...'

'By the way,' asked Radhika, 'where is Guru Vishwamitra?'

Sita hesitated.

'I am only checking because we believe Guru Vashishtha has gone to Pariha to propose Ram's candidature as the Vishnu.'

Sita was shocked. 'Guru Vishwamitra is in Pariha as well.'

Radhika sighed. 'Things will soon come to a head. You better have a plan in mind to convince Guru Vishwamitra about Ram and you partnering as the Vishnus.'

Sita took a deep breath. 'Any idea what the Vayuputras will do?'

'I have told you already. They lean towards Guru Vashishtha. The only question is whether they will give in to Guru Vishwamitra. After all, he *is* the chief of the Malayaputras and the representative of the previous Vishnu.'

'I will speak with Hanu *bhaiya*.'

Chapter 17

'But, *Didi*,' pouted Urmila, keeping her voice low as she spoke to her *elder sister*, Sita, 'why have you agreed to a *swayamvar*? I don't want you to leave. What will I do without you?'

Urmila and Sita sat on a large, well-camouflaged wooden *machan* in a tree. Their feet dangled by the side. Sita's bow lay within hand's reach, next to a quiver full of arrows. The jungle was quiet and somnolent this hot afternoon. Most of the animals, it seemed, were taking a nap.

Sita smiled and pulled Urmila close. 'I have to get married sometime, Urmila. If this is what *baba* wants, then I have no choice but to honour it.'

Urmila did not know that it was Sita who had convinced her father to arrange the *swayamvar*. The *swayamvar* was an ancient tradition where the father of the bride organised a gathering of prospective bridegrooms; and the daughter selected her husband from among the gathered men. Or mandated a competition. Sita was actively managing the arrangements. She had convinced Vishwamitra to somehow get Ram to Mithila for the *swayamvar*. An official invitation from Mithila to Ayodhya would not have gotten a response. After all, why would Ayodhya ally with a small and relatively inconsequential kingdom like Mithila? But there was no way that Ayodhya would say no to the powerful Malayaputra chief's request just to attend the *swayamvar*. And, at the *swayamvar* itself, managed by her Guru, the great Malayaputra Vishwamitra, she could arrange to have Ram as her husband. Vishwamitra had also liked the idea. This way, he would displace Vashishtha and gain direct influence over Ram. Of course, he was unaware that Sita had other plans. Plans to work with Ram in partnership as the Vishnu.

God bless Hanu bhaiya! *What a fantastic idea.*

Urmila rested her head on Sita's shoulder. Although a young woman now, her sheltered upbringing had kept her dependent on her elder sister. She could not imagine life without her nurturer and protector. 'But …'

Sita held Urmila tight. 'You too will be married. Soon.'

Urmila blushed and turned away.

Sita heard a faint sound. She looked deep into the forest.

Sita, Samichi, and a troop of twenty policemen had come to this jungle, a day's ride from Mithila, to kill a man-eating tiger that was tormenting villagers in the area. Urmila had insisted on accompanying Sita. Five *machans* had been built in a forest clearing. Each *machan* was manned by Mithila policemen. The bait, a goat, had been tied in the open. Keeping the weather in mind, a small waterhole had also been dug, lined with water-proofing bitumen. If not the meat, perhaps the water would entice the tiger.

'Listen, *Didi*,' whispered Urmila, 'I was thinking …'

Urmila fell silent as Sita raised a finger to her lips. Then, Sita turned around. Two policemen sat at the other end of the *machan*. Using hand signals, she gave quick orders. Silently, they crawled up to her side. Urmila moved to the back.

Sita picked up her bow and noiselessly drew an arrow from the quiver.

'Did you see something, My Lady?' whispered a policeman.

Sita shook her head to signal no. And then, cupped her ear with her left hand.

The policemen strained their ears but could not hear anything. One of them spoke in a faint voice, 'I don't hear any sound.'

Sita nocked the arrow on the bowstring and whispered, 'It's the absence of sound. The goat has stopped bleating. It is scared stiff. I bet it's not an ordinary predator that the goat has sniffed.'

The policemen drew their bows forward and nocked arrows. Quickly and quietly.

Sita thought she caught a fleeting glimpse of stripes from behind the foliage. She took a long, hard look. Slowly, she began to discern alternating brownish-orange and black stripes in the dark, shaded area behind the tree line. She focused her eyes. The stripes moved.

Sita pointed towards the movement.

The policeman noticed it as well. 'It's well-camouflaged ...'

Sita raised her hands, signalling for quiet. She held the bowstring and pulled faintly, ready to shoot at the first opportunity.

After a few excruciatingly long moments, the tiger stepped into view, inching slowly towards the waterhole. It saw the goat, growled softly and turned its attention back to the water. The goat collapsed on the ground in absolute terror, urine escaping its bladder in a rush. It closed its eyes and surrendered itself to fate. The tiger, though, did not seem interested in the petrified bait. It kept lapping up the water.

Sita pulled the bowstring back, completely.

Suddenly, there was a very soft sound from one of the *machans* to the right.

The tiger looked up, instantly alert.

Sita cursed under her breath. The angle wasn't right. But she knew the tiger would turn and flee in moments. She released the arrow.

It whizzed through the clearing and slammed into the beast's shoulder. Enough to enrage, but not disable.

The tiger roared in fury. But its roar was cut short just as suddenly. An arrow shot into its mouth, lodging deep in the animal's throat. Within split seconds, eighteen arrows slammed into the big cat. Some hit an eye, others the abdomen. Three missiles thumped into its rear *bicep femoris* muscles, severing them. Its rear legs debilitated, the tiger collapsed to the ground. The Mithilans quickly reloaded their bows and shot again. Twenty more arrows pierced the severely injured beast. The tiger raised its head one last time. Sita felt the animal was staring directly at her with one uninjured eye.

My apologies, noble beast. But it was either you or the villagers under my protection.

The tiger's head dropped. Never to rise again.

May your soul find purpose, once again.

— ᚱᚥ —

Sita, Urmila, and Samichi rode at the head of the group. The policemen rode a short distance behind. The party was headed back to the capital city.

The tiger had been cremated with due respect. Sita had made it clear to all that she did not intend to keep the skin of the animal. She was aware that the opportunity to acquire the tiger skin, a mark of a brave hunter, would have made her policemen careful with their arrows. They would not have liked the pelt damaged. That may have led to the tiger merely being injured rather than killed.

Sita's objective was clear. She wanted to save the villagers from the tiger attacks. An injured animal would have only become more dangerous for humans. Sita had to ensure that all her policemen shot to kill. So, she had made it clear to all that the tiger would be cremated.

'I understand why you gave that order, Prime Minister,' said Samichi, 'but it's sad that we cannot take the tiger skin home. It would have been a great trophy, displaying your skill and bravery.'

Sita looked at Samichi, then turned to her sister. 'Urmila, fall back please.'

Urmila immediately pulled the reins of her horse and fell behind the other two, out of earshot.

Samichi pulled her horse close to Sita's. 'I had to say that, Sita. It will encourage Urmila to brag about your bravery and...'

Sita shook her head and interrupted Samichi. 'Propaganda and myth-making are part and parcel of ruling. I understand that. But do not spread stories that will get debunked easily. I did not exhibit any skill or bravery in that hunt.'

'But ...'

'My shot was not good. Everyone present knows that.'

'But, Sita ...'

'Every single one knows that,' repeated Sita. 'Earlier too, you gave me all the credit for the hunt. Near the policemen.'

'But you deserved the ...'

'No, I did not.'

'But …'

'You believe you did me a service. No, Samichi, you did not. I lost respect among those men by receiving an undeserved compliment.'

'But …'

'Don't let your loyalty to me blind you. That is the worst thing you can do to me.'

Samichi stopped arguing. 'I'm sorry.'

Sita smiled. 'It's all right.' Then she turned to her younger sister and beckoned her. The three of them rode on, in silence.

— ॐ —

Sita had returned from the hunt just a few days earlier. Preparations for her *swayamvar* had begun in full swing. She personally supervised most of the work, ably assisted by Samichi and her younger sister, Urmila.

Sita sat in her chamber perusing some documents, when a messenger was announced.

'Bring him in.'

Two guards marched in with the messenger in tow. She recognised the man. He was from Radhika's tribe.

Saluting smartly, the messenger handed her a rolled parchment. Sita examined the seal. It was unbroken.

She dismissed the messenger, broke the seal and read Radhika's message.

Her anger rose even before she reached the last word. But even in her rage, she did not forget what she must do. She held the parchment to a flame till every inch of it was reduced to ashes.

Task done, she walked up to the balcony to cool her mind. *Ram ... Don't fall into Guru*ji's *trap.*

— ᛞᚷᚷ —

Mithila was a few weeks away from Sita's *swayamvar.*

Sita's spirits had been uplifted by the news that Vishwamitra was on his way to Mithila. Along with the Malayaputras and the princes of Ayodhya. Her mind had been feverishly contemplating plausible excuses to cancel the *swayamvar*. In the absence of Ram, it would have been a pointless exercise.

'Sita,' said Samichi, saluting as she entered the princess' chamber.

Sita turned. 'Yes, Samichi?'

'I have some troubling news.'

'What's happened?'

'I have heard that your uncle Kushadhwaj has been invited to the *swayamvar*. In fact, he is inviting some of his friends as well. He's behaving like a joint host.'

Sita sighed. She should have guessed that her father would invite Kushadhwaj.

Such misplaced generosity.

On the other hand, Kushadhwaj had not visited Mithila in years. Perhaps, he had made his peace with his reduced circumstances.

'I am his niece, after all,' said Sita, shrugging her shoulders. '*Chacha* may want to demonstrate to the Sapt Sindhu royalty that he retains some influence in his elder brother's household and kingdom. Let him come.'

Samichi smiled. 'As long as the one you want also comes, right?'

'Ram is coming… He is coming …'

Samichi broke into a rare smile. Though she did not understand why Sita had suddenly developed an interest in Ram, and in allying with Ayodhya, she supported her princess wholeheartedly. Allying with Ayodhya, even in its weakened state, would only benefit Mithila in the long run. And, once Sita left for Ayodhya, Samichi expected to become even more powerful. Perhaps, even rule Mithila for all practical purposes.

After all, who else was there?

Chapter 18

A nervous Samichi stood in the small clearing. The ominous sounds of the jungle added to the dread of a dark, moonless night.

Memories from the past crashed into the present. It had been so long. So many years. She had thought that she had been forgotten. Left to her own devices. After all, Mithila was a minor, insignificant kingdom in the Sapt Sindhu. She hadn't expected this. A sense of gratification meshed with the unease of the moment to altogether overwhelm her mind.

Her left hand rested on the hilt of her sheathed sword.

'Samichi, did you understand what I said?' asked the man. His gravelly voice was distinctive. The result of years of tobacco and alcohol abuse. Accompanied by uncontrolled shouting.

The man was clearly a noble. Expensive clothes. All neatly pressed. Soft, well-coiffed and completely grey hair. An array of rings on all his fingers. Jewelled pommels decorated his knife and sword. Even his scabbard was gold-plated. A thick black line, a *tilak*, plastered the middle of his wrinkled forehead.

A platoon of twenty soldiers in black uniforms stood quietly in the shadows. Out of earshot. Their swords were securely sheathed. They knew they had nothing to fear from Samichi.

She was to receive Guru Vishwamitra at Sankashya the following day. She really couldn't afford this unexpected rendezvous. Not now. She mentioned the *True Lord*, hoping it would push Akampana back.

'But, Lord Akampana ...' said Samichi uneasily, '... *Iraiva's* message ...'

'Forget everything you were told earlier,' said Akampana. 'Remember your oath.'

Samichi stiffened. 'I will never forget my oath, Lord Akampana.'

'See that you don't.' Akampana raised his hand and nonchalantly looked at his manicured nails. Perfectly cut, filed and polished. A light cream dye had been carefully painted on them. The nail on the slim pinkie finger though, had been painted black. 'So, Princess Sita's *swayamvar* will be ...'

'You don't have to repeat yourself,' interrupted Samichi. 'It will be done. It is in Princess Sita's interest as well.'

Akampana smiled. Perhaps something had gotten through Samichi's thick head after all. 'Yes, it is.'

— ᚱ —

Sita sighed and lightly tapped her head. 'Silly me.'

She walked into her private *puja* room and picked up the knife. It was the day of the *astra puja*, an ancient ritual worship of weapons. And she had forgotten the knife in the *garbha griha*, at the feet of the deities, after the *puja*.

Fortunately, she had managed without the weapon today. She had always suspected that the wealthy merchant, Vijay, was more loyal to Sankashya than Mithila. Earlier that day, in the market place, he had tried to incite the crowd to attack her, when she had intervened to save a boy-thief from mob justice.

Fortunately, it had all ended well. No one had been injured. Except that stupid Vijay who would be nursing a broken rib for many weeks. She would visit the *Ayuralay* and check on him, probably in the evening or the next day. She didn't really care what happened to Vijay. But it was important to demonstrate that she cared equally for the well-being of the rich as well, and not just the poor. Even the irredeemably stupid ones among the rich.

Where is Samichi?

The Police and Protocol Chief was expected anytime now, escorting Guru Vishwamitra and his accompanying Malayaputras to Mithila. And, of course, Ram and Lakshman.

Suddenly, the doorman announced that Arishtanemi, the military chief of the Malayaputras, had arrived.

Sita answered loudly. 'Bring him in. With respect.'

Arishtanemi walked into the room. Sita folded her hands together in a respectful *Namaste* and bowed her head as she greeted the right-hand man of Maharishi Vishwamitra. 'Greetings, Arishtanemi*ji*. I hope that you are comfortable in Mithila.'

'One is always comfortable in the place one looks upon as home,' smiled Arishtanemi.

Sita was surprised to not find Samichi with him. This was unorthodox. Samichi should have escorted the senior officer, with respect, to her chambers.

'My apologies, Arishtanemi*ji*. Samichi should have led you to my chambers. I am sure that she meant no disrespect, but I will speak with her.'

'No, no,' said Arishtanemi, raising his hand reassuringly. 'I told her that I wanted to meet you alone.'

'Of course. I hope you are satisfied with the accommodation, especially for Guru Vishwamitra and the princes of Ayodhya.'

Arishtanemi smiled. Sita had come to the point quickly. 'Guru Vishwamitra is comfortable in his usual set of rooms at the palace. But Prince Ram and Prince Lakshman have been accommodated in the Bees Quarter.'

'Bees Quarter?!' Sita was aghast.

Has Samichi gone mad?

Almost as if he had heard her thought, Arishtanemi said, 'Actually, Guru*ji* himself wanted the princes to stay in there.'

Sita raised her hands in exasperation. 'Why? They are the princes of Ayodhya. Ram is the Crown Prince of the empire. Ayodhya will see this as a terrible insult. I do not want Mithila getting into any trouble because of …'

'Prince Ram does not see it as an insult,' interrupted Arishtanemi. 'He is a mature man of great understanding. We need to keep his presence in Mithila a secret, for now. And, even you must avoid meeting him for a few days.'

Sita was losing her patience. 'Secret? He has to participate in the *swayamvar*, Arishtanemi*ji*. That's why he is here, isn't he? How can we keep this a secret?'

'There is a problem, princess.'

'What problem?'

Arishtanemi sighed. He paused for a few seconds and whispered, 'Raavan.'

— ॐ —

'It is wise of you to have not met him till now,' said Samichi.

Sita and Samichi were in the royal section of the state armoury. A special room was reserved in this wing for the favourite personal weapons of the royalty. Sita sat on a chair, carefully oiling the *Pinaka*, the great bow of Lord Rudra.

Her conversation with Arishtanemi had upset her. Frankly, she had had her suspicions about what the Malayaputras were planning. She knew that they wouldn't go against her. She was crucial to their plans. But Ram was not.

If only I had someone to talk to. I wish Hanu bhaiya *or Radhika were here …*

Sita looked up at Samichi and continued oiling the already gleaming *Pinaka*.

Samichi looked nervous. She seemed to be in a state of inner struggle. 'I have to tell you something. I don't care what the others say. But it is the truth, Sita. Prince Ram's life is in danger. You have to send him home, somehow.'

Sita stopped oiling the bow and looked up. 'His life has been in danger since the day he was born.'

Samichi shook her head. 'No. I mean real danger.'

'What exactly is unreal danger, Samichi? There is nothing that …'

'Please, listen to me …'

'What are you hiding, Samichi?'

Samichi straightened up. 'Nothing, princess.'

'You have been acting strange these past few days.'

'Forget about me. I am not important. Have I ever told you anything that is not in your interest? Please trust me. Send Prince Ram home, if you can.'

Sita stared at Samichi. 'That's not happening.'

'There are bigger forces at play, Sita. And, you are not in control. Trust me. Please. Send him home before he gets hurt.'

Sita didn't respond. She looked at the *Pinaka* and resumed oiling the bow.

Lord Rudra, tell me what to do …

— ॐ —

'My fellow Mithilans actually clapped?' asked Sita, eyes wide in incredulity.

Arishtanemi had just walked into Sita's private office. With disturbing, yet expected, news. Raavan had arrived in Mithila to participate in Sita's *swayamvar*. His *Pushpak Vimaan*, the *legendary flying vehicle*, had just landed outside the city. He was accompanied by his brother Kumbhakarna and a few key officers. His bodyguard corps of ten thousand Lankan soldiers had marched in separately and set up camp outside the city.

Sita was bemused by the news that the Mithilans had applauded the spectacle of the *Pushpak Vimaan* landing in the fields beyond the city moat.

'Most normal human beings applaud the first time they see the *Pushpak Vimaan*, Sita,' said Arishtanemi. 'But that is not important. What is important is that we stop Ram from leaving.'

'Is Ram leaving? Why? I thought he would want to prove a point to Raavan …'

'He hasn't made up his mind as yet. But I'm afraid Lakshman may talk his elder brother into leaving.'

'So, you would like me to speak with him in Lakshman's absence.'

'Yes.'

'Have you …'

'I've spoken to him already. But I don't think I had much of an impact …'

'Can you think of someone else who can speak to him?'

Arishtanemi shook his head. 'I don't think even Guru Vishwamitra will be able to convince Ram.'

'But …'

'It's up to you, Sita,' said Arishtanemi. 'If Ram leaves, we will have to cancel this *swayamvar*.'

'What in Lord Rudra's name can I tell him? He has never even met me. What do I tell him to convince him to stay?'

'I have no idea.'

Sita laughed and shook her head. 'Thank you.'

'Sita … I know it's …'

'It's okay. I'll do it.'

I must find a way. Some path will emerge.

Arishtanemi seemed unusually tense. 'There's more, Sita …'

'More?'

'The situation may be a little more complicated.'

'How so?'

'Ram was … in a way … tricked into coming here.'

'What?'

'He was made to understand that he was merely accompanying Guru Vishwamitra on an important mission in Mithila. Since Emperor Dashrath had commanded Ram to strictly follow Guru Vishwamitra's orders, he could not say no … He wasn't informed about the fact that he was expected to participate in this *swayamvar*. Till he arrived in Mithila, that is.'

Sita was shocked. 'You have got to be joking!'

'But he did agree to the *swayamvar* finally, a few days ago. On the same day that you had that fight in the marketplace to save that boy-thief …'

Sita held her head and closed her eyes. 'I can't believe that the Malayaputras have done this.'

'The ends justify the means, Sita.'

'Not when I'm expected to live with the consequences!'

'But he did agree to participate in the *swayamvar,* eventually.'

'That was before the arrival of Raavan, right?'

'Yes.'

Sita rolled her eyes. *Lord Rudra help me.*

Chapter 19

Sita and Samichi were headed for the Bees Quarter, accompanied by a bodyguard posse of ten policemen. The city was agog with the news of the appearance of Raavan, the king of Lanka and the tormentor of India; or at least, the tormentor of Indian kings. The most animated discussions were about his legendary flying vehicle, the *Pushpak Vimaan*. Even Sita's sister, Urmila, was not immune to reports about the Lankan technological marvel. She had insisted on accompanying her elder sister to see the *vimaan*.

They had marched to the end of the Bees Quarter, up to the fort walls. The *Pushpak Vimaan* was stationed beyond the city moat, just before the jungle. Even Sita was impressed by what she saw.

The *vimaan* was a giant conical craft, made of some strange unknown metal. Massive rotors were attached to the top of the vehicle, at its pointed end. Smaller rotors were attached near the base, on all sides.

'I believe,' said Samichi, 'the main rotor at the top gives the *vimaan* the ability to fly and the smaller rotors at the base are used to control the direction of flight.'

The main body of the craft had many portholes, each covered with circular metal screens.

Samichi continued. 'Apparently, the metal screens on the portholes are raised when the *vimaan* is airborne. The portholes also have a thick glass shield. The main door is concealed behind a section of the *vimaan*. Once that section swings open, the door slides sideward into the inner cabin. So the *vimaan* entrance is doubly sealed.'

Sita turned to Samichi. 'You know a lot about this *Lankan* craft.'

Samichi shook her head and smiled sheepishly. 'No, no. I just watched the *vimaan* land. That's all …'

Thousands of Lankan soldiers were camped around the *vimaan*. Some were sleeping, others eating. But nearly a third had their weapons drawn, standing guard at strategic points in the camp. Keeping watch. Alive to any potential threats.

Sita knew this camp security strategy: The staggered one-third plan. One third of the soldiers, working in rotating four-hour shifts, always on guard. While the others rest and recuperate.

The Lankans don't take their security lightly.

'How many are there?' asked Sita.

'Probably ten thousand soldiers,' said Samichi.

'Lord Rudra have mercy …'

Sita looked at Samichi. It was a rare sight. For her friend looked genuinely nervous.

Sita placed a hand on Samichi's shoulders. 'Don't worry. We can handle this.'

— ௬ா —

Samichi bent down and banged the hatch door on the Bees Quarter roof. Ten policemen stood at the back. Sita cast Urmila a quiet, reassuring look.

Nobody opened the door.

Samichi looked at Sita.

'Knock again,' ordered Sita. 'And harder this time.'

Samichi did as ordered.

Urmila still wasn't sure what her sister was up to. '*Didi*, why are we …'

She stopped talking the moment the hatch door swung open. Upwards.

Samichi looked down.

Lakshman stood at the head of the staircase that descended into the room. Muscular with a towering height, his gigantic form seemed to fill up the space. He was fair-complexioned and handsome in a rakish, flamboyant way. A bull of a man. He wore the coarse white clothes of common soldiers when off-duty: a military style *dhoti* and an *angvastram* tied from his shoulder to the side of his waist. Threaded *Rudraaksh* beads around his neck proudly proclaimed his loyalty to Lord Rudra.

Lakshman held his sword, ready to strike should the need arise. He looked at the short-haired, dark-skinned and muscular woman peering down at him. '*Namaste*, Chief Samichi. To what do we owe this visit?' he asked gruffly.

Samichi grinned disarmingly. 'Put your sword back in the scabbard, young man.'

'Let me decide what I should or should not do. What is your business here?'

'The prime minister wants to meet your elder brother.'

Lakshman seemed taken aback. Like this was unexpected. He turned to the back of the room, where his elder brother Ram stood. Upon receiving a signal from him, he immediately slipped his sword in its scabbard and backed up against the wall, making room for the Mithilans to enter.

Samichi descended the stairs, followed by Sita. As Sita stepped in through the door hole, she gestured behind her. 'Stay there, Urmila.'

Lakshman instinctively looked up. To see Urmila. Ram stood up to receive the prime minister of Mithila. The two women climbed down swiftly but Lakshman remained rooted. Entranced by the vision above. Urmila had truly grown into a beautiful young lady. She was shorter than her elder sister, Sita. Also fairer. So fair that her skin was almost the colour of milk. Her round baby face was dominated by large eyes, which betrayed a sweet, childlike innocence. Her hair was arranged in a bun. Every strand neatly in place. The *kaajal* in her eyes accentuated their exquisiteness. Her lips were enhanced with some beet extract. Her clothes were fashionable, yet demure: a bright pink blouse complemented by a deep-red *dhoti* which was longer than usual — it reached below her knees. A neatly pressed *angvastram* hung from her shoulders. Anklets and toe-rings drew attention to her lovely feet, while rings and bracelets decorated her delicate hands. Lakshman was mesmerised. Urmila sensed it and smiled genially. Then looked away with shy confusion.

Sita turned and saw Lakshman looking at Urmila. Her eyes widened, just a bit.

Urmila and Lakshman? Hmm ...

'Shut the door, Lakshman,' said Ram.

Lakshman reluctantly did as ordered.

'How may I help you, princess?' asked Ram to Sita.

Sita turned and looked at the man she had chosen to be her husband. She had heard so much about him, for so long, that she felt like she practically knew him. So far all her thoughts about him had been based on reason and logic. She saw him as a worthy partner in the destiny of the Vishnu; someone she could work with for the good of her motherland, the country that she loved, this beautiful, matchless India.

But this was the first time she saw him as a flesh-and-blood reality. Emotion arose unasked, and occupied its seat next to reason. She had to admit the first impression was quite pleasing.

The Crown Prince of Ayodhya stood at the back of the room. Ram's coarse white *dhoti* and *angvastram,* provided a startling contrast to his dark, flawless complexion. His nobility lent grace to the crude garments he wore. He was tall, a little taller than Sita. His broad shoulders, strong arms and lean, muscular physique were testimony to his archery training. His long hair was tied neatly in an unassuming bun. He wore a string of *Rudraaksh* beads around his neck; a marker that he too was a fellow devotee of the great Mahadev, Lord Rudra. There was no jewellery on his person. No marker to signify that he was the scion of the powerful Suryavanshi clan, a noble descendant of the great emperor Ikshvaku. His persona exuded genuine humility and strength.

Sita smiled. *Not bad. Not bad at all.*

'Excuse me for a minute, prince,' said Sita. She looked at Samichi. 'I'd like to speak to the prince alone.'

'Of course,' said Samichi, immediately climbing out of the room.

Ram nodded at Lakshman, who also turned to leave the room. With alacrity.

Ram and Sita were alone in no time.

Sita smiled and indicated a chair in the room. 'Please sit, Prince Ram.'

'I'm all right.'

'I insist,' said Sita, as she sat down herself.

Ram sat on a chair facing Sita. A few seconds of awkward silence passed. Then Sita spoke up, 'I believe you were tricked into coming here.'

Ram did not say anything, but his eyes gave the answer away.

'Then why haven't you left?'

'Because it would be against the law.'

So, he has decided to stay for the swayamvar. *Lord Rudra and Lord Parshu Ram be praised.*

'And is it the law that will make you participate in the *swayamvar* day after tomorrow?' asked Sita.

Ram chose silence again. But Sita could tell that there was something on his mind.

'You are Ayodhya, the overlord of Sapt Sindhu. I am only Mithila, a small kingdom with little power. What purpose can possibly be served by this alliance?'

'Marriage has a higher purpose; it can be more than just a political alliance.'

Sita smiled. 'But the world seems to believe that royal marriages are meant only for political gain. What other purpose do you think they can serve?'

Ram didn't answer. He seemed to be lost in another world. His eyes had taken on a dreamy look.

I don't think he's listening to me.

Sita saw Ram's eyes scanning her face. Her hair. Her neck. She saw him smile. Ruefully. His face seemed to …

Is he blushing? What is going on? I was told that Ram was only interested in the affairs of the state.

'Prince Ram?' asked Sita loudly.

'Excuse me?' asked Ram. His attention returned to what she was saying.

'I asked, if marriage is not a political alliance, then what is it?'

'Well, to begin with, it is not a necessity; there should be no compulsion to get married. There's nothing worse than being married to the wrong person. You should only get married if you find someone you admire, who will help you understand and fulfil your life's purpose. And you, in turn, can help her fulfil her life's purpose. If you're able to find that one person, then marry her.'

Sita raised her eyebrows. 'Are you advocating just one wife? Not many? Most people think differently.'

'Even if all people think polygamy is right, it doesn't make it so.'

'But most men take many wives; especially the nobility.'

'I won't. You insult your wife by taking another.'

Sita raised her chin in contemplation. Her eyes softened. Admiringly. *Wow ... This man is special.*

A charged silence filled the room. As Sita gazed at him, her expression changed with sudden recognition.

'Wasn't it you at the marketplace the other day?' she asked.

'Yes.'

Sita tried to remember the details. *Yes. Lakshman had been there too. Next to him. The giant who stood out. They were amongst the crowd on the other side. The onlookers. Not a part of the well-heeled mob that had wanted to lynch the poor boy-thief. I saw them as I dragged the boy away, after thrashing Vijay.* And then, she held her breath as she remembered another detail. *Hang on ... Ram was ... bowing his head to me ... But why? Or am I remembering incorrectly?*

'Why didn't you step in to help me?' asked Sita.

'You had the situation under control.'

Sita smiled slightly. *He is getting better with every moment ...*

It was Ram's turn to ask questions. 'What is Raavan doing here?'

'I don't know. But it makes the *swayamvar* more personal for me.'

Ram's muscles tightened. He was shocked. But his expression remained impassive. 'Has he come to participate in your *swayamvar*?'

'So I have been told.'

'And?'

'And, I have come here.' Sita kept the next sentence confined to her mind. *I have come for you.*

Ram waited for her to continue.

'How good are you with a bow and arrow?' asked Sita.

Ram allowed himself a faint smile.

Sita raised her eyebrows. 'That good?'

She arose from her chair. As did Ram. The prime minister of Mithila folded her hands into a *Namaste*. 'May Lord Rudra continue to bless you, prince.'

Ram returned Sita's *Namaste*. 'And may He bless you, princess.'

An idea struck Sita. 'Can I meet with your brother and you in the private royal garden tomorrow?'

Ram's eyes had glazed over once again. He was staring at Sita's hands in almost loving detail. Only the Almighty or Ram himself knew the thoughts that were running through his head. For probably the first time in her life, Sita felt self-conscious. She looked at her battle-scarred hands. The scar on her left hand was particularly prominent. Her hands weren't, in her own opinion, particularly pretty.

'Prince Ram,' said Sita, 'I asked—'

'I'm sorry, can you repeat that?' asked Ram, bringing his attention back to the present.

'Can I meet with you and your brother in the private royal garden tomorrow?'

'Yes, of course.'

'Good,' said Sita, as she turned to leave. She stopped as she remembered something. She reached into the pouch tied to her waistband and pulled out a red thread. 'It would be nice if you could wear this. It's for good luck. It is a representation of the blessings of the *Kanyakumari*. And I would like you to ...'

Sita stopped speaking as she realised that Ram's attention had wandered again. He was staring at the red thread and mouthing a couplet. One that was normally a part of a wedding hymn.

Sita could lip-read the words that Ram was mouthing silently, for she knew the hymn well.

Maangalyatantunaanena bhava jeevanahetuh may. A line from old Sanskrit, it translated into: *With this holy thread that I offer you, please become the purpose of my life ...*

She tried hard to suppress a giggle.

'Prince Ram ...' said Sita, loudly.

Ram suddenly straightened as the wedding hymn playing in his mind went silent. 'I'm sorry. What?'

Sita smiled politely, 'I was saying ...' She stopped suddenly. 'Never mind. I'll leave the thread here. Please wear it if it pleases you.'

Placing the thread on the table, Sita began to climb the stairs. As she reached the door, she turned around for a last look. Ram was holding the thread in the palm of his right hand. Gazing at it reverentially. As if it was the most sacred thing in the world.

Sita smiled once again. *This is completely unexpected ...*

Chapter 20

Sita sat alone in her private chamber. Astonished. Pleasantly surprised.

Samichi had briefed her on the conversation between Lakshman and Urmila. Lakshman was clearly besotted with her sister. He was also, clearly, very proud of his elder brother. He simply wouldn't stop talking about Ram. Lakshman had told the duo about Ram's attitude towards marriage. It seemed that Ram did not want to marry an ordinary woman. He wanted a woman, in front of whom he would be compelled to bow his head in admiration.

Samichi had laughed, while relating this to Sita. 'Ram is like an earnest, conscientious school boy,' she had said. 'He has not grown up yet. There is not a trace of cynicism in him. Or, realism. Trust me, Sita. Send him back to Ayodhya before he gets hurt.'

Sita had listened to Samichi without reacting. But only one thing had reverberated in her mind — Ram wanted to marry a woman in front of whom he would be compelled to bow his head in admiration.

He bowed to me …

She giggled. Not something she did normally. It felt strange. Even girlish …

Sita rarely bothered about her appearance. But for some reason, she now walked to the polished copper mirror and looked at herself.

She was almost as tall as Ram. Lean. Muscular. Wheat-complexioned. Her round face a shade lighter than the rest of her body. She had high cheekbones and a sharp, small nose. Her lips were neither thin nor full. Her wide-set eyes were neither small nor large; strong brows were arched in a perfect curve above creaseless eyelids. Her straight, jet-black hair was braided and tied in a neat bun. As always.

She looked like the mountain people from the Himalayas.

Not for the first time, she wondered if the Himalayas were her original home.

She touched a battle scar on her forearm and winced. Her scars had been a source of pride. Once.

Do they make me look ugly?

She shook her head.

A man like Ram will respect my scars. It's a warrior's body.

She giggled again. She had always thought of herself as a warrior. As a princess. As a ruler. Of late, she had even gotten used to being treated by the Malayaputras as the Vishnu. But this feeling was new. She now felt like an *apsara*, a *celestial nymph* of unimaginable beauty. One who could halt *her* man in his tracks by just fluttering her eyelashes. It was a heady feeling.

She had always held these 'pretty women' in disdain and thought of them as non-serious. Not anymore.

Sita put a hand on her hip and looked at herself from the corner of her eyes.

She replayed the moments spent with Ram at the Bees Quarter.

Ram ....

This was new. Special. She giggled once again.

She undid her hair and smiled at her reflection.

This is the beginning of a beautiful relationship.

— ᚱᚷ —

The royal garden in Mithila was modest in comparison to the one in Ayodhya. It only contained local trees, plants, and flower beds. Its beauty could safely be attributed more to the ministrations of talented gardeners than to an impressive infusion of funds. The layout was symmetrical, well-manicured. The thick, green carpet of grass thrown into visual relief by the profusion of flowers and trees of all shapes, sizes and colours. It was a celebration of Nature, expressed in ordered harmony.

Sita and Urmila waited in a clearing at the back of the garden. Sita had asked her younger sister to accompany her so that Urmila could spend more time with Lakshman. This would also give her some alone time with Ram, without the looming presence of Lakshman.

Samichi was at the gate, tasked with fetching the young princes of Ayodhya. She walked in shortly, followed by Ram and Lakshman.

The evening sky has increased his radiance… Sita quickly controlled her wandering mind and beating heart.

'*Namaste*, princess,' said Ram to Sita.

'*Namaste,* prince,' replied Sita, before turning to her sister. 'May I introduce my younger sister, Urmila?' Gesturing towards Ram and Lakshman, Sita continued, 'Urmila, meet Prince Ram and Prince Lakshman of Ayodhya.'

'I had occasion to meet her yesterday,' said Lakshman, grinning from ear to ear.

Urmila smiled politely at Lakshman, with her hands folded in a *Namaste*, then turned towards Ram and greeted him.

'I would like to speak with the prince privately, once again,' said Sita.

'Of course,' said Samichi immediately. 'May I have a private word before that?'

Samichi took Sita aside and whispered in her ear, 'Sita, please remember what I said. Ram is too simple. And, his life is in real danger. Please ask him to leave. This is our last chance.'

Sita smiled politely, fully intending to ignore Samichi's words.

Samichi cast a quick look at Ram before walking away, leading Urmila by the hand. Lakshman followed Urmila.

Ram moved towards Sita. 'Why did you want to meet me, princess?'

Sita checked that Samichi and the rest were beyond earshot. She was about to begin speaking when her eyes fell on the red thread tied around Ram's right wrist. She smiled.

He has worn it.

'Please give me a minute, prince,' said Sita.

She walked behind a tree, bent and picked up a long package covered in cloth. She walked back to Ram. He frowned, intrigued. Sita pulled the cloth back to reveal an intricately carved, and unusually long, bow. An exquisite piece of weaponry, it was a composite bow with recurved ends, which would give it a very long range. Ram carefully examined the carvings on the inside face of the limbs, both above and below the grip of the bow. It was the image of a flame, representative of Agni, the God of Fire. The first hymn of the first chapter of the *Rig Veda* was dedicated to the deeply revered deity. However, the shape of this flame was slightly different.

Sita pulled a flat wooden base platform from the cloth bag and placed it on the ground ceremonially. She looked at Ram. 'This bow cannot be allowed to touch the ground.'

Ram was clearly fascinated. He wondered why this bow was so important. Sita placed the lower limb of the bow on the platform, steadying it with her foot. She used her right hand to pull down the other end with force. Judging by the strain on her shoulder and biceps, Ram guessed that it was a very strong bow with tremendous resistance. With her left hand, Sita pulled the bowstring up and quickly strung it. She let the upper limb of the bow extend, and relaxed. She let out a long breath. The mighty bow adjusted to the constraints of the potent bowstring. She held the bow with her left hand and pulled the bowstring with her fingers, letting it go with a loud twang.

Ram knew from the sound that this bow was special. 'Wow. That's a good bow.'

'It's the best.'

'Is it yours?'

'I cannot own a bow like this. I am only its caretaker, for now. When I die, someone else will be deputed to take care of it.'

Ram narrowed his eyes as he closely examined the image of the flames around the grip of the bow. 'These flames look a little like —'

Sita interrupted him, impressed that he had figured it out so quickly. 'This bow once belonged to the one whom we both worship. It still belongs to him.'

Ram stared at the bow with a mixture of shock and awe, his suspicion confirmed.

Sita smiled. 'Yes, it is the *Pinaka*.'

The *Pinaka* was the legendary bow of the previous Mahadev, Lord Rudra. It was considered the strongest bow ever made. Believed to be a composite, it was a mix of many materials, which had been given a succession of specific treatments to arrest its degeneration. It was also believed that maintaining this bow was not an easy task. The grip, the limbs and the recurved ends needed regular lubrication with a special oil.

'How did Mithila come into the possession of the *Pinaka*?' asked Ram, unable to take his eyes off the beautiful weapon.

'It's a long story,' said Sita. She knew she couldn't give him the real reason. Not yet, at least. 'But I want you to practise with it. This is the bow which will be used for the *swayamvar* competition tomorrow.'

Ram took an involuntary step back. There were many ways in which a *swayamvar* was conducted. Sometimes the bride directly selected her groom. Or, she mandated a competition. The winner married the bride. However, it was unorthodox for a groom to be given advance information and help. In fact, it was against the rules.

Ram shook his head. 'It would be an honour to even touch the *Pinaka*, much less hold the bow that Lord Rudra himself graced with his touch. But I will only do so tomorrow. Not today.'

Sita frowned. *What? Doesn't he want to marry me?*

'I thought you intended to win my hand,' said Sita.

'I do. But I will win it the right way. I will win according to the rules.'

Sita smiled, shaking her head. *This man is truly special. Either he will go down in history as someone who was exploited by all. Or, he will be remembered as one of the greatest ever.*

Sita was happy that she had chosen to marry Ram. In a

tiny corner of her heart, though, she was worried. For she knew that this man would suffer. The world would make him suffer. And from what she knew about his life, he had suffered a lot already.

'Do you disagree?' asked Ram, seeming disappointed.

'No, I don't. I'm just impressed. You are a special man, Prince Ram.'

Ram blushed.

He's blushing again …!

'I look forward to seeing you fire an arrow tomorrow morning,' said Sita, smiling.

— ᚷᚷ —

'He refused help? Really?' asked Jatayu, surprised.

Jatayu and Sita had met in the patch of the jungle that was now their regular meeting place. It lay towards the north of the city, as far away as possible from Raavan's temporary camp.

'Yes,' answered Sita.

Jatayu smiled and shook his head. 'He is no ordinary man.'

'No, he isn't. But I'm not sure whether the Malayaputras agree.'

Jatayu instinctively cast a glance around the woods, as if expecting to be heard by the formidable chief of the Malayaputras. He knew Vishwamitra did not like Ram. The Prince of Ayodhya was just a tool for the *Maharishi*; a means to an end.

'It's all right. The words will not carry to …' Sita left the name unsaid. 'So, what do you think of Ram?'

'He is special in many ways, my sister,' whispered Jatayu, carefully. 'Perhaps, just what our country needs … His obsession with rules and honesty, his almighty love for this great land, his high expectations from everyone, including himself ...'

Sita finally asked him the question that had been weighing on her mind. 'Is there anything I should know about the Malayaputras' plans regarding Ram tomorrow? At the *swayamvar?'*

Jatayu remained silent. He looked distinctly nervous.

'You have called me your sister, Jatayu*ji.* And this is regarding my future husband. I deserve to know.'

Jatayu looked down. Struggling between his loyalty to the Malayaputras and his devotion to Sita.

'Please, Jatayu*ji.* I need to know.'

Jatayu straightened his back and let out a sigh. 'You do know about the attack on a motley bunch of *Asuras* close to our Ganga *ashram*, right?'

Vishwamitra had gone to Ayodhya and asked for Ram and Lakshman's help in resolving a 'serious' military problem that he was facing. He had taken them to his *ashram* close to the Ganga River. He had then asked them to lead a contingent of his Malayaputra soldiers in an assault on a small tribe of Asuras, who were apparently, attacking his *ashram* repeatedly. It was only after the 'Asura problem' had been handled that they had left for Mithila, for Sita's *swayamvar.*

'Yes,' said Sita. 'Was Ram's life in danger?'

Jatayu shook his head dismissively. 'It was a pathetic tribe of a handful of people. They were imbeciles. Incapable warriors. Ram's life was never in danger.'

Sita frowned, confused. 'I don't understand ...'

'The idea wasn't to get rid of Ram. It was to destroy his reputation with his most powerful supporters.'

Sita's eyes widened as she finally unravelled the conspiracy.

'The Malayaputras do not want him dead. They want him out of the reckoning as a potential Vishnu; and, under *their* control.'

'Are the Malayaputras intending to ally with Raavan?'

Jatayu was shocked. 'How can you even ask that, great Vishnu? They will never ally with Raavan. In fact, they will destroy him. But only when the time is right. Remember, the Malayaputras are loyal to one cause alone: the restoration of India's greatness. Nothing else matters. Raavan is just a tool for them.'

'As is Ram. As am I.'

'No. No … How can you even think that the Malayaputras would use you as a …'

Sita looked at Jatayu, silently. *Perhaps Samichi is right. There are forces far beyond my control. And Ram is …*

Jatayu interrupted Sita's thoughts and unwittingly gave her a clue as to what she should do. 'Remember, great Vishnu. You are too crucial to the Malayaputras' plans. They cannot allow anything to happen to you. No harm can come to you.'

Sita smiled. Jatayu had given her the answer. She knew what she must do.

Chapter 21

'Do I know all there is to know about the Malayaputras' plans for the *swayamvar*, Arishtanemi*ji*?' asked Sita.

Arishtanemi was surprised by the question.

'I don't understand, Sita,' he said, carefully.

'How did Raavan get an invitation?'

'We are as clueless as you, Sita. You know that. We suspect it to be the handiwork of your uncle. But there is no proof.'

Sita looked sceptical. 'Right... No proof.'

Arishtanemi took a deep breath. 'Why don't you say what is on your mind, Sita ...'

Sita leaned forward, looked directly into Arishtanemi's eyes, and said, 'I know that Raavan's family has its roots in Kannauj.'

Arishtanemi winced. But recovered quickly. He shook his head, an injured expression on his face. 'In the name of the great Lord Parshu Ram, Sita. How can you think such thoughts?'

Sita was impassive.

'You think Guru Vishwamitra has any other identity now, besides being the chief of the Malayaputras? Seriously?'

Arishtanemi looked a little agitated. It was uncharacteristic of him. Sita knew she had hit a nerve. She could not have had a conversation like this with Vishwamitra. She needed to press home the advantage. Arishtanemi was one of the rare few who could convince Vishwamitra. She unnerved him further by choosing silence. For now.

'We can destroy Raavan at any time,' said Arishtanemi. 'We keep him alive because we plan to use his death to help you. To help you be recognised, by all Indians, as the Vishnu.'

'I believe you.'

Now, Arishtanemi fell silent. Confused.

'And I also know that you have plans for Ram.'

'Sita, listen to …'

Sita interrupted Arishtanemi. It was time to deliver the threat. 'I may not have Ram's life in my hands. But I do have my own life in my hands.'

A shocked Arishtanemi did not know what to say. All the plans would be reduced to dust without Sita. They had invested too much in her.

'I have chosen,' said Sita firmly. 'Now you need to decide what to do.'

'Sita …'

'I have nothing more to say, Arishtanemi*ji*.'

— ᚱᚥ —

The *swayamvar* was held in the Hall of Dharma instead of the royal court. This was simply because the royal court was not the biggest hall in Mithila. The main building in the palace complex, which housed the Hall of Dharma, had been donated by King Janak to the Mithila University. The hall hosted regular debates and discussions on various esoteric topics — the nature of dharma, karma's interaction with dharma, the nature of the divine, the purpose of the human journey …

The Hall of Dharma was in a circular building, built of stone and mortar, with a massive dome. The delicate elegance of the dome was believed to represent the feminine, while the typical temple spire represented the masculine. The hall was also circular. All *rishis* sat as equals, without a moderating 'head', debating issues openly and without fear; freedom of expression at its zenith.

However, today was different. The Hall of Dharma was set to host a *swayamvar*. Temporary three-tiered spectator stands stood near the entrance. At the other end, on a wooden platform, was placed the king's throne. A statue of the great King Mithi, the founder of Mithila, stood on a raised pedestal behind the throne. Two thrones, only marginally less grand, were placed to the left and right of the king's throne. A circle of comfortable seats lined the middle section of the great hall, where kings and princes, the potential suitors, would sit. The spectator stands were already packed when Ram and Lakshman were led in by Arishtanemi. Most contestants too had taken their seats. Few recognised the two princes of Ayodhya, dressed as hermits. A guard gestured for them to move towards the base platform of a three-tiered stand, occupied by the nobility and rich merchants of Mithila.

Arishtanemi informed the guard that he was accompanying a competitor. The guard was surprised. He had recognised Arishtanemi, the lieutenant of the great Vishwamitra, but not Ram and Lakshman. But he stepped aside to let them proceed. After all, it would not be unusual for the devout King Janak to invite even Brahmin *rishis*, not just Kshatriya kings, for his daughter's *swayamvar*.

Ram followed Arishtanemi to the allotted seat. He seated himself, as Lakshman and Arishtanemi stood behind him.

All eyes turned to them. Many contestants wondered who these simple mendicants were, who hoped to compete with them for Princess Sita's hand. A few, though, recognised the princes of Ayodhya. A conspiratorial buzz was heard from a section of the contestants.

'Ayodhya ...'

'Why does Ayodhya want an alliance with Mithila?'

Ram, however, was oblivious to the stares and whispers of the assembly.

He looked towards the centre of the hall; to the *Pinaka* bow placed on a table. The legendary bow was unstrung. An array of arrows placed by its side. Next to the table, at ground level, was a large copper-plated basin.

A competitor was first required to pick up the bow and string it. Itself no mean task. Then he would move to the copper-plated basin. It was filled with water, with additional drops trickling in steadily into the basin through a thin tube. Excess water was drained out by another thin tube, attached to the other side. This created subtle ripples within the bowl, spreading out from the centre towards the edge. Troublingly, the drops of water were released at irregular intervals, making the ripples unpredictable.

A *hilsa* fish was nailed to a wheel, fixed to an axle that was suspended from the top of the dome. A hundred metres above the ground. The wheel, thankfully, revolved at a constant speed.

The contestant was required to look at the reflection of the fish in the unstill water below, disturbed by ripples generated at irregular intervals, and use the *Pinaka* bow to fire an arrow into the eye of the fish, fixed on the revolving wheel high above. The first to succeed would win the hand of the bride.

Sita sat in a room on the second floor adjoining the Hall

of Dharma, directly above the royal Mithilan thrones, hidden behind a latticed window. She looked at Ram, seated in the circle of contestants.

The eldest prince of Ayodhya looked around. Sita felt as though he was seeking her out. She smiled. 'I'm here, Ram. I'm waiting for you. Waiting for you to win ...'

She noticed Samichi standing with a posse of policemen a short distance from the entrance. Samichi was staring at Ram. She looked up at the latticed window where Sita sat hidden from view. She had a look of utter disapproval.

Sita sighed with irritation. *Samichi needs to relax. I can handle the situation. Ram's life is not in danger.*

She turned her attention back to the princes of Ayodhya. She saw Lakshman bend close to his elder brother and whisper something. The expression on his face mischievous. Ram looked at his brother and glared. Lakshman grinned, said something more, and stepped back.

Sita smiled. *The brothers really love each other. Surprising, given the politics of their family.*

Her attention was drawn away by the court announcer.

'The Lord of the Mithi clan, the wisest of the wise, beloved of the *rishis*, King Janak!'

The court arose to welcome their host, Janak, the king of Mithila. He walked in from the far end of the hall. In a deviation from courtly tradition, he followed the great Malayaputra chief, Vishwamitra, who was in the lead. Janak had always honoured men and women of knowledge. He followed his own personal tradition on this special day as well. Behind Janak was his younger brother, Kushadhwaj, the king of Sankashya. Those aware of the strained relations between Janak and his younger brother, were impressed by the graciousness of the king of Mithila. He had let bygones be bygones and included the entire extended family in this celebration. Unfortunately, Kushadhwaj felt otherwise. He felt his brother had been naive as usual. Besides, Kushadhwaj had just played his own cards ...

Janak requested Vishwamitra to occupy the main throne of Mithila, as he moved towards the smaller throne to the right. Kushadhwaj walked towards the seat on the left of the great *Maharishi*. This was exactly two floors below the room Sita was in, hidden behind a latticed window. A flurry of officials scuttled all over the place, for this was an unexpected breach of protocol. The king had offered his own throne to another.

A loud buzz ran through the hall at this unorthodox seating arrangement, but Sita was distracted by something else.

Where is Raavan?

She smiled.

So the Malayaputras have handled the king of Lanka. He won't be coming. Good.

The court crier banged his staff against the large bell at the entrance of the hall, signalling a call for silence.

Vishwamitra cleared his throat and spoke loudly. The superb acoustics of the Hall of Dharma carried his voice clearly to all those present. 'Welcome to this august gathering called by the wisest and most spiritual of rulers in India, King Janak.'

Janak smiled genially.

Vishwamitra continued. 'The princess of Mithila, Sita, has decided to make this a *gupt swayamvar*. She will not join us in the hall. The great kings and princes will, on her bidding, compete —'

The *Maharishi* was interrupted by the ear-splitting sounds of numerous conch shells; surprising, for conch shells were usually melodious and pleasant. Everyone turned to the source of the sound: the entrance of the great hall. Fifteen tall, muscular warriors strode into the room holding black flags, with the image of the head of a roaring lion emerging from a profusion of fiery flames. The warriors marched with splendid discipline.

Behind them were two formidable men. One was a giant, even taller than Lakshman. He was corpulent but muscular, with a massive potbelly that jiggled with every step. His whole body was unusually hirsute — he looked more like a giant bear than human. Most troubling for all those present, were the strange outgrowths on his ears and shoulders. He was a Naga. He was also Raavan's younger brother, Kumbhakarna.

Walking proudly beside him was Raavan, his head held high. He moved with a minor stoop; perhaps a sign of advancing age. Despite the stoop, Raavan's great height and rippling musculature were obvious. The muscles may have sagged a bit and the skin may have wrinkled, but the strength that remained in them was palpable. His battle-worn, swarthy skin was pock-marked, probably by a childhood disease. A thick beard, with an equal sprinkling of black and white hair, valiantly attempted to cover his ugly marks while a handlebar moustache set off his menacing features. He was wearing a violet-coloured *dhoti* and *angvastram*; only the most expensive colour-dye in the world. His headgear was intimidating, with two threatening six-inch-long horns reaching out from the top on either side.

Fifteen more warriors followed the two men.

Raavan's entourage moved to the centre and halted next to the bow of Lord Rudra. The lead bodyguard made a loud announcement. 'The king of kings, the emperor of emperors, the ruler of the three worlds, the beloved of the Gods, Lord Raavan!'

Raavan turned to a minor king who sat closest to the *Pinaka*. He made a soft grunting sound and flicked his head to the right, a casual gesture which clearly communicated what he expected. The king immediately rose and scurried away, coming to a standstill behind another competitor. Raavan walked to the chair, but did not sit. He placed his right foot on the seat and rested his hand on his knee. His bodyguards, including the giant bear-like Kumbhakarna, fell in line behind him.

Raavan finally cast a casual glance at Vishwamitra. 'Continue, great Malayaputra.'

Vishwamitra, the chief of the Malayaputras, was furious. He had never been treated so disrespectfully. 'Raavan ...' he growled.

Raavan stared at Vishwamitra with lazy arrogance.

The *Maharishi* managed to rein in his temper; he had an important task at hand. He would deal with Raavan later. 'Princess Sita has decreed the sequence in which the great kings and princes will compete.'

Raavan began to walk towards the *Pinaka* while Vishwamitra was still speaking. The chief of the Malayaputras completed his announcement just as Raavan was about to reach for the bow. 'The first man to compete is not you, Raavan. It is Ram, the prince of Ayodhya.'

Raavan's hand stopped a few inches from the bow. He looked at Vishwamitra, and then turned around to see who had responded to the sage. He saw a young man, dressed in the simple white clothes of a hermit. Behind him stood another young, though gigantic, man, next to whom was Arishtanemi.

Raavan glared first at Arishtanemi, and then at Ram. If looks could kill, Raavan would have certainly felled a few today. He turned towards Vishwamitra, Janak, and Kushadhwaj, his fingers wrapped around the macabre finger-bones pendant that hung around his neck. His body was shaking in utter fury. He growled in a loud and booming voice, 'I have been insulted! Why was I invited at all if you planned to make unskilled boys compete ahead of me?!'

Janak looked at Kushadhwaj before turning to Raavan and interjecting weakly, 'These are the rules of the *swayamvar*, Great King of Lanka …'

A voice that sounded more like the rumble of thunder was finally heard. The voice of Kumbhakarna. 'Enough of this nonsense!' He turned towards Raavan, his *elder brother*. '*Dada*, let's go.'

Raavan suddenly bent and picked up the *Pinaka*. Before anyone could react, he had strung it and nocked an arrow on the string. Everyone sat paralysed as he pointed the arrow directly at Vishwamitra.

Vishwamitra stood up, threw his *angvastram* aside, and banged his chest with his closed fist. 'Shoot, Raavan!' The sage's voice resounded in the great hall. 'Come on! Shoot, if you have the guts!'

The crowd gasped collectively. In horror.

Sita was shocked beyond words. *Guru*ji!

Raavan released the arrow. It slammed into the statue of Mithi behind Vishwamitra, breaking off the nose of the ancient king, the founder of Mithila. An unimaginable insult.

Sita was livid. *How dare he?*

'Raavan!' growled Sita, as she got up and whirled around, simultaneously reaching for her sword. She was stopped by her Mithilan maids, who held her back from rushing towards the stairs.

'No, Lady Sita!'

'Raavan is a monster …'

'*You will die ...*'

'*Look, he's leaving ...*' said another maid.

Sita rushed back to the latticed window. She saw Raavan throw the bow, the holy *Pinaka*, on the table and begin to walk towards the door. He was followed by his guards. In all this commotion, Kumbhakarna quickly stepped up to the table, unstrung the *Pinaka*, and reverentially brought it to his head. Holding it with both hands. Almost like he was apologising to the bow. Placing the *Pinaka* back on the table, he turned around and briskly walked out of the hall. Behind Raavan.

As the last of the Lankans exited, the people within the hall turned in unison from the doorway to those seated at the other end of the room: Vishwamitra, Janak and Kushadhwaj.

Vishwamitra spoke as if nothing had happened. 'Let the competition begin.'

The people in the room sat still, as if they had turned to stone. *En masse*. Vishwamitra spoke once again, louder this time. 'Let the competition begin. Prince Ram, please step up.'

Ram rose from his chair and walked up to the *Pinaka*. He bowed with reverence and folded his hands together into a *Namaste*. Sita thought she saw his lips move in a chant. But she couldn't be sure from the distance.

He raised his right wrist and touched both his eyes with the red thread tied around it.

Sita smiled. *May the* Kanyakumari *bless you, Ram. And, may she bless me with your hand in marriage.*

Ram touched the bow and tarried a while. He then brought his head down and placed it on the bow; as if asking to be blessed by the great weapon. He breathed steadily as he lifted the bow with ease. Sita looked at Ram intently. With bated breath.

Ram placed one arm of the bow on a wooden stand placed on the ground. His shoulders, back and arms strained visibly as he pulled down the upper limb of the *Pinaka*, simultaneously pulling up the bowstring. His body laboured at the task. But his face was serene. He bent the upper limb farther with a slight increase in effort, and tied the bowstring. His muscles relaxed as he let go of the upper limb and held the bow at the grip. He brought the bowstring close to his ear and plucked; his expression showed that the twang was right.

He picked up an arrow and walked to the copper-plated basin. Deliberate footsteps. Unhurried. He went down on one knee and held the bow horizontally above his head. He looked down at the water. At the reflection of the fish that moved in a circle above him. The rippling water in the basin danced as if to tantalise his mind. Ram focused on the image of the fish to the exclusion of all else. He nocked the arrow on the string of the bow and pulled slowly with his right hand. His back erect. The core muscles activated with ideal tension. His breathing steady and rhythmic.

Calmly, without any hint of nervousness or anxiety, he pulled the string all the way back and released the arrow. It shot up. As did the vision of each person in the room. The unmistakable sound of a furiously speeding arrow crashing into wood reverberated in the great hall. It had pierced the right eye of the fish, and lodged itself into the wooden wheel. The wheel swirled rhythmically as the shaft of the arrow drew circles in the air.

Sita smiled in relief. All the tension of the last few days was forgotten. The anger of the last few minutes, forgotten. Her eyes were pinned on Ram, who knelt near the basin with his head bowed, studying the rippling water; a calm smile on his face.

A part of Sita that had died years ago, when she had lost her mother, slowly sputtered to life once again.

I am not alone anymore.

She felt a bittersweet ache as she thought of her mother. That she wasn't around to see Sita find her man.

For the first time since her mother's death, she could think of her without crying.

Grief overwhelms you when you are alone. But when you find your soulmate, you can handle anything.

What was a painful, unbearable memory had now been transformed into bittersweet nostalgia. A source of sadness, yes. But also, a source of strength and happiness.

She pictured her mother standing before her. Smiling. Nurturing. Warm. Maternal. Like Mother Nature herself.

Sita was whole once again.

After a long, long time, she felt like whispering words that lay buried deep in her consciousness. Words that she thought she would have no use for once her mother had died.

She looked at Ram in the distance and whispered, 'I love you.'

Chapter 22

'Thank you, Arishtanemi*ji*,' said Sita. 'The Malayaputras stood by me. Guru*ji* put his own life at risk. I am grateful.'

It had been announced that the wedding of Ram and Sita would be carried out in a simple set of rituals that very afternoon. To Ram's surprise, Sita had suggested that Lakshman and Urmila get married in the same auspicious hour of the day. To Ram's further disbelief, Lakshman had enthusiastically agreed. It was decided that while both the couples would be wed in Mithila — to allow Sita and Urmila to travel with Ram and Lakshman to Ayodhya — a set of grand ceremonies would be held in Ayodhya as well. Befitting the descendants of the noble Ikshvaku.

In the midst of the preparations for the wedding ceremonies, Arishtanemi had sought a meeting with Sita.

'I hope this puts to rest any suspicions about where the Malayaputra loyalties lie,' said Arishtanemi. 'We have always been, and always will be, with the Vishnu.'

You will be with the Vishnu only as long as I do what you want me to do. Not when I do something that does not fit in with your plans.

Sita smiled. 'My apologies for having doubted you, Arishtanemi*ji*.'

Arishtanemi smiled. 'Misunderstandings can occur within the closest of families. All's well that ends well.'

'Where is Guru Vishwamitra?'

'Where do you think?'

Raavan.

'How is the demon king taking it?' asked Sita.

Vishwamitra had gone out on a limb to aggressively stop Raavan during the *swayamvar*. The King of Lanka had felt insulted. There could be consequences. Raavan's almighty ego was as legendary as his warrior spirit and cruelty. But would he take on the formidable Malayaputras?

Arishtanemi looked down thoughtfully before returning his gaze to Sita. 'Raavan is a cold and ruthless man, who makes decisions based on hard calculations. But his ego ... His ego gets in the way sometimes.'

'Cold and ruthless calculations would tell him not to take on the Malayaputras,' said Sita. 'He needs whatever it is we give him from the cavern of the Thamiravaruni.'

'That he does. But like I said, his ego may get in the way. I hope Guru Vishwamitra can handle it.'

Arishtanemi was astonished that Sita had not uncovered the entire secret of the aid that the Malayaputras provided Raavan. Perhaps, there were some things beyond even the redoubtable Sita's abilities. But he kept his surprise from showing on his face.

— ॐ —

The two weddings were simple sets of rituals, concluded quickly in the afternoon of the day of the *swayamvar*.

Sita and Ram were alone at last. They sat on floor cushions

in the dining hall, their dinner placed on a low stool. It was late in the evening, the sixth hour of the third *prahar*. Notwithstanding their relationship being sanctified by dharma a few hours earlier, an awkwardness underlined their ignorance of each other's personalities.

'Umm,' said Ram, staring at his plate.

'Yes, Ram?' asked Sita. 'Is there a problem?'

'I'm sorry, but ... the food ...'

'Is it not to your liking?'

'No, no, it's good. It's very good. But ...'

Sita looked into Ram's eyes. *I am your wife. You can be honest with me. I haven't made the food in any case.*

But she kept these thoughts in her head and asked, 'Yes?'

'It needs a bit of salt.'

Sita was irritated with the Mithila royal cook. *Daya! I'd told him that the central Sapt Sindhuans eat more salt than us Easterners!*

She pushed her plate aside, rose and clapped her hands. An attendant rushed in. 'Get some salt for the prince, please.' As the attendant turned, Sita ordered, 'Quickly!'

The attendant broke into a run.

Ram cleaned his hand with a napkin as he waited for the salt. 'I'm sorry to trouble you.'

Sita frowned as she took her seat. 'I'm your wife, Ram. It's my duty to take care of you.'

He's so awkward ... and cute ...

Ram smiled. 'Umm, may I ask you something?'

'Of course.'

'Tell me something about your childhood.'

'You mean, before I was adopted? You do know that I was adopted, right?'

'Yes ... I mean, you don't have to talk about it if it troubles you.'

Sita smiled. 'No, it doesn't trouble me, but I don't remember anything. I was too young when I was found by my adoptive parents.'

Ram nodded.

Will you also judge me by my birth?

Sita answered the question that she thought was on Ram's mind. 'So, if you ask me who my birth-parents are, the short answer is that I don't know. But the one I prefer is that I am a daughter of the earth.'

'Birth is completely unimportant. It is just a means of entry into this world of action, into this *karmabhoomi*. Karma is all that matters. And your karma is divine.'

Sita smiled. She was charmed by her husband's ability to constantly surprise her. Positively surprise her. *I can see what Maharishi Vashishtha sees in him. He is special …*

Ram was about to say something when the attendant came rushing in with the salt. He added some to his food and resumed eating. The attendant retreated from the room.

'You were saying something,' said Sita.

'Yes,' said Ram, 'I think that …'

Ram was interrupted again, this time by the doorkeeper announcing loudly, 'The chief of the Malayaputras, the *Saptrishi Uttradhikari*, the protector of the way of the Vishnus, Maharishi Vishwamitra.'

Sita was surprised. *Why is Guruji here?*

She looked at Ram. He shrugged. He did not know what this visit was about. Ram and Sita rose as Vishwamitra entered the room, followed by Arishtanemi. Sita gestured to her attendant to get some washing bowls for Ram and herself.

'We have a problem,' said Vishwamitra, not feeling the need to exchange pleasantries.

Sita cursed under her breath. *Raavan* ...

'What happened, Guru*ji*?' asked Ram.

'Raavan is mobilising for an attack.'

'But he doesn't have an army,' said Ram. 'What's he going to do with ten thousand bodyguards? He can't hold a city of even Mithila's size with that number. All he'll achieve is getting his men killed in battle.'

'Raavan is not a logical man,' said Vishwamitra. 'His ego is hurt. He may lose his bodyguard corps, but he will wreak havoc on Mithila.'

Ram looked at his wife.

Sita shook her head with irritation and addressed Vishwamitra. 'Who in Lord Rudra's name invited that demon for the *swayamvar*? I know it was not my father.'

Vishwamitra took a deep breath as his eyes softened. 'That's water under the bridge, Sita. The question is, what are we going to do now?'

'What is your plan, Guru*ji*?' asked Ram.

'I have with me some important material that was mined at my *ashram* by the Ganga. I needed it to conduct a few science experiments at Agastyakootam. This was why I had visited my *ashram*.'

'Science experiments?' asked Ram.

'Yes, experiments with the *daivi astras*.'

Sita drew a sharp breath. She knew the power and ferocity of the *divine weapons*. 'Guru*ji*, are you suggesting that we use *daivi astras*?'

Vishwamitra nodded in confirmation. Ram spoke up. 'But that will destroy Mithila as well.'

'No, it won't,' said Vishwamitra. 'This is not a traditional *daivi astra*. What I have is the *Asuraastra*.'

'Isn't that a biological weapon?' asked Ram. Deeply troubled now.

'Yes. Poisonous gas and a blast wave from the *Asuraastra* will incapacitate the Lankans, paralysing them for days on end. We can easily imprison them in that state and end this problem.'

'Just paralyse, Guru*ji*?' asked Ram. 'I have learnt that in large quantities, the *Asuraastra* can kill as well.'

Vishwamitra knew that only one man could have possibly taught this to Ram. His best friend-turned-foe, Vashishtha. The Chief of the Malayaputras was immediately irritated. 'Do you have any better ideas?'

Ram fell silent.

Sita looked at Ram and then at Vishwamitra. *I know exactly what Guru*ji *is trying to do.*

'But what about Lord Rudra's law?' asked Sita, a little aggressively.

It was well known that Lord Rudra, the previous Mahadev, had banned the unauthorised use of *daivi astras* many centuries ago. Those who broke the law would be punished with banishment for fourteen years, he had decreed. Breaking the law for the second time would be punishable by death.

The Vayuputras would be compelled to enforce the Mahadev's law.

'I don't think that law applies to the use of the *Asuraastra,*' said Vishwamitra. 'It is not a weapon of mass destruction, just mass incapacitation.'

Sita narrowed her eyes. Clearly, she wasn't convinced. 'I disagree. A *daivi astra* is a *daivi astra*. We cannot use it without the authorisation of the Vayuputras, Lord Rudra's tribe. I am a Lord Rudra devotee. I will not break his law.'

'Do you want to surrender, then?'

'Of course not! We will fight!'

Vishwamitra laughed derisively. 'Fight, is it? And who, please explain, will fight Raavan's hordes? The namby-pamby intellectuals of Mithila? What is the plan? Debate the Lankans to death?'

'We have our police force,' said Sita, annoyed at this disrespect shown to her force.

'They're not trained or equipped to fight the troops of Raavan.'

'We are not fighting his troops. We are fighting his bodyguard platoons. My police force is enough for them.'

'They are not. And you know that.'

'We will not use the *daivi astras*, Guruji,' said Sita firmly, her face hardening.

Ram spoke up. 'Samichi's police force is not alone. Lakshman and I are here, and so are the Malayaputras. We're inside the fort, we have the double walls; we have the lake surrounding the city. We can hold Mithila. We can fight.'

Vishwamitra turned to Ram with a sneer. 'Nonsense! We are vastly outnumbered. The double walls ...' He snorted with disgust. 'It seems clever. But how long do you think it will take a warrior of Raavan's calibre to figure out a strategy that works around that obstacle?'

'We will not use the *daivi astras*, Guruji,' said Sita, raising her voice. 'Now, if you will excuse me, I have a battle to prepare for.'

— ट॑ऽ —

'Where is Samichi?' asked Sita, surprised that the Mithila Chief of Police and Protocol was not in her office.

The sun had already set. Sita was marshalling her forces for an expected attack from Raavan. She did not think the demon king of Lanka would honour the rules of war. It was quite likely that he would attack at night. Time was of the essence.

'My Lady,' said an officer. 'We don't know where she has gone. She left immediately after your wedding ceremony.'

'Find her. Tell her to come to the fort walls. The Bees Quarter.'

'Yes, My Lady.'

'Right now!' ordered Sita, clapping her hands. As the officer hurried out, Sita turned to the others. 'Round up all the officers in the city. Get them to the Bees Quarter. To the inner wall.'

As the policemen rushed out, Sita walked out of her office to meet her personal bodyguards — the Malayaputras embedded in the Mithila police force. She checked to see if they were out of earshot. Then, she whispered to Makrant, a guard she had come to trust. 'Find Captain Jatayu. Tell him that I want all of you to protect the eastern secret tunnel on our inner wall. He knows where it is. Preferably, find a way to collapse that tunnel.'

'My Lady, do you expect Raavan to …'

'Yes, I do,' interrupted Sita. 'Block that tunnel. Block it within the hour.'

'Yes, My Lady.'

— ᡏ ᠄ —

'I cannot do that!' hissed Samichi, looking around to ascertain that nobody was near.

Akampana, unlike his usual well-groomed self, was dishevelled. The clothes, though expensive, were rumpled.

Some of the rings on his fingers were missing. The knife lay precariously in the scabbard, the blood-stained blade partly exposed. Samichi was shocked. This was an Akampana she did not know. Crazed and violent.

'You must do as ordered,' growled Akampana softly.

Samichi glared angrily at the ground. She knew she had no choice. Because of what had happened all those years ago …

'Princess Sita cannot be hurt.'

'You are in no position to make demands.'

'Princess Sita cannot be hurt!' snarled Samichi. 'Promise me!'

Akampana held his fists tight. His fury at breaking point.

'Promise me!'

Despite his anger, Akampana knew they needed Samichi if they were to succeed. He nodded.

Samichi turned and hurried off.

Chapter 23

It was late at night; the fourth hour of the fourth *prahar*. Ram and Sita had been joined by Lakshman and Samichi on top of the Bees Quarter, close to the inner wall edge. The entire Bees Quarter complex had been evacuated as a precautionary step. The pontoon bridge that spanned the moat-lake had been destroyed.

Mithila had a force of four thousand policemen and policewomen. Enough to maintain law and order for the hundred thousand citizens of the small kingdom. But against the Lankans, they were outnumbered five to two. Would they be able to thwart an attack from the Lankan bodyguards of Raavan?

Sita believed they could. A cornered animal fights back ferociously. The Mithilans were not fighting for conquest. Or wealth. Or ego. They were fighting for their lives. Fighting to save their city from annihilation. And this was not a traditional war being fought on open ground. The Mithilans were behind defensive walls; double walls in fact; a war-battlement innovation that had rarely been tried in other forts in the recent past. The Lankan generals were unlikely to have war-gamed this scenario. A lower ratio of soldiers was not such a huge disadvantage with this factor thrown in.

Ram and Sita had abandoned efforts to secure the outer wall. They wanted Raavan and his soldiers to scale it and launch an assault on the inner wall; the Lankans would, then, be trapped between the two walls, which the Mithilan arrows would convert into a killing field. They expected a volley of arrows from the other side too. In preparation for which the police had been asked to carry their wooden shields, normally used for crowd control within Mithila. Lakshman had quickly taught them some basic manoeuvres to protect themselves from the arrows.

'Where are the Malayaputras?' asked Lakshman.

Sita looked around, but did not answer. She knew the Malayaputras would not abandon her. She hoped they were carrying out last-minute parleys, laced with adequate threats and bribes, to convince the Lankans to back off.

Ram whispered to Lakshman, 'I think it's just us.'

Lakshman shook his head and spat, saying loudly, 'Cowards.'

Sita did not respond. She had learnt in the last few days that Lakshman was quite hot-headed. And she needed his short temper in the battle that was to follow.

'Look!' said Samichi.

Sita and Lakshman turned in the direction that Samichi had pointed.

Torches lined the other side of the moat-lake that surrounded the outer wall of Mithila. Raavan's bodyguards had worked feverishly through the evening, chopping down trees from the forest and building rowboats to carry them across the lake.

Even as they watched, the Lankans began to push their boats into the moat-lake. The assault on Mithila was being launched.

'It's time,' said Sita.

'Yes,' said Ram. 'We have maybe another half hour before they hit our outer wall.'

— ☌Ⰻ —

Conch shells resounded through the night, by now recognised as the signature sound of Raavan and his men. As they watched in the light of the flickering flames of torches, the Lankans propped giant ladders against the outer walls of Mithila.

'They are here,' said Ram.

Sita turned to her messenger and nodded.

Messages were relayed quickly down the line to the Mithila police-soldiers. Sita expected a shower of arrows from Raavan's archers. The Lankans would fire their arrows only as long as their soldiers were outside the outer wall. The shooting would stop the moment the Lankans climbed over. The archers would not risk hitting their own men.

A loud whoosh heralded the release of the arrows.

'Shields!' shouted Sita.

The Mithilans immediately raised their shields. Ready for the Lankan arrows that were about to rain down on them.

Sita's instincts kicked in. *Something's wrong with the sound. It's too strong even for thousands of arrows. Something much larger has been fired.*

Hiding behind her shield, she looked at Ram. She sensed that he too was troubled.

Their instincts were right.

Huge missiles rammed through the Mithilan defences with massive force. Desperate cries of agony along with sickening thuds were heard as shields were ripped through. Many in the Mithilan ranks were brought down in a flash.

'What is that?' screamed Lakshman, hiding behind his shield.

Sita saw Ram's wooden shield snap into two pieces as a missile tore through it like a hot knife through butter. It missed him by a hair's breadth.

Spears!

Their wooden shields were a protection against arrows, not large spears.

How can spears be flung to this distance?!

The first volley was over. Sita knew they had but a few moments before the next one. She lowered her shield and looked around, just as Ram did.

She heard Ram exclaim, 'Lord Rudra, be merciful ...'

The destruction was severe. At least a quarter of the Mithilans were either dead or heavily injured, impaled on massive spears that had brutally ripped through their shields and bodies.

Ram looked at Sita. 'Another volley will be fired any moment! Into the houses!'

'Into the houses!' shouted Sita.

'Into the houses!' repeated the lieutenants, as everybody ran towards the doors, lifted them, and jumped in. It was a most disorganised retreat, but it was effective. In a few minutes, practically every surviving Mithilan police soldier had jumped to safety within the houses. As the doors closed, the volley of spears resumed on the roofs of the Bees Quarter. A few stragglers were killed as the rest made it to safety; for now.

As soon as they were secure within a house, Ram pulled Sita aside. Lakshman and Samichi followed. Samichi looked ashen-faced and nervous as she stood behind her princess, helplessly rubbing her forehead.

Sita was breathing hard, her eyes flitting like that of a cornered tigress, anger bursting through every pore.

'What now?' Ram asked Sita. 'Raavan's soldiers must be scaling the outer walls. They will be upon us soon. There's no one to stop them.'

Sita had run out of ideas. She felt helpless. And livid. *Dammit!*

'Sita?' prompted Ram.

Sita's eyes suddenly opened wide. 'The windows!'

'What?' asked Samichi, surprised by her prime minister.

Sita immediately gathered her lieutenants around her. She ordered that the wood-panel seals on the windows of the houses be broken open; the ones that shared the inner fort wall.

The Bees Quarter windows overlooked the ground between the two fort walls. Sita had found her vantage point. Arrows would be fired at the charging Lankans, after all.

'Brilliant!' shouted Lakshman, as he rushed to a barricaded window. He pulled back his arm, flexed his muscles, and punched hard at the wood. Smashing the barricade with one mighty blow.

All the houses in this section of the Bees Quarter were internally connected through corridors. The message travelled rapidly. Within moments, the Mithilans smashed open the sealed windows and began firing arrows. The Lankans were caught between the outer and inner wall. They had expected no resistance. Caught off guard, the arrows shredded through their lines. The losses were heavy.

The Mithilans fired arrows without respite, killing as many of the Lankans as they could. Slowing the charge dramatically. Suddenly, the conch shells sounded; this time it was a different tune. The Lankans immediately turned and ran, retreating as rapidly as they had arrived.

A loud cheer went up from the Mithilan quarters. They had beaten back the first attack.

— ௳ㅅ —

Ram, Sita, and Lakshman stood on the roof of the Bees Quarter as dawn broke through. The gentle rays of the sun fell on the harsh devastation of Lankan spears. The damage was heart-rending.

Sita stared at the mutilated Mithilan corpses strewn all around her; heads hanging by sinew to bodies, some with their guts spilled out. Many simply impaled on spears, having bled to death.

'At least a thousand of my soldiers ...'

'We too have hit them hard, *Bhabhi*,' said Lakshman to his *sister-in-law*. 'There are at least a thousand dead Lankans lying between the inner and outer wall.'

Sita looked at Lakshman, her eyes brimming with tears. 'Yes, but they have nine thousand left. We have only three thousand.'

Ram surveyed the Lankan camp on the other side of the moat-lake. Sita's gaze followed his eyes. Hospital-tents had been set up to tend to the injured. Many Lankans, though, were furiously at work; hacking trees and pushing the forest line farther with mathematical precision.

Clearly, they did not intend to retreat to Lanka.

'They will be better prepared next time,' said Ram. 'If they manage to scale the inner wall ... it's over.'

Sita placed her hand on Ram's shoulder and sighed as she stared at the ground. She seemed to gather strength from the simple touch. It was like she had a dependable ally now.

Sita turned around and looked towards her city. Her eyes

rested on the steeple of the massive temple dedicated to Lord Rudra, which loomed beyond the garden of the Bees Quarter. Fierce determination blazed from her eyes, resolve pouring steel into her veins.

'It's not over yet. I'll call upon the citizens to join me. Even if my people stand here with kitchen knives, we will outnumber the Lankan scum ten to one. We can fight them.'

Sita could feel Ram's shoulder muscles tensing under her touch. She looked at his eyes. She saw only confidence and trust.

He believes in me. He trusts me to handle this. I will handle this. I will not fail.

Sita nodded, like she had made up her mind. And rushed away, signalling some of her lieutenants to follow her.

Ram and Lakshman followed her too, trying to keep pace. She turned around. 'No. Please stay here. I need someone I can trust, someone who understands war, to stay here and rally the forces in case the Lankans launch a surprise attack.'

Lakshman tried to argue, but fell silent at a signal from Ram.

'We will stay here, Sita,' said Ram. 'No Lankan will enter the city as long as we are standing here. Rally the others quickly.'

Sita smiled and touched Ram's hand.

Then she turned and ran.

— ᚱᚷ —

The third hour of the second *prahar* was almost ending. It was three hours before noon, in clear daylight. But this light had not blessed the city's residents with more wisdom. The news of the death of over one thousand courageous Mithilan policemen, and the devastation of the battle at the Bees Quarter, had not stirred the citizens to anger. Tales of the outnumbered and under-equipped Mithilan police, led by Prime Minister Sita, heroically fighting back the Lankans, had not inspired them. In fact, talks of surrender, compromise and negotiations were in the air.

Sita had gathered the local leaders in the market square in an effort to rally a citizen army to fight back the Lankans. This had been a few hours ago. That the rich would not think of risking their lives or property for their motherland wasn't surprising. It was shocking, though, that even the poor, who had benefited greatly from Sunaina's and then Sita's reforms, did not feel the need to fight for their kingdom.

Sita thought she would burst a capillary in utter fury, listening to the arguments being put forth by her fellow Mithilans; excuses to give a moral veneer to their cowardice.

'We must be pragmatic …'

'We haven't emerged from poverty, earned all this money, ensured good education for our children, built property, to just lose it all in one war …'

'Seriously, has violence ever solved any problem? We should practise love, not war …'

'War is just a patriarchal, upper-class conspiracy …'

'The Lankans are also human beings like us. I am sure they will listen, if we talk to them …'

'Really, is our conscience clean? We can say all we want about the Lankans, but didn't we insult Emperor Raavan at the swayamvar *…'*

'What's the big deal if so many police officers died? It's their job to protect us. And die for us. It isn't as if they are doing this for free. What do we pay taxes for? Speaking of taxes, Lanka apparently has much lower tax rates …'

'I think we should negotiate with the Lankans. Let's vote on that …'

At the end of her tether, Sita had even asked Janak and

Urmila to help her rouse the citizenry. Janak, respected as a saintly figure by the Mithilans, tried his best to urge them to fight. To no avail. Urmila, popular among the women, had no impact either.

Sita's fists were clenched tight. She was about to launch into an angry tirade against the cowardly citizenry when she felt a hand on her shoulder. She turned around to find Samichi standing there.

Sita quickly pulled her aside. 'Well, where are they?'

Samichi had been dispatched to find Vishwamitra or Arishtanemi. Sita refused to believe that the Malayaputras would abandon her at a time like this, especially when her city was threatened with annihilation. She was sure they knew she would die with her city. And she also knew that her survival mattered to them.

'I have searched everywhere, Sita,' said Samichi. 'I can't find them anywhere.'

Sita looked down and cursed under her breath.

Samichi swallowed hard. 'Sita …'

Sita looked at her friend.

'I know you don't want to hear this, but we're left with no choice. We must negotiate with the Lankans. If we can get Lord Raavan to …'

Sita's eyes flared up in anger. 'You will not say such things in my …'

Sita stopped mid-sentence as a loud sound was heard from the Bees Quarter.

There were some explosions from a section of the roof of the Bees Quarter, hidden from where the battle with the Lankans had taken place just a few hours ago. A few seconds later, a small missile flew up from the same section. It sped off in a mighty arc, moving farther and farther away in a few short seconds. Towards the city moat, where Sita knew the Lankans were camped.

Everyone in the market square was transfixed, their eyes glued in the same direction. But none had any idea of what had just happened. None, except Sita.

She immediately understood what the Malayaputras had been up to all night. What they had been preparing. What they had done.

The Asuraastra.

As the missile flew high above the moat-lake, there was a flash of a minor detonation. The *Asuraastra* hovered for an instant above the Lankan camp. And then exploded dramatically.

The spectators in Mithila saw a bright green flash of light emerge from the splintered missile. It burst with furious intensity, like a flash of lightning. Fragments of the exploded missile were seen falling down.

As they witnessed this terrifying scene play out in the sky, the ear-shattering sound of the main explosion shook the very walls of Mithila. Right up to the market square where the citizens had been debating themselves to paralysis a few moments back.

The Mithilans covered their ears in shock. Some began to pray for mercy.

An eerie silence fell on the gathering. Many cowering Mithilans looked around in dazed confusion.

But Sita knew Mithila had been saved. She also knew what would follow. Devastation had fallen on Raavan and his fellow Lankans. They would be paralysed. In a deep state of coma. For days, if not weeks. Some of them would even die.

But her city was safe. It had been saved.

After the reversal at the battle of the Bees Quarter, perhaps this had been the only way to stop Raavan's hordes.

As relief coursed through her veins, she whispered softly, 'Lord Rudra, bless the Malayaputras and Guru Vishwamitra.'

Then, like a bolt from the blue, her elation suddenly evaporated. Raw panic entered her heart.

Who had fired the Asuraastra?

She knew that an *Asuraastra* had to be fired from a substantial distance. And only an extremely capable archer could do so successfully. There were just three people in Mithila right now who could shoot an arrow from the distance required to ignite and launch an *Asuraastra*. Vishwamitra, Arishtanemi and ...

Ram ... Please ... No ... Lord Rudra, have mercy.

Sita began sprinting towards the Bees Quarter. Followed by Samichi and her bodyguards.

Chapter 24

Sita bounded up the stairway of the Bees Quarter, three steps at a time. A grim-faced Samichi followed close behind. She was up on the roof in no time. Even from the distance, she could see the devastation in the Lankan camp. Thousands lay prone on the ground. Deathly silent. Demonic clouds of green viscous gas had spread like a shroud over the paralysed Lankans.

There was not a whisper in the air. The humans had fallen silent. So had the animals. The birds had stopped chirping. The trees did not stir. Even the wind had died down. All in sheer terror of the fiendish weapon that had just been unleashed.

The only sound was a steady, dreadful hiss, like the battle-cry of a gigantic snake. It was the sound of the thick viscous green gas that continued to be emitted from the fragments of the exploded *Asuraastra* missile that had fallen to the ground.

Sita held her *Rudraaksh* pendant in fear. *Lord Rudra, have mercy.*

She saw Arishtanemi and the Malayaputras standing in a huddle. She ran up to them.

'Who shot it?' demanded Sita.

Arishtanemi merely bowed his head and stepped aside; and, Ram came into Sita's view. Her husband was the only one holding a bow.

Vishwamitra had managed to pressure Ram into firing the *Asuraastra*. And thus, breaking Lord Rudra's law.

Sita cursed loudly as she ran towards Ram.

Vishwamitra smiled as he saw her approach. 'Sita, it is all taken care of! Raavan's forces are destroyed. Mithila is safe!'

Sita glared at Vishwamitra, too furious for words.

She ran to her husband and embraced him. A shocked Ram dropped his bow. They had never embraced. Until now.

She held him tight. She could feel his heartbeat pick up speed. But his hands remained by his side. He did not embrace her back.

She pulled her head back and saw a solitary tear trickle down her husband's face.

Guilt gnawed at her. She knew Ram had been forced to commit a sin. Forced due to his love for her. Forced due to his sense of duty, which compelled him to protect the innocent: The citizens of Mithila, even if they were selfish and cowardly.

She held Ram and looked deep into his empty eyes. Her face was creased with concern. 'I am with you, Ram.'

Ram remained silent. But his expression had changed. His eyes didn't have an empty look anymore. Instead they had a dreamy sparkle, as if he were lost in another world.

Oh Lord Rudra, give me the strength to help him. To help this magnificent man. Suffering because of me.

Sita continued to hold Ram in a tight embrace. 'I am with you, Ram. We will handle this together.'

Ram closed his eyes. He wrapped his arms around his wife. He rested his head on her shoulder. She could hear him release a deep, long breath. Like he had found his refuge. His sanctuary.

Sita looked over her husband's shoulder and glared at Vishwamitra. It was a fearsome look, like the wrathful fury of the Mother Goddess.

Vishwamitra glared right back, unrepentant.

A loud sound disturbed them all. They looked beyond the walls of Mithila. Raavan's *Pushpak Vimaan* was sputtering to life. Its giant rotor blades had begun to spin. The sound it made was like that of a giant monster cutting the air with his enormous sword. Within moments the rotors picked up speed and the conical flying vehicle rose from the earth. It hovered just a few feet above the ground; pushing against inertia, against the earth's immense pull of gravity. Then, with a great burst of sound and energy, it soared into the sky. Away from Mithila. And the devastation of the *Asuraastra*.

Raavan had survived. Raavan had escaped.

— ॐ —

The following day, a makeshift *Ayuralay* was set up outside the city. The Lankan soldiers were housed in large tents. The Malayaputras trained the Mithilan doctors to tend to those who had been rendered comatose by the lethal weapon. To keep them alive till they naturally emerged from the coma; a few days or maybe even a few weeks later. Some would never surface and pass away in their sleep.

Sita sat in her office, contemplating Mithila's governance after her impending departure to Ayodhya. There was too much to take care of and the conversation with Samichi was not helping.

The police and protocol chief stood before her, shaking like a leaf. Sita had never seen her friend so nervous. She was clearly petrified.

'Don't worry, Samichi. I'll save Ram. Nothing will happen to him. He won't be punished.'

Samichi shook her head. Something else was on her mind. She spoke in a quivering voice. 'Lord Raavan survived... the Lankans... will come back... Mithila, you, I... we're finished ...'

'Don't be silly. Nothing will happen. The Lankans have been taught a lesson they will not forget in a hurry ...'

'They will remember... They always remember... Ayodhya... Karachapa... Chilika ...'

Sita held Samichi by her shoulders and said loudly, 'Pull yourself together. What's the matter with you? Nothing will happen!'

Samichi fell silent. She held her hands together in supplication. Praying. She knew what she had to do. She would appeal for mercy. To the True Lord.

Sita stared at Samichi and shook her head. Disappointed. She had decided to leave Samichi in charge of Mithila, under the titular rule of her father, Janak. Ensuring that there would be continuity in leadership. But now, she began to wonder whether Samichi was ready for additional responsibilities. She had never seen her friend so rattled before.

— ᚱᚷ —

'Arishtanemi*ji*, please don't make me do this,' pleaded Kushadhwaj.

Arishtanemi was in the section of the Mithila Palace allotted to Kushadhwaj, the king of Sankashya.

'You will have to,' said Arishtanemi, dangerously soft. The steel in his voice unmistakable. 'We know exactly what happened. How Raavan came here ...'

Kushadhwaj swallowed nervously.

'Mithila is precious to all who love wisdom,' said Arishtanemi. 'We will not allow it to be destroyed. You will have to pay for what you did.'

'But if I sign this proclamation, Raavan's assassins will target me ...'

'And if you don't, *we* will target you,' said Arishtanemi, stepping uncomfortably close, menace dripping from his eyes. 'Trust me, we will make it far more painful.'

'Arishtanemi*ji* ...'

'Enough.' Arishtanemi grabbed the royal Sankashya seal and pressed it on the proclamation sheet, leaving its imprint. 'It's done ...'

Kushadhwaj sagged on his seat, sweating profusely.

'It will be issued in the name of King Janak *and* you, Your Majesty,' said Arishtanemi, as he bowed his head in mock servility.

Then he turned and walked out.

— ॐ —

King Janak and his brother, King Kushadhwaj, had authorised the imprisonment of the Lankan prisoners of war left behind by Raavan. Vishwamitra and his Malayaputras had promised that they would take the Lankan prisoners with them when they left for Agastyakootam. The sage intended to negotiate with Raavan on Mithila's behalf, guaranteeing the kingdom's safety in return for the release of the prisoners of war.

This news had been greeted with relief by the Mithilans, and not the least, Samichi. They were petrified of the demon king of Lanka, Raavan. But now, the people felt more at ease knowing that the Malayaputras would ensure that the Lankans backed off.

'We're leaving tomorrow, Sita,' said Arishtanemi.

The military chief of the Malayaputras had come to Sita's chamber to speak with her in private. Sita had refused to meet Vishwamitra since the day Ram had fired the *daivi astra*.

Sita folded her hands together into a respectful *Namaste* and bowed her head. 'May Lord Parshu Ram and Lord Rudra bless you with a safe journey.'

'Sita, I am sure you are aware that the time to make the announcement draws close ...'

Arishtanemi was referring to the declaration that would publicly announce Sita's status as the Vishnu. Once it was made, not just the Malayaputras, but the whole of India would recognise her as the saviour who would lead the people of this land to a new way of life.

'It cannot happen now.'

Arishtanemi tried to control his frustration. 'Sita, you can't be so stubborn. We had to do what we did.'

'*You* could have fired the *Asuraastra*, Arishtanemi*ji*. In fact, Guru*ji* could have fired it as well. The Vayuputras would have understood. They would have even seen it as a Malayaputra effort to protect themselves. But you set Ram up ...'

'He volunteered, Sita.'

'R-i-g-h-t ...' said Sita, sarcastically. She had already heard from Lakshman how Vishwamitra had emotionally blackmailed Ram into firing the divine weapon, exhorting him to protect his wife's city.

'Sita, have you forgotten what state Mithila was in? You are not appreciating the fact that we saved your city. You are not even appreciating the fact that Guru Vishwamitra will handle the crisis with Raavan, ensuring that you do not face any retaliation after what happened here. Seriously, what more do you expect?'

'I would have expected you to behave with ...'

Arishtanemi interrupted Sita, guessing what she would have said. '*Honour?* Behave with honour? Don't be childish, Sita. What I have always liked about you is the fact that you are practical. You are not taken by silly theoretical ideas. You know you can do a lot for India. You must agree to make the announcement of your Vishnuhood ...'

Sita raised an eyebrow. 'I wasn't talking about honour. I was talking about wisdom.'

'Sita ...' growled Arishtanemi, clenching his fists. He took a deep breath to control himself. 'Wisdom dictated that we not fire the *Asuraastra*. There are ... We have enough problems with the Vayuputras already. This would have further complicated our relationship. It had to be Ram.'

'Right,' said Sita. 'It *had* to be Ram ...'

Is she worried about Ram being punished for firing the Asuraastra?

'Ram will not be banished, Sita. The *Asuraastra* is not a weapon of mass destruction. Guru*ji* has already told you. We can manage the Vayuputras ...'

Arishtanemi knew the Vayuputras liked Ram and would probably agree to waive the punishment for the eldest prince of Ayodhya. And if they didn't ... Well, the Malayaputras wouldn't be too troubled by that. Their main concern was Sita. Only Sita.

'Ram believes that he should be punished,' said Sita. 'It is the law.'

'Then, tell him to grow up and not be silly.'

'Try and understand Ram, Arishtanemi*ji*. I am not sure you realise how important a man like that is for India. He can transform us into law-abiding citizens. He can lead by example. He can do a lot of good. I have travelled the length and breadth of this country. I don't think the ruling nobility, including yourselves, understand the simmering anger among the common folk against the elite. Ram, by subjecting himself to the same laws that apply to them, increases the credibility of the establishment. People will eventually listen to a message delivered by Ram.'

Arishtanemi shifted on his feet, impatiently. 'This is a pointless conversation, Sita. The Malayaputras, the only ones authorised to recognise a Vishnu, have chosen you. That's it.'

Sita smiled. 'Indians don't take kindly to choices imposed from above. This is a country of rebels. The people have to accept me as the Vishnu.'

Arishtanemi remained silent.

'Perhaps you didn't understand the point I was trying to make earlier about wisdom,' said Sita.

Arishtanemi frowned.

'I suppose the Malayaputras want to keep Raavan alive till, at some stage, I kill him and hence am accepted by all Sapt Sindhuans. Who would deny a leader who delivers them from their most hated enemy ... Raavan.'

Arishtanemi's eyes widened, as he understood what Sita was saying. The Malayaputras had just committed a major blunder. That too on a strategy that they had been planning for decades.

'Yes, Arishtanemi*ji*. You thought you were setting Ram up for punishment. But instead, you have made him into a hero for the common man. The entire Sapt Sindhu has suffered Raavan's economic squeeze. And they now see Ram as their saviour.'

Arishtanemi fell silent.

'Arishtanemi*ji*, sometimes, a too-clever-by-half plan can backfire,' said Sita.

— ॐ —

Sita looked at her husband as he rode beside her. Lakshman and Urmila rode behind them. Lakshman was talking non-stop with his wife as she gazed at him earnestly. Urmila's thumb kept playing with the massive diamond ring on her left forefinger; an expensive gift from her husband. Behind them were a hundred Mithilan soldiers. Another hundred soldiers rode ahead of Ram and Sita. The convoy was on its way to Sankashya, from where it would sail to Ayodhya.

Ram, Sita, Lakshman, and Urmila had set off from Mithila two weeks after the *Asuraastra* laid waste the Lankan camp. True to their word, Vishwamitra and his Malayaputras had left for their capital, Agastyakootam, taking the Lankan prisoners with them. They would negotiate with Raavan on Mithila's behalf, guaranteeing the kingdom's safety in return for the release of the prisoners of war. The Malayaputras had also taken the bow of Lord Rudra, the *Pinaka*, which had been their treasure for centuries. It would be returned to Sita when she took on the role of the Vishnu.

Noting Samichi's improved state of mind, once the Lankan problem had been taken care of, Sita had made her friend Mithila's *de facto* prime minister. She would work in consultation with a council of five city elders established by Sita. Of course, all under the guidance of King Janak.

'Ram ...'

Ram turned to his wife with a smile as he pulled his horse close to hers. 'Yes?'

'Are you sure about this?'

Ram nodded. There was no doubt in his mind.

Sita was impressed and worried at the same time. He truly did live by the law.

'But you are the first in a generation to defeat Raavan. And, it wasn't really a *daivi astra*. If you —'

Ram frowned. 'That's a technicality. And you know it.'

Sita paused for a few seconds and continued. 'Sometimes, to create a perfect world, a leader has to do what is necessary at the time; even if it may not appear to be the 'right' thing to do in the short term. In the long run, a leader who has the capacity to uplift the masses must not deny himself that opportunity. He has a duty to not make himself unavailable. A true leader will even take a sin upon his soul for the good of his people.'

Ram looked at Sita. He seemed disappointed. 'I have done that already, haven't I? The question is, should I be punished for it or not? Should I do penance for it? If I expect my people to follow the law, so must I. A leader is not just one who leads. He must also be a role model. He must practise what he preaches, Sita.'

Sita smiled. 'Well, Lord Rudra had said: "A leader is not just one who gives his people what they want. He must also be the one who teaches his people to be better than they imagined themselves to be."'

Ram smiled too. 'And I'm sure you will tell me Lady Mohini's response to this as well.'

Sita laughed. 'Yes. Lady Mohini said that people have their limitations. A leader should not expect more from them than what they are capable of. If you stretch them beyond their capacity, they will break.'

Ram shook his head. He did not agree with the great Lady Mohini. Ram expected people to rise above their limitations and better themselves; for only then was an ideal society possible. But he didn't voice his disagreement aloud. He knew that Sita passionately respected Lady Mohini.

'Are you sure? Fourteen years outside the boundaries of

the Sapt Sindhu?' Sita looked at Ram seriously, returning to the original discussion.

Ram nodded. 'I broke Lord Rudra's law. And this is his stated punishment. It doesn't matter whether the Vayuputras pass the order to punish me or not. It doesn't matter whether my people support me or not. I must serve my sentence.'

She smiled. *He will not stray. He is truly incredible. How did he survive in Ayodhya all these years?*

Sita leaned towards him and whispered, 'We ... not I.'

Ram frowned.

Sita reached out and placed her palm on Ram's hand. 'You share my fate and I share yours. That is what a true marriage is.' She entwined her fingers through his. 'Ram, I am your wife. We will always be together; in good times and bad; through thick and thin.'

We will come back in fourteen years. Stronger. More powerful. The Vishnuhood can wait till then.

She had already decided that she would ask Jatayu for large quantities of the legendary *Somras*, the anti-ageing medicine created by the great Indian scientist, Brahma, many millennia ago. She would administer the medicine to Ram and herself to retain their vitality and youth in their fourteen years of exile. So that when they returned, they would be ready for the task ahead. Ready to change India.

She remembered a line she had read. A line supposedly spoken by Lady Varahi, the third Vishnu. *India will rise, but not for selfish reasons. It will rise for Dharma ... For the Good of all.*

She looked at Ram and smiled.

Ram squeezed her hand. His horse snorted and quickened its pace. Ram pulled back the reins gently, keeping it in step with his wife's steed.

Chapter 25

The two young couples sailed into the Ayodhya port to an overwhelming sight. It was as if all of Ayodhya had stepped out of their homes to greet them.

Sita had enjoyed her conversations with Ram during their journey. They had brainstormed on how best an empire can be organised for the good of the people. She had spoken about the concept that the state compulsorily adopt young children to break the evils of the birth-based caste system. Sita had not mentioned that she had grown to believe in the idea relatively recently; or that it was originally Vishwamitra's idea. Ram did not like or trust the Maharishi. Why taint a good idea with that dislike? They had also spoken about the *Somras* mass-manufacturing technology developed by Guru Vashishtha. Ram believed that the *Somras* should either be made available to all or none. Since taking away the *Somras* might be difficult, he suggested that Vashishtha's technology be used to make it available to all.

Enjoyable as those conversations had been, Sita knew they would probably not find the time to have more of them for a while. Ram had his work cut out in Ayodhya. To begin with, he had to ensure that he was not stopped from going on exile.

And, of course, he also had to explain his marriage to the adopted princess of the powerless kingdom of Mithila. Jatayu had quipped to Sita, that had the Ayodhyans known that she was the Vishnu, they would have realised that Ram had married up! Sita had simply smiled and dismissed his observation.

Standing at the ship's balustrade, Sita looked at the grand, yet crumbling, port of Ayodhya. It was several times larger than the Sankashya port. She observed the barricaded man-made channel that allowed the waters of the Sarayu River to flow into the massive Grand Canal that surrounded *Ayodhya*, the *unconquerable city*.

The canal had been built a few centuries ago, during the reign of Emperor Ayutayus, by drawing in the waters of the feisty Sarayu River. Its dimensions were almost celestial. Stretching over fifty kilometres, it circumnavigated the third and outermost wall of the city of Ayodhya. It was enormous in breadth as well, extending to about two-and-a-half kilometres across the banks. Its storage capacity was so massive that for the first few years of its construction, many kingdoms downriver had complained of water shortages. Their objections had been crushed with brute force by the powerful Ayodhyan warriors.

One of the main purposes of this canal was militaristic. It was, in a sense, a moat. To be fair, it could be called the Moat of Moats, protecting the city from all sides. Prospective attackers would have to row across a moat with river-like dimensions. The fools would be out in the open, vulnerable to a barrage of missiles from the high walls of the unconquerable city. Four bridges spanned the canal in the four cardinal directions. The roads that emerged from these bridges led into the city through four massive gates in the outermost wall: North Gate, East

Gate, South Gate and West Gate. Each bridge was divided into two sections. Each section had its own tower and drawbridge, thus offering two levels of defence at the canal itself.

Even so, to consider this Grand Canal a mere defensive structure was to do it a disservice. It also worked as an effective flood-control mechanism, as water from the tempestuous Sarayu could be led in through control-gates. Floods were a recurrent problem in India. Furthermore, its placid surface made drawing water relatively easy, as compared to taking it directly from the feisty Sarayu. Smaller canals radiated out of the Grand Canal into the hinterland of Ayodhya, increasing the productivity of farming dramatically. The increase in agricultural yield allowed many farmers to free themselves from the toil of tilling the land. Only a few were enough to feed the massive population of the entire kingdom of Kosala. This surplus labour transformed into a large army, trained by talented generals into a brilliant fighting unit. The army conquered more and more of the surrounding lands, till the great Lord Raghu, the grandfather of the present Emperor Dashrath, finally subjugated the entire Sapt Sindhu; thus, becoming the *Chakravarti Samrat* or *Universal Emperor*.

Dashrath too had built on this proud legacy, conquering far and wide to become a Chakravarti Samrat as well. That was until the demon of Lanka, Raavan, destroyed the combined might of the Sapt Sindhuan armies at Karachapa around twenty years ago.

The subsequent punitive trade levies that Raavan had imposed on all the kingdoms of the Sapt Sindhu, and mostly on Ayodhya, had sucked the treasury dry. It showed in the crumbling grandeur of the Grand Canal and its surrounding structures.

Despite its obviously fading glory, Ayodhya overwhelmed Sita. The city was bigger than any other in the Sapt Sindhu. Even in its decline, Ayodhya was many times grander than her Mithila. She had visited Ayodhya in the past, but incognito. This was the first time she was visible to all. Being gawked at. Being judged. She could see it in the eyes of the nobles and citizenry standing at a distance, held back by the Ayodhya royal bodyguards.

The gangplank hit the port deck with a loud bang, clearing her mind of the profusion of thoughts. A rakishly handsome man was bounding up the plank. He was shorter than Ram but far more muscular.

This must be Bharat.

He was closely followed by a diminutive, immaculately attired man with calm, intelligent eyes. He walked with slow, measured steps.

Shatrughan …

'*Dada!*' hollered Bharat, as he ran up to Ram and embraced him.

Sita could see why Radhika had fallen for Bharat. He had obvious charisma.

'My brother,' smiled Ram, as he embraced Bharat.

As Bharat stepped back and embraced Lakshman, Shatrughan quietly embraced his eldest brother.

Within a flash, the four brothers were facing Sita and Urmila.

Ram held his hand out and said with simple pride, 'This is my wife, Sita, and next to her is Lakshman's wife, Urmila.'

Shatrughan smiled warmly and folded his hands together. '*Namaste*. It is an honour to meet both of you.'

Bharat smacked Shatrughan on his stomach. 'You are

too formal, Shatrughan.' He stepped forward and embraced Urmila. 'Welcome to the family.'

Urmila smiled, her nervousness dissipating a bit.

Then Bharat stepped towards his *elder sister-in-law,* Sita, and held her hands. 'I have heard a lot about you, *Bhabhi* ... I always thought it would be impossible for my brother to find a woman better than him.' He looked at Ram, grinned and turned his attention back to her. 'But my *dada* has always had the ability to manage the impossible.'

Sita laughed softly.

Bharat embraced his sister-in-law. 'Welcome to the family, *Bhabhi.*'

— ௬ ⅄ —

The roads of Ayodhya were clogged with people waiting to receive their crown prince. A few had even extended their enthusiasm to welcome his bride. The procession inched forward at a snail's pace. The lead chariot had Ram and Sita. The prince was awkwardly acknowledging the wild cheering in the streets. Two chariots followed behind them. One had Bharat and Shatrughan, while Lakshman and his wife Urmila rode the second. Bharat flamboyantly acknowledged the multitude, waving his hands and blowing kisses with trademark flourish. Lakshman waved his trunk-like arms carefully, lest he hurt the petite Urmila, who stood demurely by his side. Shatrughan, as always, stood stoic, unmoved. Staring into the throngs. Almost like he was academically studying crowd behaviour.

The chanting of the crowd was loud and clear.

Ram!

Bharat!

Lakshman!

Shatrughan!

Their four beloved princes, the protectors of the kingdom, were finally together again. And most importantly, their crown prince had returned. *Victorious!* The defeater of the hated Raavan had returned!

Flowers were strewn, holy rice was showered, all were gay and happy. Though it was daytime, the massive stone lamp towers were lit up festively. Many had placed lamps on the parapets of their homes. Resplendent sunshine blazed with glory, as if in obeisance to the prince from the great clan of the Sun God himself. Ram of the Suryavanshis!

It took four hours for the chariots to traverse a distance that normally took less than thirty minutes. They finally reached the wing of the palace allocated to Ram.

A visibly weak Dashrath sat on his travelling throne, with Kaushalya standing next to him, waiting for his sons. A proper welcome ceremony had been laid out to receive the new brides. The eldest queen was a scrupulous upholder of tradition and rituals.

Kaikeyi had not deigned to reply to the invitation sent by Kaushalya, regarding the welcoming ceremony. Sumitra, of peace-loving Kashi, stood on the other side of Dashrath. Kaushalya leaned on her for support, always. Of course, Sumitra too was welcoming home a daughter-in-law!

Loud conch shells were heard as the *swagatam* ceremony began at the palace gate.

The four princes of Ayodhya and the two princesses of Mithila finally emerged from the melee. The Ayodhya royal guards, nervous as cats on a hot metal roof, heaved a visible sigh of relief as the royal youngsters entered the palace compound. Away from the multitude.

The royal procession moved along the elegant, marble-encrusted walkway in the compound. Verdant gardens were laid out on both sides. They slowed on reaching the entrance of Prince Ram's wing of the palace.

Sita hesitated as her eyes fell on Kaushalya. But she dismissed the thought that had struck her.

Kaushalya walked to the threshold holding the *puja thali* in her hands. It contained a lit lamp, a few grains of rice and some vermilion. She looped the *prayer plate* in small circles, seven times, around Sita's face. She picked up some rice and threw it in the air, above Sita's head. She took a pinch of vermilion and smeared it on Sita's parting on the hairline. Sita bent down to touch Kaushalya's feet in respect. Kaushalya handed the *thali* to an attendant, and placed her hands on Sita's head and blessed her. '*Ayushman bhav*, my child.'

As Sita straightened, Kaushalya indicated Dashrath. 'Accept your father-in-law's blessings.' Pointing towards Sumitra, she continued, 'And then, from your *chhoti maa*. We will then do the other ceremonies.'

Sita moved ahead to follow Kaushalya's instructions. Ram stepped forward and touched his mother's feet. She blessed him quickly and indicated that he seek his father's blessings.

Then she beckoned Urmila and Lakshman. Urmila, unlike Sita, did not dismiss the thought; the same one that had struck Sita earlier.

Kaushalya reminded her of her mother Sunaina. She had the same diminutive appearance and calm, gentle eyes. Kaushalya's skin was darker and her facial features were different, no doubt. Nobody could say that they were related. But there was something similar about them. The spiritually inclined would call it a soul connection.

Urmila waited for Kaushalya to finish the *aarti* ceremony, then bent down to touch her feet. Kaushalya blessed the younger princess of Mithila. As Urmila rose, she impulsively stepped forward and embraced Kaushalya. The Queen of Ayodhya was surprised at this unorthodox behaviour and failed to react.

Urmila pulled back, her eyes moist with emotion. She faintly voiced a word she had been unable to utter without crying, since Sunaina had died. '*Maa.*'

Kaushalya was moved by the innocence of sweet Urmila. Perhaps for the first time, the queen faced a woman shorter than herself. She looked at the round baby face, dominated by large child-like eyes. An image rose in her mind of a tiny sparrow that needed protection from the big, threatening birds around it. She smiled fondly, and pulled Urmila back into her arms. 'My child ... Welcome home.'

— ⟨ ⟩ —

A palace maid in the service of Queen Kaushalya stood, head bowed. Waiting for her instructions.

She was in the residential office of Manthara, the richest businesswoman in Ayodhya; arguably, the richest in the Sapt Sindhu. Rumours suggested that Manthara was even richer than Emperor Dashrath. Druhyu, her closest aide, could swear that there was substance to these rumours. Indeed. Very substantial substance.

'My Lady,' whispered the maid, 'what are my instructions?'

The maid fell silent, as Druhyu signalled her discreetly. She waited.

Druhyu stood submissively next to Manthara. Silent.

The disfigured Manthara sat on a specially designed chair that offered a measure of comfort to her hunched back. The scars on her face, remnants of a childhood affliction of small pox, gave her a forbidding appearance. At the age of eleven she had fallen ill with polio, leaving her right foot partially paralysed. Born to poverty, her physical disfiguration had added prejudice, not sympathy, to her formative years. She had, in fact, been teased mercilessly. Now that she was rich and powerful, no one dared say anything to her face. But she knew exactly what was said about her behind her back. For now, she was not only reviled for her deformed body, but also hated fiercely for being a Vaishya; for being a very rich businessperson.

Manthara looked out of the window to the large garden of her palatial estate.

The maid fidgeted impatiently on her feet. Her absence would be noticed in the palace before long. She had to return quickly. She cast a pleading look at Druhyu. He glared back.

Druhyu had begun to doubt the usefulness of remaining loyal to Manthara. The woman had lost her beloved daughter, Roshni, to a horrific gangrape and murder. The gang had been tried by the courts and executed. However, Dhenuka, the most vicious of them all, and the leader of the gang, had been let off on a legal technicality. He was a juvenile; and, according to Ayodhyan law, juveniles could not be awarded the death penalty. Ram, the prince of Ayodhya and chief of police, had insisted that the law be followed. *No matter what.* Manthara had sworn vengeance. Spending huge amounts of money, she had ferreted Dhenuka from jail and had had him killed in a slow, brutal manner. But her thirst for vengeance had not been quenched. Her target now was Ram. She had been patiently waiting for an opportunity. And one had just presented itself.

Druhyu stared at his mistress, his face devoid of expression.

The old bat has been wasting too much money on her revenge mission. It is affecting business. She has lost it completely. But what can I do? Nobody knows the condition of the True Lord. *I am stuck with her for now …*

Manthara made up her mind. She looked at Druhyu and nodded.

Druhyu rocked back with shock, but controlled himself.

One thousand gold coins! That's more than this miserable palace maid will earn in ten years!

But he knew there was no point arguing. He quickly made a *hundi* in lieu of cash. The maid could encash it anywhere. After all, who would refuse a *credit document* with Manthara's seal?

'My Lady …' whispered Druhyu.

Manthara leaned forward, pulled out her seal from the pouch tied to her *dhoti*, and pressed its impression on the document.

Druhyu handed the *hundi* to the maid, whose face could barely contain her ecstasy.

Druhyu quickly brought her down to earth. His cold eyes pinned on her, he whispered, 'Remember, if the information does not come on time or isn't true, we know where you live …'

'I will not fail, sir,' said the maid.

As the maid turned to leave, Manthara said, 'I've been told that Prince Ram will soon be visiting Queen Kaushalya's wing of the palace to speak with Emperor Dashrath.'

'I will inform you about everything that is discussed, My Lady,' said the maid, bowing low.

Druhyu looked at Manthara and then the palace maid. He sighed inwardly. He knew that more money would be paid out soon.

— ᳵ —

'Didi, just my section of the palace here is bigger than the entire Mithila palace,' said Urmila excitedly.

Urmila had carefully guided her maids in settling her belongings in her husband's chambers. Having put them to work, she had quickly rushed to meet Sita. Lakshman had been tempted to ask his wife to stay, but gave in to her desire to seek comfort in her sister's company. Her life had changed dramatically in a short span of time.

Sita smiled, as she patted her sister's hand. She still hadn't told Urmila that Ram and she would be leaving the palace shortly, to return only after fourteen years. Urmila would be left behind, without her beloved sister, here in this magnificent palace.

Why trouble her right now? Let her settle in first.

'How are things with Lakshman?' asked Sita.

Urmila smiled dreamily. 'He is such a gentleman. He does not say no to anything that I ask for!'

Sita laughed, teasing her sister gently. 'That's exactly what you need. An indulgent husband, who treats you like a little princess!'

Urmila indicated her diminutive structure, straightened her back and retorted with mock seriousness, 'But I am a little princess!'

The sisters burst into peals of laughter. Sita embraced Urmila. 'I love you, my little princess.'

'I love you too, *Didi*,' said Urmila.

Just then, the doorman knocked and announced loudly, 'The Queen of Sapt Sindhu and Ayodhya, the Mother of the Crown Prince, Her Majesty Kaushalya. All rise in respect and love.'

Sita looked at Urmila, surprised. The sisters immediately came to their feet.

Kaushalya walked in briskly, followed by two maids bearing large golden bowls, the contents of which were covered with silk cloths.

Kaushalya looked at Sita and smiled politely, 'How are you, my child?'

'I am well, *Badi Maa*,' said Sita.

The sisters bent to touch Kaushalya's feet in respect. The Queen of Ayodhya blessed them both with a long life.

Kaushalya turned to Urmila with a warm smile. Sita noticed that it was warmer than the one she had received. This was a smile suffused with maternal love.

Sita smiled. Happy. *My little sister is safe here.*

'Urmila, my child,' said Kaushalya, 'I had gone to your chambers. I was told I would find you here.'

'Yes, *Maa*.'

'I believe you like black grapes.'

Urmila blinked in surprise. 'How did you know, *Maa*?'

Kaushalya laughed, with a conspiratorial look. 'I know everything!'

As Urmila laughed delicately, the queen pulled away the silk cloths with a flourish, to reveal two golden bowls filled to the brim with black grapes.

Urmila squealed in delight and clapped her hands. She opened her mouth. Sita was surprised. Urmila had always asked to be fed by their mother, Sunaina; but not once had she asked her sister.

Sita's eyes moistened in happiness. Her sister had found a mother once again.

Kaushalya picked a grape and dropped it into Urmila's open mouth.

'Mmm,' said Urmila, 'It is awesome, *Maa*!'

'And, grapes are good for your health too!' said Kaushalya. She looked at her elder daughter-in-law. 'Why don't you have some, Sita?'

'Of course, *Badi Maa*,' said Sita. 'Thank you.'

Chapter 26

A few days later, Sita sat in solitude in the royal garden.

It lay adjunct to the palace, within the compound walls. Laid out in the style of a botanical reserve, it was filled with flowering trees from not only the Sapt Sindhu but other great empires of the world. Its splendid diversity was also the source of its beauty, reflecting the composite character of the people of the Sapt Sindhu. Winding paths bordered what had once been a carefully laid out lush carpet of dense grass in geometric symmetry. Alas, like the main palace and the courts, the royal garden also had the appearance of diminishing grandeur and patchy upkeep. It was, literally, going to seed; a sorry reminder of Ayodhya's depleting resources.

But Sita was neither admiring the aching beauty nor mourning the slow deterioration that surrounded her.

Ram had gone to speak with Dashrath and his mother. He would insist that he be punished for the crime of using the *daivi astra* in Mithila without Vayuputra authorisation.

While that was Ram's conversation to handle, Sita was busy making plans to ensure that their lives would not be endangered in the jungle. She had asked Jatayu to meet her outside the city. She would ask him to shadow them during the exile, along with his team. She had no idea how the Malayaputras would react to her request. She knew that they were upset with her for refusing to be recognised publicly as the Vishnu. But she also knew that Jatayu was loyal to her and would not refuse.

'The revenue of a hundred villages for your thoughts, *Bhabhi* ...'

Sita turned to see Bharat standing behind her. She laughed. 'The revenue of a hundred villages from your wealthy Kosala or my poor Mithila?'

Bharat laughed and sat next to her.

'So, have you managed to talk some sense into *dada*?' asked Bharat. 'To make him drop his insistence on being exiled?'

'What makes you think that I don't agree with him?'

Bharat was surprised. 'Well, I thought ... Actually, I have done some background check on you, *Bhabhi* ... I was told that you are very ...'

'Pragmatic?' asked Sita, completing Bharat's statement.

He smiled. 'Yes ...'

'And, what makes you think that your brother's path is not pragmatic?'

Bharat was at a loss for words.

'I am not suggesting that your brother is being pragmatic consciously. Just that the path he has chosen — one of unbridled commitment to the law — may not *appear* pragmatic. But counter-intuitively, it may actually be the most pragmatic course for some sections of our society.'

'Really?' Bharat frowned. 'How so?'

'This is a time of vast change, Bharat. It can be exciting. Energising. But many are unsettled by change. The Sapt Sindhu society has foolishly decided to hate its Vaishyas. They see their businessmen as criminals and thieves. It is over-simplistic to assume that the only way a Vaishya makes money is through cheating and profiteering. It is also biased. Such radicalisation increases in times of change and uncertainty. The fact is that while a few businessmen may be crooks, most Vaishyas are hardworking, risk-taking, opportunity-seeking organisers. If they do not prosper, then society does not produce wealth. And if a society does not generate money, most people remain poor. Which leads to frustration and unrest.'

'I agree with …'

'I am not finished.'

Bharat immediately folded his hands together into a *Namaste*. 'Sorry, *Bhabhi*.'

'People can adjust to poverty, if they have wisdom and knowledge. But even Brahmins command very little respect in India these days. They may not be resented like the Vaishyas, but it is true that the Brahmins, or even the path of knowledge, are not respected today. I know what people say about my knowledge-obsessed father, for instance.'

'No, I don't think …'

'I'm still not finished,' said Sita, her eyes twinkling with amusement.

'Sorry!' Bharat surrendered, as he covered his mouth with his hand.

'As a result, people do not listen to the learned. They hate the Vaishyas and in the process, have ensured poverty for themselves. The people who are idealised the most today are the Kshatriyas, the warriors. "Battle-honour" is an end in itself! There's hatred for money, disdain for wisdom and love of violence. What can you expect in this atmosphere?'

Bharat remained silent.

'You can speak now,' said Sita.

Bharat removed the hand that covered his mouth and said, 'When you speak about the need to respect the Vaishya, Brahmin, or Kshatriya way of life, you obviously mean the characteristics and not the people born into that caste, right?'

Sita wrinkled her nose. 'Obviously. Do you really think I would support the evil birth-based caste system? Our present caste system must be destroyed ...'

'On that, I agree with you.'

'So, coming back to my question. In an atmosphere of hatred for money-makers, disdain for wisdom-givers, and love only for war and warriors, what would you expect?'

'Radicalisation. Especially among young men. Usually, they are the biggest fools.'

Sita laughed. 'They are not *all* foolish ...'

Bharat nodded. 'You're right, I suppose. I am a young man too!'

'So, you have a situation where young men, and frankly some women too, are radicalised. There is intelligence, but little wisdom. There is poverty. There is love of violence. They don't understand that the absence of balance in their society is at the root of their problems. They look for simplistic, quick solutions. And they hate anyone who doesn't think like them.'

'Yes.'

'Is it any surprise then that crime is so high in the Sapt Sindhu? Is it any surprise that there is so much crime against women? Women can be talented and competitive in the fields of knowledge, trading and labour. But when it comes to violence, the almighty has not blessed them with a natural advantage.'

'Yes.'

'These radicalised, disempowered, violence-loving youth,

looking for simplistic solutions, attack the weak. It makes them feel strong and powerful. They are especially vulnerable to the authoritarian message of the Masculine way of life, which can lead them astray. Thus, creating chaos in society.'

'And, you don't think *dada's* ideas are rooted in the Masculine way? Don't you think they're a little too simplistic? And, too top-down? Shouldn't the solution be the way of the Feminine? To allow freedom? To let people find balance on their own?'

'But Bharat, many are wary of the uncertainties of the Feminine way. They prefer the simple predictability of the Masculine way. Of following a uniform code without too much thought. Even if that code is made by others. Yes, Ram's obsession with the law is simplistic. Some may even call it authoritarian. But there is merit in it. He will give direction to those youth who need the certainties of the Masculine way of life. Radicalised young people can be misused by a demonic force in pursuit of endless violence and hatred. On the other hand, Ram's teachings can guide such people to a life of order, justice, and fairness. He can harness them for a greater good. I am not suggesting that your elder brother's path is for everyone. But he can provide leadership to those who seek order, certainty, compliance, and definite morals. To those who have a strong dislike of decadence and debauchery. He can save them from going down a path of hatred and violence and instead, build them into a force for the good of India.'

Bharat remained silent.

'Ram's true message can provide an answer, a solution, to the radicalisation that plagues so many young people today.'

Bharat leaned back. 'Wow ...'

'What's the matter?'

'I have argued with my brother all my life about his faith

in the Masculine way. I always thought that the Masculine way will inevitably lead to fanaticism and violence. But you have opened my mind in just one conversation.'

'Seriously, can you say that the Feminine way never degenerates? The only difference, Bharat, is that it deteriorates differently. The Masculine way is ordered, efficient and fair at its best, but fanatical and violent at its worst. The Feminine way is creative, passionate and caring at its best, but decadent and chaotic at its worst. No one way of life is better or worse. They both have their strengths and weaknesses.'

'Hmmm.'

'Freedom is good, but in moderation. Too much of it is a recipe for disaster. That's why the path I prefer is that of Balance. Balance between the Masculine and the Feminine.'

'I think differently.'

'Tell me.'

'I believe there is no such thing as too much freedom. For freedom has, within itself, the tools for self-correction.'

'Really?'

'Yes. In the Feminine way, when things get too debauched and decadent, many who are disgusted by it, use the same freedom available to them, to revolt and speak out loud. When society is made aware, and more importantly, is in agreement, reforms will begin. No problem remains hidden in a Feminine society for too long. But Masculine societies can remain in denial for ages because they simply do not have the freedom to question and confront their issues. The Masculine way is based on compliance and submission to the code, the law. The questioning spirit is killed; and with that, the ability to identify and solve their problems before they lead to chaos. Have you ever wondered why the Mahadevs, who had come to solve problems that nobody else could, usually had to fight whoever represented the Masculine force?'

Sita rocked back. She was startled into silence, as she considered what Bharat had said about the Mahadevs. *Oh yes ... He's right ...*

'Freedom is the ultimate answer. Despite all the uncertainties it creates, freedom allows regular readjustment. Which is why, very rarely does a problem with the Feminine way become so big that it needs a Mahadev to solve it. This magical solution is simply not available to the Masculine way. The first thing it suppresses is freedom. Everyone must comply ... Or, be kicked out.'

'You may have a point. But freedom without laws is chaos. I'm not sure ...'

Bharat interrupted his sister-in-law, 'I am telling you, *Bhabhi*. Freedom is the ultimate silver arrow; the answer to everything. It may appear chaotic and difficult to manage on the surface. I agree that laws can be flexibly used to ensure that there isn't *too much* chaos. But there is no problem that cannot ultimately be solved if you grant freedom to a sufficiently large number of argumentative and rebellious people. Which is why I think freedom is the most important attribute of life, *Bhabhi*.'

'More important than the law?'

'Yes. I believe there should be as few laws as possible; enough just to provide a framework within which human creativity can express itself in all its glory. Freedom is the natural way of life.'

Sita laughed softly. 'And what does your elder brother have to say about your views?'

Ram walked up to them from behind and placed his hands on his wife's shoulders. 'His elder brother thinks that Bharat is a dangerous influence!'

Ram had gone to his wing of the palace and had been told that his wife was in the royal gardens. He had found her deep in conversation with Bharat. They had not noticed him walk up to them.

Bharat burst out laughing as he rose to embrace his brother. '*Dada* ...'

'Should I be thanking you for entertaining your *bhabhi* with your libertarian views?!'

Bharat smiled as he shrugged. 'At least I won't convert the citizens of Ayodhya into a bunch of bores!'

Ram laughed and said, tongue in cheek, 'That's good then!'

Bharat's expression instantly transformed and became sombre. 'Father is not going to let you go, *Dada*. Even you know that. You're not going anywhere.'

'Father doesn't have a choice. And neither do you. You will rule Ayodhya. And you will rule it well.'

'I will not ascend the throne this way,' said Bharat, shaking his head. 'No, I will not.'

Ram knew that there was nothing he could say that would ease Bharat's pain.

'*Dada*, why are you insisting on this?' asked Bharat.

'It's the law, Bharat,' said Ram. 'I fired a *daivi astra*.'

'The hell with the law, *Dada*! Do you actually think your leaving will be in the best interests of Ayodhya? Imagine what the two of us can achieve together; your emphasis on rules and mine on freedom and creativity. Do you think either you or I can be as effective alone?'

Ram shook his head. 'I'll be back in fourteen years, Bharat. Even you just conceded that rules have a significant place in a society. How can I convince others to follow the law if I don't do so myself? The law must apply equally and fairly to every single person. It is as simple as that.' Then Ram stared directly into Bharat's eyes. 'Even if it helps a heinous criminal escape death, the law should not be broken.'

Bharat stared right back, his expression inscrutable.

Sita sensed that the brothers were talking about a sensitive issue. Things were getting decidedly uncomfortable. She rose from the bench and said to Ram, 'You have a meeting with General Mrigasya.'

— ௬ —

Sita and her entourage were in the market. She didn't intend to buy anything. She had come out of the palace to give one of her guards the opportunity to slip away unnoticed. Had he left from the palace compound, his movements would have been tracked. But here, in the crowded marketplace, no one would miss one bodyguard from the large posse that guarded Sita.

From the corner of her eye, Sita saw him slip into a tiny lane that led out of the market. He had been ordered to arrange a meeting with Jatayu the following day.

Satisfied that her message would be delivered, Sita walked towards her palanquin to return to the palace. Her path was suddenly blocked by a grand palanquin that appeared out of nowhere. Covered with gold filigree, it was an ornate bronze litter with silk curtains covering the sides. It was obviously a very expensive and comfortable palanquin.

'Stop! Stop!' A feminine voice was heard from inside the curtained litter.

The bearers stopped immediately and placed the palanquin down. The strongest of the attendants walked to the entrance, drew aside the curtain and helped an old woman step out.

'*Namaste*, princess,' said Manthara, as she laboriously came to her feet. She folded her hands together and bowed her head with respect.

'*Namaste*, Lady Manthara,' said Sita, returning her greeting.

Sita had met the wealthy businesswoman the previous day. She had immediately felt sympathy for her. People did not speak kindly of Manthara behind her back. It did not seem right to Sita, especially keeping in mind that she had lost her beloved daughter, Roshni, in tragic circumstances.

One of Manthara's aides quickly placed a folded chair behind her, allowing her to sit. 'I am sorry, princess. I find it difficult to stand for too long.'

'No problem, Manthara*ji*,' said Sita. 'What brings you to the market?'

'I'm a businesswoman,' smiled Manthara. 'It's always wise to know what's happening in the market.'

Sita smiled and nodded.

'In fact, it's also wise to know what is happening everywhere else since the market is impacted by so many things.'

Sita groaned softly. She expected the usual question: Why was Ram insisting on being punished for the crime of firing a *daivi astra*?

'Manthara*ji*, I think it's best if we wait for ...'

Manthara pulled Sita close and whispered, 'I've been told that the Emperor may choose to abdicate, making Ram the king. And that he may choose to undertake the banishment of fourteen years himself. Along with his wives.'

Sita had heard this too. She also knew that Ram would not allow it. But what troubled her was something else. *Where did Manthara*ji *hear this?*

Sita maintained a straight face. Something didn't feel right.

She noticed that Manthara's bodyguards were keeping other people in the market at bay. A chill ran down her spine.

This meeting wasn't an accident. It was planned.

Sita replied carefully, 'I have not heard this, Manthara*ji*.'

Manthara looked hard at Sita. After a few moments, she smiled, slightly. 'Really?'

Sita adopted nonchalance. 'Why would I lie?'

Manthara's smile broadened. 'I have heard interesting things about you, princess. That you are intelligent. That your husband confides in you. That he trusts you.'

'Oh, I am a nobody from a small city. I just happened to marry above myself and arrive in this big, bad metropolis where I don't understand much of what you people say. Why should my husband trust my advice?'

Manthara laughed. 'Big cities are complex. Here, often, the diffused light of the moon lends greater insight. Much is lost in the glare of the sun. Therefore, the wise have held that for real wisdom to rise, the sun must set.'

Is that a threat?

Sita feigned confusion.

Manthara continued, 'The city enjoys the moon and the night. The jungle always welcomes the sun.'

This is not about business. This is about something else.

'Yes, Manthara*ji*,' said Sita, pretending to be puzzled. 'Thank you for these words of wisdom.'

Manthara pulled Sita closer, staring directly into her eyes. 'Is Ram going to the jungle or not?'

'I don't know, Manthara*ji*,' said Sita, innocently. 'The Emperor will decide.'

Manthara narrowed her eyes till they were thin, malevolent slits. Then she released Sita and shook her head dismissively.

As if there was nothing more to be learnt here. 'Take care, princess.'

'You take care, Mantha*raji*.'

'Druhyu …' said Manthara loudly.

Sita saw the right-hand man of Manthara shuffle up obsequiously. Though the look on his face was at odds with his manner.

Sita smiled innocently. *Something's not right. I need to find out more about Manthara.*

Chapter 27

Sita read the coded message quickly. It had come via Radhika. But the sender was someone else.

The message was terse, but clear: *I will speak to Guruji; it will be done.*

There was no name inscribed on the message. But Sita knew the sender.

She held the letter to a flame, letting it burn. She held on to it till it had reduced completely to ashes.

She smiled and whispered, 'Thank you, Hanu *bhaiya*.'

—*द्द्र*—

Sita and Jatayu stood in the small clearing. It was their predetermined meeting place in the jungle, an hour's ride from the city. Sita had made it in half that time. She had covered her face and body in a long *angvastram*, so that she wouldn't be identified. She had a lot to discuss with Jatayu. Not the least being her encounter with Manthara.

'Are you sure about this, great Vishnu?' asked Jatayu.

'Yes. I had initially thought that the city would be more dangerous for Ram. He has so many enemies here. But now I think the jungle may be where the true danger lies.'

'Then why not stay in the city?'

'Can't be done. My husband won't agree to it.'

'But...Why not? Who cares about what others ...'

Sita interrupted Jatayu, 'Let me give you an insight into my husband's character. General Mrigasya, one of the most powerful men in Ayodhya, was willing to back Ram replacing Dashrath *babuji* as king. In fact, my father-in-law himself wants to abdicate in Ram's favour. But my husband refused. He said it's against the law.'

Jatayu shook his head and smiled. 'Your husband is a rare jewel among men.'

Sita smiled. 'That he is.'

'So, you think Manthara will ...'

'Yes. She is not interested in the game of thrones. She wants vengeance, especially against Ram for having followed the law; for not executing her daughter's juvenile rapist-murderer. It's personal.'

'Any idea what she is planning?'

'She will not do anything in Ayodhya. Assassinating a popular prince within the city is risky. I suspect she will try something in the jungle.'

'I have visited Ayodhya before. I know her and her cohort. I also know whom she depends on.'

'Druhyu?'

'Yes. I suspect he will be the one who will organise the assassination. I know whom he will try to hire. I can handle it.'

'I have a suspicion about Manthara and Druhyu. I suspect they are loyal to ...'

'Yes, great Vishnu,' interrupted Jatayu. 'Raavan is their true lord.'

Sita took a deep breath. Things were beginning to make sense.

'Do you want us to take care of Manthara as well?' asked Jatayu.

'No,' answered Sita. 'It's been difficult enough to stop Raavan from retaliating after what happened in Mithila. Manthara is his key person in Ayodhya, his main cash cow in the north. If we kill her, he may break his pact with the Malayaputras to not attack Mithila.'

'So ... just Druhyu, then.'

Sita nodded.

'Let us meet tomorrow. I should know more by then.'

'Of course, Jatayu*ji*,' said Sita. 'Thank you. You are like a protective elder brother.'

'I am nothing but your devotee, great Vishnu.'

Sita smiled and folded her hands into a *Namaste*. 'Goodbye. Go with Lord Parshu Ram, my brother.'

'Go with Lord Rudra, my sister.'

Sita mounted her horse and rode away quickly. Jatayu picked up some dust from the ground where she had stood and brought it reverentially to his forehead. He whispered softly, *'Om Namo Bhagavate Vishnudevaya. Tasyai Sitadevyai namo namah.'*

He mounted his horse and rode away.

— ꝱᚼ —

Sita waited outside Vashishtha's private office. The guards had been surprised at the unannounced arrival of the wife of Prince Ram. They had asked her to wait since the *Raj Guru* of Ayodhya was in a meeting with a foreign visitor.

'I'll wait,' Sita had said.

The last few days had been action-packed. It had almost been decided by Dashrath that he would abdicate and install

Ram as king. Ram and Sita had decided that if that happened, Ram would abdicate in turn and banish himself, leaving Bharat to take over. Ideally, though, he didn't want to do that, as it would be a public repudiation of his father's orders. But it had not come to that.

On the day before the court ceremony to announce Emperor Dashrath's abdication, some dramatic developments had taken place. Queen Kaikeyi had lodged herself in the *kopa bhavan,* the *house of anger.* This was an institutionalised chamber created in royal palaces many centuries ago, once polygamy had become a common practice among the royalty. Having multiple wives, a king was naturally unable to spend enough time with all of them. A *kopa bhavan* was the assigned chamber a wife would go to if angry or upset with her husband. This would be a signal for the king that the queen needed redressal for a complaint. It was believed to be inauspicious for a husband to allow his wife to stay overnight in the *kopa bhavan.*

Dashrath had had no choice but to visit his aggrieved spouse. No one knew what had happened in the chamber, but the next day, Dashrath's announcement had been very different from what the rumours had suggested. Ram had been banished from the Sapt Sindhu for a period of fourteen years. Bharat had been named the crown prince in Ram's stead. Ram had publicly accepted the banishment with grace and humility, praising the wisdom of his father's decision. Sita and Ram were to leave for the jungle within a day.

Sita had little time left. She needed to tie up all the loops to ensure their security in the forest.

Vashishtha had not met Sita at all, since their arrival. Was the *Raj Guru* of Ayodhya avoiding her? Or had an opportunity not presented itself thus far? Anyway, she wanted to speak to him before she left.

She looked up as she saw a man emerge from Vashishtha's office. He was a tall, unusually fair-skinned man. He wore a white *dhoti* and an *angvastram*. But one could tell by the deliberate way he walked that he was distinctly uncomfortable in the *dhoti*. Perhaps, it wasn't his normal attire. His most distinguishing features were his hooked nose, beaded full beard and drooping moustache. His wizened face and large limpid eyes were an image of wisdom and calm.

He's a Parihan. Probably a Vayuputra.

The Parihan walked towards the main door, not noticing Sita and her maids in the sitting area.

'My Lady,' a guard came up to Sita, his head bowed in respect. 'My sincere apologies for the delay.'

Sita smiled. 'No, no. You were only doing your job. As you should.'

She stood up. Guided by the guard, she walked into Vashishtha's office.

— ᘰᚷ —

'It must be done outside the boundaries of the Sapt Sindhu,' said Druhyu.

He was in a small clearing in the forest, having ridden east from the boundaries of the Grand Canal for around three hours. He waited for a response. There was none.

The assassin was seated in the distance, hidden by dark shadows. His *angvastram* was pulled close around his face and torso. He was sharpening his knife on a smooth stone.

Druhyu hated this part of his job. He had done it a few times, but there was something about Mara that spooked him.

'The Emperor has announced the banishment of Prince

Ram. His wife and he will be leaving tomorrow. You will have to track them till they are out of the empire.'

Mara did not respond. He kept sharpening his knife.

Druhyu held his breath in irritation. *How sharp does he need that damned knife to be!*

He placed one large bag of gold coins on the tree stump near him. Then he reached into his pouch and took out a *hundi*. It was stamped with a secret seal recognised only by one specific moneylender in Takshasheela, a city far in the northwestern corners of India.

'One thousand gold coins in cash,' said Druhyu, 'and a *hundi* for fifty thousand gold coins to be picked up at the usual place.'

Mara looked up. Then, he felt the tip and edges of his blade. He seemed satisfied. He got up and started walking towards Druhyu.

'Hey!' Druhyu gasped in panic as he turned quickly and ran back some distance. 'Don't show me your face. I'm not going to see your face.'

Druhyu knew no living person had seen Mara's face. He didn't want to risk his life.

Mara stopped at the tree stump, picked up the bag of gold coins and judged its weight. He set it down and picked up the *hundi*. He didn't open the document, but slipped it carefully into the pouch tied to his waistband.

Then, Mara looked at Druhyu. 'It doesn't matter now.'

It took a few moments for Druhyu to realise the import of what had been said. He shrieked in panic and ran towards his horse. But Mara, lean and fit, could move faster than Druhyu. Silent as a panther, fast as a cheetah. He was upon Druhyu in almost no time. He caught hold of Druhyu from the back, holding his neck in his left arm, pinioning him against his own body. As Druhyu struggled in terror, Mara hit him hard on a pressure point at the back of his neck with the knife hilt.

Druhyu was immediately paralysed from the neck down. Mara let the limp body slip slowly to the ground. Then he bent over Druhyu and asked, 'Who else has been contracted?'

'I can't feel anything!' screamed Druhyu in shock. 'I can't feel anything!'

Mara slapped Druhyu hard. 'You are only paralysed from the neck down. I can release the pressure point. But first, answer ...'

'I can't feel anything. Oh Lord Indra! I can't ...'

Mara slapped Druhyu hard, again.

'Answer me quickly and I will help you. Don't waste my time.'

Druhyu looked at Mara. His *angvastram* was tied across his face. Only the assassin's eyes were visible.

Druhyu hadn't seen his face. Maybe he could still come out of this alive.

'Please don't kill me ...' sobbed Druhyu, a flood of tears streaming down his face.

'Answer my question. Has anyone else been contracted? Is there any other assassin?'

'Nobody but you ... Nobody but you ... Please ... by the great Lord Indra ... Let me go ... please.'

'Is there anybody besides you who can find an assassin like me for Lady Manthara?'

'No. Only me. And you can keep the money. I will tell that old witch that you have taken the contract. You don't have to kill anyone. How will she know? She will probably be dead before Prince Ram returns ... Please ... Let me ...'

Druhyu stopped talking as Mara removed the *angvastram*

that veiled his face. Sheer terror gripped Druhyu's heart. He had seen Mara's face. He knew what would follow.

Mara smiled. 'Don't worry. You won't feel a thing.'

The assassin got down to work. Druhyu's body had to be left there. It had to be discovered by Manthara and the others in her employ. It was supposed to send a message.

— ⌁ —

Sita was sitting with her younger sister, Urmila, who had been crying almost incessantly.

Despite all that had been happening for the last few days, Sita had found time to come and meet Urmila repeatedly. Lakshman had insisted on coming along with Ram and Sita for the fourteen-year banishment. Initially, Lakshman had thought Urmila could also come along. He had later realised that the delicate Urmila would not be able to survive the rigours of the jungle. It was going to be a tough fourteen years. The forests could be survived only if you were sturdy and hard. Not if you were delicate and urbane. It had been tough for Lakshman, but he had spoken to Urmila and she had, reluctantly, agreed to not come along with the three of them. Though she was unhappy about it.

Sita too was constrained to admit that Lakshman was right. And she had come repeatedly to meet Urmila to help her younger sister make peace with the decision.

'First *maa* left me,' sobbed Urmila, 'Now you and Lakshman are also leaving me. What am I supposed to do?'

Sita held her sister warmly, 'Urmila, if you want to come, I will push for it. But before I do so, I need you to realise what jungle life means. We won't even have a proper shelter over our heads. We'll live off the land, including eating meat; and I know how you despise that. These are minor things and I know you will adapt to what needs to be done. But there is also constant danger in the jungle. Most of the coastline south of the Narmada River is in Raavan's control. So, we can't go there unless we intend to get tortured to death.'

Urmila cut in, 'Don't say such things, *Didi*.'

'We cannot go to the coast. So, we will have to remain deep inland. Usually, within the forests of *Dandakaranya*. The Almighty alone knows what dangers await us there. We will have to sleep lightly every night, with our weapons next to us, in case any wild animals attack. Night is their time for hunting. There are so many poisonous fruits and trees; we could die just by eating the wrong thing. I'm sure there will be other dangers we are not even aware of. All of us will need our wits about us at all times to survive. And in the midst of all this, if something were to happen to you, how would I face *maa* when I leave this mortal body? She had charged me with protecting you ... And, you are safe here ...'

Urmila kept sniffing, holding on to Sita.

'Did Kaushalya *maa* come today?'

Urmila looked up, smiling wanly through her tears. 'She is so wonderful. I feel like our *maa* has returned. I feel safe with her.'

Sita held Urmila tight again. 'Bharat is a good man. So is Shatrughan. They will help Kaushalya *maa*. But they have many powerful enemies, some even more powerful than the king. You need to be here and support Kaushalya *maa*.'

Urmila nodded. 'Yes, Lakshman told me the same thing.'

'Life is not only about what we want, but also about what we must do. We don't just have rights. We also have duties.'

'Yes, *Didi*,' said Urmila. 'I understand. But that doesn't mean it doesn't hurt.'

'I know, my little princess,' said Sita, holding Urmila tight, patting her back. 'I know ...'

—— ༀ ——

Only a few hours were left for Ram, Sita, and Lakshman to leave for the jungle. They had changed into the garb of hermits, made from rough cotton and bark.

Sita had come to meet Guru Vashishtha.

'I've been thinking since our meeting yesterday, Sita,' said Vashishtha. 'I regret that we didn't meet earlier. Many of the issues that arose could have been avoided.'

'Everything has its own time and place, Guru*ji*.'

Vashishtha gave Sita a large pouch. 'As you had requested. I am sure the Malayaputras will also get you some of this. But you are right; it's good to have back-up.'

Sita opened the pouch and examined the white powder. 'This is much finer than the usual *Somras* powder I have seen.'

'Yes, it's made from the process I have developed.'

Sita smelt the powder and grinned. 'Hmmm ... it becomes finer and smells even worse.'

Vashishtha laughed softly. 'But it's just as effective.'

Sita smiled and put the pouch in the canvas bag that she had slung around her shoulder. 'I am sure you have heard what Bharat has done.'

A tearful Bharat had come to Ram's chambers and taken his brother's royal slippers. If and when the time came for Bharat to ascend to kingship, he would place Ram's slippers on the throne. With this one gesture, Bharat had effectively declared that Ram would be the king of Ayodhya and he, Bharat, would function as a mere caretaker in his elder brother's absence.

This afforded a powerful shield of protection to Ram from assassination attempts. Any attempts to murder the future king of Ayodhya would invite the wrath of the Empire, as mandated by the treaties between the various kingdoms under the alliance. Added to the cold reality of treaty obligations was the superstition that it was bad karma to kill kings and crown princes, except in battle or open combat. While this afforded powerful protection to Ram, it would severely undercut Bharat's own authority and power.

Vashishtha nodded. 'Bharat is a noble soul.'

'All four of the brothers are good people. More importantly, they love each other. And this, despite being born in a very dysfunctional family and difficult times. I guess credit must be given where credit is due.'

Vashishtha knew this was a compliment to him, the *guru* of the four Ayodhya princes. He smiled politely and accepted the praise with grace.

Sita folded her hands together in respect and said, 'I've thought about it. I agree with your instructions, Guru*ji*. I will wait for the right time. I'll tell Ram only when I think we are both ready.'

'Ram is special in so many ways. But his strength, his obsession with the law, can also be his weakness. Help him find balance. Then, both of you will be the partners that India needs.'

'I have my weaknesses too, Guru*ji*. And he can balance me. There are so many situations in which he is much better than I am. That's why I admire him.'

'And, he admires you. It is a true partnership.'

Sita hesitated slightly before saying, 'I must ask you something.'

'Of course.'

'I guess you must also have been a Malayaputra once ... Why did you leave?'

Vashishtha began to laugh. 'Hanuman was right. You are very smart. Scarily smart.'

Sita laughed along. 'But you haven't answered my question, Guru*ji*.'

'Leave the subject of Vishwamitra and me aside. Please. It's too painful.'

Sita immediately became serious. 'I don't wish to cause you any pain, Guru*ji*.'

Vashishtha smiled. 'Thank you.'

'I must go, Guru*ji*.'

'Yes. It's time.'

'Before I go, I must say this. I mean it from the bottom of my heart, Guru*ji*. You are as great a guru as the one who taught me.'

'And I mean it from the bottom of my heart, Sita. You are as great a Vishnu as the one I taught.'

Sita bent and touched Vashishtha's feet.

Vashishtha placed his hands on Sita's head and said, 'May you have the greatest blessing of all: May you be of service to our great motherland, India.'

'Salutations, great *Rishi*.'

'Salutations, great Vishnu.'

Chapter 28

Eleven months had passed since Ram, Sita, and Lakshman had left Ayodhya on their fourteen-year exile in the forest. And a lot had happened.

Dashrath had passed away in Ayodhya. The three of them had received this heartbreaking news while still in the Sapt Sindhu. Sita knew it had hurt Ram that he had not been able to perform the duties of an eldest son and conduct the funeral rites of his father. For most of his life, Ram had had almost no relationship with his father. Most Ayodhyans, including Dashrath, had blamed the 'bad fate' of Ram's birth for the disastrous loss to Raavan at the Battle of Karachapa. It was only over the last few years that Ram and Dashrath had finally begun building a bond. But exile and death had forced them apart again. Returning to Ayodhya was not possible as that would break Lord Rudra's law, but Ram had performed a *yagna* in the forest for the journey his father's soul had undertaken.

Bharat had remained true to his word and placed Ram's slippers on the throne of Ayodhya. He had begun to govern the empire as his brother's regent. It could be said that Ram had been appointed emperor *in absentia*. An unorthodox move. But Bharat's liberal and decentralising style of governance had made the decision palatable to the kingdoms within the Sapt Sindhu.

Ram, Lakshman, and Sita had travelled south. Primarily walking by the banks of rivers, they moved inland only when necessary. They had finally crossed the borders of the Sapt Sindhu near the kingdom of South Kosala, ruled by Ram's maternal grandfather. Lakshman and Sita had suggested visiting South Kosala and resting there for a few months. But Ram believed that it was against the spirit of the punishment they were serving to exploit the comforts of the palace of royal relatives.

They had skirted South Kosala and travelled deeper south-west, approaching the forest lands of *Dandakaranya*. Lakshman and Ram had expressed some concern about travelling south of the Narmada. Lord Manu had banned the Sapt Sindhuans from crossing the Narmada to the South. If they did cross, they were not to return. Or, so it had been decreed. But Sita had pointed out that Indians had, for millennia, found creative ways to travel to the south of the Narmada without actually 'crossing' the river. She suggested that they follow the letter of Lord Manu's law, but not the spirit.

While Ram was uncomfortable with this, Sita had managed to prevail. Living close to the coast was dangerous; Raavan controlled the western and eastern coastlines of the subcontinent. The safest place was deep inland, within the *Dandakaranya*, even if that meant being south of the Narmada. They had travelled in a southwesterly direction, so that the source of the west-flowing Narmada remained to their north. They had, thus, reached land that was geographically to the south of the Narmada without technically 'crossing' the river. They were now at the outskirts of a very large village, almost a small town.

'What is this town called, Captain Jatayu?' asked Ram, turning to the Malayaputra. 'Do you know these people?'

Jatayu and fifteen of his soldiers had been trailing Ram, Sita, and Lakshman, ensuring their safety. As instructed by Sita, they had remained hidden. Ram and Lakshman did not know of their presence for a long time. However, despite their best efforts to stay hidden, Ram had begun to suspect that someone was shadowing them. Sita had not been sure how Ram would react to her seeking protection from some Malayaputras. So she had not told Ram about her decision to ask Jatayu to act as a bodyguard for them. However, as they crossed the borders of the Sapt Sindhu, the risks of assassination attempts had increased. Sita had finally been forced to introduce Jatayu to Ram. Trusting Sita, Ram had accepted the Malayaputra and his fifteen soldiers as members of his team. Together they were one short of twenty now; more defendable than a group of just three. Ram understood this.

'It's called Indrapur, Prince Ram,' said Jatayu. 'It is the biggest town in the area. I know Chief Shaktivel, its leader. I'm sure he will not mind our presence. It's a festive season for them.'

'Festivities are always good!' said Lakshman, laughing jovially.

Ram said to Jatayu, 'Do they celebrate *Uttarayan* as well?'

The *Uttarayan* marked the beginning of the *northward movement* of the sun across the horizon. This day marked the farthest that the nurturer of the world, the sun, moved away from those in the northern hemisphere. It would now begin its six-month journey back to the north. It was believed to be that part of the year which marked nature's renewal. The death of the old. The birth of the new. It was, therefore, celebrated across practically all of the Indian subcontinent.

Jatayu frowned. 'Of course they do, Prince Ram. Which Indian does not celebrate the *Uttarayan*? We are all aligned to the Sun God!'

'That we are,' said Sita. '*Om Suryaya Namah.*'

Everyone repeated the ancient chant, bowing to the Sun God. '*Om Suryaya Namah.*'

'Perhaps, we can participate in their festivities,' said Sita.

Jatayu smiled. 'The Indrapurans are a martial, aggressive people and their celebrations can be a little rough.'

'Rough?' asked Ram.

'Let's just say you need bulls among men to be able to participate.'

'Really? What's this celebration called?'

'It's called *Jallikattu.*'

— ᘓᙆ —

'By the great Lord Rudra,' whispered Ram. 'This sounds similar to our *Vrishbandhan* festival ... But very few play this game in the Sapt Sindhu anymore.'

Ram, Sita, Lakshman, Jatayu, and the bodyguards had just entered Indrapur. They had gone straight to the ground next to the town lake. It had been fenced in and prepared for the *Jallikattu* competition the next day. Crowds were milling around the fence, taking in the sights and sounds. Nobody was allowed to cross the fence into the ground. The bulls would be led there soon to acclimatise them for the competition the next day.

Jatayu had just explained the game of *Jallikattu* to them. It was, in its essence, a very simple game. The name literally meant a tied bag of coins. In this case, gold coins. The contestant had to yank this bag to be declared a winner. Simple? Not quite! The challenge lay in the place this bag of coins was tied. It was tied to the horns of a bull. Not any ordinary bull, mind you. It was a bull especially bred to be aggressive, strong and belligerent.

'Yes, it is similar to *Vrishbandhan, embracing the bull*,' explained Jatayu. 'The game itself has been around for a long time, as you know. In fact, some say that it comes down from our Dwarka and Sangamtamil ancestors.'

'Interesting,' said Sita. 'I didn't know it was so ancient.'

Many bulls, which would participate in the *Jallikattu*, were specially bred in the surrounding villages and within Indrapur itself. The owners took pride in finding the best bulls to breed with the local cows. And, they took even more pride in feeding, training and nurturing the beasts to become fierce fighters.

'There are lands far to the east, outside India's borders,' said Jatayu, 'where you find bull-fighting competitions as well. But in their case, the dice is loaded against the bulls. Those people keep the bulls hungry for a few days before the contest, to weaken them. Before the main bull-fighter gets into the ring, his team further weakens the beast considerably. They do this by making the poor bull run a long distance and stabbing it multiple times with long spears and blades. And despite weakening the bull so much, the bull-fighter still carries a weapon to fight the beast, and ultimately kill it.'

'Cowards,' said Lakshman. 'There is no *kshatriyahood* in fighting that way.'

'Exactly,' said Jatayu. 'In fact, even in the rare case that a bull survives that competition, it is never brought back into the arena again because it would have learnt how to fight. And that would tilt the scales in its favour instead of the bull-fighter. So, they always bring in a new, inexperienced bull.'

'And, of course, this is not done in *Jallikattu* ...' said Ram.

'Not at all. Here, the bull is well fed and kept strong and

healthy, all the way. Nobody is allowed to spear or weaken it. Experienced bulls, which have performed well in previous competitions, are allowed to participate as well.'

'That's the way to do it,' said Lakshman. 'That will make it a fair fight.'

'It gets even fairer,' continued Jatayu. 'None of the men competing against the bull are allowed to carry any weapons. Not even small knives. They only use their bare hands.'

Lakshman whistled softly. 'That takes real courage.'

'Yes, it does. In that other bull-fighting competition I told you about, the one outside India, the bulls almost always die and the men rarely suffer serious injury, let alone die. But in *Jallikattu*, the bulls never die. It's the men who risk serious injury, even death.'

A soft, childish voice was heard. 'That's the way real men fight.'

Ram, Sita, Lakshman, and Jatayu turned almost in unison. A small child, perhaps six or seven years of age, stood before them. He had fair skin and small animated eyes. For his young age, he was extraordinarily hairy. His chest was puffed with pride. His arms akimbo as he surveyed the ground beyond the wooden fence.

He's probably a Vaanar.

Sita went down on her knees and said, 'Are you participating in the competition tomorrow, young man?'

The child's body visibly deflated. His eyes downcast, he said, 'I wanted to. But they say I cannot. Children are not allowed. By the great Lord Rudra, if I could compete I am sure I would defeat everyone.'

Sita smiled broadly. 'I'm sure you would. What's your name, son?'

'My name is Angad.'

'A-N-G-A-D!'

A loud booming voice was heard from a distance.

Angad turned around rapidly. Fear in his eyes. 'My father's coming... I gotta go ...'

'Wait ...' said Sita, stretching her hand out.

But Angad wriggled out and ran away quickly.

Sita rose up and turned towards Jatayu. 'The name rang a bell, right?'

Jatayu nodded. 'I didn't recognise the face. But I know the name. That is Prince Angad. The son of King Vali of Kishkindha.'

Ram frowned. 'That kingdom is deep in the south of *Dandakaranya*, right? Isn't it aligned to ...'

Ram was interrupted by another booming voice. 'I'll be damned!'

The crowd made way as the chief of Indrapur, Shaktivel, walked up to them. His voice aggressive. 'You come to my town and nobody informs me?'

Shaktivel was a massive man. Swarthy. Tall. Muscled like an *auroch* bull, with a large belly, his arms and legs were like the trunks of a small tree. His most striking feature, however, was his extra-large moustache, which extended grandly down his cheeks. Despite his obvious strength, he was also getting on in age, as evidenced clearly by the many white hairs in his moustache and on his head. And, the wrinkles on his forehead.

Jatayu spoke calmly, 'We've just arrived, Shaktivel. No need to lose your temper.'

To everyone present, Shaktivel's eyes conveyed immense anger. Suddenly, he burst into loud laughter. 'Jata, you stupid bugger! Come into my arms!'

Jatayu laughed as he embraced Shaktivel. 'You will always be a ridiculous oaf, Shakti!'

Sita turned to Ram and arched an eyebrow. Amused at seeing two males express love for each other through expletives and curses. Ram smiled and shrugged his shoulders.

The crowds around began cheering loudly as the two friends held each other in a long and warm embrace. Clearly, the relationship meant a lot to them. Equally clearly, they were more brothers than friends. Finally, Shaktivel and Jatayu stepped back, still holding each other's hands.

'Who are your guests?' asked Shaktivel. 'Because they are my guests now!'

Jatayu smiled and held his friend's shoulder, as he said, 'Prince Ram, Princess Sita, and Prince Lakshman.'

Shaktivel's eyes suddenly widened. He folded his hands together into a *Namaste*. 'Wow ... the royal family of Ayodhya itself. It is my honour. You must spend the night in my palace. And, of course, come and see the *Jallikattu* tomorrow.'

Ram politely returned Shaktivel's *Namaste*. 'Thank you for your hospitality. But it's not correct for us to stay in your palace. We will stay in the forest close by. But we will certainly come for the competition tomorrow.'

Shaktivel had heard of Ram's punishment, so he didn't press the matter. 'You could at least give me the pleasure of having dinner with you.'

Ram hesitated.

'Nothing fashionable at my palace. Just a simple meal together in the forest.'

Ram smiled. 'That would be welcome.'

— ᚱᚷ —

'Look at that one,' whispered Lakshman to Sita and Ram.

It was just after noon the next day. Massive crowds had gathered at the lake-side ground, where the contest between man and beast was about to take place. The ground had a small entry on the eastern side, from where bulls would be led in, one by one. They had been trained to make a run for the exit at the western end, a good five hundred metres away. The men, essentially, had that distance to try and grab hold of the bull and pull out the bag of coins. If the contestant won, he would keep the bag of gold coins. More importantly, he would be called a *Vrishank*; a *bull warrior!* Of course, if any bull reached the western gate and escaped, without losing its bag, the owner of the bull would be declared winner. Needless to say, he would keep the bag of coins.

There were various breeds of bulls that were used in the *Jallikattu* competitions. Among the most popular was a type of zebu bulls that were specifically cross-bred for aggression, strength, and speed. They were extremely agile and could turn around completely at the same spot in a split second. More importantly, they also had a very pronounced hump; this was a requirement for any bull competing in the *Jallikattu*. Some believed that the humps were essentially fat deposits. They couldn't be more wrong. These humps were an enlargement of the *rhomboideus* muscle in the shoulder and back. The size of the hump, thus, was a marker of the quality of the bull. And, judging by the size of the humps on these bulls, they were, clearly, fierce competitors.

In keeping with tradition, proud owners were parading the bulls in the ground. This was so that human contestants could inspect the beasts. As tradition also dictated, the owners, one by one, began to brag about the strength and speed of their bulls; their genealogy, the diet they were fed, the training they had received, even the number of people they had gored! The greater the monstrosity of the bull, the louder and lustier the cheers of the crowd. And as the owner stood with his bull, many from the crowd would throw their *angvastrams* into the ring to signify their intention to compete with that beast.

But they all fell silent as a new bull was led in.

'By the great Lord Rudra ...' whispered Lakshman, in awe.

Sita held Ram's hand. 'Which poor sod is going to grab the coins from that bull's horns?'

The owner of the bull was aware of the impact of the mere presence of his beast. Sometimes, silence speaks louder than words. He didn't say anything; nothing about its heredity, its awesome food habits, or fearsome training. He simply looked at the crowd, arrogance dripping from every pore of his body. In fact, he didn't expect any contestant to even try to compete against his bull.

The bull was massive, larger than all the others that had been paraded so far. The owner didn't clarify, but it seemed like a cross-breed between a wild gaur and the faster sub-breed of the domesticated zebu. Clearly though, the gaur genes had dominated in the making of this beast. It was gigantic, standing over seven feet tall at the shoulders with a length of nearly ten feet. It must have weighed in at one thousand five hundred kilograms. And practically all that one could see rippling under its skin was pure hard muscle. Its two horns were curved upwards, making a hollow cup on the upper part of the head, like a typical gaur bull. Zebu genes had prevailed in the make of the beast's skin. It was whitish grey and not dark brown like gaur skins usually are. Perhaps the only other place where the zebu genes had won was the hump. Normally, a gaur has an elongated ridge on its back; it's flat and long. But this bull had a prominent and very large hump on its upper shoulders and back. This was very, very important. For without that hump, this beastly bull would have been disqualified from the *Jallikattu*.

If a competitor managed to grab hold of the hump of a bull, his main task was to hold on tight, even as the bull bucked aggressively, trying to shake the human off. Through the tussle, the man had to somehow hold on; and if he held on long enough and pulled tight, the bull would finally slow down and the man could grab the bag.

The owner suddenly spoke. Loudly. Disconcertingly, considering the demonic animal he led, the voice of the man was soft and feminine. 'Some of you may think this bull is all about size. But speed matters as well!'

The owner let go of the rope and whistled softly. The bull charged out in a flash. Its speed blinding. It was faster than any other bull on this day.

Lakshman stared, awestruck. *Gaurs are not meant to be this fast!*

The bull turned rapidly in its spot, displaying its fearsome agility. As if that wasn't enough, it suddenly started bucking aggressively, and charging towards the fence. The crowd fell back in terror. Its dominance established, the bull sauntered back to its owner, lowered its head and snorted aggressively at the crowd.

Magnificent!

Loud and spontaneous applause filled the air.

'Looks like the hump and skin colour are not the only things it inherited from its zebu ancestor,' whispered Sita.

'Yes, it has inherited its speed as well,' said Lakshman. 'With that massive size and speed... It's almost like me!'

Sita looked at Lakshman with a smile. It disappeared as she saw the look on her brother-in-law's face.

'Don't ...' whispered Sita.

'What a beast,' said Lakshman, admiringly. 'It will be a worthy competitor.'

Ram placed his hand on his brother's shoulder, holding him back. But before Lakshman could do anything, a loud voice was heard. 'I will compete with that bull!'

Everyone's eyes turned towards a violet-coloured, obviously expensive *angvastram* flying into the ring. Beyond the wooden fence stood a fair, ridiculously muscular and very hairy man of medium height. He wore a simple cream-coloured *dhoti* with one end of it sticking out like a tail. The clothes may have been simple, but the bearing was regal.

'That's Vali,' said Jatayu. 'The King of Kishkindha.'

— ᛭ —

Vali stood close to the barricaded entrance. The gaur-zebu bull was about to be let loose. It was a covered gate and the bull couldn't see who or what was waiting on the other side. Three bulls had already run. Two had been baited and their gold coins grabbed. But one bull had escaped with its package. It was a rapid game. Individual races rarely lasted more than a minute. There were at least a hundred more bulls to run. But everyone knew that this was the match to watch.

The priest of the local temple bellowed out loud. 'May the *Vrishank* above all *Vrishanks*, Lord Rudra, bless the man and the beast!'

This was the standard announcement before any *Jallikattu* match in Indrapur. And as usual, it was followed by the loud and reverberating sound of a conch shell.

After a moment's silence, the loud clanking of metal gates was heard.

'*Jai Shri Rudra*!' roared the crowd.

From the dark interiors of the covered gate, the beast emerged. Usually, bulls charged out, thundering past the press of humans who tried to lunge from the sides and grab the hump of the animal.

Getting in front of the bull was dangerous for it could gore you with its horns. Being at the back was equally dangerous for it could kick outwards with its formidable hind legs. Its side was the best place to be. Which is why, bulls were trained to dash across, giving men less time to try and grab from the two sides.

But this gaur-zebu bull simply sauntered out. Supremely sure of its abilities. Vali, who was waiting beside the gate, hidden from view, leapt up as soon as the bull emerged. Considering Vali was nearly one-and-a-half feet shorter than the bull, it was a tribute to his supreme physical fitness that he managed to get his arms around the bull's massive hump as he landed. The bull was startled. Someone had dared to hold its hump. It started bucking wildly. Bellowing loudly. Banging its hooves hard on the ground. Suddenly, showing awe-inspiring dexterity, it whirled almost a complete circle with monstrous speed. Vali lost his grip. He was flung away.

The bull suddenly calmed down. It stared at the prone Vali, snorted imperiously and began walking away. Slowly. Towards the exit. Staring into the crowds, nonchalantly.

Someone from the crowd shouted an encouragement to Vali. 'Come on! Get up!'

The bull looked at the crowd and stopped. It then turned towards the lake, presenting its backside to the crowd. It slowly raised its tail and urinated. Then, maintaining its blasé demeanour, it started walking again. Towards the exit. Just as leisurely.

Lakshman laughed softly, as he shook his head. 'Forget about baiting this bull. The bull is, in fact, baiting us!'

Ram tapped Lakshman on his shoulder. 'Look at Vali. He's getting up.'

Vali banged his fists hard on his chest and sprinted ahead. Light on his feet. His long hair flying in the wind. He came up from behind the bull.

'This man is a maniac!' said Lakshman, worried but animated. 'That bull can crush his chest with a single blow from its hind legs!'

As Vali came close to the bull, he jumped up, soaring high. He landed on top of the bull. The surprised beast, which hadn't seen Vali come up from behind, bellowed loudly and went up on its hind legs. Trying to shake the king off. But Vali held on firmly. Screaming at the top of his lungs!

The outraged bull roared. Louder than the man who clung to it. Letting its front legs fall to the ground, it lowered its head and bucked wildly. But Vali held on, screaming all the time.

The bull suddenly leapt into the air and shook its body. It still could not get rid of the man holding on desperately to its hump.

The entire crowd had fallen silent. In absolute awe. They had never seen a *Jallikattu* match last so long. The only sounds were the loud bellows of the bull and the roars of Vali.

The bull leapt up again and readied to fall to its side. Its weight would have crushed Vali to death. He quickly let go of the bull. But not fast enough.

The bull landed on its side. Vali escaped the bulk, but its front legs lashed Vali's left arm. Lakshman heard the bone crack from where he stood. To his admiration, Vali did not scream in pain. The bull was up on its feet in no time and trotted away.

From a distance, it looked at Vali. Anger blazing in its eyes. But it kept its distance.

'The bull is angry,' whispered Ram. 'I guess it has never had a human go so far.'

'Stay down,' said Sita, almost willing Vali to remain on the ground.

Lakshman stared at Vali silently.

If a man remained curled up on the ground, unmoving like a stone, a bull normally would not charge. But if he stood up …

'Fool!' hissed Sita, as she saw Vali rising once again, his bloodied and shattered left arm dangling uselessly by his side. 'Stay down!'

Lakshman's mouth fell open in awe. *What a man!*

The bull too seemed shocked and enraged that the man had risen once again. It snorted and shook its head.

Vali banged his chest repeatedly with his right fist and roared loudly, 'Vali! Vali!'

The crowd too began shouting.

'Vali!'

'Vali!'

The bull bellowed loudly, and banged its front hooves hard on the ground. A warning had been given.

Vali banged his chest again, his shattered left arm swinging uselessly by his side. 'Vali!'

The bull came up on its hind legs and bellowed once again. Much louder this time. Almost deafeningly loud.

And then, the beast charged.

Lakshman jumped over the fence, racing towards the bull at the same time.

'Lakshman!' screamed Ram, as he and Sita also leapt over and sprinted after Lakshman.

Lakshman ran diagonally, bisecting the path between Vali and the animal. Luckily for the prince of Ayodhya, the bull did not see this new threat.

Lakshman was much taller than Vali. He was also far more bulky and muscular. But even Lakshman knew that brute strength was useless against this gargantuan beast. He knew he would have only one chance. The bull's horns were unlike the pure zebu breed; pure zebu bulls had straight, sharp horns which worked like blunt knives while goring. The gaur-zebu bull's horns, on the other hand, were curved upwards, making a hollow in the upper part of the head.

The bull was focused on Vali. It had lowered its head and was thundering towards him. It didn't notice Lakshman come up suddenly from the side. Lakshman leapt forward, timing his jump to perfection, pulling his legs up. As he soared above the bull's head, he quickly reached out with his hand and yanked the bag off the horns. For that split second, the bull kept charging forward and Lakshman's feet came in line with the bull's head. He pushed out with his legs. Hard. Effectively using the bull's head as leverage, he bounced away. Lakshman's weight and size were enough to push the head of the bull down. As he bounded away, rolling on the field, the bull's head banged into the hard ground and it tripped, falling flat on its face.

Ram and Sita used the distraction to quickly pick up Vali and sprint towards the fence.

'Leave me!' screamed Vali, struggling against the two. 'Leave me!'

Vali's struggle led to more blood spilling out of his shattered arm. It increased the pain dramatically. But Ram and Sita did not stop.

Meanwhile, the bull quickly rose to its feet and bellowed

loudly. Lakshman raised his hand, showing the bag he held.

The bull should have charged. But it had been trained well. As soon as it saw the bag of coins, it lowered its head and snorted. It looked behind at its owner, who was standing close to the exit. The owner smiled and shrugged, mouthing the words, 'You win some. You lose some.'

The bull looked back at Lakshman, snorted, and lowered its head again. Almost as if it was accepting defeat gracefully. Lakshman pulled his hands together into a *Namaste* and bowed low to the magnificent beast.

The bull then turned around and started walking away. Towards its owner.

Vali, meanwhile, had lost consciousness, as Sita and Ram carried him over the fence.

Chapter 29

Late in the evening, Shaktivel came to the forest edge where Ram and his band were resting. A few men followed the Chief of Indrapur, bearing large bundles of weapons in their hands.

Ram stood up, folding his hands together in a *Namaste*. 'Greetings, brave Shaktivel.'

Shaktivel returned Ram's greeting. '*Namaste*, great Prince.' He pointed to the bundles being carefully laid on the ground by his men. 'As requested by you, all your weapons have been repaired, shone, polished, and sharpened.'

Ram picked up a sword, examined its edge and smiled. 'They are as good as new.'

Shaktivel's chest swelled with pride. 'Our metalsmiths are among the best in India.'

'They clearly are,' said Sita, examining a spear closely.

'Prince Ram,' said Shaktivel, coming close, 'a private word.'

Ram signalled Sita to follow him, as he was pulled aside by Shaktivel.

'You may need to leave in haste,' said Shaktivel.

'Why?' asked a surprised Sita.

'Vali.'

'Someone wanted him dead?' asked Ram. 'So, they're angry with us now?'

'No, no. Vali is the one who is angry with Princess Sita and you.'

'What?! We just saved his life.'

Shaktivel sighed. 'He doesn't see it that way. According to him, the two of you and Prince Lakshman made him lose his honour. He'd rather have died in the *Jallikattu* arena than be rescued by someone else.'

Ram looked at Sita, his eyes wide in surprise.

'It is not in my town's interest to have royal families fight each other here,' said Shaktivel, folding his hands together in apology. 'When two elephants fight, the grass is the first to get trampled.'

Sita smiled. 'I know that line.'

'It's a popular line,' said Shaktivel. 'Especially among those who are not from the elite.'

Ram placed his hand on Shaktivel's shoulder. 'You have been our host. You have been a friend. We do not want to cause you any trouble. We'll leave before daybreak. Thank you for your hospitality.'

— ௶ —

Ram, Sita, and Lakshman had been in exile for twenty-four months now. The fifteen Malayaputra soldiers accompanied them everywhere.

Each member of the small party had settled into an established routine, as they moved deeper into the forests of Dandak. They were headed in the westward direction, but had not been able to find a suitable enough permanent camp. They usually stayed in one place for a short while before moving on. Standard perimeter and security formations had been agreed upon. Cooking, cleaning, and hunting duties were shared by rotation. Since not everyone in the camp ate meat, hunting wasn't required often.

On one of these hunting trips, a Malayaputra called Makrant had been gored by a boar while trying to save Sita's life. The wild boar's tusk had cut upwards through the upper quadriceps muscles on his thigh, piercing the femoral artery. Fortunately, the other tusk of the boar had hit the hard pelvic bone; thus, it had not pushed through and penetrated deeper where it would have ruptured the intestines. That would have been fatal as the resultant infection would have been impossible to treat in their temporary camp. Makrant had survived, but his recovery had not been ideal. His quadriceps muscles were still weak and the artery had not healed completely, remaining partially collapsed. He still limped a great deal; a condition which could be dangerous for a soldier in the hazardous jungle.

Because of the injury it was impossible for Makrant to move easily through the forest. So, they had not moved camp for some time.

Makrant had been suffering for a few months. Jatayu knew something had to be done. And, he knew the cure as well. He simply had to steel himself for the journey …

'The waters of Walkeshwar?' asked Sita.

'Yes,' said Jatayu. 'The holy lake emerges from a natural spring bursting out from deep underground, which means it picks up specific minerals on its way to the surface. Those minerals infuse the waters with their divine goodness. That water will help Makrant's arteries recover quickly. We can also get some medicinal herbs from the island which will help his partly atrophied muscles to recover fully. He can have the full use of his legs again.'

'Where is Walkeshwar, Jatayu*ji*?'

'It's in a small island called Mumbadevi on the west coast. Specifically, the northern part of the Konkan coast.'

'Weren't we supposed to stop at an island close to it for supplies on our way to Agastyakootam? An island called Colaba?'

'Yes. Our captain had thought it would be a good idea to stop there. I had advised against it.'

'Yes. I remember.'

'Mumbadevi is the big island to the northwest of Colaba.'

'So, Mumbadevi is one of that group of seven islands?'

'Yes, great Vishnu.'

'You had advised against stopping there since it is a major sea base for Raavan's forces.'

'Yes, great Vishnu.'

Sita smiled. 'Then, it's probably not a good idea for Ram and me to accompany you.'

Jatayu didn't smile at Sita's wry humour. 'Yes, great Vishnu.'

'But the Lankans will not dare hurt a Malayaputra, right?'

Fear flashed momentarily in Jatayu's eyes, but his voice was even and calm. 'No, they won't ...'

Sita frowned. 'Jatayu*ji*, is there something you need to tell me?'

Jatayu shook his head. 'Everything will be fine. I will take three men with me. The rest of you should stay here. I will be back in two months.'

Instinct kicked in. Sita knew something was wrong. 'Jatayu*ji*, is there a problem in Mumbadevi?'

Jatayu shook his head. 'I need to prepare to leave, great Vishnu. You and Prince Ram should remain encamped here.'

— ᚱᚷ —

It was dark when Jatayu and the three soldiers reached the shoreline of the mainland. Across a narrow strait, they saw the seven islands that abutted the south of the far larger Salsette Island. Torchlights on houses and tall lamp towers on streets and public structures had lit up the central and eastern side of Salsette Island. Clearly, the town had expanded on this, the largest island, in the area. It was ten times bigger than the seven islands to the south put together! It was logical that a fast-growing town had come up here. There were large freshwater lakes in the centre of the island. And enough open area to build a large town. Crossing into the mainland was easy since the creek that separated it was narrow and shallow.

There had been a time when the seven islands to the south of Salsette had been the centre of all civilisation in the area. The island of Mumbadevi had a wonderful harbour on its eastern shores, which worked well for larger ships. The port built at that harbour still existed. And clearly, it was still busy. Jatayu could also see lights on the other four smaller islands on the eastern side: Parel, Mazgaon, Little Colaba, and Colaba. But the western islands of Mahim and Worli were not clearly visible.

The hills at the western end of Mumbadevi, where Walkeshwar was, were tall enough to be seen from across the straits, during the day. In fact, the hills had once been visible at night as well. For that's where the main palaces, temples, and structures of the old city were. And they had always been well lit.

But Jatayu couldn't see a thing there. No torchlights. No lamp towers. No sign of habitation.

Walkeshwar remained abandoned. It remained in ruin.

Jatayu shivered as he remembered those terrible days. The time when he had been a young soldier. When Raavan's hordes had come … He remembered only too well. For he had been one of the horde.

Lord Parshu Ram, forgive me … Forgive me for my sins …

'Captain,' said one of the Malayaputra soldiers. 'Should we cross now or …'

Jatayu turned around. 'No. We'll cross in the morning. We'll rest here for the night.'

— ᚱᚷ —

Jatayu tossed and turned as he tried to sleep. Memories that he had buried deep within himself were bursting through to his consciousness. Nightmares from his long-hidden past.

Memories of when he was younger. Many, many years ago.

Raavan used our own people to conquer us.

Jatayu sat up. He could see the islands across the creek.

When he had been a teenager, Jatayu had carried the pain, the anger, of being ill-treated as a Naga. As someone who was deformed. But Nagas weren't the only ones ill-treated. Many communities had complaints against the rigid, supercilious, and chauvinistic elite of the Sapt Sindhu. And Raavan had seemed like a rebel-hero, a saviour of sorts to many of them. He took on the powers-that-be. And, the disenchanted flocked to him. Fought for him. Killed for him.

And, were used by him.

Jatayu had, at that time, enjoyed the feeling of vengeance. Of hitting out at the hated, self-absorbed elite. Until the time that his unit had been ordered to join an *AhiRaavan*.

Raavan's forces were divided into two groups. One group commanded the land territories, with commanders called *MahiRaavans* in charge. And the other group commanded the seas and the ports, with commanders called *AhiRaavans* in control.

It was with one such *AhiRaavan* called Prahast that Jatayu had been ordered to come to Mumbadevi and its seven islands.

These seven islands were peopled by the Devendrar community at the time, led by a kindly man called Indran. Mumbadevi and the other six islands were an entrepot, *with goods stored for import and export with minimal custom duties. The liberal Devendrars provided supplies and refuge to any seafarer, without favour or discrimination. They treated everyone with kindness. They believed it was their sacred duty to do so. One such seafarer, who had been provided refuge for some time, was Jatayu, when he was very young. He remembered that kindness well. It was a rare place in India, where Jatayu had not been treated like the plague. He had been welcomed like a normal person. The shock of the compassion had been so overwhelming that he had cried himself to sleep that first night in Mumbadevi, unable to handle the flood of emotions.*

And many years later, he had returned, as part of an army sent to conquer that very same Mumbadevi Island.

Raavan's strategic reasons were obvious. He wanted absolute control over all the sea trade in the Indian Ocean; the hub of global trade. Whoever dominated this Ocean, dominated the entire world. And only with absolute control could Raavan enforce his usurious customs duties. He had conquered or managed to gain control over most of the major ports across the Indian subcontinent and the coasts of Arabia, Africa, and South-east Asia. Those ports followed his rules.

But Mumbadevi stubbornly refused to charge high custom or turn away any sailor who sought refuge there. Its inhabitants believed this service was their duty. Their dharma. Raavan had to gain control over this important harbour on the sea route between the Indus-Saraswati coasts and Lanka.

AhiRaavan Prahast had been sent to negotiate a solution. And, if needed, force a solution. The Lankan Army had been waiting, camped in their ships, anchored at the Mumbadevi harbour, off its eastern coast. For a week. Nothing had happened. Finally, they had been ordered to march to Walkeshwar, the western part of Mumbadevi, where the palace and a temple dedicated to Lord Rudra had been built, right next to a natural-spring-filled lake.

Jatayu, being a junior soldier, was at the back of the line.

He knew the Devendrars couldn't fight. They were a peaceful community of seafarers, engineers, doctors, philosophers, and storytellers. There were very few warriors among them. Jatayu hoped desperately that a compromise had been reached.

The scene he saw at the main town square, outside of the palace, baffled him.

It was completely deserted. Not a soul in sight. All the shops were open. Goods displayed. But nobody to tend to, or even secure them.

At the centre of the square was a massive pile of corkwood, with some mixture of holy sandalwood. It was held in place by a metallic mesh. All drenched in fresh ghee. It had clearly been built recently. Perhaps, the previous night itself.

It was like a very large unlit cremation pyre. Humongous. Massive enough to potentially accommodate hundreds of bodies.

It had a walkway leading up to its top.

Prahast had come in expecting a ceremonial surrender, as he had demanded, and then the peaceful expulsion of the Devendrars. This was unexpected. He immediately made his troops fall into battle formations.

Sanskrit chants were emanating from behind the palace walls. Accompanied by the clanging of sacred bells and the beating of drums. It took some time for the Lankans to discern the words of the chants.

They were from the Garuda Purana. *Hymns usually sung during a death ceremony.*

What were the Devendrars thinking? Their palace walls

were not tough enough to withstand an assault. They did not have enough soldiers to take on the five-thousand-strong Lankan Army.

Suddenly, smoke began to plume out of the palace compound. Thick, acrid smoke. The wooden palace had been set on fire.

And then, the gates were flung open.

Prahast's order was loud and clear. 'Draw! And hold!'

All the Lankans immediately drew their weapons. Holding their line. In military discipline. Expecting an attack …

Indran, the king of the Devendrars, led his people out of the palace. All of them. His entire family. The priests, traders, workmen, intellectuals, doctors, artists. Men, women, children. All his citizens.

All the Devendrars.

They all wore saffron robes. The colour of fire, of Lord Agni. The colour of the final journey.

Every single face was a picture of calm.

They were still chanting.

Every Devendrar carried gold coins and jewellery. Each one carried a fortune. And each one carried a small bottle.

Indran walked up the pathway to the stand that overhung the massive pile of wood. He nodded at his people.

They flung their gold coins and jewellery at the Lankan soldiers.

Indran's voice carried loud and clear. 'You can take all our money! You can take our lives! But you cannot force us to act against our dharma!'

The Lankan soldiers stood stunned. Not knowing how to react. They looked at their commander for instructions.

Prahast bellowed loudly. 'King Indran, think well before you act. Lord Raavan is the King of all three Worlds. Even the Gods fear him. Your soul will be cursed. Take your gold and leave. Surrender and you shall be shown mercy!'

Indran smiled kindly. 'We will never surrender our dharma.'

*Then the king of the Devendrars looked at the Lankan soldiers.
'Save your souls. You alone carry the fruit of your karma. No one else.
You cannot escape your karma by claiming that you were only following
orders. Save your souls. Choose well.'*

*Some Lankan soldiers seemed to be wavering. The weapons in their
hands shaking.*

'Hold your weapons!' shouted Prahast. 'This is a trick!'

*Indran nodded to his head priest. The priest stepped up to the pile of
wood and stuck a burning torch deep into it. It caught fire immediately.
The pyre was ready.*

*Indran pulled out his small bottle and took a deep swig. Possibly a
pain reliever.*

*'All I ask is that you not insult our Gods. That you not defile our
temples.' Indran then stared at Prahast with pity. 'The rest is for you
to do as you will.'*

Prahast ordered his soldiers again. 'Steady. Nobody move!'

Indran pulled his hands together into a Namaste *and looked up at
the sky.* 'Jai Rudra! Jai Parshu Ram!'

Saying this, Indran jumped into the pyre.

Jatayu screamed in agony. 'Noooo!'

The Lankan soldiers were too shocked to react.

'Don't move!' screamed Prahast at his soldiers again.

*All the other Devendrars took their potions and started running up
the walkway. Jumping into the mass pyre. Rapidly. In groups. Every single
one. Men, women, children. Following their leader. Following their king.*

*There were one thousand Devendrars. It took some time for all of
them to jump in.*

*No Lankan stepped up to stop them. A few officers close to Prahast,
to the disgust of many, started picking through the gold jewellery thrown
by the Devendrars. Selecting the best for themselves. Discussing the value
of their loot with each other. Even as the Devendrars were committing*

mass suicide. But the majority of the Lankan soldiers just stood there. Too stunned to do anything.

As the last of the Devendrars fell to his fiery end, Prahast looked around. He could see the shocked expressions of many of his soldiers. He burst out laughing. 'Don't be sad, my soldiers. All the gold will be divided up equally among you. You will all make more money today than you have made in your entire lives! Smile! You are rich now!'

The words did not have the desired impact. Many had been jolted to their souls. Sickened by what they had witnessed. Within less than a week, more than half of Prahast's army had deserted. Jatayu was one of them.

They couldn't fight for Raavan anymore.

The loud sound of the waves crashing against hard rocks brought Jatayu back from that painful memory.

His body was shaking. Tears pouring from his eyes. He held his hands together in supplication, his head bowed. He gathered the courage to look across the straits at Mumbadevi. At the hills of Walkeshwar.

'Forgive me, King Indran … Forgive me …'

But there was no respite from the guilt.

— ௴ —

It had been a few months since Jatayu's return from Mumbadevi.

The medicine from Walkeshwar had done wonders for Makrant. The limp had reduced dramatically. He could walk almost normally again. The atrophied muscles were slowly regaining strength. It was obvious that within a matter of months Makrant would regain the full use of his legs. Some Malayaputras were even planning hunts with him.

Sita had tried a few times to ask Jatayu why the mention

of Mumbadevi caused him such distress. But had given up over time.

Early today, she had stolen away from the group to meet Hanuman at a secret location.

'Prince Ram and you need to settle down at one place, princess,' said Hanuman. 'Your constant movement makes it difficult for me to keep track of you.'

'I know,' said Sita. 'But we haven't found a secure place yet.'

'I have a place in mind for you. It's close to water. It's defendable. You will be able to forage food easily. There is enough hunt available. And, it's close enough for me to track you.'

'Where is it?'

'It's near the source of the holy Godavari.'

'All right. I'll take the details from you. And, how's ...'

'Radhika?'

Sita nodded.

Hanuman smiled apologetically. 'She's ... She's moved on.'

'Moved on?'

'She's married now.'

Sita was shocked. 'Married?'

'Yes.'

Sita held her breath. 'Poor Bharat ...'

'I have heard that Bharat still loves her.'

'I don't think he'll ever get over her ...'

'I'd heard something once: Better to have loved and lost than never to have loved at all.'

Sita looked at Hanuman. 'Forgive me, Hanu *bhaiya*, I don't mean to be rude. But only someone who has never loved at all can say something like that.'

Hanuman shrugged his shoulders. 'Point taken. In any case, the location for the camp ...'

Chapter 30

Six years had lapsed since Ram, Sita, and Lakshman had gone into exile.

The band of nineteen had finally settled along the western banks of the early course of the mighty Godavari, at *Panchavati*. Or the *place of the five banyan trees*. The site suggested by Hanuman. The river provided natural protection to the small, rustic, yet comfortable camp. The main mud hut at the centre of the camp had two rooms — one for Ram and Sita, and the other for Lakshman — and an open clearing for exercise and assembly.

Another cluster of huts to the east housed Jatayu and his band.

The perimeter of this camp had two circular fences. The one on the outside was covered with poisonous creepers to keep animals out. The fence on the inside comprised *nagavalli* creepers, rigged with an alarm system. It consisted of a continuous rope that ran all the way to a very large wooden cage, filled with birds. The birds were well looked after and replaced every month with new ones. If anyone made it past the outer fence and attempted to enter the *nagavalli* hedge, the alarm system would trigger the opening of the birdcage roof. The noisy flutter of escaping birds would offer precious minutes of warning to the inmates at the camp.

Ram, Sita, and Lakshman had faced dangers in these six years, but not due to any human intervention. The occasional scars served as reminders of their adventures in the jungle, but the *Somras* had ensured that they looked and felt as young as the day they had left Ayodhya. Exposure to the harsh sun had darkened their skin. Ram had always been dark-skinned, but even the fair-skinned Sita and Lakshman had acquired a bronze tone. Ram and Lakshman had grown beards and moustaches, making them look like warrior-sages.

Life had fallen into a predictable pattern. Ram and Sita liked to go to the Godavari banks in the early morning hours to bathe and share some private time together. Their favourite time of the day.

This was one such day. They had washed their hair the previous day. There was no need to wash it again. They had tied it up in a bun while bathing. After their bath in the clear waters of the river, they sat on the banks eating a repast of fresh berries and fruit.

Ram lay with his head on Sita's lap. She was playing with his hair. Her fingers got stuck in a knot. She gently tried to ease it out and untangle the hair. Ram protested mildly, but the hair came loose easily, without any need to yank it.

Sita smiled. 'See, I can do it gently as well.'

Ram laughed. 'Sometimes ...'

Ram ran his hand through Sita's hair. It hung loose over her shoulder, down to where his head lay on her lap. 'I am bored with your ponytail.'

Sita shrugged. 'It's up to you to tie some other knot. It's open now ...'

'I'll do that,' said Ram, holding Sita's hand and looking lazily towards the river. 'But later. When we get up.'

Sita smiled and continued to ruffle Ram's hair. 'Ram ...'

'Hmm?'

'I need to tell you something.'

'What?'

'About our conversation yesterday.'

Ram turned towards Sita. 'I was wondering when you would bring that up.'

Sita and Ram had spoken about many things the previous day. Most importantly, of Vashishtha's belief that Ram would be the next Vishnu. Ram had then asked who Sita's guru was. But Sita had sidestepped the answer.

'There should be no secrets in a marriage. I should tell you who my guru is. Or was.'

Ram looked directly into Sita's eyes. 'Guru Vishwamitra.'

Sita was shocked. Her eyes gave it away. Ram had guessed correctly.

Ram smiled. 'I'm not blind, you know. Only a favourite student could get away with saying the kind of things that you had said to Guru Vishwamitra in my presence that day in Mithila.'

'Then why didn't you say anything?'

'I was waiting for you to trust me enough to tell me.'

'I have always trusted you, Ram.'

'Yes, but only as a wife. Some secrets are too big even for a marriage. I know who the Malayaputras are. I know what your being Guru Vishwamitra's favourite disciple means.'

Sita sighed, 'It was silly of me to wait for so long. Passage of time makes a simple conversation more complicated than necessary. I probably should not have listened to ...'

'That's water under the bridge.' Ram sat up and moved close to Sita. He held her hands and said, 'Now, tell me.'

Sita took a deep breath. Nervous for some reason. 'The Malayaputras believe I am their Vishnu.'

Ram smiled and looked directly into Sita's eyes, with respect. 'I have known you for years. Heard so many of your ideas. You will make a great Vishnu. I will be proud to follow you.'

'Don't follow. Partner.'

Ram frowned.

'Why can't there be two Vishnus? If we work together, we can end this stupid fight between the Malayaputras and Vayuputras. We can all work together and set India on a new path.'

'I'm not sure it is allowed, Sita. A Vishnu cannot begin her journey by breaking the law. I will follow you.'

'There is no rule that dictates that there can be just one Vishnu.'

'Umm ...'

'I know, Ram. There is no such rule. Trust me.'

'All right, assuming there isn't, you and I can certainly work together. I'm sure that even the Malayaputras and Vayuputras can learn to work together. But what about Guru Vashishtha and Guru Vishwamitra? Their enmity runs deep. And the Malayaputras will still have to acknowledge me. With things between our gurus being the way they are ...'

'We'll handle that,' said Sita, as she inched close to Ram and embraced him. 'I'm sorry I didn't tell you for so long.'

'I thought you would tell me yesterday, when you were tying my hair. That's why I touched your cheeks and waited. But I guess you weren't ready ...'

'You know, Guru Vashishtha believes ...'

'Sita, Guru Vashishtha is just like Guru Vishwamitra. He is brilliant. But he is human. He can sometimes read situations incorrectly. I may be a devotee of the law, but I am not an idiot.'

Sita laughed. 'I'm sorry I didn't trust you earlier.'

Ram smiled. 'Yes. You should be. And remember, we are married. So, I can use this against you anytime in the future.'

Sita burst into peals of laughter and hit her husband's shoulder playfully. Ram held her hands, pulled her close and kissed her. They held each other in companionable silence. Looking at the Godavari.

'What do we do for now?' asked Sita.

'There's nothing to do till our exile is over. We can just prepare ...'

'Guru Vashishtha has accepted me. So, I don't think he will have a problem with our partnership.'

'But Guru Vishwamitra ... He'll not accept me.'

'You don't hold anything against him? For what he did in Mithila?'

'He was trying to save his Vishnu. His life's work. He was working for the good of our motherland. I'm not saying I condone his cavalier attitude towards the *daivi astras*. But I understand where he was coming from.'

'So, we don't tell the Malayaputras anything about what we have decided for now?'

'No. In fact, I'm not even sure we can tell the Vayuputras for now ... Let's wait.'

'There is one Vayuputra we can tell.'

'How do you know any Vayuputra? Guru Vashishtha had consistently refused to introduce me to any of them till I was accepted by all as a Vishnu. It could have caused problems.'

'I wasn't introduced to him by Guru Vashishtha either! I got to know him through sheer good fortune. I met him through a friend at my *gurukul*. I believe he can advise and help us.'

'Who is he?'

'He is Radhika's cousin.'

'Radhika! Bharat's Radhika?'

Sita smiled sadly. 'Yes ...'

'You know Bharat still loves her, right?'

'I have heard ... But ...'

'Yes, the law in her tribe ... I had told Bharat to not pursue her ...'

Sita knew Radhika's reasoning was different. But there was no point in revealing that to Ram. It was water under the bridge.

'What is her brother's name? The Vayuputra?'

'Hanu *bhaiya*.'

'Hanu *bhaiya*?'

'That's what I call him. The world knows him as Lord Hanuman.'

— ᳶᳵ —

Hanuman smiled, folded his hands together and bowed his head. 'I bow to the Vishnu, Lady Sita. I bow to the Vishnu, Lord Ram.'

Ram and Sita looked at each other, embarrassed.

Sita and Ram had told Lakshman and the Malayaputras that they were going on a hunt. They had, instead, stolen away to a clearing at least a half-day away. They had taken a boat ride downstream on the Godavari, where Hanuman was waiting for them. Sita had introduced Ram to Hanuman. And told him of their decision. Hanuman seemed to accept the decision very easily. Even welcoming it.

'But do you think Guru Vishwamitra and Guru Vashishtha will agree?' asked Sita.

'I don't know,' said Hanuman. Then looking at Ram, he continued, 'Guru Vishwamitra was very angry that Guru Vashishtha has told you that he expects you to be the Vishnu.'

Ram remained silent.

Hanuman continued. 'Your brother Lakshman is a brave and loyal man. He will die for you. But he can, sometimes, let out secrets that he shouldn't.'

Ram smiled apologetically. 'Yes, he said it in front of Arishtanemi*ji*. Lakshman doesn't mean any harm. He is ...'

'Of course,' agreed Hanuman. 'He is very proud of you. He loves you a great deal. But because of that love, he sometimes makes mistakes. Please don't misunderstand. But I would suggest that you don't tell him about your little arrangement. Or, about me for that matter. At least for now.'

Ram nodded. Agreeing.

'What is the reason for the enmity between Guru Vashishtha and Guru Vishwamitra?' asked Sita. 'I have never been able to find out.'

'Yes,' said Ram. 'Even Guru Vashishtha refuses to speak about it.'

'I am not sure either,' said Hanuman. 'But I have heard that a woman called Nandini may have played a role.'

'Really?' asked Sita. 'A woman caused the rift between them? What a cliché.'

Hanuman smiled. 'Apparently, there were other problems as well. But nobody is sure. These are just speculations.'

'Anyway, what's more important is, do you think the Malayaputras and Vayuputras can come together on this?' asked Ram. 'Will they agree to the two of us being Vishnus?

I've been told by Sita that there is no law against it. But it is certainly against the standard protocol for Vishnus and Mahadevs, right?'

Hanuman laughed softly. 'Prince Ram, do you know how long the institutions of the Vishnu and Mahadev have been running?'

Ram shrugged. 'I don't know. Thousands of years? Since Lord Manu's times, I guess. If not earlier.'

'Right. And do you know exactly how many Vishnus and Mahadevs, in the many millennia, have actually emerged according to the plans and protocols laid down by the tribes left behind by the previous Vishnu or Mahadev?'

Ram looked at Sita. And then, back at Hanuman. 'I don't know.'

Hanuman's eyes were twinkling. 'Precisely zero.'

'Really?'

'Not once, not once has any Vishnu or Mahadev emerged exactly according to plan. The best laid plans always have a tendency to get spoilt. There have always been surprises.'

Ram laughed softly. 'We are a country that does not like order and plans.'

'That we are!' said Hanuman. 'The Mahadevs or the Vishnus didn't succeed in their missions because "plans were implemented exactly". They succeeded because they were willing to give their all for our great land. And they were followed by many who also felt exactly the same way. That is the secret. Passion. Not plans.'

'So, you think we will succeed in getting the Malayaputras and Vayuputras to agree?' asked Sita.

'Of course we will,' answered Hanuman. 'Don't they love India? But if you ask me how exactly we will succeed, my answer is: I don't know. No plans as of yet! But we have time. Nothing can be done till the both of you return to the Sapt Sindhu.'

—⌐⌐⌐—

It had been more than thirteen years of exile now. In less than a year, Ram, Sita, and Lakshman would head back to the Sapt Sindhu and begin their life's greatest karma. Hanuman had, over time, managed to get the Vayuputras to accept Sita. And Arishtanemi, along with a few other Malayaputras, had begun to favour Ram. Vashishtha, of course, had no problem with Ram and Sita being the Vishnus together. But Vishwamitra ... well, he was another matter altogether. If he held out, the Malayaputras could not be counted on to be completely on board. After all, they were a relatively disciplined organisation that followed their leader.

But this was not occupying the minds of Ram and Sita right now. They lounged around in their section of the camp, watching the setting sun as it coloured the sky with glorious hues. Unexpectedly, the avian alarm system was triggered; the flock of birds in the cage had suddenly fluttered away noisily. Someone had breached their camp perimeter.

'What was that?' asked Lakshman.

Ram's instincts told him that the intruders were not animals.

'Weapons,' ordered Ram calmly.

Sita and Lakshman tied their sword scabbards around their waist. Lakshman handed Ram his bow, before picking up his own. The brothers quickly strung their bows. Jatayu and his men rushed in, armed and ready, just as Ram and Lakshman tied quivers full of arrows to their backs. Sita picked up a long spear, as Ram tied his sword scabbard to his waist. They already wore a smaller knife scabbard, tied horizontally across the small of their backs; a weapon they kept on their person at all times.

'Who could they be?' asked Jatayu.

'I don't know,' said Ram.

'Lakshman's Wall?' asked Sita.

Lakshman's Wall was an ingenious defensive feature designed by him to the east of the main hut. It was five feet in height; it covered three sides of a small square completely, leaving the inner side facing the main hut partially open; like a cubicle. The entire structure gave the impression that it was an enclosed kitchen. In fact, the cubicle was bare, providing adequate mobility to warriors. But unseen by enemies on the other side of the wall. They would have to be on their knees, though. A small *tandoor*, a *cooking platform*, emerged on the outside from the south-facing wall. Half the enclosure was roof-covered, completing the camouflage of a cooking area. It afforded protection from enemy arrows.

The south, east, and north-facing walls were drilled with well-spaced holes. These holes were narrow on the inner side and broad on the outer side, giving the impression of ventilation required for cooking. Their actual purpose was to give those on the inside a good view of the approaching enemy, while preventing those on the outside from looking in. The holes could also be used to shoot arrows. Made from mud, it was not strong enough to withstand a sustained assault by a large force. Having said that, it was good enough for defence against small bands sent on assassination bids. Which is what Lakshman suspected they would face.

Designed by Lakshman, it had been built by everyone in the camp; Makrant had named it 'Lakshman's Wall'.

'Yes,' said Ram.

Everyone rushed to the wall and crouched low, keeping their weapons ready. Waiting.

Lakshman hunched over and peeped through a hole in the south-facing wall. Straining his eye, he detected a small band of ten people marching into the camp premises. Led by a man and a woman.

The man in the lead was of average height. Unusually fair-skinned. His reed-thin physique was that of a runner; this man was no warrior. Despite his frail shoulders and thin arms, he walked as if he had boils in his armpits; pretending to accommodate impressive biceps. Like most Indian men, he had long, jet black hair that was tied in a knot at the back of his head. His full beard was neatly trimmed, and coloured a deep brown. He wore a classic brown *dhoti* and an *angvastram* that was a shade lighter. His jewellery was rich but understated: pearl ear studs and a thin copper bracelet. He looked dishevelled. As though he had been on the road for too long, without a change of clothes.

The woman beside him faintly resembled the man, possibly his sister. Bewitching. Almost as short as Urmila. Skin as white as snow. It should have made her look pale and sickly. Instead, she was distractingly beautiful. Sharp, slightly upturned nose. High cheekbones. She almost looked like a Parihan. Unlike them, though, her hair was blonde, a most unusual colour. Every strand of it was in place. Her eyes were magnetic. Perhaps she was the child of Hiranyaloman Mlechchas: fair-skinned, light-eyed, and light-haired foreigners who lived half a world away towards the north-west. Their violent ways and incomprehensible speech had led to the Indians calling them barbarians. But this lady was no barbarian. Quite the contrary, she was elegant, slim, and petite, except for breasts that were disproportionately large for her body. She wore a classic, expensively dyed purple *dhoti*, which shone like the waters of the Sarayu. Perhaps it was the legendary silk cloth from the far-eastern parts of India; one that only the richest could afford now. For Raavan had established a complete monopoly on it and had jacked up the prices. The *dhoti* was tied fashionably low, exposing her flat tummy and slim, curvaceous waist. Her silken blouse was a tiny sliver of cloth, affording a generous view of her cleavage. Her *angvastram* had deliberately been left hanging loose from a shoulder, instead of across the body. Extravagant jewellery completed the picture of excess. The only incongruity was the knife scabbard tied to her waist. She was a vision to behold.

Ram cast a quick glance at Sita. 'Who are they?'

Sita shrugged.

It was quickly clarified by the Malayaputras that the man was Raavan's younger half-brother Vibhishan, and the woman his half-sister Shurpanakha.

A soldier next to Vibhishan held aloft a white flag, the colour of peace. They obviously wanted to parley. The mystery was, what did they want to talk about?

And whether there was any subterfuge involved.

Ram looked through the hole again, and then turned towards his people. 'We will all step out together. It will stop them from attempting something stupid.'

'That is wise,' said Jatayu.

'Come on,' said Ram, as he stepped out from behind the protective wall with his right hand raised, signifying that he meant no harm. Everyone else followed Ram's example and trooped out to meet the half-siblings of Raavan.

Vibhishan nervously stopped in his tracks the moment his eyes fell on Ram, Sita, Lakshman, and their soldiers. He looked sideways at his sister, as if uncertain about the next course of action. But Shurpanakha had eyes only for Ram. She stared at him, unashamedly.

A look of recognition flashed across a surprised Vibhishan's face when he saw Jatayu.

Ram, Lakshman, and Sita walked in the lead, with Jatayu and his soldiers following close behind. As the forest-dwellers reached the Lankans, Vibhishan straightened his back, puffed up his chest and spoke with an air of self-importance. 'We come in peace, King of Ayodhya.'

'We want peace as well,' said Ram, lowering his right hand. His people did the same. He made no comment on the 'King of Ayodhya' greeting. 'What brings you here, Prince of Lanka?'

Vibhishan preened at being recognised. 'It seems Sapt Sindhuans are not as ignorant of the world as many of us like to imagine.'

Ram smiled politely. Meanwhile, Shurpanakha pulled out a small violet kerchief and covered her nose delicately. Lakshman noticed her fashionable and manicured finger nails, each one shaped like a winnowing basket. That was perhaps the root of her name. Shurpa was Old Sanskrit for a winnowing basket. And nakha meant nails.

'Well, even I respect and understand the ways of the Sapt Sindhuans,' said Vibhishan.

Sita watched Shurpanakha, hawk-eyed, as the lady continued to stare at her husband. Unabashedly. Up close, it was clear that the magic of Shurpanakha's eyes lay in their startling colour: bright blue. She almost certainly had some Hiranyaloman Mlechcha blood. Practically nobody east of Egypt had blue eyes. She was bathed in fragrant perfume that overpowered the rustic, animal smell of the Panchavati camp; at least for those in her vicinity. Not overpowering enough for her, evidently. She continued to hold the stench of her surroundings at bay, with the kerchief pressed against her nose.

'Would you like to come inside, to our humble abode?' asked Ram, gesturing towards the hut.

'No, thank you, Your Highness,' said Vibhishan. 'I'm comfortable here.'

Jatayu's presence had thrown him off-guard. Vibhishan was unwilling to encounter other surprises that may lie in store for them, within the closed confines of the hut. Before they came to some negotiated terms. He was the brother of the enemy of the Sapt Sindhu, after all. It was safer here, out in the open; for now.

'All right then,' said Ram. 'To what do we owe the honour of a visit from the prince of golden Lanka?'

Shurpanakha spoke in a husky, alluring voice. 'Handsome one, we come to seek refuge.'

'I'm not sure I understand,' said Ram, momentarily flummoxed by the allusion to his good looks by a woman he did not know. 'I don't think we are capable of helping the relatives of ...'

'Who else can we go to, O Great One?' asked Vibhishan. 'We will never be accepted in the Sapt Sindhu because we are Raavan's siblings. But we also know that there are many in the Sapt Sindhu who will not deny you. My sister and I have suffered Raavan's brutal oppression for too long. We needed to escape.'

Ram remained silent.

'King of Ayodhya,' continued Vibhishan, 'I may be from

Lanka but I am, in fact, like one of your own. I honour your ways, follow your path. I'm not like the other Lankans, blinded by Raavan's immense wealth into following his demonic path. And Shurpanakha is just like me. Don't you think you have a duty towards us, too?'

Sita cut in. 'An ancient poet once remarked, "When the axe entered the forest, the trees said to each other: do not worry, the handle in that axe is one of us."'

Shurpanakha sniggered. 'So the great descendant of Raghu lets his wife make decisions for him, is it?'

Vibhishan touched Shurpanakha's hand lightly and she fell silent. 'Queen Sita,' said Vibhishan, 'you will notice that only the handles have come here. The axe-head is in Lanka. We are truly like you. Please help us.'

Shurpanakha turned to Jatayu. It had not escaped her notice that, as usual, every man was gaping intently at her; every man, that is, except Ram and Lakshman. 'Great Malayaputra, don't you think it is in your interest to give us refuge? We could tell you more about Lanka than you already know. There will be more gold in it for you.'

Jatayu stiffened. 'We are the followers of Lord Parshu Ram! We are not interested in gold.'

'Right ...' said Shurpanakha, sarcastically.

Vibhishan appealed to Lakshman. 'Wise Lakshman, please convince your brother. I'm sure you will agree with me when I say that we can be of use to you in your fight when you get back.'

'I could agree with you, Prince of Lanka,' said Lakshman, smiling, 'but then we would both be wrong.'

Vibhishan looked down and sighed.

'Prince Vibhishan,' said Ram, 'I am truly sorry but—'

Vibhishan interrupted Ram. 'Son of Dashrath, remember the battle of Mithila. My brother Raavan is your enemy. He is my enemy as well. Shouldn't that make you my friend?'

Ram kept quiet.

'Great King, we have put our lives at risk by escaping from Lanka. Can't you let us be your guests for a while? We will leave in a few days. Remember what the *Taittiriya Upanishad* says: "*Athithi Devo Bhava*". Even the many *Smritis* say that the strong should protect the weak. All we are asking for is shelter for a few days. Please.'

Sita looked at Ram. And sighed. A law had been invoked. She knew what was going to happen next. She knew Ram would not turn them away now.

'Just a few days,' pleaded Vibhishan. 'Please.'

Ram touched Vibhishan's shoulder. 'You can stay here for a few days; rest for a while, and then continue on your journey.'

Vibhishan folded his hands together into a *Namaste* and said, 'Glory to the great clan of Raghu.'

Chapter 31

'There is no salt in this food,' complained Shurpanakha.

It was the first hour of the fourth *prahar* and those in the Panchavati camp had settled down for their evening meal. It had been Sita's turn to cook. While Ram, Lakshman, and the rest were enjoying the food, Shurpanakha had found much to complain about. The lack of salt was just the latest in a litany of complaints.

'Because there is no salt in Panchavati, princess,' said Sita, trying very hard to be patient. 'We make do with what we have. This is not a palace. You can choose to stay hungry, if the food is not to your liking.'

'This food is worthy of dogs!' muttered Shurpanakha in disgust, as she threw the morsel of food she had in her hand back on the plate.

'Then it should be just right for you,' said Lakshman.

Everyone burst out laughing. Even Vibhishan. But Ram was not amused. He looked at Lakshman sternly. Lakshman looked at his brother in defiance, then shook his head and went back to eating.

Shurpanakha pushed her plate away and stormed out.

'Shurpa ...' said Vibhishan, as if in entreaty. Then he too got up and ran after his sister.

Ram looked at Sita. She shrugged her shoulders and continued eating.

— र्ँ ⅄ —

An hour later, Sita and Ram were in their hut. By themselves.

While no Lankan except Shurpanakha had been troublesome, Lakshman and Jatayu remained suspicious of them. They had disarmed the visitors and locked their weapons in the camp armoury. They also maintained a strict and staggered twenty-four-hour vigil, keeping a constant watch on the guests. It was Jatayu's and Makrant's turn to stay up all night and keep guard.

'That spoilt princess fancies you,' said Sita.

Ram shook his head, his eyes clearly conveying he thought this silly. 'How can she, Sita? She knows I'm married. Why should she find me attractive?'

Sita lay down next to her husband on the bed of hay. 'You should know that you are more attractive than you realise.'

Ram laughed. 'Nonsense.'

Sita laughed as well and put her arms around him. 'But you are mine. Only mine.'

'Yes, My Lady,' said Ram, smiling and putting his arms around his wife.

They kissed each other, languid and slow. The forest was gradually falling silent, as though settling in for the night.

— र्ँ ⅄ —

The guests had been in Panchavati with the forest-dwellers for a week now.

Lakshman and Jatayu had insisted on continuing the staggered vigil, keeping a constant watch on the guests.

Vibhishan had announced that they would be leaving in a few hours. But Shurpanakha had insisted that she had to wash her hair before leaving. She had also demanded that Sita accompany her. To help her with her hair.

Sita had no interest in going with Shurpanakha. But she wanted to get rid of the spoilt Lankan princess as soon as possible. This had encouraged her to say yes.

Shurpanakha had insisted on taking the boat and going a long way downriver.

'Don't think I'm not aware that your disgusting camp-followers have been taking the opportunity to spy on me at my bath time!' Shurpanakha said with pretended outrage.

Sita grimaced and took a deep breath, not saying anything.

'Not your goody-goody husband, of course,' said Shurpanakha, coquettishly. 'He has eyes only for you.'

Sita, still silent, got into the boat, with Shurpanakha climbing in daintily. Sita waited for Shurpanakha to pick up one of the oars. But she just sat there, admiring her nails. Grunting angrily, Sita picked up both the oars and started rowing. It took a long time. Sita was irritated and tired before Shurpanakha directed her into a small hidden lagoon by the river, where she wanted to bathe.

'Go ahead,' said Sita. As she turned around and waited.

Shurpanakha disrobed slowly, put all her clothes into the cloth bag she had carried and dived into the water. Sita settled back, her head on the stern thwart, her body stretched out on the bottom boards, and waited. Feeling uncomfortable after some time, Sita pulled up some jute sacks, bundled them together into a pillow on the plank and rested her head again. The lazy daylight filtering through the dense foliage was calming her down slowly, lulling her to sleep.

She lost track of time as she fell into a short nap. A loud bird call woke her up.

She heard Shurpanakha frolicking in the water. She waited for what she thought was a reasonable time. Finally, Sita edged up on her elbows. 'Are you done? Do you want your hair untangled and tied?'

Shurpanakha stopped swimming for a bit and faced Sita with a look of utter contempt and disgust. 'I'm not letting you touch my hair!'

Sita's eyes flew open in anger. 'Then why the hell did you ask me to come h …'

'I couldn't have come here alone now, could I,' interrupted Shurpanakha, like she was explaining the most obvious thing in the world. 'And, I wasn't about to bring one of the men along. Lord Indra alone knows what they would do if they saw me in this state.'

'They would drown you, hopefully,' muttered Sita, under her breath.

'What did you say?' snapped Shurpanakha.

'Nothing. Finish your bath quickly. Your brother wants to leave today.'

'My brother will leave when I tell him we can leave.'

Sita saw Shurpanakha looking into the forest beyond the banks of the lagoon. Sita followed Shurpanakha's gaze. Then she shook her head in irritation. 'Nobody has followed us here. No one can see you. In the name of all that is good and holy, finish your bath!'

Shurpanakha didn't bother to answer. Casting Sita a contemptuous look, she turned and swam away.

Sita held her fist to her forehead and repeated softly to herself. 'Breathe. Breathe. She's leaving today. Just breathe.'

Shurpanakha continued to steal glances at the forest. She couldn't see anyone. She muttered under her breath, 'None of these idiots are reliable. I have to do everything myself.'

— ⹐⹑ —

At the Panchavati camp, Vibhishan had come to speak to Ram.

'Great one,' said Vibhishan, 'you know we are leaving soon. Is it possible to return our weapons to us so that we may get going?'

'Of course,' said Ram.

Vibhishan looked at Jatayu and his Malayaputras a short distance away, then in the direction of the Godavari, the great river hidden by the dense foliage. His heart was beating fast.

I hope they have reached.

— ⹐⹑ —

'Enough!' said Sita, in irritation. 'You're as clean as you can be. Get out of the water now. We're leaving.'

Shurpanakha looked once again into the forests.

Sita picked the oars. 'I'm leaving. You can choose to stay or come along.'

Shurpanakha shrieked in anger, but surrendered.

— ⹐⹑ —

Sita rowed the boat back in short order. It was a ten-minute uphill walk thereafter to the camp. She waited for Shurpanakha to step out of the boat.

Sita didn't expect, nor get, any help from Shurpanakha to pull the boat onto the banks so that it could be tied securely to a tree with a hemp rope. Shurpanakha was behind Sita as she bent, wrapped the boat-rope around her right hand, held on to the gunwale of the boat, and began to tug.

Focused as she was on her task, as well as the physical strain of pulling a boat up the bank all by herself, she didn't notice Shurpanakha reach into her bag, pull out some herbs and creep up on her.

Shurpanakha used a specific kind of soap and perfume that she had carried with her for her bath. It had a distinctive fragrance. Very different from the feral smell of the jungle.

It was this smell that saved Sita.

She reacted almost immediately, letting go off the boat. Just as Shurpanakha jumped at her and tried to stuff the herbs into Sita's mouth, she turned and hit the Lankan princess hard with her elbow. Shurpanakha fell back, screaming in agony. Sita lunged forward towards the princess of Lanka but the rope wrapped around her wrist made her lose balance. Sensing an opportunity, Shurpanakha pushed Sita into the water. But as Sita fell, she elbowed the princess of Lanka again. Shurpanakha recovered quickly and jumped into the water after Sita, trying again to push the herbs into her mouth.

Sita was taller, tougher and more agile than the posh Shurpanakha. She pushed Shurpanakha hard, flinging her some distance away. She spat out the herbs, quickly pulled out her knife from the scabbard and cut the rope loose. She glanced at the herbs floating in the water, recognising them almost immediately. She pushed through the water to reach Shurpanakha.

Shurpanakha, meanwhile, had recovered. She swam towards Sita and tried to hit her with her fists. Sita grabbed and held both her wrists in her left hand; then yanked hard till the princess of Lanka was forced to turn around. Then Sita wrapped her arm around Shurpanakha's throat, holding her hard against her own body.

Then Sita brought the knife close to Shurpanakha's throat. 'One more move, you spoilt brat, and I will bleed you to death.'

Shurpanakha fell silent and stopped struggling. Sita pushed the knife back in its scabbard. Then used the remnants of the rope around her own wrist to restrain Shurpanakha's hands. She pulled Shurpanakha's *angvastram* and tied it across her mouth.

She reached into Shurpanakha's bag and found some more of the herbs.

'I'll push this into your mouth if you make any more trouble.'

Shurpanakha remained quiet.

Sita started dragging her towards the camp.

A short distance from the camp, the *angvastram* across Shurpanakha's mouth came loose and fell away. She immediately began screaming.

'Stay quiet!' shouted Sita, dragging her along.

Shurpanakha, though, kept screaming at the top of her voice.

A short while later, they emerged from the woods. Sita tall, regal but dripping wet and furious. Muscles rippling with the strain of dragging Shurpanakha along. The Lankan princess' hands remained securely tied.

Ram and Lakshman immediately drew their swords, as did everyone else present.

The younger prince of Ayodhya was the first to find his voice. Looking at Vibhishan accusingly, he demanded, 'What the hell is going on?'

Vibhishan couldn't take his eyes off the two women. He seemed genuinely shocked, but quickly gathered his wits and replied. 'What is your sister-in-law doing to my sister? She is the one who has clearly attacked Shurpanakha.'

'Stop this drama!' shouted Lakshman. *'Bhabhi* would not do this unless your sister attacked her first.'

Sita walked into the circle of people and let go of Shurpanakha. The Lankan princess was clearly livid and out of control.

Vibhishan immediately rushed to his sister, drew a knife and cut the ropes that bound her. He whispered into her ear. 'Let me handle this. Stay quiet.'

Shurpanakha glared at Vibhishan. Like this was all his fault.

Sita turned to Ram and gestured towards Shurpanakha. She held out some herbs in the palm of her hand. 'That pipsqueak Lankan stuffed this in my mouth as she pushed me into the river!'

Ram recognised the herbs. They were normally used to render people unconscious before surgeries. He looked at Vibhishan, his piercing eyes red with anger. 'What is going on?'

Vibhishan stood up immediately, his manner placatory. 'There has obviously been some misunderstanding. My sister would never do something like that.'

'Are you suggesting that I imagined her pushing me into the water?' asked Sita, aggressively.

Vibhishan stared at Shurpanakha, who had also stood up by now. He seemed to be pleading with her to be quiet. But the entreaty was clearly lost in transmission.

'That is a lie!' screeched Shurpanakha. 'I didn't do anything like that!'

'Are you calling me a liar?' growled Sita.

What happened next was so sudden that very few had the time to react. With frightening speed, Shurpanakha reached to her side and drew her knife. Lakshman, who was standing to the left of Sita, saw the quick movement and rushed forward, screaming, *'Bhabhi!'*

Sita moved quickly to get out of the way and avoid the strike. In that split second, Lakshman lunged forward and banged into a charging Shurpanakha, seizing both her arms and pushing her back with all his brute strength. The elfin princess of Lanka went flying back. Her own hand, which held the knife, struck her face as she crashed into the Lankan soldiers who stood transfixed behind her. The knife hit her face horizontally, cutting deep into her nose. It fell from her hand as she lay sprawled on the ground, the shock having numbed any sensation of pain.

As blood gushed out alarmingly, her conscious mind asserted control. She touched her face and looked at her blood-stained hands. The horror of it all reverberated through her being. She knew she would be left with deep scars on her face. Painful surgeries would be required to remove them.

She screeched with savage hate and lunged forward again, this time going for Lakshman. Vibhishan rushed to her and caught hold of his rage-maddened sister.

'Kill them!' screamed Shurpanakha. 'Kill them all!'

'Wait!' pleaded Vibhishan, stricken with visceral fear. He knew they were outnumbered. He didn't want to die. And he feared something even worse than death. 'Wait!'

Ram held up his left hand, his fist closed tight, signalling his people to stop but be on guard. 'Leave now, prince. Or there will be hell to pay.'

'Forget what we were told!' screeched Shurpanakha. 'Kill them all!'

Ram spoke to a clearly stunned Vibhishan, who held on to a struggling Shurpanakha for all he was worth. 'Leave now, Prince Vibhishan.'

'Retreat,' whispered Vibhishan.

His soldiers began to withdraw, their swords still pointed in the direction of the forest-dwellers.

'Kill them, you coward!' Shurpanakha lashed out. 'I am your sister! Avenge me!'

Vibhishan dragged a flailing Shurpanakha, his eye on Ram. Mindful of any sudden movement.

'Kill them!' shouted Shurpanakha.

Vibhishan continued to pull his protesting sister away as the Lankans left the camp and escaped from Panchavati.

Ram, Lakshman and Sita stood rooted to their spot. What had happened was an unmitigated disaster.

'We cannot stay here anymore,' Jatayu stated the obvious. 'We don't have a choice. We need to flee, now.'

Ram looked at Jatayu.

'We have shed Lankan royal blood, even if it is that of the royal rebels,' said Jatayu. 'According to their customary law, Raavan has no choice but to respond. It would be the same among many Sapt Sindhu royals as well, isn't it? Raavan will come. Have no doubt about that. Vibhishan is a coward, but Raavan and Kumbhakarna aren't. They will come with thousands of soldiers. This will be worse than Mithila. There it was a battle between soldiers; a part and parcel of war; they understood that. But here it is personal. His sister, a member of his family, has been attacked. Blood was shed. His honour will demand retribution.'

Lakshman stiffened. 'But I didn't attack her. She—'

'That's not how Raavan will see it,' interrupted Jatayu. 'He will not quibble with you over the details, Prince Lakshman. We need to run. Right now.'

Chapter 32

They had been on the run for thirty days. Racing east through the *Dandakaranya*, they had moved a reasonable distance parallel to the Godavari, so that they couldn't be easily spotted or tracked. But they couldn't afford to stray too far from the tributary rivers or other water bodies, for the best chance of hunting animals would be lost.

They had been surviving on dried meat and jungle berries or leaves, for long. Perhaps the Lankans had lost track of them, they thought. With the frugal food and constant marching, their bodies were weakening. So Ram and Lakshman had set out to hunt, while Sita and the Malayaputra soldier Makrant had gone to fetch banana leaves.

Secrecy was of the essence. So they were cooking their food in holes dug deep into the ground. For fire they used a very specific type of coal; anthracite, which let out smokeless flames. As added precaution, the buried cooking pot was also covered with a thick layer of banana leaves to ensure that even by chance, no smoke escaped, which could give their position away. It was for this that Sita and Makrant were cutting banana leaves. It was Sita's turn to cook.

Unknown to Sita, Raavan's *Pushpak Vimaan* had landed a short distance from the camp. Its ear-splitting noise drowned out by thunderous howling winds. Unseasonal rains had just lashed the area. A hundred Lankan soldiers had disgorged from the *Vimaan*, attacking the camp and killing most of the Malayaputras rapidly.

Some Lankans had fanned out to search for Sita, Ram, and Lakshman. Two of them had ambushed Sita and Makrant, who were on their way back to the camp. Makrant had died, hit by two arrows. One through his shoulder and the other through his neck. Sita had, through sheer skill, managed to kill these two Lankans, steal their weapons and reach the camp. There she had found that every single Malayaputra, except for Jatayu was dead. She had tried, heroically, to save Jatayu, but had failed. The Naga had been grievously injured trying to protect the one he worshipped as the Vishnu.

Kumbhakarna, the younger brother of Raavan, had ordered that Sita was to be captured alive. Many Lankan soldiers had charged at Sita at the same time. She had fought bravely, but was ultimately captured, incapacitated and rendered unconscious with a Lankan blue-coloured toxin.

They had quickly bundled her into the *Pushpak Vimaan* and taken off, just as Ram and Lakshman had reached the camp to find dead bodies strewn everywhere and the severely injured figure of Jatayu.

— ᚱᚷ —

Sita couldn't remember how long she had been unconscious. It must have been hours. She still felt a little groggy. Light was streaming in through the porthole windows on the walls of the *vimaan*. A constant, dull repetitive sound was causing her pain in her head. It took her some time to realise that it was the sound of the *vimaan's* rotors, muffled by the soundproof walls.

Not soundproofed enough.

Sita pressed her temples to ease the pain in her head. It worked only for a few moments. The pain was back soon.

Then she realised something odd.

My hands aren't tied.

She looked down at her legs. They weren't tied either.

She felt her hopes rise.

Almost immediately, it deflated and she laughed softly at her own stupidity.

Where am I planning to go? I'm thousands of feet up in the sky. That blue toxin has made me slow.

She shook her head slowly. Trying to clear it.

She was on a stretcher fastened onto a platform close to the wall.

She looked around. The *vimaan* was truly huge. She looked up. It was perfectly conical from the inside as well. Smooth metal all the way to the tapering top, high up. There was a painting at the summit. Her vision was a little clouded so she couldn't see what it was. At the exact centre of the *vimaan* was a tall, perfectly cylindrical pillar, stretching all the way to the top. It was solid metal, obviously sturdy. She felt like she was inside a giant temple spire. But the interiors, while spacious and comfortable, had frugal furnishing. None of the luxurious and expensive accoutrements of most royal vehicles; or at least the royal vehicles in the Sapt Sindhu. The *Pushpak Vimaan* was basic, sparse, and efficient. Clearly, more of a military vehicle than one for pomp and show.

Because it placed function over form, the *Pushpak Vimaan* was able to comfortably accommodate more than a hundred soldiers. They all sat silently, disciplined, in regular concentric arcs on the floor, right up to the *vimaan* walls.

She could see Raavan and Kumbhakarna seated on chairs that had been fastened to the floor. Their seating area had been screened partially. A curtain hung from an overhanging rod. They weren't too far. But they whispered. So, Sita could not hear much of what they were saying.

Still on the stretcher, she came up on her elbows. Making a heaving sound. She still felt weak.

Raavan and Kumbhakarna turned to look at her. They got up and started walking towards her. Raavan stumbled on his *dhoti*. Distracted.

Sita had managed to sit up by now. She sucked in her breath and looked defiantly at the two brothers.

'Kill me now,' growled Sita. 'Otherwise, you will regret it.'

All the Lankan soldiers stood up, drawing their weapons. But at a signal from Kumbhakarna, they held their positions.

Kumbhakarna spoke, surprisingly gently, 'We don't want to hurt you. You must be tired. You woke up very quickly. The toxin given to you was strong. Please rest.'

Sita didn't answer. Surprised by Kumbhakarna's kind tone.

'We didn't know,' said a hesitant Kumbhakarna. 'I ... I didn't know. We wouldn't have used that toxin otherwise ...'

Sita remained silent.

Then she turned towards Raavan. He was just staring at her. Unblinking. There was sadness on his face. Melancholy. And, his eyes appeared strange. Almost like there was love in them.

Sita shrank to the wall, pulling her *angvastram*, covering herself.

Suddenly, a hand appeared. A neem leaf. And, the blue-coloured paste. Her nose.

Sita felt darkness enveloping her vision. Slowly.

She saw Raavan looking to Sita's right, where the person

who had drugged her was standing. There was anger on his face.

And, darkness took over.

— ᚛᚜ —

Her eyes opened.

Diffused light streamed through the porthole windows. The sun was close to the horizon.

How long have I been unconscious?

Sita couldn't be sure. Was it a few hours? Or many *prahars*?

She edged up, again. Slowly. Weakly. She could see that most of the soldiers were asleep on the floor.

But there were no soldiers around the platform where she had been sleeping.

She had been left alone.

Raavan and Kumbhakarna were standing near their chairs. Stretching their legs. Whispering to each other.

Her vision cleared slowly. Allowing her to judge the distance. Raavan and Kumbhakarna were not more than fifteen or twenty feet from her. Their backs to Sita. They were in deep conversation.

Sita looked around. And smiled.

Someone has been careless.

There was a knife lying close by. On the platform where her stretcher was affixed. She edged over. Noiselessly. Carefully. Picked up the scabbard and unsheathed the blade. Slowly. Without making any sound.

She held the knife tight in her hand.

She took some deep breaths. Firing energy into her body.

She remembered what she had heard.

Kill the chief and the Lankans capitulate.

She tried to get up. The world spun around her.

She sat back on the platform. Breathing deeper. Firing more oxygen into her body.

Then, she focused. She got up stealthily and crept towards Raavan.

When she was just a few feet from Raavan's back, she raised her knife and lunged forward.

A loud scream was heard as someone grabbed Sita from behind. An arm around her neck. A knife pressed close to her throat. Sita could feel that her attacker was a woman.

Raavan and Kumbhakarna whirled around almost immediately. Most of the Lankan soldiers got up too.

Kumbhakarna raised his hands slowly. Carefully. He spoke in a calm but commanding voice. 'Drop the knife.'

Sita felt the arm around her throat tighten. She could see that by now, all the Lankan soldiers were on their feet. She surrendered and dropped her knife.

Kumbhakarna repeated. A little harsher this time. 'I said, drop the knife.'

Sita knit her brow. Confused. She looked down at the knife she had dropped. She was about to say that she had no other knife, when she felt a prick on her neck. The attacker, holding her from behind, had brought the knife in closer. Its tip drawing blood.

Kumbhakarna looked at Raavan before turning back to the attacker holding Sita. 'Khara is dead. This will not bring him back. Don't be silly. I am ordering you. Drop the knife.'

Sita could feel the arm clasped around her neck tremble. Her attacker was struggling with deep emotions.

Finally, Raavan stepped closer and spoke in a harsh, commanding, almost terrifying tone. 'Drop the knife. Now.'

Sita felt the arm clasped around her throat relax. It was suddenly pulled back. And a soft whisper was heard.

'As you command, Iraiva.'

Sita was stunned as she heard the voice. She spun around. Staggered. She fell back, holding the wall of the *vimaan* for support.

Willing breaths into her body, she looked again at the face of her attacker. The one who had wanted to kill her a few moments ago. The one who obviously had strong emotions for Khara. The one who obviously was under the complete control of Raavan.

The one who had saved her life once ...

The one she had thought was her friend.

Samichi.

... *to be continued.*

Other Titles by Amish

Shiva Trilogy

Ram Chandra Series